Index to the archives of Richard Bentley & Son 1829-1898

Compiled by Alison Ingram

Chadwyck-Healey, Cambridge

Somerset House, Teaneck

1977

Chadwyck-Healey Ltd
21 Bateman Street
Cambridge CB2 1NB

ISBN 0 85964 018 3

Somerset House
417 Maitland Avenue
Teaneck, NJ 07666

ISBN 0 914146 21 1

Printed in England

This index has been compiled by Alison Ingram for use with the microfilm publication <u>The archives of Richard Bentley & Son 1829-1898</u>, Chadwyck-Healey, 1976. This publication is part II of the series <u>British publishers' archives on microfilm</u> which also includes:

Part I   George Allen & Co. 1893-1915
             Cambridge University Press 1696-1902
             Kegan Paul, Trench, Trübner & Henry S.King 1858-1912
             Elkin Mathews 1811-1938
             George Routledge & Co. 1853-1902
             Swan Sonnenschein & Co. 1878-1911

Part III   The House of Longman 1794-1914
             Grant Richards 1872-1948

Companion publications to the archives and the index are:

<u>The Lists of the publications of Richard Bentley & Son 1829-1898</u> on microfiche

with

<u>Index and guide to the lists of the publications of Richard Bentley & Son 1829-1898</u> by Michael L. Turner

5000 pages on microfiche with 388pp. printed index, published 1975

Chadwyck-Healey Ltd ISBN 0 85964 013 2

Somerset House   ISBN 0 914146 15 7

Readers using the Bentley archives are strongly urged to use this very extensive bibliography of Bentley publications.

Publisher's Note

The most significant thing about this index is that through it the three major parts of the Bentley archives are at last united. The division of the archives between England and America is so haphazard that it has made the researcher's task immeasurably more difficult - as Royal Gettmann has attested.

We believe that now that the archives are united on microfilm and through this index their full value will come to be realised.

We wish to thank Scott Bennett for his expert work in the preparation of the Bentley archives at the University of Illinois. While this work was done primarily to make the archives more accessible for researchers in the Rare Book Room in the Library of the University of Illinois, without it the microfilm publication would not have been possible.

We also wish to thank Brooke Whiting, Curator of Rare Books at the Library of the University of California at Los Angeles for his help in the preparation of the microfilm and Alison Ingram for compiling the index.

Readers using the index should remember that much of the material that is indexed is internal documents - ledgers, diaries, and other office records which may themselves be inaccurate or inconsistent. For instance ledger headings are often abbreviated working titles of books and may bear little relation to the final published titles. Where possible the index gives both working titles and published titles but assumes that the reader is also using Michael Turner's Index to the Bentley Lists.

Using the Index

This is an index to the archives of Richard Bentley & Son on microfilm from the collections at the British Library, the University of Illinois and the University of California at Los Angeles. It contains a detailed synopsis of each collection and an index of correspondents, authors and titles which consolidates references in all three collections. It also contains a summary of Bentley items in the Bodleian Library, and the Berg Collection at the New York Public Library.

It is assumed that the index will be used in conjunction with The Lists of the publications of Richard Bentley & Son 1829-1898 on microfiche and with Michael Turner's Index and guide to the lists of the publications of Richard Bentley & Son; these give invaluable information about authors, editors and titles which it has been considered unnecessary to duplicate.

Entries are by correspondents or authors, with titles listed under each author. Bentley periodicals and Publisher's Series are listed separately at the end of the index, followed by a list of titles by anonymous or unidentified authors.

Inevitably the amalgamation of three separate collections, each with its own classification system, has revealed inconsistencies of spelling and nomenclature, as well as bringing to light new information about names. For this reason the alphabetical systems do not always tally precisely, and this fact should be borne in mind when using the index. In addition, it should be remembered that some correspondents, due to uncertainty of identification, may have more than one main entry (e.g. Smith, J. Smith and J.C. Smith); others, whose signatures are indecipherable, none at all. It is hoped, however, that the detailed synopses give enough shape and chronology to the mass of material to enable the researcher to use the available information as efficiently as possible, and to repair some of the inaccuracies and omissions.

British Library (L)

Each reference is to a volume and page (see Examples of entries). The synopsis shows on which reel a volume is located and gives a description of material not included in the index. The following sections are fully indexed: authors' ledgers, publication ledgers, agreement and memorandum books, lawsuits and agreements, letterbooks and incoming correspondence, with the exception of the post-1874 sections of volumes 96 and 104, which are in copyright; all other items in copyright are indexed, although the items themselves are not reproduced on the microfilm. In addition, occasional items outside these areas are indexed (e.g. readers' reports where the manuscripts can be identified, or parts of volumes 6 and 22 which deal with periods not referred to elsewhere). Members of the Bentley family are not indexed unless they feature as authors themselves.

University of Illinois (IU)

The first part of the collection contains material relating to the Bentley family and the Bentley firm, including employees. The synopsis is the only guide to this material. The alphabetically arranged correspondence files which follow are fully indexed, except for the Unidentified section at the end. The simple reference IU indicates inclusion in the correspondence files. There are no volume or folio numbers, although the letters of each individual correspondent are numbered. Additional information is given when an item is not in its expected alphabetical position (see Examples of entries), and the synopsis gives the location of alphabetical sections on film.

University of California at Los Angeles (UC)

The alphabetically arranged correspondence files are indexed as above, under the reference UC, with additional information as to position when necessary. Again, reference should be made to the Examples of entries and the synopsis. The Manuscripts and Ephemera are arranged in numbered sections, and have been indexed as far as possible; in addition, the synopsis gives a detailed description of the contents of each section.

Abbreviations

L	British Library
IU	University of Illinois
UC	University of California at Los Angeles
(c)	in copyright
orig.	indicates the original title of a work prior to publication
prop.	indicates that only the proposal for the work is referred to
[ ]	indicates some query about the enclosed item, usually due to lack of verification or illegibility

Examples of entries

British Library

L2,76	Volume 2, page 76 (using the new folio nos., not the original pagination)
L117A	The first part of Volume 117, which is in two volumes
L85,2(c)	in copyright
L2,23a	Lower case letter indicates unnumbered page after L2,23

University of Illinois

IU	The alphabetically arranged correspondence files (reels 19-57)
IU(Albemarle)	See under Albemarle in the correspondence files
IU Unidentified	The unidentified section at the end of the correspondence files (see synopsis)
IU Richard Bentley I,3	The third letter in the correspondence of the first Richard Bentley
IU Richard Bentley II,180+	Letter(s) between 180 and 181 in the correspondence of the second Richard Bentley

University of California at Los Angeles

UC	The alphabetically arranged correspondence files
UC(Albemarle)	See under Albemarle in the correspondence files
UC(end of C)	A group of letters at the end of section C in the correspondence files (see synopsis for grouping)
UC(Carr-end of C)	As above, in the group of Carr letters
UC Miscellaneous	See Miscellaneous unidentified correspondence
UC Manuscripts,4	Section 4 of the Manuscripts and Ephemera

Bentley Archives/British Library (L)

Synopsis

Reel	Volume		
1	1	General authors' ledger	1829-30; 1855-61 (see vol.117)
	2	"	1861-72
	3	"	1872-96
	4	"	1896-8
2	5	<u>Temple Bar</u> Authors' ledger	1868-99
	6	Outlay Day book (trade and authors)	1837-54
	7	Publication ledger (catalogues, books, excerpts etc. printed; arranged and indexed by title)	1836-53
3	8	Summary ledger of customers for whom printing is undertaken; mainly trade, private institutions, societies	1846-54
	9	Summary ledger: miscellaneous	1861-3
		<u>London Society</u>	1872
	10	Summary ledger (see vols.16-22)	1863-72
4	11	"	1872-8
	12	"	1878-82
5	13	"	1882-7
6	14	"	1887-96
	15	"	1895-8
7	16	Cash book (summarized in above ledgers)	1861-8
	17	"	1868-74
8	18	"	1874-9
	19	"	1879-84
9	20	"	1884-9
10	21	"	1890-5
11	22	"	1895-1901
	23	Magazine and newspaper ledger: monthly summary of trade accounts	1895-8
12	24	Private cash book	1890-99
	25	Outlay Day book (trade and authors)	1861-9
	26	"	1869-77
13	27	Authors' Day book, with copyright details	1877-88
	28	"	1888-1900
	29	Trade Day book	1877-83
14	30	"	1883-9
	31	"	1888-94
15	32	"	1894-8
	33	Outlay ledger	1884-95
	34	"	1896-8
16	35	Summary ledger: miscellaneous	1861-99
	36	Publication ledger (arranged by title)	1855-66
17	37	"	1866-72
18	38	"	1872-7
19	39	"	1877-82
20	40	"	1882-7
21	41	"	1887-93
22	42	"	1893-8
23	43	Magazine and newspaper ledger	1896-8
	44	Sales ledge	1896-8
	45	<u>Temple Bar</u> decennial statistics	1860-98
	46	Mrs.Henry Wood's novels: Cash sales	1888-97
	47	"	1898
24	48	Town sales	1888-98
	49	Country sales	1891-6
	50	"	1896-8
25	51	Foreign sales	1888-98
	52	Agreement memorandum books	1827-33
26	53	"	1833-7

Reel	Volume		
27	54	Agreement memorandum books	1837–40
28	55	"	1840–6
	56	"	1846–51
29	57	"	1851–4
	58	"	1856–63
30	59	"	1864–75
31	60	"	1875–81
	61	"	1881–3
32	62	"	1883–5
	63	"	1885–8
33	64	"	1888–90
	65	"	1890–3
34	66	"	1893–5
	67	"	1895–9
35	68	"	1828–31; 1853–6
	69	Agreement and publication register	1829–59
	70	"	1860–86
36	71	"	1887–98
	72	Agreement memorandum notebook	1861–70
	73A, B	Lawsuits and agreements	1823–34; 1835–9
37	74	"	1834–8
	75	"	1839–66
38	76	"	1837–40
	77	"	1835–41
39	78	Publication list	c. 1829–73
	79	"	1873–98
	80	Letterbooks	1829–54
	81	"	1830–9
40	82	"	1849–54
	83	"	1854–64
41	84	"	1864–76
	85	"	1876–84
42	86	"	1885–92
	87	"	1892–5
43	88	"	1895–7
	89	"	1897–1908
	90	Incoming correspondence	1830–8
44	91	"	1839–43
	92	"	1844–9
	93	"	1849–58
45	94	"	1860–5
	95	"	1866–73
46	96	" (1873–4 indexed; post-1874 in copyright, so unindexed)	1873–1909
	97	Reports of Geraldine Jewsbury	1860–3
47	98	"	1864–6
	99	"	1867–9
48	100	"	1870–2
	101	"	1873–5
49	102	Reports of other readers	1860–74
	103	Incoming trade letters and receipts, mainly connected with London Society	1829–72
	104	Receipts and letters (post-1874 material unindexed because in copyright)	1872–1900
	105	Incoming receipts for London Society illustrations and engravings	1870–3
50	106	Trade accounts and receipts	1867–70
	107	London Society financial statements and receipts (mainly for drawings)	1866–70
51	108	Trade subscription lists, arranged by title	1829–30
	109	"	1831–2

Reel	Volume		
	110	Trade subscription lists, arranged by title	1833–41
52	111	"	1842–7
	112	"	1848–60
	113	"	1862–8
53	114	"	1869–75
	115	Miscellaneous account sheets	1826–1901
54	116	<u>Miscellany</u> lists nos.1–47	1837–40
	117A,B	Authors' accounts: summary of old authors' ledgers (presumed missing)	1832–55
	118	Notes on business transfer, with stock list	1897
	119	Customs registration	1893–8
	120	Notes on authors' accounts	1898
	121	Address book	1879–98
55	122	Agreements and other legal documents	1833–65
	123	Miscellaneous correspondence, proofs, reviews, cuttings etc.	1831–1915
		Includes publication list 1879, with notes, and information concerning imprints and the accounts system	

Bentley Archives/University of Illinois (IU)

Synopsis (Reels 1–18 are not indexed)

Reel

	Bentley family	
	Bentley family	
1	Bentley family	Miscellaneous documents
	Richard Bentley I	Letters 1821–71, numbered 1–50
		Diary 1827
		Diary, 17 vols. 1859–70
		Bibliography of source material on naval defence 1588–1845
		Documents, manuscripts, proofs 1829–70, including recollections of Edward Bentley (b.1753), autobiographical manuscripts and material concerning Walpole's letters, Samuel Bentley, W.H.Ainsworth and H.Colburn
2		Colburn proofs continued
	George Bentley	Letters 1844–95, numbered 1–468
3		After Business Diary vols.1–6, 1850–70
4		" " 7–11, 1871–80
5		" " 12–16, 1880–87
6		" " 17–21, 1887–95
7		Notebook, c.1885, with contents page at end
		Cashbook of personal expenses, 6 vols. 1853–85
		Various documents
		Manuscripts, including a memoir of Richard Bentley I
		Proofs
8	Richard Bentley II	Letters 1868–93, numbered 1–499
9		" 1893–9, " 500–674
		Documents
		Notes on Publication lists
		Source material on Henry Colburn
	Bentley family letters	?... Bentley
		Alfred Bentley
		Amy Georgiana Bentley
		Annette Bentley (Williams)
		Annie Bentley
		Cara Bentley

Reel		
	Bentley family letters /	Charlotte Bentley
		Clara Bentley
		E.I. Bentley
		Edith Bentley
		Fred. W. Bentley
		Frederick Bentley
		Horatio Halliburton Bentley
		John Bentley, brother of Richard Bentley I
		John Bentley, nephew of Richard Bentley I
		Julia Bentley
		Louey Bentley
		Samuel Bentley (c.1878)
		Samuel Bentley (1785-1868)
		Letters, numbered 1-60
		Documents, notes, manuscripts, including materials for a memoir of Thomas Tomkins
		Mrs. Samuel Bentley
		Thomas Charles Bentley
		William Bentley
10	Henry Colburn (firm)	Colburn & Bentley letters
		Various documents
		Publication lists 1806-29, compiled by Richard Bentley II, with worksheets
	Colburn & Bentley (firm)	Documents
		Partnership account 1829-37
		Office account 1829-35
		Publication lists 1829-32
	Richard Bentley & Son	
11	Accounts department	Miscellaneous records, with a printed guide to departmental procedures
	Advertising department	A printed guide to departmental procedures, with various lists and clippings
		Advertisements scrapbook
	Audit department	Statements 1861-3, from Quilter & Co.
	Bentley's Favourite Novels	Financial statement and sales, 1886-91
	Cashier's department	Mainly cancelled cheques 1875-99
	Catalogues 1846-97	Stray lists: Special Creditors Accounts current; valuations for balance sheets 1855-7 (bound) vol.1 (also includes printed articles concerning the Bentleys, and business forms)
12		Stray lists vol.2
	Copyright	Various documents
	Country department	Various documents
	Culinary delights	Food and wine invoices etc.
	Employees	Reginald Alford
		Edward Augustus Arnold
		Nathaniel Thomas Beard
		Benjamin Cousens
		Henry Fry
		William F. Green
		Robert Keith Johnston
		Letters 1885-98, numbered 1-96
		Letterbook vol.1, 1890-92
13		Letterbook vols.2-5, 1892-8, with fragments from vols.2 and 5 after the appropriate volumes
		John Thomas Marsh

Reel	Employees /	Edward Samuel Morgan
		Letters 1832-73, numbered 1-136
		Documents, including an autobiographical account of his service with Colburn and the Bentleys
14		James Munnings
		Letters 1870-6, numbered 1-50
		Ratcliffe, Frank J.
		Ratcliffe, H.W.
		Rivenhall, Edward
		Van Homrigh, B.A.
		Letters 1874-89, numbered 1-144
		Van Homrigh, W.D.
	Foreign & Colonial department	Trade list and prices
	General management	Documents concerning the organization of account books, personnel, business premises etc.
		Miscellaneous memoranda 1828-9
		Reference book 1829-32
		Various memoranda, lists and addresses
		Note book
		Memoranda, caller and address book vols.1-2, 1872-87
15		" vol.3, 1888-93
		Note book 1876-87, kept by Richard Bentley II
		Includes floor plans, list of translators and trade addresses
		Memoranda of works under consideration or in progress 1886-98
		George Bentley's Letts's Diary vols.1-5, 1890-4
16		" vol.6, 1895
		Printed Inventory of titles ?1898
	Inspectorate	Documents 1861-2
		Minute book 1855-8
		" 1861-71
	Manuscript department	Various documents 1883-96
	Outlay department	Printed guide to departmental procedures, 1885
		Claims and receipts for copyrighted books 1831, 1836-58
17		" 1858-98
	Periodicals	Bentley's Miscellany
		Various documents, mainly receipts
		Bentley's Quarterly Review
		Two printed notices
		London Society
		Statements of account to Charles Riley, 1870-2
		Temple Bar
		Letters, documents and proofs 1874-95
		Monthly authors' list 1899-1900
		List of articles in type 1877-1900 (incomplete)
		Manuscript reports on two articles 1893-4
		Production schedules 1881-5
		'Renewed riots in London': a brief 'jeu d'esprit'
		Reference table of contents: annual index of Temple Bar articles 1860-98
	Publication lists	List of publications, vol.2, 1829-39, compiled by Richard Bentley II
		Worksheets for list of publications 1829-39
		Corrigenda et addenda to publication lists 1818-56, 1858
18		" 1818
		" 1825-9
		" ?1818

Reel
18
	Stock department	Documents 1865-87, including lists of plates in the
		    hands of printers
		Memoranda of stock, plates and rights for individual
		    works, c.1898 (incomplete)

	Town department	Various documents, mainly concerning dinner sales
		Entries of days of subscription: prices of books
		    published, 2 vols. 1806-58
		Subscription lists 1856-63: lists of trade sales for each
		    title

	Correspondence	Mainly letters, with a few documents and manuscripts
19		Abbott, Augustus - Atcherley, Rowland J.
20		Auckland - Bate, Samuel S.
21		Baten - Bourrienne, Louis A.F. de
22		Bowden, A. - Broughton, Rhoda (letter 362)
23		Broughton, Rhoda (letter 363) - Byron, George
24		Cadell, Robert - Clifford, Lucy
25		Clifford, Lucy M.H. - Costello, Louisa S.
26		Costenoble, Hermann - Dalling & Bulwer
27		D'Almeida, W.B. - Dixon, Frederick
28		Dobell, Sydney T. - Edwards, Amelia B.
29		Edwards, Annie - Everett, George
30		Eversley - Fothergill, Caroline
31		Fothergill, Jessie - Fyfe, J.H.
32		Gad & Keningale - Gray, John A.
33		Gray, Russell - Hartlett, E.
34		Hartley, May - Hewlett, Joseph T.J.
35		Hickman, Walter - Hook, Theodore
36		Hook, Walter - Hullmandel, Charles
37		Humboldt, C.H. - Jesse, John H.
38		Jeune, F.H. - Kettle, Mary R.S.
39		Kiegan, John - Le Marchant, Denis
40		Le Marchant, Henry D. - Londonderry
41		Lonergon, E.Argent - Macquoid, Katharine
42		Macquoid, Thomas R. - Maxwell, Mary E.
43		Maxwell, William H. - Montgomery, Fanny
44		Montgomery, Florence - Nast, C.L.R.
45		*Nature* - Palmer, E.H.
46		Palmer, H.V. - Phipps, Pownoll W.
47		Phipps, Ramsay W. - Quivogne de Montifaud, Marie A.
48		Rachel, Mme. - Richards, James Brinsley
49		Richards, W.L. - Saint John, Bayle
50		Saint John, Isabella - Shakespeare, William
51		Sharpe, J.E. - Spencer, Mary J.
52		Spencer, William R. - Strickland, W.J.
53		Stronach, George - Trollope, Frances E.
54		Trollope, Thomas A. - Waugh, John
55		Weatherly, Frederick E. - Wollaston, J.T.
56		Wolseley, Garnet J. - Yates, Edmund H.
57		Yonge, C.M. - Zimmern, Helen

Unidentified authors:

(A) Correspondence indexed by recipient or person
    referred to;
(B) Correspondence or manuscripts, indexed as far
    as possible;
(C) Miscellaneous fragments, lists, correspondence -
    unindexed;
Correspondence signed by initials, alphabetically
    arranged - indexed.

Bentley Archives/University of California (UC)

Synopsis

Reel

1	Correspondence A-J	Includes the following groups of letters at the end of alphabetical sections (with the number of letters indicated in brackets):

	B	Bancroft, Sir Squire and Lady M. (11) Bentley, various (34) Diehl, Alice M. (11)
	C	Carr, Ralph (13) Clifford, Lucy (9)
	D	Desart, 4th Earl of (10)
	F	Forster, Charles (70)
	G	Garcia, Manuel (6)

2	Correspondence K-V	L	Landon, Letitia E. (29) Lucy, Sir Henry W. (12)

	M	Majendie, Lady Margaret (9)
	P	Pollock, Emma J. (4) Pollock, Juliet (42) Pollock, Walter H. (85)
	R	Reeves, Helen (15) Roberts, Lord Frederick S. (16)
	S	Sargent, Herbert H. (5) Simeon, Stephen (5) Symons, George J. (7)
	T	Thurston, B.W. (4)

3	Correspondence W-Z	W	Williams, Francis E. (82)

Miscellaneous Unidentified Correspondence

Manuscripts and Ephemera 1-24

1	Barham, R.H.	Ingoldsby Legends: miscellaneous records
2	Bentley, George	Bentley's Dinner Sale. Notes
3	"	Miscellaneous manuscripts
4	"	Manuscripts fragments by J.H.Newman and George Bentley
5	"	Review of Viel-Castel, Memoirs sur le regende Napoleon III
6	Bentley records	Accounts
7	"	Book lists
8	"	Notebook, December 1872, of jobs to be done
9	"	Catalogues: notes for the Bentley lists, 1875, 1876
10	"	Contracts and agreements
11	"	Correspondence
12	"	Reviews
13	"	Diary of business matters, March 1875
14	"	Instructions and memos to employees
15	"	Miscellaneous; includes manuscript account of Edmund Appleyard
16	"	List of works by Robert Montgomery (incomplete)
17	"	Items relating to Jane Porter
18	"	Proof sheets
19	"	Rejection letter
20	"	Annual report of London Library committee, 1892
21	"	Roberts, F.S.: items relating to Forty-one years in India

Reel	22	Bentley records /	Tales from Bentley: incomplete list of contents
	23	"	Varty Smith, A.: printed correspondence
	24	"	Wood, Charles W.: lay-out sheet for list of works

4   Manuscripts and Ephemera 25-47

	25	Richard Bentley II	Two schoolboy manuscripts
		Richard Bentley I	Manuscript prayer
	26	Bentley, Samuel	Excerpta Historica: various items
	27	"	Miscellaneous manuscripts
	28	"	Letters from various persons
	29	"	Letters to various persons
	30	"	Records and accounts 1819-31
	31	Burnaby, Frederick G.	Manuscript fragments
	32	Fairfax, Thomas	The Fairfax Correspondence: various items
	33	The French are on the Sea	Manuscripts, 1797
	34	Gordon, Adam L.	Various items
	35	Halls, John H.	Synopsis of The Life ... of Henry Salt
	36	Kingsley, Henry	Review of Oak Stow Castle
	37	Kuhe, William	Synopsis of My musical recollections
	38	Life is a Nightwatch	Manuscript
	39	Miscellaneous manuscripts	Includes copies of letters from Robert Burns, Robert Southey, Charles Lamb and Thomas Gray
	40	Molloy, James Lynam	Manuscript of a poem
	41	Montgomery, Florence	Misunderstood: typed fragment
	42	Moodie, Susanna	Letter and manuscript
	43	Timbs, John	Autobiographical material
	44	W.H.O.	Manuscript of a poem
	45	Bentley, Samuel	Concio de puero Jesu: various items
	46	Tomkins, Thomas	Title page
	47	Temple Bar	Book reviews, proofs

Bentley items in the Bodleian Library, Oxford

1) Miscellaneous Bentley family papers, 1829-1936, including cashbooks, notebooks, diaries, inventories and letters of condolence.

2) Papers (1882-1935) of Richard Bentley II:

Manuscripts and proofs
Papers relating to the publication lists
Proofs of items by: Henniker, Mrs. Florence E.H.
                     Junot, Laura
                     Keppel, Sir Henry
                     Mallett, J. Reddie
                     Ransom, Arthur
                     W., B.O.

3) Business papers, including a cashbook (1829-48) and material relating to Edward Bulwer Lytton.

4) Correspondence with: Bull, Edward
                        Bulwer, Edward G.E. (1st Baron Lytton)
                        Bulwer, Sir Henry
                        Clifford, Lucy
                        Daniel, George
                        Godwin, Mrs.
                        Holland, Sir Henry
                        Hood, Thomas
                        Jerdan, William
                        Lyne, Joseph L.
                        Lytton, Lady (Rosina)
                        Shelley, Percy B.
                        Smith, Horace
                        Talfourd, Sir Thomas Noon

5) Letters arranged in alphabetical order of the writers' names

Bentley items in the Berg collection at the New York Public Library

1) Correspondence with or relating to:

              Ainsworth, W.H.
              Barham, R.H.
              Barham, R.H.D.
              Blackett, Spencer
              Bond, C.F.
              Bond, Mildred Barham
              Browning, Robert
              Bryce, Mr.
              Buckstone, John Baldwin
              Bunn, Alfred
              Collins, Wilkie
              Cruikshank, George
              Dickens, Charles
              Dickens, Charles jnr.
              Du Pontivac de Heussy, Robert
              Faulkner, G.
              Forster, John
              Gissing, George
              Gregory, John
              Haggard, Sir Henry Rider
              Hawthorne, Nathaniel
              Hogarth, George
              I., W.
              Irving, Washington
              Jerdan, William
              Leech, John
              Macmillan & Co.
              Mahony, Francis Sylvester
              Mitford, George
              Mitford, Mary Russell
              Morgan, E.S.
              Morton, Caroline (Sheridan)
              Murray, John
              Oliphant, Cyril Francis
              Oliphant, Margaret O.Wilson
              Reade, Charles
              Reade, Compton
              Reade, Emma
              Reade, Gertrude
              Reade, William Winwood
              Rivington, Charles
              Roberts, C.J.
              Smythies, Harriet M.G.
              Taylor, Cooke
              Tenniel, John
              Unwin, T.Fisher
              Watt, A.P.
              Waugh, John
              Wood, Ellen Price
              Woods, Margaret L.

2) Miscellaneous papers, letters, agreements and other legal documents relating to Charles Dickens.

GENERAL
Accounts system L123,237-58; IU Richard
Bentley & Son,Accounts Dept.; IU Richard
Bentley & Son,General Management
American authors L83,62; L93,238-40
Copyright, notes on L88,194; L122,3 52
Electricity, installation of L86,297 333 344
353

Abbot, Reginald C.E.(Lord Colchester) L3,66;
L59,299; L60,196; L84,252; L85,163;
IU(Colchester)
Abbott, Augustus
The Afghan war L39,305 309; L40,419; L41,
511; L42,508; L123,181-2; IU
Abbott, Dr.Evelyn L3,103; L5,112 266; L60,
17; L85,369-70(c); IU
Abdy, Miss L5,206
Abell, Frank L5,221
Abell, H.F. L22,357 367
Aberdeen, Lord
see Gordon, George J.J.H.
Abram, Edmund W. L5,290
Abrantes, Laure
see Junot, L.
The Academy IU
Ackermann, Arthur IU
Ackermann & Co. L55,199
Ackroyd, Miss Laura L5,28
Adam, Stevenson & Co. L84,171
Adams, Captain L85,127
Adams, Mrs.B.J.Leith IU(Laffan)
Adams, Henry B.(Frances Snow Compton pseud.)
Esther L40,409; L41,494; L42,482; L62,304
Adams, Rev.Henry C. L3,71; L4,83; L95,
186; IU
Frank Lawrence L38,279; L39,440; L100,
232
Adams, J.W.Richard L64,32
Adams, R.D. IU
Adams, W.M. IU
Adams, W. & Son L59,246; L83,247 276; L84,
295(c)
Adams, William Davenport IU
Adderley, C.F.
Our town L53,60; L117A,20
Addison, Charles G.
Damascus and Palmyra L54,52-7; L81,192
Addison, H.B. IU
Addison, Henry R. L91,158 176 181 183 186-9
246-8 286-7; L92,209
The Admiralty L94,109
Adolphus, John IU
Memoirs of John Bannister L54,38; L117A,38
Adye, Sir John M.
Sitana L2,19; L3,77; L37,22; L38,81; L39,
196 400; L40,420
Adye, Willett L. IU; IU Richard Bentley I,34
Musical notes L37,196; L38,79; L39,196;
L42,401
Aflalo, Frederick George IU; UC

The Age, Melbourne IU; UC
Agnew, Mrs. L5,291
Agnew, Georgette IU
Aide, Charles H. L1,166; L2,15; L5,103;
L83,213; IU
Rita L36,40 43; L37,226; L58,171
Aikin, Lucy IU
Aikman, Charles M. L5,219; IU
Aincotts, Vincent IU
Ainscough, James
The Man who disappeared L42,421; L67,113;
L88,193
Ainslie, Douglas G.D. IU(Woods,M.L.)
Ainsworth, T. & Sons L81,182 202-3
Ainsworth, William H. L6,103; L53,333; L54,
171 179 236-7a; L58,9; L59,94 109 157 166;
L70,219; L75,355; L81,237-8; L83,57 223-4
226; L84,88-9; L90,60-1; L91,86 88 141 195;
L93,234; L94,267-71; L117A,27; IU; UC
Crichton L53,339-47; L56,12
Guy Fawkes L7,147; L54,179 237-9; L55,
43; L56,12
Jack Sheppard L7,142; L54,157-9 239; L55,
45; L56,12; L75,159 200-87
Old St.Paul's (pub.Hugh Cunningham) L7,147
Rookwood L53,87-91; L56,12; L122,92
The Tower of London L6,65; L55,99-101
Aird & Coghill L85,370-1
Aitken, George Atherton IU
Akerman, John Y. L93,36-7; IU
London legends L7,148
Spring-tide L7,113 169; L8,119 174
Alabama (Confederate states cruiser)
The Alabama claims; case of the United States
L37,318; L38,77; L39,401 431; L40,419;
L123,236
Alban, S. IU
Albemarle, Earl of
see Keppel
Alberg, Albert L5,174
Albrecht, Prof. IU
Aldine Press IU
Aldis, Mrs.H.G. L5,298; L22,363
Alecto (pseud.) IU
Alexander, Mrs.
see Hector, A.F.
Alexander, A. L74,181-218
Alexander, Miss Dorathea A. L5,208
Alexander, Henrietta
see Thomson, Henrietta
Alexander, Sir James E. L1,67; L81,100;
L117A,20; IU
Incidents in the Maori war L36,114; L37,16;
L58,311
Transatlantic sketches L52,326; L53,49
Travels to the seat of war L52,131; L68,60
Alford, Henry L89,119
Alfred, A. IU
Alger, J. L5,28; L86,256
Ali Muhammad Khan
The political and statistical history of Gujarat
L36,117; L90,72
Alison, Sir Archibald L1,136; L58,97-103;

L83, 86 89 91 101 103 113 117 144 166 169 180
197; L93,295; IU
All the year round L123,153-5; IU
Allan, A. L5,301
Allan, W.Alex L88,156
Allanson, E.P. IU
Allder, Hannah IU
Alldridge, Miss Lizzie L3,41; L5,224
  The Queen's house L40,442; L41,529; L63,
  49
Allen, Miss L91,43 153; L117B,18
Allen, A. IU
Allen, Carl F.
  Appeal to the people of Europe L36,131
Allen, Eliza L91,163
Allen, F. L5,24
Allen, Grant L5,111
Allen, Miss Phoebe L86,437
Allen, Raymund L5,295
Allen, W.H. & Co. L55,337; L66,16; L85,
  373-4; L86,303-5 307 309
Allen, William L91,44
  A narrative of the expedition to the River Niger
  L36,98; L42,405; L56,80; L117B,44
Allen, Colley & Edwards IU
Alleyne, Sarah F. L3,169
Allhusen, Mrs. L5,104
Allhusen, Alice E. IU
Allhusen, Beatrice M. IU
Allison, W. IU
Allport, Miss Ellen L3,100; L4,26; L88,60
  140 356; IU
  The Desire of the moth L42,427; L66,258-84;
  L88,358
Alma Tadema, Laurence IU
Almond, W.Russell IU
Almy, Percival H.W. L5,299
Althaus, T.F. L5,187
Amari, Michele L82,118-19; L117B,41
  History of the war of the Sicilian Vespers L36,
  148; L56,246
Amazon steam-ship
  Narrative of the loss of the Amazon L36,186
Amherst, Countess Alice IU
Amherst, William Pitt (1st Earl Amherst) IU
The Amicable Society L83,187
Amos, Andrew
  Four lectures L6,125 173; L7,160 162; L36,
  97; L117A,21
  The Great Oyer of poisoning: the trial of the
  Earl of Somerset L36,99; L55,334
Ampère, André M.
  The Story of his love L3,48; L38,278; L39,
  433
Anderson L87,120(c)
Andersen, Hans C. L1,155; L5,71; L83,134;
  L93,294; L117B,39; IU
  A Christmas greeting L36,100
  The Ice-maiden L2,55; L36,307; L37,17
  The Improvisatore L122,80 124
  In Spain L2,55; L36,154; L37,16; L38,82
  Only a fiddler L55,274
  Pictures of Sweden L36,101 284

A Poet's bazaar L55,324
A Poet's day dreams L36,100; L37,21
The Sand-hills of Jutland L1,156; L36,246
To be, or not to be L1,156; L36,80 284
The Two baronesses L7,166; L8,53; L56,
131
Andoe, William L90,74 94; L117A,18
Andrew, John L83,26 33 36 43 120; IU
Andrews, Alexander L1,174; L83,155
  History of British journalism L36,63; L58,
  159
Andrews, George L83,62-3
Andrews, J. L81,163
Andrews, Walter IU
Anglia Christiana Society IU
Anneslie, Major T. L5,189; IU(Aunestie)
Anonymous IU
  see Unidentified titles
Ansted, Prof. L2,66
Anstruther, Hon.Mrs. L5,277; L66,188
Antrobus, Mrs.Clara L. L3,73; L5,294; L22,
  359; L87,207; IU; UC
  Wildersmoor L42,436; L66,137
Ap George, T.George F. IU; IU(George,G.)
Apperley, Charles J. L91,202; IU
Apperson, G.L. L5,208
Appleton & Co. L60,164; L61,214; L63,1;
  L65,145 319-21; L66,254; L82,246 329 331-2;
  L83,40 65 81 105-6; L84,176 212; L85,58 117
  126 179 188 279(c) 331 337 350 358 [364] 377
  393 412 415 432; L86,59 92 246 395 418 421
  439; L87,41 55 61 76 119 139 151 169 171-2
  176-7 183 202 266; L88,50 91 239 242 249 308
  348 354; L117B,12; IU; IU(Curtis,G.T.)
Appleton's Journal IU
Appleyard, Edmund UC Manuscripts,15
Arbroath Guide L86,238 242 244; IU
Archdale, George L5,82 120 143 148; L87,
  130(c) 179; IU
Archdale, Mary IU
Archer, Edward C.
  Tours in Upper India L52,296; L117A,27
Archer, H.M. IU
Archer, Isabel M. IU
Archibald L81,184
Arfwedson, Carl D.
  The United States and Canada L53,115; L81,
  126 145; L117A,24
Argles, Miss Daisy L5,277
Argles, Mrs.Margaret (M.Hungerford) L5,94
  209; L85,402; IU(Angles); IU(Hungerford)
The Argus IU
Argyll, Duke of
  see Campbell, J.G.E.
Arleer, Edward IU
Arlincourt, Charles d' L117B,29
Armitage, Harold L5,39
Armitage, Rev.Robert L82,110; L92,63;
  L117B,42; IU
  Doctor Hookwell L7,149; L55,126-31
  Doctor Johnson: his religious life and his
  death L6,180; L36,176; L56,212
  Ernest Singleton L7,164; L8,35; L56,31

The Primitive church L55,202
Armstrong L5,98
Armstrong IU
Armstrong, A. L91,79-81
Armstrong, Clara IU
Armstrong, Cosmó IU
Armstrong, E. IU
Armstrong, Ella Evelyn IU
Armstrong, Miss F. L5,227
Armstrong, Florence E. IU
Armstrong, G. IU
Armstrong, George L86,232
  Names and places of the Old Testament L41,
  324
Armstrong, Isabella IU
Army & Navy Magazine IU
Army & Navy Stores L88,328
Armytage, Hon.Mrs. L86,311; L88,81 118
Armytage, Hon.Fenella F.
  Old court customs L40,379; L41,524; L42,
  516; L61,298; IU
Árnason, Jón
  Icelandic legends L2,27; L36,147; L37,217
Arnold, Arthur L2,71
Arnold, C.J. L91,128
Arnold, E.Lester L5,305
Arnold, Edward A. L3,33; L86,98;
  IU(Murray's Magazine)
Arnold, Miss Ethel M. L5,199; IU
Arnold, F. IU
Arnold, Rev.Frederick L2,32; L3,43 110; L5,
  72; L86,146; L95,93 111 114-15 164; L96,23
  53-6 62
  Christ Church days L37,87; L38,115; L41,
  506
  Turning points in life L3,41; L38,275; L39,
  453 455; L40,333 459; L41,165; L42,323;
  L60,133; L61,138 173; L102,89
Arnold, R.A. L5,68
Arnold, Samuel J. L92,283 290-1
Arnold, Rev.T.H. L1,183
Arnold, Thomas J.
  Dramatic stories L52,252
Arnold, Rev.W.F. L2,29
Arnold, William T. IU
Arrom de Ayala, C.F.J.
  The Sea-gull L2,25; L37,239; L38,232
Arrowsmith, John L84,185-6; IU
Art & Book Co., Leamington L85,448
Artell, E.J. IU
Arundell, Mr. L80,14
Arundell, Rev.Francis V.J.
  Discoveries in Asia Minor L53,78; L117A,26
Arundell, Rev.Thomas IU; IU George Bentley,
  170
  Historical reminiscences of the City of London
  L37,24; L38,78
Arundell, William G.M.(Lord Galway)
  IU(Galway)
Asarta, F. de IU(De Asarta)
Ashbee, H.S. L5,126
Ashburnham, Sir William
  The Restoration of the Jews L36,102; L38,

82; L117B,9
Ashby-Sterry, Joseph IU
Ashe, Rev.T. L5,80
Ashe, Thomas IU
Asher & Co. L88,186; IU
Ashley, Hon.A.Evelyn M. L3,74; L4,83;
  L84,238 253; L86,156; IU; UC
  The Life of Viscount Palmerston L38,356;
  L39,182-3 312; L40,203-4 312; L41,166-7
  266; L42,253-4; L60,198; L123,208-9
Ashton, Captain J. L57,142-4; L82,229;
  L117A,30
  The Pappenheimers (trans.) L36,216; L57,41
Ashton, Ralph L22,356
Ashton, Thomas
  Bannerford L36,105; L57,206
Ashurst,Morris,Crisp & Co. L89,132
Ashworth, Henry IU
Asiatic Society of Bengal IU
Aspinwall, Thomas L52,272 301; L54,7 14 28
  87; L55,46 186 254 279; L56,14-16 154; L74,
  166; L82,296 308; L90,102; L91,211; L92,
  66; L93,196; IU
Associated Booksellers of Great Britain &
Ireland
  see Burleigh, T.
Association to protect the rights of authors IU
Asthmatics' Institute IU
Astle, John IU
Astley, Sir John IU Unidentified,(A)
Aston, J.C. L89,105
Atcherley, Rowland J.
  A Trip to Boerland L39,323; L40,465; L42,
  404; L60,186; L123,205-6; IU
The Athenaeum L83,261; L84,32; L86,59 251
  255; L93,238-40; IU George Bentley,258;
  IU(MacColl) UC(Francis)
Atherstone, Edwin L1,164; L83,169
  Handwriting on the wall L36,227
Atkins, G.
  History of popular science (prop.) L52,178
Atkinson, Miss Blanche L22,354; L87,55
Atkinson, Charles L.
  Otterbourne L52,274; L90,16 21; L117A,5
Atkinson, E. L86,91
Atkinson, W.E.G. UC
Atlas Insurance Co. L85,337; L86,79 116 283
  285; L88,109
Atmaram,Sagoon & Co. L85,182
Auckland, Lord
  see Eden, William
Audin, Jean M.V.
  French dialogues L37,109; L38,135; L39,
  145
Auerbach, Berthold
  The Country house on the Rhine L2,68; L37,
  81; L38,107; L39,449; IU
Augener & Co. L84,133
Auguet de Saint-Sylvain, L.X.(Baron de los
Valles)
  The Career of Don Carlos, or a chapter in the
  history of Charles V L53,170; L90,73;
  L117A,29

Aumale, Henry E.P.L.(Duke d')
  see Henry Eugene P.L.
Aundell, Rev.Thomas L5,70
Aunet, Léonie d'
  The Notary's daughter L3,17 149; L39,276;
  L40,446; L60,58
Austen, Rev.Henry T. L52,305 311 313;
  L117A,5
Austen, Jane L36,246 284-5; L37,15 21 33 37
  323-4; L40,364; L41,191; L52,305 311 313;
  L88,126; IU
  Emma L37,17; L38,30; L39,15-16; L40,16;
  L41,18; L42,8-9
  Letters of Jane Austen L3,14; L40,191; L41,
  517; L42,511; L62,177
  Mansfield Park L37,18; L38,27; L39,18;
  L40,19; L41,20 31; L42,10-11
  Northanger Abbey L37,19; L38,28; L39,
  19-20; L40,20-1; L41,21 31; L42,11-12
  Persuasion L39,19-20; L40,20-1; L41,21 31;
  L42,11-12
  Pride and prejudice L37,18; L38,29; L39,21;
  L40,22-3; L41,22 32; L42,12-13; L53,38
  Sense and sensibility L37,17; L38,31; L39,
  22-3; L40,23-4; L41,23 32; L42,13-13a
Austen, La[yard] IU
Austen-Leigh
  see Leigh
Austin, Alfred L2,19; L5,26 37; L58,298;
  L70,89; L84,160; IU; UC
  The Poetry of the period L37,25; L38,76;
  L39,196
Austin, Frank L5,223
Austin, George L5,198
Austin, Hester IU
Austin, J.
  see Mudie, C.E.
Austin, L.F. L5,184
Austin, Wiltshire S. L1,81; L2,49; L58,65;
  L83,218 235; L93,128 154-6 173-7 179 191-4
  211 269-70; L117A,30; IU
  The Lives of the Poets-Laureate L36,103;
  L57,138
The Australasian L62,249-51
The Authors' Syndicate L5,58; L66,77-82;
  L67,183 257-8; L86,346(c) 481 494; L87,158
  192 275; L88,57 94 99 199 220(c) 220 224 246
  279 299 302 309 333 338; L89,42 45 52 57; IU;
  IU(Society of authors)
Autotype Company L85,4 49; L87,165; IU; UC
[Avalson], William W. IU
Aveline, M.G.
  Fairy tale charades L1,132; L36,93; L58,
  163
Avonmore, Lady M.T.
  see Longworth, M.T.
Aylat & Jones L82,225
Aylmer, Miss L81,141

B., J.J. IU Unidentified
Babington, J.Henry IU

Bacon, Rev.J.Mackenzie L22,349 368
Baconnier-Salverte, Anne J.E.
  The Occult sciences L55,296
Badcock, Lovell
  Rough leaves L54,40; L81,126; L117A,35
Badeley, Mrs. UC
Baden-Powell, Agnes S. IU
Baden-Powell, Baden F.S. L5,207; IU
  In savage isles L41,378; L42,244-5
Baden-Powell, Sir George S. L5,76; IU
  New homes for the old country L37,316; L38,
  261; L39,424 427; L40,447; L41,387 524;
  L42,516
  That unconscionable Turk L39,264; L40,458;
  L41,535; L42,522
Baden-Powell, Henrietta G. IU
Badham, Charles L5,128
Badham, Rev.Henry L5,187; IU
Baedeker, Karl IU
Bagenal, Philip H. L5,56; L85,430; IU
  Life of Ralph B.Osborne L3,184; L40,225;
  L41,517; L42,509
Bagg, Thomas IU
Bagot, Richard IU
Bagster, Mr. L93,47
Bagwell, Richard L5,57
Baildon, H.Bellyse L5,282; IU
Bailey, John C. L5,239; IU
Bailey, Shaw & Gillett L85,5-8; IU
Baillie, Dr. L83,136
Baillie, Mrs.F.S. L5,127
Baillière, F.F. IU(Ballière)
Bailliere, Jean Baptiste L74,1-33
Baillot L59,14-19; L83,274 277
Baily, Alfred H. L55,113; L75,291-334
Baily, Emily IU
Baily, John IU
Baily, Olive IU
Baily & Roberts IU
Bain, Mrs.Charlotte L5,103 124 141-2; L86,
  354 433 435-6 438; L87,250-1; IU
Bain, James IU
Bain, John L5,214; L83,32
Bain, Thomas George IU
Baines, Frederick E. L3,129; L4,26; L87,
  227; L88,104; IU; UC
  Forty years at the Post Office L42,353 357;
  L66,166
  On the track of the Mail Coach L42,364; L67,
  44-6
Baird, Alexander L5,38
[Baissier] L82,101
Bake, Miss L89,67
Bake, R.B. IU
Baker, A. L5,101
Baker, A. IU
Baker, Augustus A.
  Servia and the Servians (prop.) L60,132; L85,
  105; L123,215
Baker, G. UC
Baker, George IU
Baker, Georgina (Mrs.Eric Baker) L5,101; IU
Baker, Henry B. L3,116; L5,41 46 51 54 71;

L89,73; L95,91; IU
French society L38,305; L39,197
Our old actors L39,295 379; L40,213 215
448; L41,176
Baker, M.A. IU
Baker, Mary IU(Stiles)
Baker, Victoria (Mrs.V.Rybot; J.Masterman
pseud.) L3,58; L86,266; L87,140;
IU(Masterman)
A Devoted couple (orig.Six sons) L42,447;
L66,64
The Scotts of Bestminster (orig.Was he a
widower) L41,450; L64,144
Baker, Folder & Upperton L87,188
Baker & Scribner L82,64 68 80-1 87
Balbo, Cesare
The Life and times of Dante Alighieri L36,115
Balch, William Ralston UC
Baldwin, Astley H. L96,12
Baldwin, Charles IU
Baldwin, Edward T. L5,306
Baldwin, William C. L2,54; L83,230; L87,
275; L88,231; IU
African hunting L36,291 297; L37,38; L42,
352 374; L58,282
Baldwin & Cradock L81,63 67
Balestier, Wolcott
see Lovell, John W.
Balfour, Lady Blanche M.H.G. IU
Balfour, Frederic H. L3,55; L4,27; L5,233;
L22,361; L87,103 106(c) 286 295; L88,55 58
66 172 230 296; IU
Cherryfield Hall L42,431; L66,296 319-22
Dr.Mirabel's theory L42,451; L65,292-5
The Undergraduate L41,427; L42,497; L65,
32
Unthinkables L42,384; L67,176-9
Balfour & Macdonald, Emperor (pseud.) IU
Ball, Robert H. L85,22
Ball, W. L90,321; L117A,37
Ball, W.E.
see Moore, J.J. & Co.
Ballantine, Walter L65,51-6
Ballantine, William L3,143 187; L4,83; L5,
187-8; L85,312-13 438 459 464; IU
The Old world and the new L40,265; L41,290;
L42,516; L62,143
Some experiences of a barrister's life L14,
301; L39,380; L40,322 332 335 454; L41,291
355; L42,314; L61,13-75; L65,51-8; L79,64;
L119,98
Ballantine, Mrs.William L65,58; L86,394
Ballantyne, Archibald L5,279; IU
Lord Carteret L40,154; L41,316; L42,503;
L63,177
Ballantyne, Hanson & Co. L62,324; L66,178;
L84,30; L85,154 154(c) 157; L86,109 358 397
417 428 461; L87,242 250 253 258; L88,138
340; L89,45 68; IU
Ballantyne's Novelists Library L52,220; L73A,
35-7
Ballenden, John IU
Balley, Georgina IU

Balls, Charles IU
Balt, B.M. IU
Balzac, Honoré de IU(Lordwell)
The Correspondence L3,96 111; L38,365;
L39,228; L40,422; L41,521; L42,513; L60,
21
Eugenie Grandet (prop.) L3,126; L39,330;
L123,215
Bamford, Samuel L83,34
Bancroft, George L82,177 191 193 199 211 216
235 245 256 282; L83,28 39 47 49 51; L117A,
33; IU
History of the American Revolution L36,27;
L57,91
Bancroft, Lady Marie E. IU George Bentley,
261; UC(end of B)
Mr.& Mrs.Bancroft on and off the stage L14,
300; L41,325 337 341 393; L42,281 514; L63,
289; L64,138-41; L65,20; L86,470
Bancroft, Sir Squire L3,81 91; L86,156 184
477(c) 480-1; IU; UC(end of B)
Mr.& Mrs.Bancroft on and off the stage
see Bancroft, Lady M.E.
Bandinel, James L94,304; IU
Bandmann, Daniel E. L5,96; IU
Bangor, J.C. IU
Bangs, Lemuel, W. L86,84 87 89 102 117 130
166(c) 231 260 372 457 467-8; L87,73 75 101
130 137 137(c) 151 161 181 195 282 290; L88,
145 165 168
see Scribner & Welford
Bangs Brothers & Co. L82,206 213; L83,50
Banim, John L1,23; L68,79; L81,50 98;
L117A,13; IU
The Denounced L52,5; L68,16-17
The Smuggler L68,60; L122,56 121
Banim, Michael
The Denounced
see Banim, J.
Banister, Caroline H.
Angelo L36,103; L57,300
Bank of England L86,337; IU
Banks, D.C. L5,301
Banks, G.Linnaeus L84,43
Banks, Mrs.G.Linnaeus
see Varley, I.
Banks, Percival W. L55,87 89; L91,216-18;
IU
Barber, C.M.
see Russell, Lord John
Barbier, G.E. IU
Barclay, A.A.(Armiger Barczinsky pseud.)
L5,259
Barclay, George IU
Barclay, Hugh
The Sinaitic inscriptions L37,49
Barclay, Mrs.Robert IU
Barczinsky, Armiger
see Barclay, A.A.
Barford, Miss L82,330
Barham, Rev.C.N. L5,268
Barham, Richard H. L80,22-5; L81,237; L90,
145; L91,255 258 279-81; L117B,2; IU; UC

The Ingoldsby legends   L2,71; L3,116; L7,
143-66 passim   L8,49 52-3 94; L12,172;
L13,192; L36,22-3 137 171 254-5 301-5 312
315; L37,152-8 162-3 168-9 172 175 306 309;
L38,157-64 311 337; L39,iii 153-4 156-63 165;
L40,184 273-82; L41,256-64 266 391; L42,
232-40; L54,261; L75,291; L123,
203-4 206-7; UC Manuscripts,1
The Ingoldsby lyrics   L39,356; L40,283;
L41,391; L42,240
The Jackdaw of Rheims   L37,162; L38,166;
L39,164
The Smugglers leap   L39,272; L40,282; L41,
264; L42,241
Some account of my cousin Nicholas   L7,146;
L122,76 124
The Witches' frolic   L38,367; L39,164; L40,
282; L60,20
Barham, Rev.Richard H.D.   L2,71; L3,134;
L5,45; L92,89; L117B,16; IU
The Life of the Rev.Richard H.Barham   L37,
38; L38,86; L39,198-9 232; L40,205-6; L41,
168-9; L42,251-2; L55,345
The Life of Theodore E.Hook   L7,166 168;
L8,53 94 111; L36,106; L37,142; L39,267
289; L40,206-7; L41,175; L42,252-3
Rubber of life   L55,9
Baring, Hon.Maurice   L5,167; IU
Barker, Lady   IU
Barker, Edward H.   L3,62 108; L4,27; L5,67
164-5 275; L86,295; L87,97 184(c) 254; IU;
UC
Two summers in Guyenne   L42,345 351; L66,
182; L87,196; L119,158
Wanderings by southern waters   L41,379; L42,
331; L65,259-64; L119,128
Wayfaring in France   L41,350; L42,331; L65,
9-12; L86,381; L119,127; UC Manuscripts,12
Barker, Mrs.Elizabeth R.   L3,119; IU
Barker, John
Angling excursions in France and Belgium
(prop.)   L55,310
Barker, M.A.   IU
Barker, Matthew H.   L54,152; L81,198-9
210-12; L117B,4; IU; IU(United Service
Gazette)
Hamilton King   L54,153
Barker, Robert E.   IU
Barker, W.G.J.   IU
Barker, William A.   L90,220
Barker, Edward   UC
Barlow, Mr.   L81,147 157 159 163 169
Barlow, Frank Pratt   IU
Barnard, B.T.   L5,261
Barnard, Frederick L.
A Three years' cruise   L36,106; L42,402;
L56,84
Barnard, Harry   UC
Barnard, Rev.Mordaunt R.   L2,24; L3,60;
L5,83; L59,126; L84,75; IU
Barnes, F.E.   L88,135(c)
Barratt, James   IU
Barraud, Herbert   L63,282; L64,211; L86,182

202 207 210 217 220-2 224 226 228 235 283
289-90 292-3 316-18
Barrera, Mme.A. de
Gems and jewels   L2,52; L36,251; L37,45;
L58,241
Barrère, Camille E.P.   IU
Barrett, Mr.   L85,190
Barrett, Charles R.B.   IU
Barrett, Elizabeth (Mrs.E.B.Browning)
Letters to R.H.Horne   L3,99; L38,362; L39,
228; L40,423; L60,8
Barrett, Frank   L3,133; L5,106; L85,206 257
310 434 437; L86,63-5; IU
Folly Morrison   L39,349; L40,430; L60,247
Honest Davie   L40,375; L61,302
Lieutenant Barnabas (orig.Lady Betty)   L39,
367; L40,288; L60,307-8
Little Lady Linton   L40,394; L41,517; L62,
169-72
A Prodigal's progress   L39,390; L40,350;
L61,146
Barrett, R.Henry   IU
Barrett, William A.   IU
Barrow, E.P.   L5,79
Barrow, John
The Life of Admiral Sir W.S.Smith   L7,164;
L8,107; L55,317 343; L56,3-5; L117B,32
Barry, Alfred   IU
Barry, Miss Fanny   L5,256
Barry, M.J.   L90,324
Barry, Octavia   IU
Barry, William W.   L2,74; L5,21; IU
A Walking tour in Normandy   L37,281; L59,
170
A Walking tour round Ireland   L37,278;
[L38,80]
Barstow, Mrs.   IU
Barters, M.E.   IU
Barthélemy Saint-Hilaire, Jules
Egypt and the Great Suez Canal   L1,154
Bartholeyns, A.O.   L5,156
Bartholomew, J.   L88,89(c)
Bartlett, Sir Ellis A.   IU
Barton, Gustave   IU
Barton, R.S.   IU
Barton, William Henry   UC
Bartram & Son   L81,165-6
Bartrum, A.C.   IU
Barttelot, Sir Walter G.   L3,67; IU; UC
The Life of Edmund M.Barttelot   L41,357-8;
L42,265; L64,305-13
Barz, G.H.   L90,144
Basire, James   IU
Bastow, A.   L83,231
Bate, Samuel Stringer   IU
Bateman, A.   L94,211
Bateman, Mrs.Jane C.
The Netherwoods of Otterpool   L1,167; L36,
228 235; L58,155
Bateman, Miss May   L5,289
Baten, Mrs.   IU
Bates, C.H.   IU
Bates, Miss Emily K.   IU

Egyptian bonds   L3,118; L39,294; L60,142;
L123,192-3
Bates, Henry W.   L3,64; IU
Bath, Marquis of
see Thynne, John A.
The Bath Herald   L82,100
Bathurst, Lord Henry   IU
Bathurst, Selina   IU
[Batistouifur, Ettore]   IU
Battersby, C.J.   L5,126
Battersby, W.H.(Francis Prevost pseud.)
L5,245
Batthyany, Casimir   IU
Batty, Beatrice
see Stebbing, B.
Baudry   L83,26
Baumann, M.   L85,180
Baxter, Walter R.   L91,275; L117B,14
Baxter, Rt.Hon.William E.
The Tagus and the Tiber   L36,107; L82,198
200 204; L83,73
Baylis, Alexander J.   L58,304 321
Bayliss, Wyke   L86,307
Bayly, Helena Haynes   L55,195 199 253; IU
Bayly, Thomas H.   L90,137; L117A,40; IU
Complete poetical works (prop.)   L40,166;
L41,324
Kindness in women (orig.Marriage settlements)
L53,335; L54,36
Songs, ballads and other poems   L36,108;
L54,207 307; L55,38 195 199 253
Bayly, N.T.H.
see Bayly, T.H.
Baynard, Rev.J.B.   L5,232
Baynes, Adam C.   L77,110-59
The Bazaar,Exchange & Mart   L88,242 251
Bazancourt, César de (Baron)
History of the Crimean War (prop.)   L58,53
Beach, Charles
Andrew Deverel   L2,18 54; L36,306; L37,18;
L94,74 87; L97,190
Beach, George   L87,283
Beaconsfield, Earl of
see Disraeli, B.
Beadfield, Thomas   L86,44
Beadon, Mrs.Harriette (H.Musgrave pseud.)
L3,64; L5,230; L86,167
Illusions   L41,478; L63,257
Beal, Robert W.   L5,88
Beale, Miss Anne   L1,128; L2,17; L5,18;
L83,216 270; L94,200; L95,101 108; L100,
283; IU
Country courtships (orig.Married in haste)
L37,80; L38,99; L39,398 450; L59,205; L65,
304; [L97,145] ; L99,96
Gladys the reaper   L36,233 241
Nothing venture; nothing have   L36,160; L38,
201; L39,430 433; L40,448; L41,523; L59,20
Simplicity and fascination   L36,92; L58,32;
L68,100
Beale, Lionel   L83,182; IU; UC Manuscripts,
47
Beale, Marie Christine   IU

Beale, Miss Sophia   L22,360
Beale, T.Willert   L3,59; IU
The Light of other days   L41,351; L42,274;
L64,243
Beard, Lessey   L89,43
Beard, Nathaniel T.   L5,127; UC
Beau, Adolphe   L85,478
Beauclerk, Grace (Duchess of St.Albans)
IU(St.Albans)
Beauclerk, [N]   IU
Beauclerk, William A.(Duke of St.Albans)
L3,184; L85,310 338 340 411; IU(St.Albans)
Beauclerk, William N.   L3,125; L4,83; L22,
338; L86,206 216
Rural Italy   L41,334 389; L42,308; L64,320
Beaufort, Emily A.(Lady Strangford)   L2,46;
L3,19; L26,55; L59,203; L84,135 138 276;
IU(Strangford); IU George Bentley,176+1
The Eastern shores of the Adriatic   L36,150
153; L37,230; L58,339; [L97,226]
Beaufort, Raphael Ledos de   L3,186; L62,270;
L85,469; L86, 52-3 59 76-7 434; IU(Ledos)
Beaumont, Lord   IU
Beavan, Arthur H.   IU
Beazley, Dr.C.   IU
Beazley, S.   L91,108
Beck, Baroness Wilhelmina von   L82,162-5 227;
IU; UC(Carr-end of C)
see Derra de Moroda, C.
Personal adventures   L36,83; L56,259-68;
L117B,9
Becker, A.B.   L53,93
Becker, Bernard H.   L3,127; L86,312; IU
Adventurous lives   L39,285
Beckett, Arthur William à   IU(à Beckett)
Beckett, G. à   L90,134; L91,225 276; L95,25;
IU(à Beckett)
Beckford, William T.   L90,41 62-3; L92,21;
L117A,12 22
Italy, with sketches of Spain and Portugal
L7,143; L74,37 181
Recollections of an excursion   L36,193
Beckwith, Charles   L1,97; L55,324; L92,198;
L93,287; L117B,14
Bede, Cuthbert
see Bradley, E.
Bedford, Henry C.G.   L1,146; L83,116; L93,
271
Bedford, Miss Jessie   L3,141; L5,226; L87,
224; L88,150
Cornish diamonds   L42,435; L66,162
Bedford, Rev.W.K.   L86,409
Beechey, E.M.   IU
Beechey, Frederick W.   L1,71; L81,29 44 46
55-6 59-62 66 75; L90,14; L117B,38; IU
Narrative of a voyage to the Pacific   L52,71
325; L68,39
A Voyage of discovery towards the North Pole
L7,150; L36,108; L55,143
Beechey, St.Vincent   UC
Beeching, Henry Charles   UC
Beeker, Bernard   L86,314
Beerbohm, Mr.   L85,209

Beerbohm, Miss Constance L5,198
Beerbohm, Julius L5,112; IU
Begbie, A.G. IU
Begbie, Miss A.H. L5,302
Begbie, Harold L22,367
Behrens, Bertha
  Lizzie of the mill L3,92; L39,348; L60,242
Belfast, Earl of
  see Chichester, F.R.
Belford Brothers L85,53
Belford,Clarke & Co. L63,150
Bell, Arthur L89,89
Bell, C.Moberly
  see The Times
Bell, Mrs.Florence (Reid Kerr pseud.) L4,75;
  L5,187 228; L86,406; L88,152(c) 153; L89,
  89; IU; UC
  Conversational openings and endings L41,362;
  L42,505 510; L65,81
  Miss Tod and the prophets L42,400; L67,
  294-6
Bell, George L85,219; IU
Bell, Miss Gertrude L5,296
  Safar Nameh Persian pictures L42,303; L66,
  126
Bell, H.T.Mackenzie L5,230; IU
Bell, Miss J.B. L85,268
Bell, Mrs.Martin
  see Martin, Mrs.Mary B.
Bell, Matthew L85,233 381 387 426
Bell, Robert L56,333; L82,95; L117B,20;
  IU; UC
  The Ladder of gold L56,197
  Wayside pictures L36,109; L56,105
Bell & Bradfute L81,35 38 40 64-103 passim
  119 175 189; L82,176; L86,197 350; IU
Bell & Curll L81,29 37
Bellew, John C.M. IU
Belloc, Mme. L117A,10
Beltz, George F. L90,62; IU
Bemrose L81,153
Benedict, Ernest L87,218
Benett, William L92,55; L117B,30
Bengifer Brothers L85,398
Bengough, Miss Marion A. L3,127; L86,395;
  L87,67; IU
  In a promised land L41,407; L42,475; L65,
  282-4
  So near a kin (orig.From one stem) L41,425;
  L42,496; L65,45
[Bengurnsa, N.] L85,165
Benham, Rev.William IU
Benham & Tindal L84,62
Benkhausen, G. L68,32
Bennett, Mrs. L85,20
Bennett, Sir Ernest N. IU
Bennett, Frederick D.
  Gleanings in Polynesia (prop.) L54,202
  Narrative of a whaling voyage L55,182;
  L117A,5
Bennett, George L117A,24
Bennett, Miss Helen A. IU; UC
Bennett, J.W. L80,21

Bennett, Joseph IU
Bennett, S. IU
Bennett, Miss Susan E.
  Bewitched (orig.A Pious fraud) L3,104; L42,
  446; L66,56
Bennett, W. IU
Bennett, W.S. IU
Bennoch, Francis IU
Benoit, Mme. de L84,226
Benson, Arthur C. L5,215; L88,155; IU
Benson, E.F. L5,293; L67,95-8
Benson, E.J. L5,261
Benson, Miss M.E. L5,209
Bent, T.Theodore L5,224
Bentinck, Miss L1,172; L83,170
Bentinck family IU
Bentley
  The Bentley ballads L1,132; L2,73; L36,79 229
  229 232 235; L37,35-6 103 249 290; L38,88
  264 360; L39,97-8; L40,194-5; L41,183;
  L42,170; L84,196
  Bentley's cook's every day book L36,30
  Old 'Miscellany' days L40,181; L41,293;
  L42,295
  Tales from Bentley L36,74 249 269 298 318;
  L37,43; UC Manuscripts,22
Bentley, Miss L1,143; L92,211; L93,86 120
  205 217-22
Bentley, Miss L5,25
Bentley, Anna C. UC
Bentley, Miss C. L5,33; L37,31
Bentley, Dr.Edward L117A,35
Bentley, G.Samuel UC
Bentley, George L5,23 54; UC Manuscripts,
  2-5
  The Rock inscriptions in the Peninsular of
  Sinai L37,43; L38,89; L39,198
Bentley, Rev.Horatio L84,187 189;
  [UC Miscellaneous]
  A Sermon on the death of Lord Beaconsfield
  L39,358
Bentley, Joseph Clayton UC
Bentley, Richard I
  The Persecution of the Baroness von Beck
  UC(Carr-end of C)
Bentley, Richard II L5,138; UC Manuscripts,
  25
Bentley, Rev.S. L5,109
Bentley, Samuel L1,98; L2,19; L81,30; L93,
  293; L117A,3; L122,8 11 15; UC Manuscripts,
  27-30 45-6
  Excerpta historica L36,83; L37,109; UC
  Manuscripts,26
Benziger Brothers L67,71; L87,290; L88,48
  139 147
Beresford, Rev.John Jervis L5,216 229; IU
Beresford, Margaret IU
Berger, Miss Adele L86,408
Berger, Mme.Florence K. L3,101; L5,93 119
  126; L85,358; IU
  A Winter in the city of pleasure L38,364; L39,
  233; L40,464
Berggreu, G. L67,242

Berkeley, Hon.George C.G.F. L2,23; L84,84
  127; L117A,32; IU
  Anecdotes of the Upper Ten Thousand L37,22
  49 290; L38,89; L59,131
  Berkeley Castle L53,248 277
Bernard, Charles de L55,11
Bernard, John
  Retrospections of the stage L1,45; L52,76
  108 277; L68,42 53
Bernard, William Baile L1,45; L52,76 108;
  L68,42 53; [L81,112; L101,103] ; L117B,45
  Retrospections of America (prop.) L52,319
Bernard-Beere, F. IU
Berry, Miss Mary
  Social life in England and France L36,110;
  L117A,24; IU
Berry, Miss Sarah L84,256-7; L122,136
Bertram, J.G. L5,91
Bertram, James G. L84,30 33; IU
Bertrand & Son L1,35; L82,174 207; L90,106;
  IU
Besant, Sir Walter L3,83; L4,28; L5,38 50 59
  68; L41,viii; L61,131-2; L62,260; L63,161;
  L84,287 335; L85,358; L86,204 270 270-4(c)
  277 346; L123,263; IU(Palestine...)
  The French humourists L38,296; L39,200;
  L40,224; L41,183a 510; L42,190
  Jerusalem L37,293; L38,88; L39,98-9;
  L40,435; L41,332 364; L42,247; L63,323;
  L119,86; UC Manuscripts,6 11
  Our work in Palestine L3,33; L38,274; L39,
  179; L40,310
  Twenty-one years work in the Holy Land L40,
  166; L41,299
Bethell, Hon.Augusta (Mrs.Parker) L2,25;
  L62,100; L85,418; L86,101; IU(Parker)
Bethune, Lord
  see Lindesay-Bethune
Bettany, George Thomas L85,470; L86,136
  139 142; UC
Bettany, Mrs.Jeanie Gwynne L5,211
Beukhausen, G. L52,38
Bevan, T.B. L5,19
Bevington, L.S. L5,95
Bewicke, Miss Alicia (Mrs.Little) L2,76; L3,
  68; L4,83; L84,261 270; IU(Little)
  Flirts and flirts L37,128; L38,131; L59,165
  Lonely Carlotta L38,315; L39,434; L59,322;
  L101,144
  Love me for my love L37,172; L38,175;
  L39,398; L40,442
  One foot on shore L37,212; L38,203
Bewicke, Nora IU
Bickers, H. L55,162
Bickers & Bush L83,44
Bickers & Son L62,322; L84,76; L85,281
Bickerstaffe-Drew, Francis L5,244; L89,61
  113 114(c); IU
Bicknell, Algernon S. IU
Bicknell, Walter L. IU
Bida L84,205
Bigot, Mme.Marie (Miss Healy) L5,85; IU
Billing & Sons L64,262; L66,320; L85,173

305 308 332 356 475; L86,72 91 164 199 286(c)
  288(c) 335 362 422(c) 425 431; L87,148 156 196
  276; L88,258-9 261 277 322 329(c); L89,87;
  IU; UC
Billings, H.I. IU
Bilton, Rev.William L1,99; L117B,14
Bindley, Charles L92,266
Bindloss, H. L5,297
Binett, John L92,9-10
Bingley, Charles S. IU
Binney, Frederick A. IU
Binyon, Robert Laurence L5,218
Birch, William J. L90,318
Bird, Mr.
  see Autotype Company
Bird, Miss H.M. UC(Riddell)
Bird, Mrs.Mary P.(Mrs.Bonham Bird) L3,141;
  L5,261; L87,140; IU
  Wedded to a genius (orig.The House of bondage)
  L42,446; L66,62
Bird, Dr.Robert M.
  Nick of the woods L54,34; L117A,24
  Peter Pilgrim L54,162
Birt, Captain W.J. L5,99; IU
Bishop, Florence IU
Bishop, H. L53,320-5
Bishop, Mrs.Maria C. L3,134; L4,29; L22,
  336; L88,280; IU
  A Memoir of Mrs.Augustus Craven L42,352
  369; L66,168 309-11; L67,71; L119,160
Bisset L90,310
Bisset, Catherine IU
Blachford, John L117B,32
Black, Mrs. L87,65(c) 66
Black, A. & C. L67,77
Black, Alexander L83,232 254
Black, Charles L88,66
Black, Charles E.D. L5,282; IU
Black, Clementina IU
Black, Robert L3,110 123; L85,63 68-84; L87,
  110; IU
  Horse racing in England L42,338; L66,21
  Love or lucre L39,276; L40,440; L41,518;
  L60,63; L123,52-115
Black, William L5,25; IU
Black, William Henry IU
Black and White IU
Blackburn, E.Owen IU
Blackburn, Henry L95,104 106 152 174-5; IU
Blackett, Arthur IU
Blackett, Henry IU
Blackett, Spencer L63,278; L64,237-40; L68,
  178; IU(Blackett and Watt)
Blackford, John L55,317
Blackmore, Richard D. L88,206(c); UC
Blackwell, Anna IU
Blackwell, Richard G. IU
Blackwood, A. L81,48 231
Blackwood & Sons L57,247; L61,305; L65,48;
  L66,198; [L84,144] ; IU; UC
Blaede, Gertrude IU
Blaikie, Mrs.J.Lang L5,121
Blake, Mrs.Agnes J. L22,356

Blake, Mrs.Cecilia M.   L94,194-6 240 247
Blake, Edith   IU
Blake, George   L83,266 268; IU
Blake, H.A.   L5,81
Blake, Sir Henry A.   IU
Blake, R.   IU
Blake, Sophia J.   IU(Jex-Blake)
Blake & Co.   L85,386; IU
Blaker, Mrs.Mary (Miss M.Mark-Lemon)
  L5,215
Blakey, Robert
  The History of political literature   L1,108;
  L36,94; L117B,39
Blakiston, Peyton   IU
Blanc, Jean J.L.
  Threatened social disorganization   [L6,180] ;
  L36,186
Blanch, Henry M.   L75,348-55
Blanchard, Samuel L.   IU
Blanchard & Lea
  see Lea & Blanchard
Bland, Mrs.(E.Nesbit)   L5,168
Blandford, George F.   IU
Blaquiere, J. de   L95,27
Blaze de Bury, M.elle   L5,194
Blaze de Bury, Marie P.R.   L82,231 279 324;
  L93,76 124 206 213; L117A,24; IU
  Leonie Vermont   L56,186
  Memoirs of the Princess Palatine   L36,116;
  L82,364
[Blenkinsop]
  Memoirs   L36,111
Blessington, Lady
  see Gardiner, M.
Blissett, Miss Nellie K.   L5,281; L22,355 359
  361; L67,268 317
Blomfield, Miss D.F.   L5,192
Blott, J.S.   IU
Blount, Miss Constance S.   L3,91; IU
  Little Lady Lorraine   L38,301; L39,447;
  L59,308; L101,54 57
  A Losing hazard   L38,340; L39,440; L59,
  339
  Our next neighbour   L38,371; L39,442
Bloxam, Mrs.   L81,53 59
Bloxsome, Edward   L1,191; L58,189
Bluhm, Miss Elizabeth   L87,274
Blumenthal, Louise   IU
Blundell, Mrs.   L5,223; L67,38
Blundell, Charles J.W.   IU
Blundell, Mary E.   IU
Blunt, Reginald   L86,265
Blyth, Harry   L87,110
Blyth, Mary P.   L3,83; L94,278; UC
  Antoinette (orig.Chateau Boisfontaine)   L41,
  468; L63,313
  The Queen's jewel   L41,457; L42,471
Boaden, James   L52,302; L90,17 22; L117A,
  32; IU
Board of Trade, London   L84,35-7
Board of Trade, Toronto   L87,264-5(c)
Boards, J.   IU
Bock, Carl A.   L85,240; IU

Boddam, A.   L59,320(c)
Boddington, Miss H.   L22,365
Boddy, Mary E.   IU(Broddy)
Bode, Clement A. de (Baron)   IU(De Bode)
Bodenstedt, Friedrich M. von
  The Morning-land   L36,204; L56,319; L82,
  170
Bodichon   L5,27
Bogue, David   L117B,27
Bohn, de E.F.   L85,54 176 180
Bohn, Henry G.   L53,226; L57,62; L58,239;
  L82,181 183 186 188 190; L83,71 80-1 212-13;
  L117B,5; IU
Boissier, Rev.G.R.   L93,24; L117B,40; IU
Bojanowski, E. von   L86,466
Bompas, George   L86,57
Bon Marché, Liverpool   L86,445; L87,252;
  L88,353
Bond, Dr.   L88,65 65(c)
Bond, Mrs.   L88,199-200(c)
Bond, Lady Caroline F.   L3,116; L86,439;
  IU; UC
Bond, Sir Edward A.   IU
Bond, R.Warwick   L5,164
Bond, Thomas   L85,372 378
Boner, Charles   UC
  Memoirs and letters   L2,87; L3,56; L37,257;
  L38,87; L39,201; L59,232
Boner, Emma   IU
Bonneau-Avenant, Alfred de   L2,89; L84,140
  183; IU
  The Life of Madame de Beauharnais de
  Miramion   L2,40; L37,184; L38,181; L39,
  216 401; L40,444; L59,211; L99,256
Bonner, George W.   IU
Bonsey, M.E.   IU
Bonstetten, Charles Victor de   UC Manuscripts,
  39
Booksellers & Stationers' Association of
  Victoria, Australia   IU
Booksellers' Provident Institution, London   IU
Boon & Co.   L88,240
Boosey, Mrs.Ph.Solms
  Gordon of Duncairn   L1,191; L36,67; L58,
  189
Boosey, Thomas   L93,251
Boosey, William   L5,125
Booth, Mrs.   L5,180
Booth, Miss E. Gore   L5,271
Booth, J.   L117B,7
Booth, Lionel   L83,250; L84,52
Booth, Mrs.Y.M.H.   L85,145; IU
Boothby, L.C.   IU
Boothman, C.   L95,32
Borlase   L5,65
Borthwick, Rev.Robert B.   L2,84; L3,34; L84,
  148 174 211 213 240; IU
  Fourfold message of Advent   L37,22; L38,130;
  L39,207 222; L40,431; L41,219
  The Praise of God   L37,322; L38,212; L39,
  423; L40,450; L41,219
  What is unity?   L37,322; L38,254; L39,423;
  L40,461; L41,219

Bosanquet, G.W.   L2,70
Bosh   L26,7
Bossange & Co.   L81,33; L84,157
Boswell, James
  Letters of James Boswell   L1,148; L36,248
Bosworth   L84,83
Bosworth, Annie   IU
Boteler, Miss Maria   L53,111; L92,85; L117B, 16
Boteler, Thomas
  Narrative of a voyage to Africa   L42,403; L53,111
Bothmer, Marie von   IU
Botten, C.   IU
Bouchette, Joseph
  The British dominions   L52,232 234
  A Topographical dictionary   L52,232 234
Boulger, Demetrius C.   IU
Boulger, Dorothy H.
  see Havers, D.H.
Boulnois, Miss Helen   L22,355
Boult, S.H.   L5,72
Boulton, Oscar   L5,202; L87,143; IU
Boulton, William B.   L22,357
Bourcicault, Dion   IU(Boucicault); UC
Bourke, H.   IU
Bourn, H.M.   L85,192
Bourne, H.R.Fox   L2,63; L3,76; L5,32;
  L59,190-2; L84,95; L102,81; IU
  English merchants   L37,47; L40,429; L59, 124; L107,1
  English seamen under the Tudors   L37,50;
  L38,92; L39,429; L59,137
Bourrienne, L.A.Fauvelet de
  see Fauvelet de Bourrienne, L.A.
Boussod, Valadon & Co.   L66,203; L86,116
  159 171 204; L87,182 186(c); L88,281 333; UC
Boutell, Rev.Charles   L2,57; L83,271 274-6
  Heraldry   L36,151; L37,34-5; L38,84; L59,2
Bouton D'Or (pseud.)   UC Manuscripts,12
Boutourlin, M.
  see Buturlin, M.
Bow Bells   L67,125
Bowden, A.   IU
Bowden, Edward   IU
Bowden, Mary   IU
Bower, Cotton & Bower   L88,88
Bowers, William
  Naval adventures   L53,28 103
Bowie, A.G.   IU
Bowker, James   L2,15
Bowlby, G.B.   IU
Bowles, Mr.   L84,140
Bowles, Emily   L2,33; IU
Bowles, Marie   IU
Bowles, Thomas G.   IU
Bowles & Gardiner   IU(Gardiner)
Bowman, F.E.   UC
Bowman, Walter   L5,110
Bowstrad, Miss   L89,90
Boyce, John C.
  Nigh unto the end   L39,347; L40,308; L41, 525; L42,516; IU

Boyce, M.A.B.   IU
Boyce, William   L62,290-1
Boyd   L93,141-3
Boyd, Alexander & Sons   L87,170
Boyd, Rev.Andrew K.H.   L5,79; IU
Boyd, Archibald   L1,143; L82,143; L117A,37; IU
  The Cardinal   L36,118 231; L57,278 287
  The Crown ward   L36,89; L58,51
  The Duchess   L37,67; L56,269; L57,287
Boyd, Archibald   IU
Boyd, C.W.   IU
Boyd, John   IU
Boyd, Percy   L93,207
Boyd, T.J.   L82,170-2
Boyd, Sir Thomas J.   IU
Boykin, Edward M.   IU
Boyle, Frederick   L2,75; L3,182; L5,16 35
  50 139; L84,319; L85,467; IU; UC
  A Good hater   L40,400; L41,511; L62,263-4
  The Narrative of an expelled correspondent
  L39,275; L40,429
  A Ride across a continent   L37,51; L99,72
  A Trio of worthies: early exhibitions of art in
  Liverpool   L38,253; L39,258
Boyle, R.W.   IU
[Boyne]   L82,57
Boys, Augusta   IU
Boys, H.   L86,389
Brabant, William F.   IU
Brabner, W.A.   L5,29
Brabourne, Lord
  see Hugessen, E.H.K.
Brace, Charles L.   L1,160; L2,20; L82,280;
  L83,128; L117B,42
  The Norse-folk   L36,41; L83,136
Bradbury, Edward   L5,99; IU
Bradbury, W.H.   IU
Bradbury & Evans   L82,214; L83,86 159 176
Bradby, Edward H.   IU
Braddon, Julia   IU
Braddon, Mary E.
  see Maxwell, M.E.
Braddyll, Mrs.Mary M.   L87,190
Bradfield, Thomas   L5,185
Bradford, Rev.William   L56,193; L83,77
The Bradford Observer   IU
Bradley, Miss   L5,182
Bradley, Rev.Edward (Cuthbert Bede pseud.)
  L1,156; L83,141-2 148; L93,299 304; L95,73
  160; L98,156; IU
  Fairy fables   L36,230; L58,148
  Nearer and dearer   L36,95
  A Tour in tartan-land   L36,127; L37,39;
  L58,310 318
Bradley, Emily T.   L86,265; IU(Smith,E.T.)
  Life of the Lady Arabella Stuart   L41,346;
  L42,264; L64,186-8
Bradley, George Granville   UC
Brady   L83,202
Brady & Scott   L83,196
Braim, Thomas H.   L1,72; L117B,17
  A History of New South Wales   L55,298

Braine, C.Dimond H.   IU

Braithwaite, J.   L88,197(c)

Brand, Ferdinand   L81,203

Brand, Henry B.W.   IU

Brand, W.F.   L86,452

Brandaid, John   IU

Brandes, Georg M.C.
Lord Beaconsfield   L3,110; L39,322; L40,
424 426; L41,504 506; L60,172;   IU

Brandon, Henry
Statistics of crime (prop.)   L54,154

Branfill, Benjamin A.   IU

Brassey, Annie   IU

Braumüller & Son   L85,126 149-52 158 161 224
226-8 231 249;   IU

Bray, Mrs.Anna E.
see Stothard, A.E.

Bray, Sir Claude A.   L3,49; L4,68; L5,276;
L22,333; L86,365-6; L87,60 63; L88,182 184
The King's revenge   L42,419; L67,131
Last of the Dynmokes   L41,405; L42,467;
L65,266
To save himself   L41,432; L42,496; L64,339

Bray, Lady Emily O.   IU

Bray, Reginald   IU

Braybrooke, Lord Charles   L82,362; UC

Braybrooke, Lady Jane   IU

Braybrooke, Richard G.   IU

Brayley, Edward W.   IU

Bread Relief Fund   IU

Brebrier, Arthur   L22,361

Breidenbach, H.   IU

Breitkopf & Härtel   L86,365;   IU

Brenan, J.G.   L5,219

Brereton, Austin   IU

Breslin, J.William   L5,308

Breton, Mrs.Florence Barbara (F.B.Slade)   UC

Breton, Frederic   L3,144; L87,103 212; L89,
118; L117A,22;   IU
A Heroine in homespun   L42,452; L65,326;
L66,44-8

Breton, William H.
Excursions in New South Wales   L53,23

Brett, John   IU

Brette, Phillippe H.E.
A French reader   L37,109; L38,135; L39,145

Bretton, W.   L81,58

Breunel, Miss F.   IU

Brew, Miss M.   UC

Brewer, John S.   L53,349; L117A,18

Brewster, Dr.   L81,32 80

Brewster, Sir David   IU

Brice, Arthur Montefiore (A.Montefiore pseud.)
L5,218 310; L22,354 358

Bricknell, J.L.   L5,240

Bridge, Rev.Arthur   L3,144; L85,259 314 344;
IU; UC
Poems   L39,377; L40,224; L41,196; L42,171

Bridge, Miss C.H.M.   L5,100;   IU

Bridge, Sir Cyprian A.G.   IU

Bridge, G.W.   IU

Bridgeman, J.   L57,93; L117A,7

Bridges, Emily   IU

Briefless, Jeremiah (pseud.)   [L123,22]
Maidenthorpe   L2,47; L9,149; L36,285;
L37,197; L38,199; L70,87; L83,235

Brierley, Thomas   IU

Brierly, Lady   L86,370

Briggs, Rev.Thomas   L61,315

Bright, Augustus   IU

Brinville, A.   L93,58

Briscoe, J.Potter   IU

Bristed, A.H.   L5,282

Bristol, Dean of   L88,99

British Medical Journal   L87,189(c)

British Museum   IU

British Ornithologists' Union   L64,40

British Orphan Asylum, Slough   IU(Barry,A.)
UC Manuscripts,9

Britton, William   L85,420

Broad, Charles E.   IU

Broadwood, Miss Alice   L5,297

Brock, Mrs.Clutton   L5,267

Brockedon   L81,54

Brockhaus, F.A.   L88,200 210-11

Brockman, Janie   IU

Broderip, Mrs.Frances F.   L2,76; L3,32;   IU;
UC
Tib's tit-bits   L37,253; L38,235; L39,225;
L59,179-81

Broderip, John S.   IU

Brodhead, John R.   L56,148; L82,15 313

Brodie, Miss H.S.   L5,156

Brodie, Mrs.Jessy A.   L3,132; L60,230-5;
L85,191 236;   IU; UC

Brodie, [T.]   IU

Brodribb, W.B.   L5,167

Brodrick, Rev.Alan   L5,277

Bromley, Frederick   IU

Brooke, Miss   L5,253; L88,279

Brooke, Sir Arthur de Capell   L81,51
Sketches in Spain   L52,155 157; L68,69

Brooke, Emma F.(E.Fairfax Byrrne pseud.)
L3,162; L86,137 143 231
A Fair country maid   L40,383; L62,41
The Heir without a heritage   L40,89; L41,491;
L42,484; L63,209

Brooke, Sir James
The Private letters   L36,113; L57,140 169
289

Brooke, Samuel   L91,191

Brooke, W.A.   IU

Brooke, W.H.   IU

Brooker, Thomas & Co.   L85,282; L88,305-6;
IU; IU(Brooker & Harrison); IU(Copper &
Steel...)

Brooker & Jepson   L88,319 321

Brookes, W.Murray   L94,296

Brookfield, Mrs.Frances M.   L5,178

Brookfield, Jane O.   IU

Brooks, Mr.   L2,61

Brooks, Cecil   L85,435

Brooks, Charles W.S.   L1,100; L2,18; L82,
291; L83,55 57 141-2 144 152 155 171 178-81
183-4; L93,254 307; L117B,30;
IU(Brooks,S.); UC

Aspen Court L36,225 235; L38,372; L58,144
The Gordian Knot L36,223 236 240-1; L37,44
194; L86,111; IU; UC
L38,147
Brooks, George IU
Brooksbank, Thomas IU Unidentified,(A)
Broome, H. L86,110(c)
Bross L91,93-4
Brotherton, Mrs.Mary L2,62; L5,27 258;
L84,66; IU
Brough
Heads and tales L38,96
Brougham, Lady Emily F. IU
Brougham, Lord Henry L56,186; L82,32 267;
IU
Brougham, Lord William UC
Broughton, Mrs.Augusta Delves L3,76; L63,
194; L86,111; IU; UC
Broughton, Miss Rhoda L2,26 86; L3,37 167;
L4,30; L5,32 38 132 139170; L22,339 361;
L60,164 178; L61,214-16; L84,104-5 124 154
157 172 201 272 321; L85,166 336; L86,160;
L87,41; L88,48(c) 210; L89,77-8 82; L96,63;
IU; IU George Bentley,178-9; IU Richard
Bentley II,589 659+1; UC
Alas L41,32 455; L42,14-15 478 497; L64,
100-2 202 266; L65,1; L66,34-7; L119,11
A Beginner L42,25-6 442; L66,60 133-5;
L119,147
Belinda (orig.Miss Watson's victims) L40,
46-7 347; L41,40; L42,15-16; L61,143 180-3
237; L119,9
Cometh up as a flower L37,58 69 87 301;
L38,33; L39,31; L40,36; L41,33 129; L42,
16-17; L59,128; L60,1; L99,18; L119,1
Dear Faustina (orig.Female friendships) L42,
27; L67,163-5 246
Doctor Cupid (orig.Peggy and Prue) L40,46
441; L41,41 129 507; L42,17-18 481; L63,
73-5 169; L119,10
The Game and the candle (pub.McM.) L42,
200; L67,287-9
'Goodbye,sweetheart!' L37,317; L38,51-51a
258; L39,32-3; L40,37-8; L41,34; L42,
18-19; L59,222; L119,4
Joan L38,373; L39,38-9 451; L40,39 436;
L41,35 515; L42,19-20 486; L59,344; L60,
30; L119,7
Mrs.Bligh L41,97 408; L42,20-1; L65,177
247; L119,12
Nancy L38,74 302; L39,34 402 424; L40,
40-1 447; L41,36 42 523; L42,21-2 27 492;
L59,304-5 310; L119,6
Not wisely but too well L38,338; L39,35-6;
L40,42; L41,37; L42,22-3 27; L59,85; L98,
217-19; L99,71; L119,2
Red as a rose is she L37,53 235; L38,34-5
214; L39,37; L40,43-4; L41,38 42; L42,
23-4 29; L59,193 208-10; L119,3
Scylla or Charybdis L41,26; L42,429; L66,
248; L67,22 50-1 62 66; L119,148
Second thoughts L39,338 358; L40,45; L41,
39; L42,24-5; L60,194 243; L119,8
Tales for Christmas Eve L38,275; L39,224

L59,270-1; L119,5
Twilight stories L39,417; L40,177; L41,155
158; L42,158; L119,5; L123,207-8
[Browhill, Bertrand] IU
Brown, Mr. L84,146
Brown, A. & Son L85,299 299-300(c) 300
Brown, Alfred H. IU
Brown, Andrew M.
Life and labours of John Campbell L59,143;
L84,98
Brown, Arthur IU
Brown, G.M. L92,178
Brown, Helen Kier IU
Brown, J.B. L90,304
Brown, John F. IU
Brown, Joseph IU
Brown, Lewis L92,105
Brown, Peter Blazes IU
Brown, Robert B.
see Borthwick, R.B.
Brown, Thomas B. IU
Brown, Roberts & Co. L85,387; L88,305 307
Browne, C.F. L2,65
Browne, Charles L2,68
Browne, E.J. L88,240-1(c)
[Browne], F.Napier IU
Browne, Mrs.Fielding L5,36
Browne, Frances IU
The Hidden sin L36,324; L37,142 147; L38,
149; L63,118
Browne, H. L82,179
Browne, H.Devey IU
Browne, H.L. L91,203; L92,116
Browne, Hablot Knight IU; UC
Browne, Hamilton IU
Browne, J. L81,151
Browne, J.H. L91,256
Browne, John H.Balfour IU
Browne, Richard Charles L5,219; IU
Browne, Richard G.M. L2,16; L84,41; L94,
279 313-15; IU
Astronomical geology L36,244; L37,46;
L38,93
Browne, Robert L86,118 233(c) 234-5
Browne, Rev.Robert W. L56,327; L83,78
A History of Greek classical literature L6,
134; L7,171; L8,150 200; L36,30; L56,289;
L117A,14
A History of Roman classical literature L36,
30 111; L37,36 242; L38,93; L40,263; L41,
226 229; L42,204; L56,289; L117A,14
Browne, Zoe Houston IU
Browning, Elizabeth B.
see Barrett, E.
Browning, George L5,100; IU
Browning, William Ernst L84,288; IU(Ernst-
Browning)
Bruce, Alice IU
Bruce, John L57,81-3; L82,189; L117B,7;
IU
Bruce, Knight L91,98-9
Bruce, Miss Polly L5,284
Brunton, Dr. L81,71

Bruton, H.W. L86,81; UC
Bruylant-Christophe & Co. IU
Bryan, Henry IU
Bryans, Clement L3,44; L4,31; L63,137-40;
  L86,92 94 114; L88,198
Bryant, W.Charles L5,202
Bryant, William IU
Bryce, D. & Son L86,314; L88,59
Bryce, David L83,88 105
Bryce, William L86,433
Bryden, Henry A. IU
Brydges, Sir S.Egerton L117B,3; IU
Buchanan, George L65,329-34; IU
Buchanan, Prof.Robert
  Tales of the two rebellions L56,184
  see Fillan, A.D.
Buchanan, Robert W. L2,67; L3,84-5; L5,102;
  L82,86; L84,323; L85,20 239 249 447; L86,
  123 128-9 212 258 329; IU; UC(Bentley-end of
  B)
  Autobiography (prop.) L40,221; L41,196;
  L62,212
  A Child of nature (orig.The Story of Madeline)
  L39,299 305; L40,425; L60,139
  A Hero in spite of himself (prop.) L40,398;
  L41,490; L42,485; L62,198
  The Master of the mine L40,344; L41,521;
  L62,184
  The Shadow of the sword L38,373; L39,253
  452; L60,9
Buckingham, Lord
  see Chandos, R.T.N.
Buckingham, Leicester S.F.
  Memoirs of Mary Stuart L1,72; L55,192;
  L117B,40
Buckland, Francis T. L1,149; L2,16; L5,43;
  L83,157 190 212 217; L93,305; IU
  Curiosities of natural history L36,224 245
  250-1 265 294 308; L37,40-2 291; L38,90-2;
  L39,127-8 137 142; L40,91 226-8; L41,201-5;
  L42,173-5; L58,118 213 248; L59,92; L119,
  123-6; L123,204
Buckle, George Earle IU; UC
Buckle, Mary S. IU
Buckley, William IU
Buckstone, John B. IU
Buckton, Catherine M. IU
Buckton, George Boudler UC
Buckton, Mrs.K.
  see Carter, Miss K
Buée, Henry S.B. IU
Buél, Kenneth F. UC
Buerstenbinder, Elizabeth (E.Werner pseud.)
  IU(Bürstenbinder)
  Beacon fires L3,63; L41,433; L42,480; L64,
  295-9; L67,253
  Fickle fortune L3,92; L39,369; L40,113 430;
  L41,105-6; L42,125; L60,236-7
  A Heavy reckoning L3,33; L41,444; L42,486
  Her son (orig.Old Mike or Wild Mike) L3,92;
  L40,453; L41,483; L63,135-6
  No surrender (orig.Dearly bought) L3,92;
  L39,309 378; L40,112-13; L41,102-3; L42,

126; L123,196-7
  Raymond's atonement L3,92; L40,387-8;
  L41,531; [L62,27]
  Success: and how he won it L3,92; L38,368;
  L39,96 448; L40,110; L41,104-5; L42,126-7
  Under a charm (orig.Vineta) L3,92; L39,231
  280 292; L40,111-12 460; L41,103-4; L42,127
Buffum, Edward G.
  Six months in the gold mines L36,114
The Builder L88,248; IU
Bull, John IU(Bull,S.)
Bull, Samuel IU
Bullen, William IU
Bulley, Miss A.Amy L5,161
Bullfinch, Thomas L83,48 88
Bulloch, James D. L3,163; L22,367; L42,541;
  L85,395 399; IU
  The Secret service L40,329; L41,531 540;
  L62,54
Bullock, William L84,257; IU
Bulman, G.W. L5,290
Bulmer, Miss Maud A. L5,278
Bulwer, Edward G.E.L.(Lord Lytton) L1,30;
  L2,23; L6,48 106; L36,158; L80,17-19; L81,
  38 223 230; L82,146 168 180; L83,90; L84,105
  201-2 206 221; L117B,43; L122,91; IU(Lytton);
  [IU(Pollak)] ; IU Unidentified,(A); UC(Lytton)
  England and the English L53,3 107; L74,37
  181
  Eugene Aram L54,284-98
  The Fall of Florence (prop.) L56,82
  Godolphin L52,321 323
  Harold L6,118; L56,82
  The Last days of Pompeii L53,3; L54,284-98;
  L74,37 181
  Miscellaneous prose works L37,182; L38,176;
  L39,426; L59,151
  Paul Clifford L54,284-98
  The Siamese twins L52,172; L68,78
Bulwer, Lady Georgiana C.M.(Lady Dalling)
  L59,274-89 291-4 302; IU(Dalling and
  Bulwer,G.)
Bulwer, Rosina D.(Lady Lytton) L80,17-18 20;
  L81,224-5; IU(Lytton)
Bulwer, Sir W.H.Lytton (Lord Dalling) L2,31;
  L3,18 55; L5,248; L59,302; L81,144; L82,
  44; L84,93 110 126 146 154 165-8 174 180;
  L117A,7; IU(Dalling and Bulwer,W.); IU
  George Bentley,113+1; IU Unidentified,(A)
  France: social, literary, political L53,105;
  L74,37 181
  Historical characters L37,37 48 313; L38,95
  366; L39,99-100; L40,202 230; L41,178;
  L59,136 185 274-89 291-4
  The Life of Viscount Palmerston L37,223 260;
  L38,208 288 313; L39,181-2; L40,312; L41,
  266; L42,253; L59,185-7 274-89 291-4
  The Monarchy of the middle classes L53,148
  Sir Robert Peel L38,285; L39,203; L123,
  30-51
Bulwer-Lytton
  see Bulwer
Bumpus, J. IU

Bunbury, Mrs. L1,81
Bunbury, Clement L5,176
Bunbury, Mrs.Frances J. L82,169; L117A,13
Bunbury, Sir Henry E. L93,232; L117B,10
  Narratives of some passages in the Great War
  L36,117; L57,304; L82,346 352; L83,38
Bunbury, Mervyn R. L84,321
Bunbury, Miss Selina IU
  Evelyn L56,158; L117B,28
Bunch, R.Stanton UC
Bundy, Sir Thomas IU
Bunn, A. L81,58
Bunn, Alfred L1,101; L117B,10; IU
  Old England and New England L57,267
  The Stage L54,269
Bunnett, Mrs. L5,64
Bunnett, Miss Fanny E. L2,68; L3,48; L59,
  90; L83,249 277-8; L84,83 125
Bunnett, Miss S.E. L87,134
Bunnètt, V.E. IU; IU(Bunnitt)
Bunney, A.H. L88,249; L89,87
[Bunser, E.] IU
Burbidge, James I. L122,15
Burckhardt, John L.
  Notes on the Bedouins L1,52; L52,4 29 31;
  L68,14 28-9
Burd, R.S. L5,133
Burdo, Adolphe M.L.
  The Niger and the Benueh L3,110; L39,335;
  L40,336; L42,404
Burdon, Miss Hannah D.
  Seymour of Sudley L53,144; L81,164; L117A,
  11
Burette, F.H.Apel L59,155
Burgess, M.A. IU
Burghes, A.M. L86,76 190
Burgoyne, Miss L3,53
Burgoyne, Sir John F.
  The Military opinions L1,126; L3,53; L36,
  73 78; L37,45; L58,201; IU
Burgoyne, Miss Margarett A. IU
Burgoyne, Roderick H. L3,157; L85,356 400;
  L88,103; IU
  Historical records of the 93rd Sutherland
  Highlanders L40,380; L41,226; L42,204
Burke, Christian L5,276; L22,363; L88,159
Burke, J.Bernard IU
Burke, John L1,21; L52,126-9; L68,71 76-7;
  IU
  Official Kalendar L52,48; L68,34
Burke, Ulick IU
Burleigh, T. L86,374; L87,138 214; L88,
  75(c) 75 230
Burlingham, Charles Culp UC
Burlington, R. L88,316
Burmester, F.G. L5,62
Burn, J.H. L90,120-1; L117A,30; IU
Burn, James & Co. L86,240; L87,280; L89,
  96; IU
Burnaby, Frederick G.
  Our radicals (orig.Politics and passion) L3,
  48; L40,103 462; L41·,487 525; L42,470;
  L63,104-7; UC Manuscripts,31

Burnand, F.C. L95,113; IU
Burne IU
Burney & Wills, Misses IU
Burns, Robert UC Manuscripts,39
Burns & Oates L62,278; L85,394
Burrell, William S.
  Indian memories
  see Cuthell, E.E.
Burrow, C.Kennett L5,141; L22,360
Burrow, John H. IU
  Jabez Oliphant L2,25; L37,159 171; L38,
  168; L59,221; L100,11
Burrows, Rev.F.R. L5,204
Burrows, Prof.Montagu L85,446; IU
Bürstenbinder, E.
  see Buerstenbinder, E.
Burt, R.K. & Co. IU
Burton, Isabel L85,53; IU
Burton, L.W. IU
Burton, Mrs.Mina E. L3,65; L5,48; L86,
  392-3; IU
  Ruling the planets L41,427; L42,495; L65,41
Burton, Sir Richard F. L1,101; L3,106; L85,
  19 21; L117B,15; IU
  Goa and the Blue Mountains L7,171; L8,150;
  L36,115; L56,291
  Scinde L36,86; L57,22
  Sind revisited L38,371; L39,256; L41,510;
  L60,46
Burton, Thomas S. L56,191
Bury, Lady Charlotte
  see Campbell, C.S.M.
Bury, Viscount W.
  see Keppel, W.C.
Bury, Rev.W.E. IU
Bush, H. L83,204
Bush, R.J. L83,268
Bushby, Mrs.Anne S. L1,156; L2,55; L82,310;
  L83,140; L93,186-7; L94,166; L117A,13; IU
  Poems L38,44
  The Danes sketched by themselves L36,145;
  L37,42
Bushby, H.N.G. L5,220
Bushby, Miss Jane L2,55; L3,83; IU
Bushe, John L55,30 168 319; L56,141; L57,70;
  L82,181; IU(Bush)
Bushell, Samuel L75,198-287
Bushnell, Miss Margaret L22,353
Buss, R.W. IU
Butcher, Mr. L86,133
Butcher, Charles H.
  Sir Gilbert L1,173; L36,61-2
Butcher, Mrs.Edith L.
  see Floyer, E.L.
Bute, K. UC
Butland, George T. L83,69
Butler, Alfred
  Elphinstone L1,102; L54,316; L117A,34
Butler, E.H. & Co. L86,311
Butler, Fanny L94,258
Butler, Harriet IU
Butler, Lady Rachel E.
  see Russell, R.E.

Butler, Richard (Earl of Glengall)
 The Follies of fashion L1,40; L52,52; L68,
 36; IU(Glengall)
Butler, Weeden IU
Butler, Sir William F. IU
Butler & Tanner L64,7-9; L86,219
Butt, Geraldine R.(Mrs.Glasgow) IU
Butt, Isaac IU
Butterworth, C. L67,133
Butterworth, Joshua L83,71-2
Buturlin, Mikhail IU
Buxton, Mrs.Bertha H. L3,89; L5,90 93; IU
 Jennie of 'The Princes' L38,367; L39,442
 Won! L39,243; L60,53
Buxton, Sir Edward L83,34
Buxton, Sydney C. IU
Buzzard, Thomas L83,186
Bye-Gones IU
Byerley, Sir John L53,158; L117A,18
Byers, Mr. L81,157 162
Byng, F.E.C.
 Fourfold messge of Advent
 see Borthwick, R.B.
Byrde, Mrs.M.B. L5,297
Byrne, Eleanor R. IU
Byrne, J.H. L92,184
Byrne, John F.D.
 Australian writers L42,375; L67,129; L88,
 184
Byrne, Joseph C.
 Twelve years' wanderings L36,116; L56,61-2
Byrne, Mrs.Julia C. L1,179; [L83,204]
 Undercurrents overlooked L36,211; L58,206
Byrne, Oliver L3,95; L84,226; IU
 Byrne's treatise on navigation L38,234; L39,
 260; L40,225; L41,536-7; L42,324; L60,38
Byron, Lord George G.
 The Unpublished letters (prop.) L37,321;
 L38,264; L39,201; L40,423; L41,537; L42,
 524; [L55,303]; L59,260-4; IU
 see Young, Henry S.
Byrrne, E.Fairfax
 see Brooke, E.F.

C., Mrs. IU Unidentified
C., C.H. IU Unidentified
C., Edward
 see Callow, E.
Cadell, Robert IU
Cadell, Thomas L1,58; L52,147; L54,6; L68,
 66; L90,111 127; L117A,32
Cadiot, E.H. IU
Cadogan, Lady Augusta S. IU
[Cadogan, F.] IU
Caignart de Saulcy, Louis F.J.
 Narrative of a journey L57,156-7
Caillié, Réné
 Travels through Central Africa L1,35 53-5;
 L42,402
Caine, T.Hall L5,224; L87,160; IU; IU
 George Bentley,285

Calabrella, Baroness E.C. de
 The Double oath L56,140; L117A,22
Calamy, Edmund
 An Historical account of my own life L1,43 59
Calcroft, M. L93,159
Calderon, G.L. L5,18; L89,70
Calderon, Philip H. L84,296
Callow, Edward L3,105; L85,52; IU
 Five years penal servitude L39,267 270 411;
 L40,168 429; L60,61-3 78-93 174
 Whitecross and the bench L39,304; L60,
 118-20 174; L123,167 187-8
Calmet, Augustin
 The Phantom world L36,126; L56,224; UC
 Manuscripts,6
Calthorpe, Lady Eliza M. IU
Calton, Robert B. L1,82; L83,244; L117B,38;
 UC Manuscripts,10
 The Bye-lanes and downs of England L36,77;
 L37,235; L38,229; L39,403 422; L40,456;
 L41,504; L42,501
 Rambles in Sweden L7,164; L8,34
Calvary, S. & Co. IU
Cambridge, Ada (Mrs.G.F.Cross) L3,124;
 L4,84; L86,315; L87,259; IU(Cross);
 UC(Cross)
 In two years time L39,321; L60,191; L123,
 199-200
 A Mere chance L39,381; L40,444; L61,117
 189-90
Cameron, C.F. IU
Cameron, Mary Lovett L5,98; IU
Campan, Jeanne L.H.
 The Private life of Marie Antoinette L40,
 313-14; L41,291 296; L42,299 303; L119,164
Campanella, Catherine IU
Campanella, Guiseppe M. L3,65; L84,320;
 L85,107(c); IU
 Life in the cloister L39,202 205; L40,288;
 L41,267; L42,512; L61,315
 My life and what I learnt in it L38,309; L39,
 202 209; L59,313; L101,113 118
Campbell L81,207
Campbell, Alice M. IU
Campbell, Andrew Fletcher IU
Campbell, Charlotte S.M.(Lady Bury) L1,42;
 L80,4; L81,54 56; L90,83; L117A,4;
 IU(Bury,C.)
 Concealment L53,246; L81,156; L117A,35
 The Devoted L52,140; L53,195
 The Disinherited L52,317; L53,195
 The Divorced (prop.) L53,194
 [The Exclusives L78,5]
Campbell, Colin F.
 Letters from camp L3,41; L4,87; L42,350
Campbell, Duncan L54,4
Campbell, E.V. IU
Campbell, Emily H. IU
Campbell, Mrs.Emma A. L59,143; IU
Campbell, Frances IU
Campbell, H. L93,48
Campbell, Mrs.Howard D. L5,138; L22,358
Campbell, J.Braadalbane IU

Campbell, Sir James
  Memoirs L37,88; L38,113; UC
Campbell, James & Son IU
Campbell, James Dykes IU
Campbell, Mrs.John L84,98 118
Campbell, John G.E.(9th Duke of Argyll)
  IU(Argyll)
Campbell, Thomas L1,26; L52,66 169 216;
  L81,41; L117A,23; UC
  Life of Sir Thomas Lawrence (prop.) L68,
  37-8
  Poetical works L52,328; L69,37-8
Campbell, Mrs.Vere L22,360
Campbell, Miss Zora L88,83(c)
Campoverde, Guiseppe L3,125; L60,187-9;
  L61,161; L85,159 313; IU
Candler, E. L81,109
Canning, George IU
Cannon, J. L5,81; IU
Canot, Theodore
  Revelations of a slave trader [L36,121];
  L42,403; L57,313-16; L123,27-9
Canton, William L5,84; IU; UC
Canvins, Joseph IU
Capel, Charles C. L87,157; IU
Capes, Rev.John M. L2,73; L3,69; L84,119
  151; L95,38-43; IU
  The Mosaic-worker's daughter L37,201; L38,
  191; L59,171; L99,163
Capper, Samuel J.
  Wanderings in war time L37,302; L38,107;
  IU(Caprer)
Capron & Co. L59,274-89 302; L61,202-6;
  L81,221-2; L82,281; L84,211 214 223; L85,
  425; L88,178; IU
Capsidy, June L85,44(c)
Capsidy, Loftus L85,44
Caracciolo, Enrichetta L2,75; L83,277; L84,
  34-7 40 43; IU
  Memoirs of Henrietta Caracciolo L36,135 146
  202; L37,83-4; L38,344; L39,202; L40,451;
  L59,57-72; L75,348
Carey, Lady L83,255
Carey, Edward F. L85,159
Carey, Edwin L94,245
Carey, Robert
  Narrative of the late war in New Zealand
  L36,128; L37,80
Carey, Miss Rosa N. L3,129 170-85 passim;
  L4,31-2; L42,395; L65,179; L67,266; L85,
  146 170-1(c) 172 216 325 328 337 381 414;
  L86,46-7 115 179 260 456 463; L87,41 164;
  L88,289 323 331 335 342 344-6; L89,126; IU;
  UC
  Barbara Heathcote's trial L40,49-50; L41,
  47 139; L42,28-9 397; L62,22; L119,68
  But men must work L41,411; L42,457; L65,
  209; L119,24
  For Lilias L40,407; L41,96 510; L42,29-30;
  L62,299-302; L119,71
  Heriot's choice L39,326; L41,70 119; L42,
  31-2 399; L60,179; L119,62; L123,210-11
  Lover or friend (orig.Mrs.Blake) L41,438;

L42,32-3 489; L64,275; L119,76
  Mary St. John L40,362; L41,78 521; L42,
  34-5; L61,195; L119,67
  The Mistress of Brae Farm L42,50; L67,
  159-62
  Mrs.Romney L42,437 455
  Nellie's memories L39,339a; L40,48; L41,
  45 53; L42,35-6 396; L60,219; L119,63
  Not like other girls L40,47 392; L41,44 116;
  L42,37-8; L62,124; L119,69
  The Old old story (orig.Pandora's box) L42,
  48 440; L66,87 141-7; L67,190
  Only the governess L41,51 473; L42,38-9;
  L63,280; L119,74
  Queenie's whim L39,356; L40,451; L41,43;
  L42,40-1 399; L119,64
  Robert Ord's atonement L40,85-6; L41,48
  119; L42,41-2 397; L62,196; L119,70
  The Search for Basil Lyndhurst L41,453;
  L42,47-8 495 499; L64,130; L119,75
  Sir Godfrey's grand-daughters L41,416; L42,
  49-50 476-7; L65,156-9; L119,77
  Uncle Max (orig.The End crowns all) L40,443;
  L41,50 53; L42,43-4 398; L63,131-3; L119,72
  Wee wifie L40,52; L41,49 116; L42,44-5 396;
  L63,216; L119,73 81
  Wooed and married L40,49-50; L41,46 62;
  L42,46-7 398; L61,197; L119,65-6
Carey & Lea L81,85; L117B,8
Carlén, Emilie
  see Flygare, E.
Carleton, William IU
[Carling, Laura Jane] L95,3
Carlisle, Earl of IU
Carlisle, Henry E. IU
Carmichael, Alison C.
  Tales of a grandmother L36,121; L54,234
Carmichael, Montgomery L88,162; UC
Carne, John IU
Carnsen, Henry L5,29-31; L85,158;
  IU(Carnsew)
Carocci, Amy IU
Carpendale, T.C. L84,49
Carpenter, Arthur B. IU
Carpenter, J.E. IU
Carr, Alfred IU
Carr, Alice (Mrs.Comyns Carr) L5,[27] 108;
  IU
Carr, Frank L83,260-1
Carr, J.W.Comyns IU
Carr, Mrs.M.E. L5,27 [108]
Carr, Ralph UC(end of C)
Carrington, Edmund L91,1
Carrington, Evelyn L5,82; IU
Carroll, W.G. IU
Carruthers, R. & Sons IU(Carrothers)
Carson, Lionel UC
Carter, C.J. L94,107
Carter, Miss Katherine (Mrs.K.Buckton) L5,
  89; L88,92 94 97 103-4 105(c)
Carter, Miss Mary E.(Mrs.M.E.Stevenson)
  L3,166; L85,404; L86,247 251 304; L87,105;
  L88,350

Juliet L40,385; L62,110
Mrs.Elphinstone of Drum L42,453; L66,3
Mrs.Severn L41,455; L64,110
Carter, S.G. IU
Cartwright, Mrs.Edward L5,304
Case, Mrs.Adelaide
  Day by day at Lucknow L1,170; L2,51; L36,
  42 [244]; L58,179; L83,163
Casey, Charles
  Two years on the farm of Uncle Sam L7,173;
  L8,174; L36,122; L82,233
Casey, Elizabeth S. L91,200-1
Cassell & Co. L84,221; L86,120 292 308;
  L87,203 205; IU; UC
Cassell's Magazine IU(Fenn,G.M.)
Cassilis, Ina Leon L85,317
Castelcicala IU
Castle, Captain L86,372 424
Castle, Mrs.Agnes Egerton L5,234 249 309;
  L22,340 354
  The Pride of Jennico
  see Castle, E.
Castle, Egerton L3,61; L4,33; L5,234 249;
  L22,340 354 358 360; L66,240-4; L87,282;
  L88,313; L89,99 104; IU; UC
  Consequences L41,431; L42,57; L65,13 38
  The Pride of Jennico L42,410
  Young April (pub.McM.) L42,250; L67,318
Castlereagh, Viscount IU
Caswall, R.C. L94,312
Cathcart, Miss L80,14
Cator, F.S.Vaughan IU
Caughey, [Anna] IU
Caussidière, Marc
  Secret history of the Revolution [L36,122];
  L56,127
Cautwell, John L86,138
Cave & Cave L85,442; UC
Cavendish
  Life of Cardinal Wolsey (prop.) L40,232
Cawse, Clara IU
Cawse, John IU
Cawthorn & Hutt L82,251
Caxton Press L85,64(c)
Cayley, Cecil L5,260
Cayley, E.S. L82,352; IU
Cayley, George J. L1,138; L82,344; L83,31;
  L117A,38
  Las Alforjas L36,123; L57,202-3
Cazalett, Rev. L2,68
Cazenave, D. L2,16
Cecil, Robert A.(Lord Salisbury) IU(Salisbury)
Celeste, Mme. IU
The Censor IU
Central Direction of the Children's Libraries of
  the Primary Schools, Norway IU
Central Educational Co., Derby L88,172
Cervantes Saavedra, Miguel de
  El Buscapié L36,123; L56,113-15
Cervati, Mme.Ada F. L5,109
Cesaresco, Contessa Martinenge L5,193
Chads, Sir Henry D. UC
Chaffers, Thomas IU

Chalcraft, Miss Harriette A.
  Lucy Aylmer L1,147; L36,91; L58,104
Chalke, G.A. L85,77; IU
Challice, Dr. L83,137 153 156 158 162 171
Challice, Annie E.
  The Sister of charity L1,159; L36,84-5
Challis, Henry W. L90,248-51 253 286; L91,67
[Challyon, F.A.] IU
Chalmers, Alexander IU
Chalvey Club, Slough IU; IU(Dean,C.F.)
Chambaud, Baron de L85,456 458
Chamberlain, Walter IU
Chambers, Miss Beatrice A. L5,266
Chambers, Miss Caroline R. L5,184
Chambers, E. L94,171 180 183
Chambers, R. IU(Chambers,N.)
Chambers, Robert IU
  History of Scotland L68,85; L81,30 93 159;
  L117A,6
Chambers, W. & R. L65,298; L88,191 341; IU
Chamier, Daniel UC
Chamier, E. IU
Chamier, Frederick L53,269; L81,175 203;
  L91,156-7; L117A,12; IU; UC
  The Arethusa L36,263; L37,231; L53,271-3
  Ben Brace L53,136; L122,68-9 106 122
  The Life of a sailor L52,270 335; L122,82
  113-14 122
  The Spitfire or the Pirate Captain (prop.)
  L53,326
  The Unfortunate man L53,66
  Walsingham, the gamester L53,142
Champion L86,147
Chandos, Richard T.N.(1st Duke of Buckingham)
  IU(Buckingham)
Chaplin, F.D.P. IU
Chaplin, W.H. & Co. L89,111(c); UC
Chapman, E.Whitaker L94,106 110 147 153
Chapman, Elizabeth R. L5,104; IU
Chapman, Florence IU
Chapman, Frederick L84,194 305
Chapman, John IU
Chapman, Samuel IU
Chapman, T. L82,237
Chapman, W. L82,236
Chapman & Hall L5,44; IU
Chappell, T. L82,159
Chappell, William IU
Chappell & Co. L86,342
Chaquire L94,276
Charity Organisation Society IU
Charles V̄
  Correspondence of the Emperor Charles V̄
  L36,112; L56,193
Charles, F. L87,286
Charlton, F.L. IU
Charmes, Gabriel
  Five months at Cairo L3,155; L40,370; L61,
  240
Charsley, G.H. IU(Charsley,S.H.)
Charsley, Mrs.Stephen IU
Chasles, Victor E.P. L56,152; L82,14; L83,
  238; IU; UC

Chasseaud, George W. L1,127
  The Druses of the Lebanon L58,11-17
Chasteauneuf, Marie de IU
Chatelain, Clara de IU
Chatelain, Jean B.F. de IU
Chater, A.G. L5,244
Chater, George IU
Chatrian, Pierre A.
  A Man of the people L37,292; L38,183; L39,
  398 448
  The Outbreak of the French Revolution L2,81;
  L37,113; L38,206 269; L39,436
Chatterton, Lady Henrietta G.M. L2,55; L3,
  17; L9,173; L58,279; L83,113-14 186 188;
  L94,55-8; IU; UC
  Aunt Dorothy's tale L6,53; L53,253
  A Good match L7,140; L54,167
  The Heiress and her lovers L36,218; L37,79;
  L58,326; L94,93; L97,261 271
  Retribution (prop.ed.) L36,242; L58,91;
  L97,3
Chatterton, Sir William L53,253; L117B,13
Chatto & Windus L3,160; L5,45 55; L60,
  180-1; L61,233-5 258; L63,91 270; L64,200;
  L85,180 210; L86,104 136 424(c); IU
Cheeseman, Clara E.
  A Rolling stone (orig.The Bitter before the
  sweet) L3,44; L40,414; L41,529; L62,
  327-8
Cheeseman, T.F. L86,51
Cheever, Henry T. L82,167 185
  The Life and trials of a youthful Christian
  L36,125
  Life in the Sandwich Islands L36,124
Cheltnam, C.Smith L2,81; L5,35; L86,56; IU
Chepman, Clarice UC
Cherbuliez, Charles V.
  Froment jeune (prop.) L3,81; L38,136; L39,
  270
  The Wish of his life L39,300
Chermside, Emily IU
Chermside, Rev.Richard S. L2,28 45;
  IU(Chermside,A.)
  Ned Locksley L36,136 157; L37,62; L38,43;
  L39,419; L40,55; L41,53; L58,330; L94,90
Cheshire, William IU
Chesneau, Ernest IU
Chesney, F.R. IU
Chesney, George IU
Chesterfield, Earl of
  see Stanhope, P.D.
Chettle, Miss L5,216
Chetwynd, Hon.Mrs.Julia L64,123-9 248-65;
  L85,270; L86,216 224 228 254 284 289 291 301
  306 308 318 320; IU
Chetwynd, Miss Katharine L3,86; L64,123-9
Chevalier, A. IU
Chevenot, Marie IU
Chichekjian, Boghos L88,105; UC
Chichester, Dean of
  see Hook, Walter F.
Chichester, Mr. IU
Chichester, Frederick R.(Earl of Belfast)

L1,98; L93,109; L117A,5; IU
  Birth, parentage and education (prop.) L56,
  286
  Two generations L56,293
Child, Harry L2,85; L3,71; L5,67; L85,408
  A Cast for a crown L37,82; L38,105; [L59,
  223]
Child, Mrs.Maria L. L81,191; L92,46 69;
  L117A,6
Child, Theodore L5,172
Childar, Miss A. IU
Childar, Miss C. L89,119 121(c)
Childe-Pemberton, H.
  see Pemberton, H.
Childs, John & Son IU
Childs, T.H. IU
Chillcott L86,349
Chillington, J.C.
  see Jenkins, Hadow
Chisholm, H.W. L5,231
Chisholm, Hugh L5,255
Chisholm, John C. IU
Chiswick Press
  see Whittingham & Wilkins
Chivers, Cedric L87,156; L88,279 334-5 337-8
  341
Chocarne IU
Cholmondeley, Earl IU
Cholmondeley, Miss Mary L3,86; L4,34; L5,
  203 225 275; L86,209 262-3(c) 303 413; L87,
  67(c) 70-1 72(c) 73 84 266; L88,160(c) 175
  251; IU
  The Danvers jewels L41,482 488; L42,410
  464
  Diana Tempest (orig.Nemesis) L41,409; L42,
  52-3 458; L65,228 321; L66,85
  Sir Charles Danvers (orig.Deceivers ever)
  L41,42 132 459; L42,53-4 58; L64,1-3 241
Chorley, Henry F. L2,88; L59,243; L81,128
  130; L92,161 239 242 267-9 272 295-6; L93,
  16 33-4; L95,97; UC(Bentley-end of B)
  Henry Fothergill Chorley: autobiography L3,
  60; L38,296; L39,203; L40,425; L41,502;
  L42,407 500; L59,243 290; L65,82
  Sketches of a sea port town L53,47
Chorley, W.B. IU
Chorlton, Miss Margaret J. L5,301
Christall, Charles W. L84,301
Christian, E.V.B.(Edmund Viney pseud.) L5,
  239
Christian, Mrs.Eleanor E. L3,71; L5,216; IU
Christie, Alice M. L5,252; IU
Christie, Mary L87,260; IU
Christie, Richard C. IU
Christie, W.D. IU
Christmas, Rev.Henry L1,180; L2,50; L56,
  224; L82,26 291; L83,76 98 197 205 209;
  L117B,40; IU
  The Cradle of the twin giants L7,169; L8,111;
  L36,126; L56,164
  Echoes of the universe L36,125; L56,253
  The Shores and islands of the Mediterranean
  L36,128; L56,251

Christmas, Julia IU
Church, Alfred IU
Church, Mrs.C.M. L5,251
Church, Eva Ross IU
Church, Frederica IU
Church, R.H. L92,14
Church, Mrs.Ross
  see Marryat, Florence
Church, [Russ] IU
Churchill, Charles R.J.(9th Duke of Marlborough)
  IU(Marlborough)
Churchill, J. L90,173; L91,32
Churchill, Lord Randolph H.S.
  Plain politics for the working classes L40,449;
  L41,526
Churchward, William B. L3,70; L86,136
  My consulate in Samoa L40,96; L41,277; L63,
  207
Churnside, Mrs. L117A,2
Churton, E. IU Unidentified,(A)
Churton, R. IU
Chuter, H. L81,33
Claassen, Emma J. IU
Clanricarde, Ulick J. IU
The Clarion L87,296
Clark L91,40
Clark, A.D. IU
Clark, Charles L86,310; L88,320
Clark, E. IU
Clark, George
  see Powell, Thomas
Clark, George W. IU
Clark, J. & W. IU
Clark, J.W. L95,139
Clark, John IU
Clark, R. & R. L85,281 286 322 347 360 363 391
  422 443 474; L86,169 191 362(c) 362 364(c);
  L87,109 129; L88,286; L89,104-5 109; IU;
  IU(Kirkwood); UC; UC(Kirkwood)
Clark, S.H. IU
Clark, W. L89,117(c) 118
Clarke, C.E. IU
Clarke, C.H. L83,209
Clarke, Mrs.Charles L85,418 421
Clarke, Rev.Charles L2,67 72; L5,17; L84,
  95 103; IU
  The Flying scud L37,126
Clarke, Charles H. L85,421
Clarke, Emily Stanley IU
Clarke, Geo. L90,52
Clarke, General George Calvert L5,177
Clarke, H. IU
Clarke, H.Saville L2,66; L5,71
Clarke, Herbert E. L5,74; IU
Clarke, J. L117A,12
Clarke, James UC Manuscripts,39
Clarke, John IU
Clarke, Joseph L122,23
Clarke, Marcus A.H. L3,93; L61,96-101;
  L67,247; L85,160 221; IU(Ballière)
  For the term of his natural life L40,189 445;
  L41,54 60 187-8 510; L42,51-2 456 459; L65,
  201-3

His natural life L3,93 96 99; L4,34a; L38,
  347 368; L39,297 431 433; L40,51; L101,192;
  L102,137; L123,233
  Sensational tales (pub.E.R.Cole: Sydney) L63,
  77-9
Clarke, Mrs.Marcus L3,93 96 99; L4,34a;
  L22,336; L61,100; L67,247; L88,106
Clarke, Mary Cowden L5,41; IU
Clarke, Sara J.(Grace Greenwood pseud.)
  Haps and mishaps of a tour in Europe L1,124;
  L36,163; L117A,40
Clarke, Stephen Hardcastle L5,300
Clarke, T.H.Shadwell IU
Clarke, W.J. L89,89
Clarke, Fynmore & Fladgah IU
Clavequin, E. L3,42; IU
Clay, H.A. L5,209
Clay, John L88,198-9 219 235
Clay, R. & Sons L83,175 232; L84,48 116; L85,
  31 272 [457] ; L86,54 167-8 173 184 280 340;
  L87,142 175; IU; IU(Clery); IU(Printing Office)
Claydon, Miss M.A. IU
Clayton, Ellen C. IU
Clayton, Mary IU
Clayton, Cookson & Co. L83,197-8
Clegg, Alice M. IU
Clegg, W.H. UC Manuscripts,15
Clegg, William H. IU
Clemens, Samuel L.(Mark Twain pseud.) L3,
  188; L5,87; IU
Clement, Charles G. IU
Clerk to the Vestry, Westminster L86,378
Clerk to St.James Vestry, Piccadilly L87,55-6
Clerke, E.M. L5,63
Clerque, Miss Helen L5,47; L22,365
Cliffe, Francis IU
Clifford, Miss E. L5,152
Clifford, Edmund
  see Seeley, R.B.
Clifford, Hugh L5,133
Clifford, Mrs.Lucy L3,176 186; L4,35; L5,149
  223; L86,60 428; L87,145 205(c); IU;
  UC(end of C)
  Aunt Anne L41,93 412; L42,54-5 479 482;
  L65,213; L119,78
  Mrs.Keith's crime L40,186 406; L41,277;
  L62,312-15; L86,67
Clifford, Lucy M.H. IU
Clifford, S.L.J.
  see Clifford, Mrs.Lucy
Clinton, H.R. IU
Clinton, Henry Fynes IU
Cloake, W.J. L86,367 491
Clodd, E. L86,67-8
Clowes, Alice A. L3,132; L4,84; L86,492
  Charles Knight L41,377; L42,181; L65,
  299-300 303
  Sunshine and shade L2,76; L3,69; L37,243;
  L38,225; L39,447
Clowes, E. IU
Clowes, Elizabeth IU
Clowes, George L2,76; L3,69; L83,67
Clowes, W. & Sons L66,270; L83,71 129 139

210 262-3; L84,85 101 117 127 153 170-1 [176]
228 279; L85,13-14 18 22 26 28 34-6 54 60 64
65(c) 65-6 142-3 153 157 219 239 243 245 249
253 255 257 298 307 312 314 329-30 335 353-4
357 357(c) 359 362 366 368 371 375 388 403 419
431 469; L86,45 60 68 97-8 101 110 132 135 141
145 161 163 189 231-2 262 280 366; L87,46
61(c) 70 72(c) 114 247 249 256 259 262; L88,86
121 122(c) 122 133 139 143 229 249 270 317;
L89,46(c) 103(c) 111; L122,129; IU; IU
Richard Bentley I,29-32; IU George Bentley,
132 171; IU Richard Bentley II,2; UC:
UC(Desart-end of D)
Clowes, Sir William Laird IU
Cluer, A.R. IU
Clulow, E. L87,185; L88,142 146
Clydesdale News IU
Coates, T.M. IU
Cobb, E. L89,92
Cobb, James F. L59,132; L84,96 99 106; IU
Cobban, J.M. L5,172
Cobbe, Miss Frances P. L2,67; L3,133 138;
L4,36; L5,92 280; L87,246 267 282; L88,45 47
267; IU
Life L42,347; L66,186
Cochrane IU
Cochrane, Alfred L5,245
Cochrane, Arthur (Arthur Stuart pseud.) L67,
136
Cochrane, Baillie (1st Baron Lamington)
IU(Lamington)
Cochrane, Douglas (12th Earl of Dundonald) L3,
43; L86,297; IU(Dundonald)
Cochrane, James IU
Cochrane, John
A Reply to the Quarterly Review L36,277;
L38,200; L58,268
Cochrane, Louisa H.(Countess of Dundonald)
IU(Dundonald)
Cochrane, Thomas (10th Earl of Dundonald)
IU(Dundonald)
The Autobiography of a seaman L1,150; L2,
25; L3,43; L36,205 259-60 306; L37,95; L38,
265; L39,111; L40,428; L41,347 501; L42,166;
L58,208 274; L64,182; L83,212; L87,159;
L94,73; L123,215
Cochrane, Thomas B.(11th Earl of Dundonald)
L84,111-12 137; IU(Dundonald)
Life of Thomas, Tenth Earl of Dundonald L2,
63; L37,100; L38,121-2; L39,206; L59,159
190-2
Cock, Lamborn IU
Cockburn, James L58,184
Cockburn, S. & Son UC
Cocks, Charles A. L1,139; L92,172 192;
L117B,34
Cocks, John S.(Earl of Somers) IU(Somers)
Cocks, Robert & Co. L83,72; L87,251
Cocks, Biddulph & Co. L57,110
Cockton, Henry L1,71; L91,150 192
The Modern rake's progress (prop.) L54,148
240-7
Stanley Thorn L54,257; L55,50

Cohen, John L81,58
Cohen, Margaret L87,231
Coignet, Clarisse G.
Francis the First and his times L40,172; L41,
220; L63,57-9
A Gentleman of the olden time L40,151; L41,
317; L63,202 212-14
Coke, Hon.Henry J.
A Ride over the Rocky Mountains L36,127;
L57,56; L117A,30
Vienna in 1848 L7,167; L8,94; L36,127
Colburn, Henry L53,16-22; L55,38 303; L73A;
L73B; L80,5 15; L81,99 106 123-7 147; L82,
301; L117B,45; L123,141-5 151 234; IU
Richard Bentley I,8 9+1
Colchester, Lord
see Abbot, R.C.E.
Cole L5,92
Cole, Alfred W. L57,18; L82,208 253 289 321;
L117B,41
The Cape and the Kafirs L7,172; L8,174;
L36,128; L42,405
Cole, Grenville A.J. L88,197 204 207-8; IU
Cole, Sir Henry L60,162; L84,182 250(c) 262;
IU
Cole, J.Jones L93,67-8
Cole, John W. L1,134; L2,46; L83,72 190;
L93,229 281; L94,62; L102,1-24; L117B,17;
IU
The Life of Charles Kean L36,75
Memoirs of British generals L58,28; L68,98
Russia and the Russians L36,139
Cole, Margaret IU
Cole, Robert L81,57
Coleman, John L5,148 181-?
Coleman & Co. L83,262
Colenso, Frances E. IU
Coleridge, Arthur D. L4,73; L5,306; L67,174;
L88,74 224 280; L89,75; IU
Eton in the forties L42,363 378; L67,6-9;
L88,120
Coleridge, Henry J. L3,149; L64,14-16; L67,
263; L85,449; UC
Coleridge, Henry Nelson IU
Coles, Henry L89,122
Coles, John L88,244
Colgan, Nathaniel L5,172; IU
Colles, William M.
see The Authors' Syndicate
Colley, John IU
Collier, Sir George
France on the eve of the Great Revolution L36,
207; L37,82
Collier, John IU
Collier, M.A. IU
Collier, W.Payne L5,154
Collier, William L90,199; L92,28; IU
Collins, Charles A. L84,55; IU
Collins, Edward J.Mortimer L2,65; L5,66;
IU(Collins,W.M.)
The British birds L3,108; L39,299
Pen sketches by a vanished hand L3,108; L39,
278; L40,465; L41,292; L42,299; L60,70;

L123,204-5
Selections from the poetical works L40,175;
  L41,292 298; L42,172; L63,87; L66,306
Thoughts in my garden L3,108; L39,347;
  L40,463 465; L41,292; L42,325; L60,240-1;
You play me false L39,293; L60,108
Collins, Frances (Mrs.E.J.M.Collins) L3,
  108; L5,66 103; L60,108 241; L63,87; L85,
  84 181; IU
You play me false
  see Collins, E.J.M.
Collins, John Churton L5,100; L85,242 246
  246-8(c); IU
Collins, Mabel
  see Cook, Mrs.Keningale
Collins, William W. L1,141; L2,22; L3,57;
  L5,42 50; L82,253; L83,44; L84,180 283
  [289] 296; L93,163-5 233 247 250 276;
  L117B,2; IU; UC
  Basil L6,148; L57,186
  The Frozen deep L38,326
  Hide and seek L36,139; L57,309
  Miss or Mrs? L38,276
  Mr.Wray's cash-box L36,129
  The New Magdalen L38,72 289; L39,436 448;
  L40,54; L41,53; L59,272
  Poor Miss Finch L37,306; L38,58-9 210;
  L39,432 448; L59,255
  Rambles beyond railways L7,170 172; L8,
  150 165; L36,85 114-15; L37,85; L38,111
  334; L56,276; L58,256; UC Manuscripts,47
  A Rogue's life L39,412; L40,170; L41,155;
  L42,157; L60,147; L64,200; L123,189-90;
  IU Unidentified,(C.,W.)
Collison-Morley, J.L. IU
Collyer, Mrs.D'Arcy L5,271
Colmache, Mme. L5,151; L82,293 299
Colman, George L1,46; L6,19; L54,6 30;
  L90,121; L117A,32; IU
  Random records L52,1; L68,15 71
Colnaghi & Co. IU(Cohiaghi); UC
Colombine, David E.
  Marcus Manlius L36,62
Colonial Booksellers Agency L87,78(c) 80
Colton, Robert B.
  see Calton, R.B.
Colvill, Helen H. L3,20; L86,290 293; L88,
  96
  Mr.Bryant's mistake L41,441; L42,491;
  [L64,172]
  The Princess Royal L42,436; L66,139
Colvin, Sidney IU
Combridge & Co. L88,49 51 93 115 161; L89,
  91
Comerford L81,180 216
Comme
  see Lomme
Commission Italienne de secours aux blessés
  IU
Compton, Florence IU
Compton, Frances S.
  see Adams, H.B.
Conder, Claude R. L5,133

Altaic hieroglyphs L41,316
Heth and Moab L40,217 272; L41,297
Syrian stone-lore L40,115; L41,299; L63,
  161
Tent work in Palestine L39,251-2 353; L40,
  327 460-1; L41,295-6
Conder, Francis R. IU
Coney, A.Whyte L86,348 372
Conn, William L3,155; L61,240
Conneau, Captain L83,37
Conolly, Arthur
  Journey to the north of India [L7,110] ; L53,
  30; L81,131; L117A,24; IU
Conpey, Augusta IU
Conroy, James L2,86 88; L3,35; IU
  The Emigrant's wife L37,215; L38,126
Conroy, Sir John IU
Constable, Edwin C. UC
Constable, Marmaduke L5,227
Constable, T. & A. IU; UC
Conte, E.W. L5,240
Conway, Mary G. IU
Cook L83,146
Cook, Dutton L2,66
Cook, E.T. L5,111
Cook, Mrs.E.T. L5,286
Cook, F. & Co. L82,289
Cook, Harriett L92,158
Cook, [James] IU
Cook, Jane E. IU
Cook, John & Brothers IU
Cook, John D. L83,166 189; IU; UC
Cook, Dr.Keningale L5,197; L95,106; IU
Cook, Mrs.Keningale (Mabel Collins) L5,176
  208; IU
Cook, Thomas Edward UC
Cooke, A.R. L82,248
Cooke, Miss Agnes L85,317
Cooke, George W. L53,182-4 196-200; L81,
  146 184; L82,320; L117A,30; IU
  Memoirs of Lord Bolingbroke L53,129 131;
  L90,81
Cooke, Henry L84,187; L92,77; IU
Cooke, Robert IU
Cooke, S.C. IU
Cooke, W. L5,22
Cooke, W.H. L5,22; IU
Cooke & Co. L84,215
Cookney, F.F. L82,365 368
Coomes, M. L83,122
Cooper, Dr. L5,86
Cooper, Anthony Ashley (Earl of Shaftesbury)
  IU(Shaftesbury)
Cooper, Charles F. L3,54
  The Ring of Gyges L40,459; L41,486; L42,
  494; L63,158
Cooper, Henry IU
Cooper, Herbert S.
  Coral lands L3,126; L39,329; L40,229 232
  426; L41,160-1 190-1; L42,177 243; L60,239;
  IU
Cooper, James F. L1,15; L52,198-203 212;
  L54,248; L81,27 31 43-8 54 75 97 137 143

173-5 189 205 236 241; L82,28 32 66 68 78
139-40 147 160; L90,4; L91,155; L92,19;
L117A,9-10; L123,152; IU; IU Henry
Colburn,3+1; UC
  The Bee-hunter L56,94
  The Borderers L54,223-34
  The Bravo L52,197; L68,87
  The Headsman L53,25; L75,1; L76,248
  Homeward Bound L6,27
  Jack O'Lantern L7,149
  Lucy Hardinge L7,157
  Mark's reef L7,164; L8,35
  Mercedes of Castile L7,144
  The Pathfinder L7,142; L54,250-5
  The Prairie L54,223-34; L57,1; L77,110-59
  The Red rover L54,223-34; L57,1; L77,
  110-59
  Satanstoe L7,159
  The Sea lions L7,167; L8,94
  The Two admirals L7,148
  The Water witch L54,223-34; L57,1
  The Ways of the hour L7,170; L8,119
  Wyandotte, the hutted knoll L7,152
Cooper, Lady M.E.White IU
Cooper, Rev.R. IU
Cooper, Miss Susan A.F. L1,103; L82,159
  269; L117B,43; IU
  Rural hours L36,85
Cooper, Thomas S. L3,69; L4,84; L86,294
  372; IU
  My life L3,76; L41,348 364; L42,283 285
  515; L65,7-8
Cooper, Mrs.Thomas S. L88,119
Cooper, William W. L1,103; L5,104; L82,194;
  L117A,28; IU; UC(Bentley-end of B)
  Zoological notes and anecdotes (orig.Anecdotes
  of animals) L7,172; L8,174; L36,167 247
  272; L37,18 247; L38,79; L39,196 198
Cooper, Madon & Co. L86,240 302 317
Cope, Charles H.
  Reminiscences of Charles W.Cope L41,366;
  L42,309; L65,104; L86,407; L88,90
Copinger, N. IU
Copinges, W. L85,323
Copyright Association L85,200; IU
Coquilla Sectorius, pseud. IU
Corballis, James H. L3,90; L4,84; L86,395
  418 446; L87,232; L88,148 230
  Forty-five years of sport L41,367; L42,198;
  L65,49
Corbet L91,47
Corbet, Mary E. IU
Corbett, Edward L3,31; L86,296 376 415; UC
  An Old coachman's chatter L41,351 387;
  L42,296 298
Corbould, E. IU
Corelli, Marie
  see Mackay, Mary
Cork, Countess of
  see Poyntz, I.H.
'Corker' IU
Corkran, Mrs. L5,137
Corkran, Alice IU

Latheby Towers (orig.Miss Saville) L3,115;
  L39,300; L40,438; L60,124; L123,187-8
Corkran, Miss Henriette L5,79 210 287; IU;
  UC
Corkran, J.F. IU
Corkran, John F.
  History of the National Constituent Assembly
  L36,130; L56,156
Corkran, Louisa IU
Cormack, Mrs. L83,76
Cormack, Miss Sarah G.
  Life in Bombay L1,82; L6,140; L57,72;
  L82,182 217; L93,302; L117B,18
Corney, Bolton
  Curiosities of literature L1,104; L54,81;
  L117B,30; IU
Cornford, L.Cope L5,274
Cornhill Magazine
  see Smith, G.
Cornish, Mrs.Blanche W. L5,276; IU
Cornish, F.Warre L5,279; IU
Cornish, Rev.J.F. L5,60
Cornish, William L84,37 334
Cornish Brothers L89,63
Cornish & Son L85,95
Cornwall, Barry
  see Procter, R.A.
Corsom
  Two months in the Confederate States L36,
  129; L37,81
Corvin-Wiersbitzki, Otto J.B. von L2,45 83;
  L3,20; L5,36 66 120; L59,199-200; L84,
  106-10 120-1 136 273 277; IU(Corving)
  Everybody his own private secretary L37,108;
  L38,212
  In France with the Germans L2,81; L37,310;
  L38,118
  A Life of adventure L37,86; L38,99
Coryton, John IU
[Cose, E.W.] L82,294
Cosson, E.A. de IU
Costello, Dorothy IU
Costello, Miss Louisa S. L1,102; L83,32;
  L91,[151] 295; L92,51 82-3; L93,158 261;
  L117B,21; IU; UC
  Béarn and the Pyrenees L36,132; L55,200
  Catherine de Medicis L122,125
  Clara Fane L56,96
  Jacques Coeur L7,163; L8,34; L36,131;
  L56,18
  Memoirs of eminent English women L36,131;
  L55,148
  Memoirs of Mary, the younger Duchess of
  Burgundy L36,133
  A Pilgrimage to Auvergne L7,148; L36,132;
  L55,59
  The Queen's poisoner L7,147; L122,89-90
  A Summer among the Bocages L7,144; L54,
  259
Costenoble, Hermann IU
Cotta, Baron L81,233
Cottee, Susanna IU
Cotter, [J.G.] IU

Cotter, L.P. IU
Cotterell, Miss Constance L3,36; L5,220; L22,368; L86,280; L87,121 209 276; IU
  Strange Gods L41,445; L42,495; L64,155
  Tempe (orig.Tempe Rivers) L42,448; L66, 38
Cotton, Charles H. L87,68
Cotton, Miss Ellen F. L5,120; L22,356
Cotton, F.Percy IU
Cotton, Frank L5,137
Cotton, Lynch Stapleton IU
Cotton, Sir Sydney J.
  Nine years on the north-west frontier L2,72; L37,89; L38,114; L99,126; IU
Council on Education L83,243
Court, M.A. L5,272
Courtauld, Sarah (Mrs.Sydney Courtauld)
  Normanstowe (orig.Truth shall thee deliver) L42,432; L66,215; L88,138
Courtauld, Sydney L87,257 261; IU
[Courtney] IU
Courtney, William P. L3,135; L4,80; L5, 257; L87,197 200; IU
  English whist L42,347; L66,120-3
Cousens IU George Bentley,400
Cousens, Benjamin L5,189
Coutts, F.B.Money IU
Coutts & Co. L91,133; IU
Couvreur, Mme.Jessie C.(Tasma pseud.) L3, 43; L4,37; L5,166; L67,251; L71,266; IU
  A Fiery ordeal L42,411; L67,249-51
  Not counting the cost L42,430; L66,250-4; L119,156
Cowan, Andrew L81,57
Cowan, Miss C.E.L.
  see Riddell, Mrs.C.E.L.
Cowan, George Inglis IU
Cowan, H.B. L94,253
Cowan, Miss Julia B. L5,195
Coward, A.William L5,236
Coward, T.L. IU
Cowdry, Mr. L85,101
Cowell, Stepney L57,173; L82,330
Cowen, Joseph IU
Cowper, John S. L66,227; L87,253
Cowtan, Robert IU(Cowten)
  Memories of the British Museum L37,261; L38,106; L39,429; L59,245
Cox, Rev.E. L94,266
Cox, Edward William UC
Cox, Miss Emily L5,128; L22,349 367
Cox, John A. L90,85
Cox, Ross L81,26 78
Cox, Rev.W.L. Paige L5,296
Coxon, Mrs. L2,67
Coxon, Miss Ethel Stuart (Mrs.A.G.Earl) L3, 128; L5,106; IU
  A Basil plant L39,373; L40,422; L61,12
  The Long lane (orig.On the rocks) L40,469; L41,518; L63,89
  'Monsieur Love' L39,325; L60,176; L123, 199-200
Coxon, Miss Lucy L2,69

Coxwell, Henry L5,172; IU
Coyne, J.Stirling L91,219; IU
Cozens, Charles
  Adventures of a guardsman L7,164; L8,35; L36,134; L56,41
Craig, Duncan L94,129
Craig, R.Manifold L5,287
Craigie & Hipgrave L86,173(c)
Craik, Mrs.
  see Mulock
Craik, George L. L83,70 90; IU; IU(Kraik)
Craik, Miss Georgiana M.(Mrs.G.May) L3, 130; L85,162-3 429; L86,60 113 162 270 401; IU; IU(May)
  A Daughter of the people L40,451; L41,485; L63,119
  Diana L41,448; L42,482; L64,153
  Godfrey Helstone L40,393; L41,511; L62,147
  Mrs.Hollyer L40,408; L41,521; L62,329
  Patience Holt L41,423; L42,494; L65,69
  Two women L39,333; L40,464; L60,201
Craske, E. IU
Craven, Mrs.Augustus
  see Craven, P.M.A.
Craven, Lady Helen E.
  Notes of a music lover L42,385; L67,244; L89,49
Craven, Pauline M.A. IU(Craven, Mrs.Augustus); IU(Craven,P.L.M.); IU(Meaven)
  Anne Severin L2,57; L37,24; L38,81; L59, 183
  Eliane L3,149; L39,392; L40,247
  Life of Lady Georgiana Fullerton L41,327; L64,14
  Natalie Narischkin L38,201; L39,259; L40, 446; [L60,58]
  A Sister's story L37,72 240 295; L38,227 233 344; L39,40; L40,52-3; L41,52; L42,67
Craven, Hon.Richard K.
  Excursions in the Abruzzi L36,134
Crawford, Eliza F.[Mrs.E.Green] L117B,31
Crawford, Miss Mabel S. L2,20; L3,22; L83, 245-6
  Through Algeria L36,304; L37,83; L58,299; [L97,155]
  The Wilmot family L36,169; L37,269; L59, 34; L98,83
Crawford, Penfound IU
Crawford, Miss Virginia M. L5,232; IU
Crawley, Rowland L2,78; L3,70; L59,175
Crawley, W.P. IU
Creagh, J.
  A Scamper to Sebastopol L38,272; L39,436
Creasy, Sir Edward S. L1,83; L2,34; L3,97; L5,67; L57,231-4; L82,39 202; L83,53-4 131 155; L84,136 143 294; L92,136; L93, 64-5 136 159 181-2 203 306 L117B,32; IU
  The Fifteen decisive battles L7,171; L8,150; L9,135-6; L36,220 256-7 281; L37,77-8 82 291; L38,109-10; L39,129-31; L40,198 233; L41,169-70 221; L42,191-2 199-200; L57,11 183 233; L58,231 245

History of the Ottoman Turks L36,44; L38, 111; L39,125-6; L40,201; L41,172; L42, 407; L57,306

The Invasions of England L36,135; L57,89

The Later decisive battles of the world L40, 212; L41,267 286; L42,268

Memoirs of eminent Etonians L36,135; L56, 255

The Old love and the new L37,208 211; L38, 202; L59,215

The Rise and progress of the English Constitution L6,165; L36,28 110-11; L37, 26 77; L38,108; L39,132; L40,200; L41,171; L42,205; L57,251; L58,231

Unsuccessful great men (prop.) L59,332

Creasy, Lady Mary IU

Creed, Miss S.M. L5,221

Creighton & Seales L84,316

Cremer, Jacob J.
  An Everyday heroine L3,100; L39,262

Crespi, A.J. L87,226(c)

Crespigny, Mme. de L92,154

Cresswell, Henry L5,149

Creswell, Margaret S. IU

Crichton, Mrs. L5,75

Criddle, J. L92,21; L117B,31

Cridland, Aurelia IU

Cridland, Fanny F. IU

Cridland, Frederick J. L59,10; IU

Cridland, [J.] IU

Cridland, Joseph L56,111 150; L84,72

Crisp, Frederick Arthur UC

Critchett, Anderson L5,105

Croft, W. IU

Crofton, Helen IU

Croker, Elizabeth L95,269 275-8 283; IU

Croker, John Wilson IU

Croker, Thomas Croftin L81,28; IU;
  UC(Bentley-end of B)

Croker, Thomas F.D. IU; UC(Bentley-end
  of B)

Croly, Dr.G. L92,132-3 135; L117B,4; IU

Crombie, J.W. L5,130

Crommelin, Maria H. IU
  Over the Andes L42,371; L67,89; L88,158

Crompton, Dr. L82,162-3

Crompton, Miss L82,276 349

Crompton, J. & T.B. L81,101 107-10 114
  116-17 120

Cromwell, Constance L. IU

Crook, J.M. L91,49-50

Crookshank, Arthur L91,2 12

Crosby & Co. L88,277

Crosby, Lockwood & Co. L86,65 77 100 197;
  IU(Crosby,Lockhart & Co.)

Cross, Mrs.G.F.
  see Cambridge, A.

Cross, Joseph
  The American pastor in Europe L1,186;
  L36,77

Crosse, Mrs.Andrew L5,225 235

Crosse, Cornelia A.H. IU
  Red letter days of my life L3,100; L41,378;

L42,311

Crosse, Ormonde IU

Crosse, W.E.Crosse L22,357

Crosse & Blackwell L83,248; L84,295(c)

Crossley & Clarke L83,100

Crossley, Moir & Co. L86,132

Crothers, W.Edmund L5,58; L85,212(c) 213
  323; IU

Crouch, Archer P. L5,127

Crouch, H.N. UC

Crowder, Curtis & Vizard IU

Crowe, Mrs. L82,235

Crowe, Eyre E. L1,44; L81,26; L82,210;
  L83,45-6; L93,149 227; L117A,11
  Charles Delmer L36,124; L57,218-20
  The English in Boulogne (prop.) L52,112;
  L68,54
  The English in Italy (prop.) L52,110; L68,54
  The Greek and the Turk L36,136; L57,99
  238
  History of the reigns of Louis XVIII and
  Charles X L36,140; L57,240

Crowe & Gladstone L85,31 38

Crowest, Frederick J. L3,79-80 83; L4,38;
  L22,341; L85,41 289 324; L87,258; L88,43
  77 81 136; IU
  A Book of musical anecdote L39,266; L40,
  446; L42,401; L61,106
  Great tone poets L38,324-5; L39,102-3;
  L40,248 254; L41,222; L42,201-2; L60,
  251-3; L101,167; L119,106
  The Story of British music L42,359 387;
  L67,10

Crowley, Walter L5,75

Crowquill, Alfred
  see Forrester, A.H.

Crowther, Alfred H. L85,460-3

Croxall, A. IU

Cruikshank, George (jnr.) [L83,255-7 262];
  L84,245; IU

Cruikshank, George (snr.) L53,328-33; L55,
  99-101; L81,233; [L83,255-7 262]; L86,75;
  L117B,8; IU; UC

Cruikshank, Percy L92,212; IU; UC

Cruikshank, Robert IU

Crump, A. L5,177

Cudlip, Mrs.Annie Thomas L2,76; L5,15 59;
  L84,234; IU

Cudlip, Pender H. IU

Cuffe, William U.(4th Earl of Desart) L5,69;
  L96,31 39 46; IU George Bentley,173;
  IU(Desart); UC(Desart-end of D)

Cullen, Jane E.B. IU

Culling, S.K. L89,94(c)

Cumberland, Stuart C. IU

Cumming, Miss Gordon L5,137; IU

Cumming, John L81,37 42 64-104 passim
  119-21 160; 176 207 212 215 217 231 235

Cumming, Rev.John L1,186; L2,21; L3,64;
  L83,200 229-30 236 248-9 256 263; L84,149;
  IU
  Fall of Babylon L37,101; L38,116; L39,103;
  L40,254; L41,198; L42,193; L59,214

The Great tribulation   L36,76 97;   L37,74 79;
L38,116;   L39,106 246;   L40,254 447;   L41,198;
L42,202;   L59,35
The Millenial rest   L36,287;   L37,75 323;
L38,117;   L39,105;   L40,255;   L41,199;   L42,
279;   L59,35
Popular lectures on 'The Essays and Reviews'
L36,268
Readings on the prophet Isaiah   L36,252-3
277;   L37,76;   L38,118;   L39,104;   L40,255;
L41,199;   L42,518
Redemption draweth nigh   L36,205 253;   L37,
75 80;   L38,117;   L39,107;   L40,464;   L41,197;
L42,312;   L58,244;   L59,35
Cundall, Joseph   IU
Cunningham, Miss   L5,171
Cunningham, Allan   L81,201;   IU
Cunningham, Charlotte F.   IU
Cunningham, Peter   L1,149;   L58,68-80;   L82,
299 312;   L83,107 116 131 149-50 152-4 156
158 161 164 167-71 173 177-9;   L92,263;   L93,
282 291;   IU;   IU George Bentley,35 457
Cunynghame, Sir Arthur A.T.   L82,132
A Glimpse at the Great Western Republic
L36,136;   L56,327
Curling, Henry   L92,102;   L93,98;   L117A,31;
IU
Shakspere   I 6,110 113;   L56,98
Curling, James B.   L1,104;   L83,139 148;
L117A,28;   IU(Blucking)
Curran, H.G.
Confessions of a whitefoot   L69,104;   L117A,
32
Currie, Donald & Co.   L87,134
Currie, Henry   L82,82
Currie, Lady M.M.
see Singleton, M.M.
Curry & Co.   L81,215 219-20
Curryer & Baynes   UC
Curtis, Miss   L85,45
Curtis, Ella J.   L95,33;   IU
Curtis, George Ticknor   IU
Curtis, George W.   L82,218
Lotos-eating   L36,137
Nile notes   L36,138
The Wanderer in Syria   L36,137
Curtius, Ernst
History of Greece   L2,68;   L3,59 78-9 115 117;
L4,39;   L36,188;   L37,74 84-5 99-100 295 301;
L38,100-4 263;   L39,134-5;   L40,114 234-6;
L41,227-8;   L42,206;   L59,39
Curzon, Millicent   IU
Cust, Hon.Sir Edward   L83,117
Custom House, London   L84,31;   L88,117 177 203
Customs Offices, Liverpool   L83,278
Customs Offices, Sydney   L88,177
Cuthell, Mrs.Edith E.   L5,265;   L87,102;   IU
Indian memories   L42,338;   L66,10-16

Dacre, Baroness
see Wilmot, B.

Dahn, Ludwig J.S.F.
A Struggle for Rome   L3,81 106;   L39,273;
L40,465;   L62,1-4;   IU
The Daily Mail   L88,318-19
Daily News   L86,48;   IU
Daily Telegraph   L87,138;   IU
Dalby, Rev.William   L86,312
Daldy, F.R.   L88,115;   IU
Daldy & Co.   L60,210-12;   L83,45;   L85,162
169
Dale, Alice M.   L5,160;   L87,161
Dallas, George M.
Letters from London   L2,86;   L37,102;   L38,
119;   L39,436
Dallaway, James   IU
Dalling
see Bulwer
D'Almeida, W.Barrington   IU
Daly, Mrs.Dominic   L5,292
Daly, Mrs.Harriet Willes   L3,114;   L4,40;
L67,28;   IU
Daly, William H.   L22,364
Dalziell   L83,260
Daman, Katharine   IU
[Damant, M.]   IU
Dana, Marvin   IU
Danford, Miss Beatrice   L5,59
Daniel, George   L76,24-36;   L81,216;   IU
Merrie England   L7,147;   L54,310
Danniel, Henry   IU
Danvers, F.D.   L90,193;   IU
D'Arcy, Miss Ella   L5,162
Darrell, Joyce
see Duffy, B.
Darter & Walton   L89,70;   IU
Dartmouth
see Legge
Dasent, Mr.   IU
Daudet, Alphonse   IU
Daugars, John W.   L5,19 137;   IU
Daunt, W.J.O'Neill   L117A,39;   IU
The Husband hunter   L54,173;   L91,116
The Old earl and his young wife   L55,25
The Wife hunter   L54,42
Davey, Richard   L5,255;   L86,492;   L87,208(c)
212(c);   IU
Sidelights of the French Revolution (prop.)
L41,381;   L42,322;   L66,128-31
Davidson, Hugh C.   L5,61;   IU
Davidson, Miss L.Campbell   L5,262
Davidson, Randall T.   IU
Davie, George J.   IU
An Elementary Greek grammar   L38,119;
L39,397 453;   L40,433;   L41,214;   L85,90
Davies, Mrs.B.   IU
Davies, B.R.   IU
Davies, Rev.Charles M.
Philip Paternoster   L1,166;   L2,24;   L36,43-4;
L58,175
Davies, E.S.   L2,57
Davies, Rev.Edward W.L.   IU
A Memoir of the Rev.John Russell   L3,116;
L39,302;   L40,321;   L60,116;   L119,101

The Out of door life of the Rev.John Russell L40,318 336; L41,159-60; L42,255; L123, 182-3

Paul Pendril L2,57; L37,221; L59,108; L98,201

Davies, Eleanor IU

Davies, George C.
The Golden shaft L3,76; L38,321; L39,440; L59,323; IU

Davies, Gerald S. IU(Davier)

Davies, H.Walford IU

Davies, James IU

Davies, Mrs.Mary L3,27; L86,60-2 133
The Menu cookery book L40,187; L41,520; L63,6-12

Davies, Phillis IU

Davies, Slade L82,328

Davies, Sir William L5,281; UC

Davis, Ellis J. IU

Davis, John L3,62; L4,40; IU
The History of the Second, Queen's Royal Regiment L41,322; L42,221 223; L63,174; UC Manuscripts,11

Davis, N. IU

Davis, Dr.Nathan L1,188; L102,31
Carthage and her remains L36,257; L37,96; L58,247

Davis, P. L85,449 451

Davis, P. & Sons L86,323 336 494 496

Davis, R.R. IU

Davis & Campbell IU(Davis,I.)

Davison L82,31

Davison, Gertrude C. IU

Davison, J.[W.] IU

Dawkins, Clinton G. L82,367

Dawnes IU

Dawson, Miss L88,98

Dawson, A.J. L5,61

Dawson, Alfred L5,85

Dawson, Mrs.Flora L2,53; IU
Princes, public men and pretty women L36, 170; L37,97

Dawson, Henry,William & Stephen L73A,1 195

Dawson, John L61,202; L73B,7; L84,287; L85,2 259; L86,358 365; IU; UC Manuscripts, 11

Dawson, Miss L.A. L5,289; IU

Dawson, Richard L5,309

Dawson, W.H. L5,216

Dawson, William & Sons L87,135

Day, Frances A. IU

Day, Frederick L94,282

Day, Julia
The Old engagement L36,214; L57,60

Day, Vincent B. & Son L83,66 238; IU; IU(Day,W.)

Day, William IU; IU(Day,V.B.)

Day, William L84,259

Day, William H. L3,28; L86,86 110(c) 260 264 331 399; L87,74; L88,282; L89,90
The Horse L40,84; L41,323 501; L42, 229-30; L63,197-8; L119,118
Reminiscences of the turf L14,301; L40,202;

L41,361 508 529; L42,304-5 518; L63,65-8 71; L65,22

Dayman, Edward Arthur IU; UC

Dayrolles, Frederick L55,277; L117A,25; IU

Deacon, W.F. L82,285 291; L117B,17; IU
The Vendean chief (prop.) L54,256

Dean, Charles F. IU

Dean, Thomas A. IU

Dean & Munday IU

Dean & Son L83,188

Deane, Rev.Anthony C. L5,262; L87,296; IU

Deane, Miss Mary B. L3,115; L5,248; L87, 67 168
Eve's apple L42,441; L66,96

Dearden, W. L81,155 188

Debory, Thomas IU

Deck, H.R. L5,65

Decker, Arthur IU

Deeley, Lydia IU

De Fonblanque, Mrs. L85,87 92

De Fonblanque, Mrs. IU Unidentified, (A)

De Fonblanque, Caroline A. IU
Five weeks in Iceland L3,132; L39,345; L40,247; L41,388 510 516; L42,507 509

De Fonblanque, Edward B. L5,246; L59,300; L84,244 254; IU(Fonblanque)

De Fonblanque, Miss Ethel A.(Mrs.Master) L5,95 149; IU(Fonblanque)

De Fonblanque, Thomas IU(Fonblanque)

De Gray, Lord Thomas P. IU

De Gruchy, Mrs. L5,224

Deighton, Bell & Co. L87,288; L88,45

De Jongh, Miss Bertha L3,56; L85,8-10; IU(Jongh)
Camille's tormentor L38,357; L39,245
Loving and loth L38,343; L39,441
Rosa Noel L38,290; L39,401 441
The Sisters Lawless L38,316; L39,441; L59, 316
We are Worldlings L38,365; L39,441; L60, 12

De Kantzow, Herbert
Summer days in Auvergne L3,77; L4,79; L38,333; L39,224; L40,324; L41,532; L42, 322; L101,200; IU

De la Condamine & Johnston IU; UC

Delane, John Thaddeus IU; UC

Delany, Mary
see Granville, M.

De Leon, Edwin IU

Delffs, Sophie IU

Delworth, W. L82,298

Demmler, Franz C.F.
Baron Rehden's memoirs (prop.) L56,48

De Morgan, Miss Mary A. L87,253; IU

De Morgan, Sophia E.
Three score years and ten L42,355; L66,222

Denbigh, Mary IU(Denleigh)

Denby, E.L. IU

Denham, Robert & Co. L85,199 339 360; L86, 410; L88,58 293; L89,113-4

Denison, Miss L85,129 440

Denison, Edward

Letters and other writings L3,50; L37,214;
  L38,121 359; L39,204 454; L40,237 427; L41,
  519; L42,512
[Denleigh, Mary] IU
Dennis, George L6,114; L117B,10
  A Summer in Andalucia L56,143-4
Dennis, John L5,112; IU
Dennis Bros. & Co. L83,276
Denny, A. & F. L88,173(c) 174
Denny, Edward IU
Dennys, Dr. L5,111
Dent, J.M. L86,283 292
Dent, John C. L5,76; IU
Dent & Hellyer L86,350; L87,223
Derby, Earl of
  see Stanley, E.H.
Derby & Jackson L83,139
Dering, E.H. IU
De Robeck, George L5,88 142; IU
Derosne, Charles B. L84,32 159; IU
Derosne, Mme.Judith L84,32
Derra de Moroda, Constant UC(Carr-end of C);
  UC(Murr..)
  see Beck, W. von
De Saint Croix, Georgie IU
Desart, 4th Earl of
  see Cuffe, William U.
Des Echerolles, A.E.M.
  Private trials L57,165
Des Granges IU
De Soyres, John IU
Despard, C. IU
Desprez, Frank L5,43; IU
De Tabley
  see Warren
Detmold, Emily IU
De Vere, Aubrey T. L82,72; L117B,23; IU
  Picturesque sketches of Greece and Turkey
  L36,141; L56,242
De Vere, Sir Stephen E. L5,201; IU
Devereux, Captain L82,28
Deverill, John IU
[Devey]
  Life of Count Cavour L36,102; L102,69
Devey, Mr. L2,15
Devey, Frederick N. L57,105; L58,26 37 76;
  L82,135 207 220 225 318 333; L83,115 124
  160; IU; IU Richard Bentley I,25
Devey, Joseph
  Life of Joseph Locke L2,19; L36,101 273;
  L58,298; L70,54
Devrient, P.Edward
  My recollection of Felix Mendelssohn Bartholdy
  L2,73; L37,202; L38,190; L42,401; L59,
  178; IU
Dewar, G.A.B. L5,155; L22,367
Dewar Brothers L85,344 362
D'Ewes, John L1,153; L83,133-4 140
  China, Australia and the Pacific islands L36,
  142; L58,126-9
D'Ewes, Sir Simonds
  The Autobiography and correspondence L7,
  158; L36,142

Dewynter, Charles L86,208 259
Dexter, Thomas A. L56,237
Dibdin, E.Raimbault L5,192
Dibdin, Thomas Frognall IU
Dibdin, Thomas John IU
Dicher, Mrs. L86,277a
Dick, Cotsford L5,177
Dickens, Charles J.H. L1,130; L6,50; L53,
  291-301; L58,144; L71,143; L76,83-245;
  L83,77 145 172; L90,113 125 130-1 156 171
  180 203-7 268 307; L117A,33; IU; UC
  Barnaby Rudge L53,291-301
  Mudfog papers L39,344; L40,179; L41,153
  159; L42,159-60
  Oliver Twist L6,30; L53,291-301; L54,239
  L55,45; L74,221-62
  The Village coquettes L39,283; L40,336;
  L41,537 540; L42,523
Dickins, Lady Frances E.
  Gatherings of a country rambler L36,143
Dickins, Miss Mary L5,265
Dickinson, Miss Evelyn L5,140
Dickinson, Fanny IU
Dickinson, John & Co. L66,43; L82,363; L83,
  235; L86,204; L87,42; L88,275; L89,53; IU
Dickinson, Lowes IU; IU(Dickinson Bros.)
Dickinson, R. & L. IU
Dickinson, William R.
  Vincent Eden (prop.) L6,58 165; L7,143;
  L54,213-21; L82,285 291; L117B,23
Dickson, Col. L56,191; L82,136
Dickson, E.W. L83,163
Dickson, George W. IU
Dickson, Nicholas L5,67
Dickson, Mrs.T.W. IU
Dickson, Rev.William P. L2,32 83; L3,34
  120-1 124; L4,41; L22,336; L58,265; L63,
  76; L83,200 232; L84,141; L85,425; L86,49;
  L87,116-17(c) 122 126(c) 126; L95,30; IU
Dickson Brothers & Co. L82,356
Didier & Co. L83,26 109; L84,100 159; IU
Didot & Co. L85,400
Diehl, Mrs.Alice M. L3,145; L4,84; L5,134;
  L85,337 422 449; L86,119 327; L87,69; L88,
  292; IU; UC(end of B)
  Elsie's art life (orig.Art and intrigue) L41,
  406; L42,458; L65,307
  Eve Lester L40,362; L61,217
  The Garden of Eden L39,383; L40,432; L61,
  111; UC(Pigott)
  Her three lovers L41,442; L63,218-20
  The Knave of hearts L40,392; L62,141
  Musical memories L42,383; L67,226
Dilke, C.W. L82,92
Dilki, W. IU
Dilks, T.Bruce L5,217
Diller, M.R. IU
Dilworth, Darren L57,214
Dimond, Miss M.A. IU
Diplock, A.H. L5,157; L22,354 358
Disraeli, Benjamin (Earl of Beaconsfield) L1,
  34; L6,102; L81,72; L83,99; L117A,20
  The 'Runnymede Letters' L3,185; L40,219;

L41,302; L42,519
The Young duke L68,65
D'Israeli, Isaac IU
Dissel, Annette von L5,73; IU
Ditchfield, P.H. IU
Ditters von Dittersdorf, Carl
The Autobiography L42,375; L67,174
Divers, Mrs.Maud L5,303; L88,148
Dixie, Lady Florence C.(Lady F.C.Douglas)
L3,133; IU
Across Patagonia L39,339 385; L40,366 422;
L60,254-68
In the land of misfortune L40,352 439-40;
L41,513; L42,404 508; L61,174
Dixon, Charles L3,88; L86,321; IU
Our rarer birds L41,336 347; L42,296 298;
L64,35-60
Dixon, Rev.E.S. L84,38 43
Dixon, Frederick L5,160-61; IU; UC
Dixon, W.Hepworth L83,221 261; L84,172;
L101,67; IU(Disern)
Doäzan, Baron L88,254 347
Dobell, Peter
Travels in Kamtchatka L1,45; L52,38; L68,
32
Dobell, Sydney Thompson L6,120; L82,195 204
284; L93,189; L117A,12; IU; UC
The Roman L36,116; L37,91; L38,124; L39,
205; L40,454; L57,194
Dobson, Austin L5,256; IU
Dobson, H.W. L2,15
Dodd, G. L2,70
Dodd, Mead & Co. L66,316; L88,44 55 70-1
Doddrell, T. IU
Dodgson, Joseph L85,441
Doidge & Co. L88,336
Dolbeshoff, Marie I. IU
Dolby, Richard
The Cook's dictionary L1,57; L52,142; L68,
65
Domestic Monthly L85,382-4(c)
Dominic, M. L86,455
Donald, Robert IU
Donegall, B. IU
Donoghue, D.J. IU
Doran, Alban IU
Doran, Emma M.H. IU
Doran, Dr.John L1,132; L2,64; L3,46; L5,
36 38 45; L36,260; L37,91; L57,74; L58,
163; L82,188 344; L83,145 192-3; L85,24;
L94,145; L117A,24; IU; UC
The Book of the Princes of Wales L36,79 88;
L37,93
Habits and men L36,145
The History of court fools L36,230; L58,163
In and about Drury Lane L39,376; L40,284;
L41,514; L42,508; [L61,89]
Knights and their days L36,61; L58,34
A Lady of the last century L38,273
Lives of the Queens of England L36,15-16;
L37,92; L38,319; L39,205 243; L40,316;
L41,518 542; L42,255; L58,20
London in the Jacobite times L39,265; L40,

442; L60,41
'Mann' and manners L38,349; L39,215 397
Memoir of Queen Adelaide L36,58 90; L37,94
Monarchs retired from business L1,135;
L36,88; L37,92
New pictures and old panels L36,58; L37,93
Table traits L36,25 39; L37,97; L38,125;
L39,110
Dorchester, Lady
see Pigott-Carleton, H.
Dorman, J. L85,367
Dormer, Lady Elizabeth A. L57,20
Lady Selina Clifford (ed.) L7,172; L8,150;
L36,144
Doty, H.H. IU
Doubre, Dr.Paul L85,389
Doudney, Miss Sarah L3,157; L85,374 438
The Missing rubies L3,122; L41,477; L42,
491
A Woman's glory L40,378; L61,319-24
Dougall, Miss Lily L3,132; L4,43; L5,241-3
291; L88,325; IU
The Madonna of a day L42,65 427; L67,34;
L119,150
The Mermaid L42,433; L66,224-6; L119,149
Doughty, Miss Fanny Albert UC
Doughty, Mrs.Frances A. L88,247
Douglas, Christianna J.
Honour and shame L55,281; L117B,5
Douglas, David IU
see Clark, R. & R.
Douglas, Lady F.C.
see Dixie, F.C.
Douglas, George B. IU
Douglas, Hannah IU
Douglas, Rev.Herman
Jerusalem the golden L2,17; L36,161; L37,
90; [L102,50]
Douglas, Sir Howard L83,181
Douglas, Lord James E.S. L3,150; L85,315;
IU
Estcourt (orig.Violet and Clarice) L40,384;
L41,508; L62,44
Queen Mab L40,396; L41,529; L62,214
Royal Angus L40,345; L61,155
Douglas, John S.(Marquis of Queensbury)
IU(Queensbury)
Douglas, William IU
History of the Tenth Royal Hussars L38,369;
L39,238
Douglas & Foulis L87,287
Douzinas, Katharine IU
Dover, Lord
see Ellis, G.J.W.
Dowcett, Mr. UC(Bentley-end of B)
Dowd, Rev.James L5,198
Dowling, Richard IU
Downes, Louisa J.C.(Vere Haldane pseud.) L2,
24; L123,13-19
Our Charlie L36,192; L37,210; L59,53
Thrice his L37,250; L38,238; L59,54
Downey & Co. L88,56; L89,49; IU(Donney)
Dowsett, J.C. IU

Dowson, Alfred C. L5,127; IU
Dowson, Ernest C. L5,215; IU
D'Oyl, Mme. L86,312
Doyle, A.Conan L5,129
Doyle, Sir Francis H. IU
Doyle, Richard IU
D'Oyly, A. IU
Dracon, J. L90,325
[Dragson, Amelia] IU
Drake, C.F.Tyrwhitt
  The Literary remains L3,123; L38,327; L39,
  251 402; L40,428; L41,517; L42,511; L60,35
Drake, Mrs.Emma Tyrwhitt L3,123; L60,35
Drake, Rev.F.W.Tyrwhitt L85,11
Drakeford, D.J.P. L117A,31
Dramatic Authors' Society IU
Drapes, Annie C.T. IU
Dray, William L85,46
Draycott, Charles L5,301
Drew, Catharine IU
Drew, Mary IU
[Dromor, Ferdinand] IU
Drought, C.E. IU
Drought, Dora A. IU
Drummond, Sir Francis W. UC
Drummond, Hamilton L5,278; L67,77; L88,
  94 143-4 147 149 152(c); IU
Drummond, Miss Maura L5,184
Drury, Miss Anna H. L2,88; L3,68; L85,27;
  IU
  Called to the rescue L39,330; L123,209-10
  Furnished apartments L38,239; L39,440
  Gabriel's appointment L39,268; L40,432;
  L41,511; L42,484; L60,44
  The Story of a shower L37,304; L38,222;
  L39,447; L100,123
Drury, Col.H. IU
Dublin, Archbishop of
  see Whately, R.
Dublin Evening Mail L82,127
Du Bois Reymond, Emil H.
  A Speech in the German war L37,269; L38,
  147; L39,427
Dubourg, Augustus W. L3,102; L5,49; L85,
  336 345 381; IU
  Angelica L41,371; L42,168; L65,187
  Four original plays L40,371; L41,220; L42,
  193; L61,228-32
  Four studies of love L38,323; L39,235; L60,
  47
  Vittoria Contarini L39,421; L40,460
Dubourg, Charles S. L90,90 290; L91,223;
  L117A,16
Du Cane, Sir Edmond F. IU
Du Casse L83,27 34
Duckworth, James L88,106
Duckworth, W.M. IU
Ducôté, A. IU
Ducoudray Holstein, H.L.V.
  Memoirs of Simon Bolivar L1,35; L52,15;
  L68,21
Duell, Reginald S. IU
Duff, Miss L5,84

Duff, Col.A.G. UC
Duff, Miss Henrietta A. L3,104; L5,101; IU;
  UC
  Honor Carmichael L39,339; L60,222
  Virginia L38,333; L39,237; L60,64
Dufferin, Earl of L85,455
Dufferin & Ava, Marquis of IU; IU Richard
  Bentley II,658; UC
Duffield, Alexander J. L5,51; L61,126; IU
  Peru in the guano age L38,129; L39,257;
  L40,451 455; L41,526; L42,517
Duffy, Bella (Joyce Darrell pseud.)
  Winifred Power L3,171; L40,390; L41,538;
  L42,498; L62,107-9
Duffy, James & Co. L89,102 105 106(c) 109
  117 117(c)
Dulwich College, Governors of L67,99
Dumas, Alexandre L2,53; L83,271-2
  Emma Lyons (prop.) L36,148; L58,324;
  L97,287 291
  San Felice (prop.) L98,77
Dunant, J.R. IU
Duncan, B.C. IU
Duncan, George IU
Duncan, John
  Travels in Western Africa L36,144; L42,
  406; L56,39; L117A,25
Duncker, Maximillian W. L3,87; L85,374-5;
  IU
  The History of antiquity L3,103; L38,345;
  L39,193-5 240 391; L40,238-40; L41,230-2;
  L42,208-9; L60,17; L123,183-4 205-6
  History of Greece L3,103 169; L39,389;
  L40,369; L41,233; L42,210; L61,128-30
Duncker & Humblot L3,140; L66,100-7; L87,
  182; IU
Dundee Evening Telegraph L85,277; L89,94-5
  103
Dundonald
  see Cochrane
Dunham, Miss E.J. L5,283
Dunham & Co. L83,50
Dunkin, Edwin IU
Dunlop, Admiral IU
Dunlop, D. L95,21
Dunlop, Madeline A.W. L1,163; L83,211
  How we spent the autumn L36,118
  The Timely retreat L36,18 87; L58,157
Dunlop, Robert H.W. L1,167; L2,23; L3,22
  Hunting in the Himalaya L36,117; L37,94
  Service and adventure L36,66; L58,184
Dunlop, Rosaline H.M.
  How we spent the autumn
  The Timely retreat
  see Dunlop, M.A.W.
Dunmore IU
Dunn, Frederick J.A. IU
Dunnill & Palmer L83,172
Dunning, John L95,153
Dunphy, Henry M. IU
Dupanloup, Félix A.P.
  Atheism and the social danger L37,98; L38,
  334; L59,132

The Last days   L3,147; L39,340; L40,428;
L123,200-1
Du Parquet, Mme.C.   L64,202; L86,119 313;
IU
Dupont, L.   IU
Durant, A. & Co.   L88,340
Durham, Cornelius   IU
Durham, Rev.Thomas Charles   L5,208
Durrant, A.W.   L5,301
Durrant, V.   L85,4
Durrant, W.S.   L22,366; L86,313-14
Dutton, Miss Annie V.   L4,78; L88,149-50
   Wisdom's folly   L42,422; L67,79 146
Dutton & Co.   L85,252; L88,324
Dyce, Alex.   IU(Dyge)
Dyer, Frederick N.   L83,58
   The Step-son   L36,145; L58,18

Eagland, W.H.   IU
The Eagle   IU
Eardley-Wilmot, Edward P.   IU
Earle, J.C.   L5,80
Earp, George B.   L1,150; L2,25; L58,110
   208 274; L83,122-3 215 224
Eason & Son   L87,249
Eastern Telegraph Company   IU
Eastlake, Charles L.   IU
Eastlake, Lady Elizabeth   IU; UC
Eastwood, J.R.   L5,204
Eaton, D.   IU
Ebeling, Adolph
   Sketches of modern Paris   L37,171; L38,172
   L39,426; L40,441; L41,535
Ebsworth, Rev.Joseph W.   UC
Eccles, G.W.   L85,380; IU
Eckley, Sophia M.   L94,192; IU
   The Oldest of the old world   L36,197; L37,108;
   L83,198 206
Ecroyd, Henry   L2,68; L5,29
Ecuyer, le Vicomte de l'   L86,135
Eden, Hon.Miss   L1,182; L84,73
Eden, Charles   IU
Eden, Hon.Eleanor   L2,53; L5,69; IU
   The Autobiography of a working man   L36,92
   100; L37,108
   Dumbleton Common   L37,98; L98,248
   Easton and its inhabitants   L37,109; L38,130
Eden, Hon.Emily   L2,53; L58,233 277; [L97,
   48-9]
   Letters from India   L5,69; L37,304; L38,
   130; L98,187
   The Semi-attached couple   L36,83 121 190;
   L37,55 237; L38,242
   The Semi-detached house   L1,178; L36,72;
   L58,196
   Up the country   L37,109-10 292; L38,126;
   L59,106 115
Eden, William (Lord Auckland)
   The Journal and correspondence   L1,182; L2,
   53; L36,247 270; L37,19; L58,233 277; L94,
   6; IU(Auckland)

Eden, Remington & Co.   IU George Bentley,
   259+1a
Edersheim, Ella (E.Overton)   L5,203;
   IU(Overton)
Edersheim, Madeleine   IU
Edgcumbe, Richard   L5,171 258; L85,453-4(c);
   IU
Edge, Geo.E.   L86,327(c)
Edgeworth, Charles S.   IU
Edgeworth, Frances A.   IU
Edgeworth, Maria   L55,237; L90,37; L117A,
   21; IU
   Helen   L53,32; L74,1 86 105 181; L82,242;
   L122 64 101 122; L123,138
Edgeworth, Richard L.
   Memoirs   L7,153; L36,146; L55,237
Edler, Carl E.
   Baldine and other tales   L40,187; L41,495;
   L42,479; L63,35
Edlmann, Miss Edith   L5,158
Edmonds & Remnants   L81,221; L83,101; L84,
   31 104
Edmonston & Co.   IU
Edmonston & Douglas   L82,229; L84,101
Edwardes, Mrs.Annie   L2,62; L3,47; L5,22
   36 47 60 158; L84,66 68 78 82 123 153; L85,
   26 270 322; L87,123 125(c); L88,186;
   IU(Edwards,Annie); UC
   The Adventuress   L42,449; L66,40
   A Ballroom repentance   L39,388; L40 61-2
   358; L41,60 504; L42,68; L61,119-21;
   L119,21
   A Blue-stocking   L38,98; L39,268 409; L40,
   165 423; L41,150 158 504; L42,156 160 479;
   L60,42; L119,18
   A Girton girl   L40,59 399; L41,61 511; L42,
   68-9 484; L62,210; L119,22
   Jet: Her face and her fortune   L39,280; L40,
   436; L60,69; L119,19
   Leah: A woman of fashion   L6,180; L38,350
   365; L39,41-2 402 427; L40,55-6 440; L41,
   58 518; L42,69-70 488; L119,17
   Ought we to visit her?   L37,208 298; L38,50
   203; L39,43; L40,57; L41,59; L42,70; L59,
   231; L119,15
   Pearl Powder   L41,62 439; L42,71 493; L64,
   74; L119,23
   Steven Lawrence, yeoman   L37,241; L38,339;
   L39,44-5; L40,60; L41,62; L42,72; L59,
   153; L119,13
   Susan Fielding   L37,255; L38,60 225; L39,
   46 403 442; L40,58 456; L41,62 532; L42,
   72-3 495; L59,176; L119,14
   A Vagabond heroine   L38,284; L39,413 420;
   L40,173 460; L41,156-7; L42,157 159; L119,
   16; L123,193 195
   Vivian the beauty   L39,326; L40,466; L119,
   20; L123,202-3
Edwardes, Charles   L5,211 230; L22,357;
   L86,126-7 216 297 400; IU; UC
   Letters from Crete   L40,92; L41,268; L63,
   188
   Sardinia and the Sardes   L41,348; L42,320;

L64,165-7

Edwardes, Lady Emma IU

Edwardes, Sir Herbert B. L82,81 104 107 110
115 264 278; L83,161 178 194; L117B,42; IU
A Year on the Pubjab frontier L36,146

Edwardes, J.G. L94,130

Edwardes, John IU

Edwards, Miss Amelia B. L85,24; IU

Edwards, Annie
see Edwardes, Annie

Edwards, Charles L84,144 179 235

Edwards, Miss E.C.Hope L3,154
Azahar L40,370; L41,503-4; L61,238-40
Eau-de-nil L39,382; L40,242; L41,509;
L61,113

Edwards, H.Sutherland IU

Edwards, J. L83,258

Edwards, Rev.Joseph L2,64; L3,30; L57,293;
L82,219; IU

Edwards, M.B.Betham L3,156; L5,15 139;
L59,161; L64,114; L86,123 180 260a 380 398
400 492-3 496-7; L88,82(c) 83 86 100; L89,
48; IU(Edwards,Betham); IU George Bentley,
217; UC
Disarmed L40,378; L61,316-18
Next of kin wanted L40,102; L41,487; L86,
139
The Parting of the ways (orig.The Rapmans)
L41,63 472; L42,66; L63,291
The Roof of France L41,449

Edwards & Peake L57,106

Edwards & Sons IU

Egan, Pierce L81,170; IU

Egbert, Henry IU

Egerton, Francis C.G.(3rd Earl of Ellesmere)
IU(Ellesmere)

Egerton, Thomas L117A,5

Eglington & Co. L64,211; L86,321

Ehemann, Rev.E.A. L60,265-6; L85,296 299

Eiloart, Mrs.Elizabeth L2,80; L3,41; L84,
151-2; IU(Eilvart)
From thistles-grapes? L37,116; L38,137;
L59,218; L99,262
Just a woman L37,114; L38,167; L59,239
Out of her sphere L37,303; L38,204; L39,
434; L40,449; L59,254
Woman's wrong L38,268; L39,439; L59,269

Elam, Charlotte S.
The Busy-body L55,139; L117A,25

Eld & Blackham L87,235; L88,206 222 253 294
312 339; L89,88

Elder, A. L91,45 174

Electric Supply Corporation, London L86,353
408 415; L87,188; L88,140

Elers, A.Maud IU

Elgin, Countess Elizabeth IU

Eliot, Edward G.(Earl of St.Germans)
IU(St.Germans)

Eliot, P.H. IU

Eliot, Samuel L82,251 300
History of the early Christians L36,147
The Liberty of Rome L7,167; L8,95; L36,
147; L56,154; L82,17

Ellenborough, Earl of
see Law, E.

Ellerbeck, J.W. L88,352

Ellermann, C. L117B,30

Ellerton, J.
Fourfold message of Advent
see Borthwick, R.B.

Ellesmere, Earl of
see Egerton, F.C.G.

Ellet, Elizabeth F.
Women artists L36,197-8; L37,107

Ellice, Rev.James
Eternal life L1,84; L36,148; L117B,19

Ellicott, Mrs.A. L5,209

Ellicott, Florence (Mrs.F.Travers) L5,39;
IU(Travers)

Elliot, Mrs. L86,100

Elliot, Miss Anne L3,167; L4,70; L85,403;
L86,178 267 373 452; L87,193; L88,295; IU
Dr.Edith Romney L40,386; L62,103
Evelyn's career L41,428; L42,483; L65,18
A Family arrangement (orig.Fellow bondsmen)
L42,437; L66,116
Her own counsel (orig.A.Pagan) L41,447;
L42,485; L64,146
My wife's niece (orig.The Tenth of June) L40,
409; L62,316
An Old man's favour (orig.Will) L41,478;
L63,254-6
Where the reeds wave L42,414; L67,230

Elliot, Arthur D. IU

Elliot, Lady Charlotte L5,85; IU

Elliot, Miss Emma (Margery Hollis pseud.)
L3,183-184; L4,69; L85,473; L87,68 224;
L88,268; IU; UC(Hollis)
Anthony Fairfax (orig.Infelix) L40,403; L41,
502; L42,477; L62,285
Audrey L41,440; L42,478; L64,233-5
Stapleton's luck L42,416; L67,197
Through thick and thin L41,404; L42,462;
L65,296-8
Up in arms L42,434; L66,164 255

Elliot, Mrs.Frances Minto L3,147; L4,85;
L85,287 314 318
The Diary of an idle woman in Sicily L39,373;
L40,237; L41,210; L42,506

Elliot, Frank L92,238

Elliot, Mrs.H.V. IU

Elliott, C.B. L81,51

Elliott, Rev.Charles B. L81,195 232; L117A
37
Letters from the north of Europe L52,243

Elliott, Emily IU

Elliott, Mrs.Grace D.
Journal of my life L1,172; L36,60 63; L37,
106

Elliott, H.J. L5,83

Elliott, Rev.W. L93,6-9

Elliott, Matilda IU

Elliott, William
Carolina sports L37,110; L38,128

Elliott, William Perceval L92,72 142

Elliott & Fry L89,79 82-3

Ellis, Alice IU
Ellis, Arthur IU
Ellis, Rev.Dudley L2,69
Ellis, Miss Dymphua Glode L5,303
Ellis, George J.W.(Lord Dover) L80,10-11;
  IU(Dover)
Ellis, Sir Henry IU
  Original letters L7,160; L36,150; L55,292;
  L117B,32
Ellis, Rev.R.S. L85,130; IU
Ellis, Mrs.Sarah (S.Stickney) L1,165; L2,26;
  L3,23; L83,186 203; IU
  Chapters on wives L36,116 125; L37,106
  Friends at their own fireside L36,42 222;
  L58,172
  The Mothers of great men L36,65 172 174;
  L37,105
Ellis, Stewart Marsh UC
Ellison, C. L92,99
Ellison, James IU
Ellison, W.A. IU
Elliston, John L84,330; L85,17; IU
Elmes, Rev.John
  The Last of the O'Mahonys [L55,83]; L117A,
  33
Elphinstone, Lord John IU
Elphinstone, Hon, Mountstuart
  An Account of the Kingdom of Caubul L36,149;
  L54,107-19
  Letters from the minutes L3,176; L40,294;
  L41,303; L42,315; L61,284-98
Elwood, Mrs.Anne K.
  Narrative of a journey L1,60; L52,122; L68,
  58
Elwood, Charles L52,122; L68,58
Ely, Marchioness of IU
Ely, George H. L5,62; L22,363
Elzevir Press IU
Emerson, Sir James E. IU(Tennent)
  Belgium L54,318-20; L117B,11; UC(Tennent)
  Travels in Germany (prop.) L54,318
Emerson, Ralph W. [L36,240]; L83,115
Emerton, Wolseley Partridge UC
Emery, Mr. L84,33
Endres, Emma R. IU(Interstate...)
Engel, Louis L3,58; L5,61 144 152; L86,182;
  IU
  From Mozart to Mario L40,166; L63,173 322
Engelhorn L86,299 303
Engelmann, Julius L85,11 15 20 25 32 89 91;
  IU; IU George Bentley,180
Engleheart, J.H. IU
The Englishman, Calcutta L85,89 95; IU
Enoch, Frederick L22,364; IU
Ensor, Alice G. IU
Ensor, Ernest L5,305
Ensor, Laura L3,63; L63,243-5; L86,153
Epen, Fanny IU
Erasmus, Desiderius UC Manuscripts,45
Erckman, E.
  A Man of the people
  The Outbreak of the French Revolution
  see Chatrian, P.A.

Ernle
  see Prothero
Ernst, J.Eugene IU
Ernst, William IU
Ernst-Browning
  see Browning, W.E.
Errol, George IU
Erroll, Henry L3,59; L5,273; L86,147 201
  294
  The Academician L41,470; L42,478; L63,
  315
  By woman's favour L41,445; L64,163
  An Ugly duckling L41,63 125 483; L42,73;
  L63,234 265
Erskine, John F.(Earl of Mar) IU(Mar)
Escott, T.B. L2,67
Escott, T.H.S. L5,17; L85,420; IU
Esmenard, J.G. d' L80,2; L81,122 128 139
  144 171; L117A,39; L117B,29
Espin, John L82,161-2
Esquier L88,247
Estes & Lauriat L85,130 410; L88,145
Euripides
  The Alcestis L3,175; L40,191; L41,193
  The Andromach L2,64; L3,30; L36,29 81;
  L37,105; L38,129; L39,133; L40,243; L41,
  192; L42,500; L57,293; L66,302
Evans, Mrs. L86,350
Evans, Rev.Albert E. L2,82; L3,50; L84,173
  211; L101,136; IU
  The Bond of honour L37,30; L38,84; L100,7
  17 30
  Fourfold message of Advent
  see Borthwick, R.B.
  Revealed at last L38,277 281; L39,446
Evans, Arthur C. IU
Evans, Edward & Son IU
Evans, F.M. L83,83-4
Evans, George L85,345; IU
Evans, Mrs.George L3,23
Evans, Miss H. L94,115
Evans, H.E.G. L5,166; IU
Evans, John L81,91
Evans, Rev.John A. L5,227; IU
Evans, Mary IU
Evans, Miss Middleton L5,210
Evans, R.H.(auctioneer) L1,58
Evans, Richard L52,169; L68,77 95; L82,42
Evans, T.J. IU
Evening Post, New York L86,325 345
Everett, Edward IU
Everett, George IU
Eversley, Viscount
  see Lefevre, C.S.
Evitt, Miss L. L84,132; IU
Ewald, A.Charles L5,52; L123,173; IU
Ewald, Hermann F.
  John Falk L2,55; L37,160; L38,169
Ewing, J.J. L5,59
Ewing, Juliana H. IU
Ewing, Thomas IU
Examiner L89,64; IU; IU(Life)
Examiner & Times, Manchester IU

Eykyn, Roger   IU George Bentley,172;
  UC(Desart-end of D)
Eyre, Rev.E.   L82,259-64 270-1
Eyre, Miss Mary A.   L2,60; L84,60 142;
  L94,213; IU
  A Lady's walks in the south of France   L36,
  185; L37,104; L38,127; L39,397 428; L59,
  36; L98,61
  Over the Pyrenees into Spain   L36,199; L37,
  104; L38,127; L39,401 428; L40,449; L59,
  52
Eyre, Selwyn   IU
Eyre & Spottiswoode   L85,298

F.C.
  see Smith, W.
Faber, Mrs.   L2,32
Faber, M.A.   IU
Faber, Reginald Stanley   IU; UC
Fabris, Col.Cecilio   IU
Fagan, Rev.H.   L5,64
Faid, John   IU
Fairbairns, W.H.   L88,243
Fairbank, Florence   IU
Fairbank, Sir William   IU; UC
Fairfax family
  The Fairfax correspondence   L6,144 165 180;
  L36,151; L56,66; L82,192 302; L117B,20 46;
  UC(Bowman); UC Manuscripts,32
Fairfield, Charles
  Some account of Baron Bramwell (pub.McM.)
  L42,259; L67,310; L88,348; L89,81
Fairholt, Frederick W.   L93,81; L117A,28;
  IU
Fairley, Mrs.   L89,87
Fairweather, James   L2,75; L5,64
  Six years in the prisons of England   L37,243;
  L38,223; IU
Falkland, Lucius B.   IU
Falkner, J.M.   L5,59; IU
Fallon, D.   L5,284
Family Grocer & Wine Merchant, Dublin   UC
The Family Herald   L86,482 482(c) 485
Fane, S.Ponsonby   IU(Great Britain: Lord
  Chancellor's dept.); UC Manuscripts,11
Fane, Violet
  see Singleton, M.
Fane, W.D.   IU
Fanshawe, Lady Anne
  Memoirs   L37,116; L82,301
Fanshawe, John G.   IU
Faraday, Prof.   L83,225; UC(Bentley-end of B)
Farmer & Sons   L87,202; L88,117(c) .
[Farnham, W.R.]   IU(Farnhaur)
Farrar, Frederic William   UC
Farrar, J.A.   L5,113; IU(Farrer)
Farrer, J.W.   IU(Favrer)
Farrie, Hugh   L3,30; L86,319 365; L89,116
  Acte   L41,442; L42,128 478; L64,219 316
  The Deliverance of Robert Carter   L41,435;
  L42,482; L64,337

Farrington & Co.   L88,264
Farrow, Morley   IU
Fauconpret, de   L81,196; L117A,36
Faulkner, Sir Arthur B.
  Visit to Germany   L52,294; L117B,3
Faulkner, C.W. & Co.   IU
Faulkner, George   L91,41 52
Fauvelet de Bourrienne, Louis A.   L6,130; L8,
  35; L117B,12
  Memoires   L1,53
  Private memoirs of Napoleon   L8,94; L40,
  229 341; L41,276 540; L42,340 343 513; L53,
  228; L62,222; L119,163; L123,141-5
  IU(Bourrienne)
Faux, William   IU; UC
Fawcett, George   L5,38
Fawcett, Rt.Hon.Henry   L85,412; IU
Fawkes, Mrs.   IU
Fawkes, Mrs.F.Hamley   IU
Fawn, J. & Son   L86,298(c) 298
Fay, Theodore S.   L117B,42; IU(Fox,T.S.)
  The Countess   L7,142; L54,191
  The Double duel   L7,150
Fayahar, Harvie   IU
Fazakerley, Jacob   IU
Fea, Allan   IU
Fearon   L92,128
Fearon, Frederick   IU
Featherstonhaugh, George W.
  A Canoe voyage up the Minnay Sotor   L1,105;
  L7,162; L55,336; L117A,31
Featherstonhaugh, J.B.   L1,105
Federal Bank   L87,48
Feeny, J.   L82,227
Feilding, Clare   IU
Felgate, William   L57,167
Fellowes, Miss C.
  see Wallop, Lady C.
Fellowes, W.B.   L5,65
Fendall, Percy   L5,83; IU
Fenn, Mr.   L94,118; L95,156
Fenn, George M.   IU
Fenn, W.W.   IU
Fenton, C.J.Kirkby   L5,251; IU
Fenton, Rev.J.Kirkby   IU
Fenwick, Bedford   IU
Fenwick, Miss Lucy   L5,239
Ferguson, A.   L5,291
Ferguson, James   IU
Ferguson, Robert
  Life and labours of John Campbell
  see Brown, A.M.
Fernie, Thomas P.   [L80,21]
Ferrier, John   L5,79; IU; UC
Ferrier, Susan E.   L36,16; L37,124; L82,223;
  L117B,2; L122,86 116; IU; UC Manuscripts,
  39
  Destiny   L39,384; L40,357; L41,492 497;
  L42,462 465; L55,17-23
  The Inheritance   L39,384; L40,356; L41,492
  497; L42,465 467; L55,17-23
  Marriage   L39,383; L40,355; L41,493 498;
  L42,466 469; L55,17-23

Ferrier, Walter IU
Festing, Miss Gabrielle L5,307; L22,361
Festing, Henry UC
Fetherstonhaugh, Hon.Maria (Minna) G. L3,
  108; L5,217; L85,78 456 463; IU; UC
  Alan Dering L39,342; L41,502
  Dream faces L40,396; L41,507; L42,481;
  L62,194; L63,293; IU George Bentley,186+2
  For old sake's sake L40,358; L41,510; L61,
  187
  Kilcorran L39,241; L41,516; L60,54
  Kingsdene L39,281; L41,516; L60,74-5
  Robin Adair L39,303; L41,529; L60,120;
  L123,181
Fewin, Simon L95,237
Ficenton, J.K. UC
Field, Julian L5,88; L86,233
Field, Roscoe & Co. L89,120-1
Field Sports Protection & Encouragement
  Association IU
Fielding, H.
  see Hall, H.F.P.
Figgis, Samuel L88,254; IU
Figuier, Guillaume L.
  The Day after death L2,81; L37,313; L38,
  125 336; L39,108-9; L40,249; L41,211;
  L42,184; L119,109
Fillan, A.D.
  Stories of the two rebellions L6,180; L36,151
  see Buchanan, Prof.R.
Finch, Mrs.Clay L5,283
Finch, John L83,73
Finch, Miss Marianne L1,84; L117B,3
  An Englishwoman's experience in America
  L36,152; L57,208
Finch-Hatton, George James (Earl of
  Winchilsea) IU(Winchilsea)
Finden L2,84
Findlay, Charles Farquharson IU
Findlay, John IU
Finnemore, John L22,361
Fircks, Mary von L86,416
Firmin, H.J.P. IU
Firth, J.B. L5,288
Fisher L87,76(c)
Fisher, Arthur A'Court
  Personal narrative L36,115; L37,114; L39,
  401; L58,308; L97,194
Fisher, Arthur T. L3,45; L4,44; L5,159;
  L22,347; L86,337 395 499; IU; UC
  The Farrier (orig.No foot: no horse) L41,
  385; L42,199 201; L65,313
  Outdoor life in England L42,360; L67,83
  Rod and river L41,373; L42,308 310; L65,
  216
  Through the stable L41,355 363; L42,326-7
  523; L64,273; L119,117
Fisher, Charles L5,289; L22,355
Fisher, Esther Y.(Mrs.Arthur T.Fisher) UC
Fisher, G. L92,50 76 109 129 160 174-5
Fisher, Harriett IU
Fisher, S. IU
Fisher, Vernon IU

Fisher, W.E.Garrett L5,279; IU; UC(Garrett)
Fishing Gazette L66,93
Fitzball, Edward L81,127 129; IU
Fitzclarence, George (1st Earl of Munster)
  L81,123; IU(Munster); IU Unidentified, (A)
Fitzgerald, Miss
  The Story of my love L2,77; L37,256; L38,
  224
Fitzgerald, Edward P. L5,53; IU
  Letters to Fanny Kemble L3,133; L42,339
  344 361; L66,244-7; L67,18
Fitzgerald, J.E. IU
Fitzgerald, Miss K.M. L5,62
Fitzgerald, Percy H. L2,43; L3,61; L4,78;
  L84,42 57; L85,469; L87,120; L94,236;
  L95,169; L96,57; L123,165-6; IU; UC
  Beauty Talbot L37,53; L38,85; L59,226;
  L100,49
  Bella Donna L36,139; L37,28; L38,94; L58,
  335
  Charles Lamb L36,315; L37,122
  Charles Townshend L37,125
  Fairy Alice L36,200; L37,121; L38,136;
  L59,41
  Jenny Bell L36,238; L37,122; L38,169;
  L39,434; L59,87; L98,142
  The Lives of the Sheridans L40,63; L41,268;
  L42,256; L63,69-70
  Memoirs of an author L42,344; L66,89-91
  The Middle-aged lover L38,291; L39,447;
  L40,445
  Mildrington the barrister L36,153; L37,191;
  L59,6
  The Parvenu family L38,341; L39,437; L59,
  336
  The Romance of the English stage L38,322;
  L39,400 428; L40,467; L41,530; L42,519
  Stonyhurst memories L42,356; L66,211-14
Fitzgibbon, Miss Mary A. L3,135; L88,57;
  IU; UC
  A Trip to Manitoba L39,337; L40,290; L41,
  536; L60,199
  A Veteran of 1812 L42,346
Fitzpatrick, William J. L2,56; L3,143; L67,
  87; L83,272; L86,87; L88,101 132 168; L94,
  159; IU; UC
  Memoirs of Richard Whately L36,160; L37,
  268; L59,26
  Memories of Father Healy L42,365 390; L67,
  24-8; UC Manuscripts,18
Fitzroy, Rev.E. L84,167
Fitzroy, Henry (5th Duke of Grafton) L80,26;
  L117B,25; IU(Grafton)
Fitzroy, Lord William IU
Fladgate & Co. L87,112-13
Flagg, Jared B.
  The Life of Washington Allston L41,383; L42,
  267; L65,280
Flammarion, Camille
  The Marvels of the heavens L2,79; L37,196;
  L38,187; L39,166 178; L40,289-90; L41,
  278 500; L42,279; L119,108
Fleischmann, Florence IU

Fleming, Albert L5,293
Fleming, Mrs.Alice M. L5,272
Fleming, J.M. L5,211
Flenzel, Emil IU
Fletcher, Mrs.Eliza L53,246; L81,156;
L117A,35
Fletcher, Elizabeth S.
see Watson, E.S.
Fletcher, Henry C. L2,57 82; L3,19; L84,
151-2
History of the American War L36,183; L37,
123 127 296-7; L38,133-4; L39,140 155;
L40,160 248; L41,235; L42,211; L59,4
Fletcher, Joseph S. L3,89; L87,90 120 177-8
When Charles the First was king (orig.Scythe
and sword) L41,409; L42,476; L65,218;
L86,488 490
Fletcher, Julia C.(George Fleming pseud.)
L3,18; L86,58 60; IU(Fletcher,C.)
Andromeda L13,131; L40,410; L41,503;
L63,14-17
Fletcher, W.J. L5,134; L22,361
Flint, Alicia UC
Flint, Montagu L5,108
Floyer, Miss Edith L.(Mrs.Butcher) L3,152;
L5,130 283; IU
A Strange journey L40,359; L61,193
Flygare, Emilie (E.Carlén) IU(Carlén)
The Brother's bet L2,55; L37,50; L38,98
The Guardian L2,55; L36,191; L37,81;
L38,145
John L36,120
Julie L36,120
The Lover's stratagem L7,173; L8,175;
L36,119
The Maiden's tower L36,118; L57,190;
L82,250
Woman's life L36,119; L57,142;
UC Manuscripts,47
Flynn, J.A. IU
Fogerty, Joseph L3,90; L86,254; IU
Robert Leeman's daughters (orig.Muriel and
Mirelle) L41,454; L42,494; L64,112
Folkard, Miss Mary H.Tennyson L5,190-1
Follyston L90,236
Folthorpe, Robert L83,239
Fonblanque, Albany de Grenier L2,33; L3,82
101; L5,32 44 52; L83,250; L84,63; L85,
271; IU; UC
Bad luck L38,332; L39,247
Cut adrift L37,56; L38,107; L59,195-6;
L99,191
A Family tree L38,347; L39,450
Jedwood justice (orig.The Gault case) L41,
420; L42,487; L65,121
Pious frauds L39,344; L60,226-7
A Tangled skein L38,346; L39,224; L97,
144 146
Fonblanque, Albany William IU
England under seven administrations L53,
213; L117B,12
Life and labours L3,62; L38,308; L39,207;
L59,300

Fonblanque, Mrs.Ch. de IU
Fontanier, Victor
Narrative of a mission to India L55,225;
L117A,12; L117B,30
Fonvielle, Wilfred de L5,71; IU
Fookes, A.B.R. IU
Foote, J.A. IU
Foote, John L5,93; L90,239
Foote, W. L117B,20
Foran, James IU
Forbes, Archibald IU
Forbes, Edward IU
Forbes, Frederick E.
Five years in China (orig.China and Labuan)
L7,165; L8,49 52; L36,153; L56,58; IU
Six months service in the African blockade
L7,168; L8,94; L36,153; L42,403
Forbes, James
Oriental memoirs [L7,110]; L53,81-5 226;
L123,236
Forbes, Jonathan
Eleven years in Ceylon L7,141 145; L36,152;
L54,209; L91,132; L117B,25
Forcols, A. UC Miscellaneous
Ford, Douglas M. L5,29
Ford, Joan IU
Ford, L. IU
Ford, Richard IU
Forde, Miss Gertrude L3,137; IU
A Lady's tour in Corsica L39,343; L40,287;
L41,518; L60,220
Forester, Thomas L93,101; L117A,8
Everard Tunstall L36,158; L56,315;
UC Manuscripts,47
Forfar, James L5,108
Forman, H.Buxton L2,69; L85,137 137-9(c);
IU
Forrest, Emma IU
Forrest, Sir George W. L3,176; L4,85; L5,
86; L61,284-98; L85,234-6 343 346 413; L86,
122; IU
Forrester, Mrs.(Mrs.Smith Brydges) L5,31 121
Forrester, Alfred H.(Alfred Crowquill pseud.)
L1,73; L2,70; L5,18; L117B,28; IU; UC
Forrester, Charles R.
Phantasmagoria of fun L7,150
Forster, Rev.Charles L1,85-86; L2,44; L3,
28; L82,151 185; L83,84 226; L84,204; L94,
146; L117B,7; IU; UC(end of F)
The Apostolic authority L36,92
Israel in the wilderness L36,186; L37,93 117;
L38,137; L39,436
The Israelitish authorship L36,55
The Life of John Jebb L36,94 155; L37,119
The One primeval language L36,55 237; L37,
118; L56,303-5
Sinai photographed L36,288-9; L37,117;
L38,334; L58,254
Six preacher sermons L36,156; L37,118
Forster, Rev.J.J. UC(end of F)
Forster, James W.
The Apocalypse its own interpreter L1,146;
L36,156; L38,136; L39,449; L57,216

Forster, John L82,369; L83,151; L84,161
302-4; L117A,39; IU
Forster, Miss Laura M. L3,141; IU; UC
Chelsea window gardening L39,334; L40,231;
L41,206; L63,60
Forsyth, Alice IU
Forsyth, Miss Ethel L63,250; IU
Forsyth, Sir Thomas D. IU
Autobiography L41,321 387; L42,501; L63,
250
Fortescue, G. L85,343
Foskett, Mrs. IU
Foster, F.W. L67,282-4; L89,50 61 63
Foster, J. IU
Foster, James Richard UC
Foster, John C. L75,1-105; L76,248-353
Foster, Margaret L5,267
Fothergill, Miss Caroline IU
Put to the proof (orig.Judith Terry) L3,159;
L40,385; L62,28
Fothergill, Miss Jessie L3,100; L5,94 101 120
142; L85,24 292 309; L86,376; IU
Aldyth L39,385; L40,366; L41,77; L42,
74-5; L61,104-5; L119,30
Borderland L40,469; L41,76; L42,75-6;
L63,127; L119,33
The First violin L38,131; L39,238 263 298
399; L40,71-2; L41,71 97; L42,76-8; L60,
43 56; L119,26; L123,193-5
From Moor Isles (orig.Ines Grey) L41,464;
L42,79-80 483; L63,283; L119,34
Healey L39,386; L40,77 367; L41,75; L42,
77; L61,104-5; L119,31
Kith and kin L39,352 391; L40,72-3 437;
L41,72; L42,78-9; L60,269; L119,29
Made or marred L39,360; L40,182; L41,
152; L60,293
One of three L39,361; L40,183; L41,152
154; L42,116; L60,293; L119,35
Peril L40,376; L41,526; L61,207-8; L119,
32
Probation L39,299 308 332a; L40,74; L41,
73 81; L42,81; L60,122; L119,27; L123,
201-2 210-11
The Wellfields (orig.Their heart's desire)
L39,332 363; L40,75-6; L41,74; L60,202
285; L119,28
Fothergill, Sophia IU
Foulds, James L. L85,462
Fowler, Mrs.Ada D. L3,145; L87,103 105
115; UC
The Bishop's wife L42,451; L66,1
Fowler, Miss E.T. L5,226; L88,75
Fowler, Rev.Montague L87,115; L89,92
Fox, Arthur IU
Fox, Major Bushe L5,222
Fox, Rt.Hon.Charles J.
Memorials and correspondence L2,41; L36,
54 176 250; L37,224; L38,217; L39,423;
L40,451
Fox, Henry R.(3rd Baron Holland)
IU(Holland,H.R.)
Fox, John L5,32; IU

Vindication of Lady Byron L37,259; L38,243;
L39,420; L40,460; L41,537; L42,523
Fox, Loftus B. L93,90 183
Fox, Lady Mary E.
Account of an expedition to New Holland L7,
167; L8,94; L36,155; L53,320-5
Fox, T.Hamilton IU
Fox, Thomas IU
Fox, Mrs.Thomas S. IU
Fox, Walter St.John IU
Foxwell, Ernest L5,189; L86,115; IU; UC
History of English trains (prop.) L88,165;
IU Unidentified, (B)
Francatelli, Charles E. L1,142; L2,27; L9,
81; L83,243; L93,267; L117A,6; IU
The Cook's guide L9,148; L36,16 206 217
273-4; L37,120-1 216; L38,132 157; L39,141;
L40,250-1; L41,224 389; L42,194; L58,
314-16; L59,246; L119,115
The Modern cook L7,159; L8,35 53 95; L36,
21 103 130; L37,115 119 129; L38,132 340;
L39,143-4; L40,251-2; L41,225 389; L42,
195; L55,217; L57,105-10
Francillon, Robert E. IU
Strange waters L3,112; L39,291; L60,105-6
Francis, A.L. IU
Francis, J.G. L5,39 72 86; IU
Francis, J.P. L5,39 72 86
Francis, John C. L3,72; L4,86; L87,109;
IU; UC
John Francis L41,330; L42,196
Francis, P.
see Francis, J.P.
Francis, Sir Philip L55,303; L83,125 128
Frankland, Mr. L86,336
Frankland, Charles C.
Narrative of a visit to Russia and Sweden L52,
236
Franklin, Lady L83,196
Franklin, John IU
Franklin, Sir John UC
Franklyn, Dr. L84,205
Franklyn, Henry Bowles IU(Franklin)
[Franklyn], Johns IU
Franks, J.W. IU
Franks, J.W. IU
Fraser L95,20
Fraser, Agnes D. L5,283; IU
Fraser, James IU
Fraser, James B. L1,51 105; L81,221; L90,
243; L117B,6; IU; UC
Alle Neemroo L36,104; L55,34
The Dark falcon L7,156
The Highland smugglers L52,283
Narrative of the residence of the Persian
princes L54,65
The Persian adventurer L52,120; L68,57
Travels in Koordistan L7,111[149]
A winter's journey [L7,139]
Fraser, Jessie IU
Fraser, John IU
Fraser, Julia A. L86,441
Fraser, W.A. L5,28; L22,366
Fraser, William L1,56; L52,11 139; L68,18

L81,28 30 34; L91,291
Freebain, A.R. IU
Freeman, Mrs. L5,277
Freeman, Mrs.(née Merivale) L85,359
Freeman, Cecil IU
Freeman, Rev.Gage Earle L5,179; L88,227;
IU; UC
  Mount Carmel L37,199
Freeman, Herbert B. IU
Freeman, Miss Margaret L3,89; IU
Freeman, Mrs.Maria L1,169; L36,229
  A Friend in need L58,161
Freeman, Samuel IU
Freese, F.W. IU
Freese, Mrs.Octavia L87,212; L88,78; IU
  More about Gordon L42,346; L66,148-50
  173-6
Freeth, C. IU
Fremantle, Mrs. Lyon L5,105; IU
Frémont, Jessie B.
  Souvenirs of my time (pub.D.Lothrop & Co:
  Boston) L63,150
French, Mrs.A.
  see Hector, Mrs.A.F.
French, Rev.T. L84,120
French & Denton L84,77
Frend, Mrs.Henry L5,309; L89,72
Frere, Bartle IU
Freytag, Gustav
  Debit and credit L1,164; L36,37 62; L58,
  125
  Reminiscences L3,86; L41,338; L64,72-3
  123-9 248-65
Friend, D.B. L88,273
Friswell, Mrs.Emma L64,149; IU
Friswell, James H. L1,163; L2,15; L84,63;
  UC
  A Daughter of Eve L36,107-8; L97,202
  Ghost stories L36,87; L64,148-9
Frith, Frederick IU
Frith, Minnie IU
Frith, Walter L5,188; IU
Frith, William P. L3,69; L86,159; IU;
  IU Unidentified (F.,W.P.)
  John Leech L3,23; L41,358 388; L42,247a;
  L64,318; L65,47-8
  My autobiography L40,83; L41,321 334-6
  362 388; L42,196 280; L63,269; L119,104
Froebel, Julius
  Seven years in Central America L1,134 154;
  L36,64; L37,121; L58,194
Frohman, Daniel L86,345
Fromme, Carl L85,130 198; IU
Frost, Anne IU
Frost, Thomas IU
Froude, James A. IU(Fronde)
Fry, Clarence E. IU
Fry, Francis IU
Fry, Henry UC
Fryer, Charles E. IU
Fryxell, Anders
  The History of Sweden L36,168; L55,231
Fuller, B. & Co. L85,478

Fuller, J.F. IU
Fuller, J.J.F. L87,147
Fuller, Sarah M.
  Memoirs of Margaret Fuller Ossoli L1,115;
  L2,40; L117B,32
Fuller, Neales & Rose L87,145
Fullerton, Lady Georgiana C. L2,56-7; L3,
  17 149; L5,34; L60,58; L67,254 259-65;
  L84,79 98-100 150; L85,13 44 257 259 304;
  L91,16; L95,2; IU
  Constance Sherwood L36,195; L37,115; L38,
  115 327; L39,47-8; L40,63; L59,46
  Ellen Middleton L40,66; L41,66; L42,83;
  L62,277-8
  Lady-bird L36,167; L37,64 68 72 270; L38,
  39; L39,49; L40,65-6; L41,64; L42,83;
  L82,274-5
  Mrs.Gerald's niece L37,135 269; L38,38
  145 199; L39,50; L40,65; [L59,183]
  A Stormy life L37,239; L38,228
  Too strange not to be true L36,155 168; L37,
  65 71 115 284; L38,40; L39,51-2; L40,67;
  L41,65; L42,84-5; L59,24; L98,22
  A Will and a way (orig.Sown in tears) L39,
  370; L40,463; L61,5
Fullom, Stephen W. L2,70; L3,72; L4,86
  Time will tell L37,252; L38,239
Funk & Wagnalls L85,471 474; L86,47; IU
Furley, Miss Catherine Grant L5,198
Furlong, Miss Mary L5,243
Furne, Jouvet & Co.
  see Jouvet & Co.
Furniss, Harry IU
Furnivall, F.J. IU
Fursdon, Charles IU
Fuseli, Henry
  Lectures on painting L1,49 58; L52,147;
  L68,66
Fyfe, Henry H. L4,69; L88,274 276;
  UC(Times)
  A Trick of fame L42,415; [L67,202]
Fyfe, J.H. L5,96; IU
Fyvie, Isabella
  see Mayo, I.F.
Fyvie, John L5,211; L22,356 360 367-8

Gad & Keningale IU
Gaffney, Thomas L87,158 160 162 169
Gage, Mr. IU
Gage, Selina IU
Galbraith, L.
  see Gibson, L.
Gale, Peter L1,106; L90,50; L117A,22
Galignani & Co. L81,63 66-7 72-3 80-2 84
  [139]; L83,265; L117A,22
Galignanis Messenger IU
Gall & Inglis L62,272-4
Gallard, M.elle de IU(Xavier)
Gallenga, Mrs.A. L5,193; L83,272
Gallenga, Antonio C.N. L2,17; IU
  The Invasion of Denmark L36,213; L37,132

L59,28
Galletti di Cadilhac, Mme.M. L3,49; L5,210
  Our home by the Adriatic L40,169; L41,524;
  L63,82-6
Gallway, Emily C. L94,311
Galt, John L1,28; L90,1-2 24; L117A,2; IU;
  UC
  Bogle Corbet (orig.The Emigrants) L52,168
  184; L68,75-6 81
  Eben Erskine L52,250
  Lawrie Todd (orig.The Settlers) L52,19 84;
  L68,22 43; L122,94
  Life of Lord Byron L1,18
  The Lives of the players L52,207; L68,89
  Southennan L52,86; [L68,44]
  Stanley Buxton (orig.The Schoolfellows) L52,
  205; L68,89
Galton, Arthur L5,244
Galway, Lord
  see Arundell, W.G.M.
Gambier, James W. IU
Gamble, Dominic J. L5,43; IU
Gane, W.Law L92,163
Gannerons, Emile L87,275 276(c); L88,73
Garcia, Manuel L85,318; UC(end of G)
Gardiner IU Unidentified,(A)
Gardiner, Miss Linda L5,159
Gardiner, Marguerite (Lady Blessington)
  L117A,13; IU(Blessington); UC(Bentley-
  end of B)
  Conversations of Lord Byron L3,57; L41,
  385; L42,182
  The Governess (prop.) L54,44
  Marmaduke Herbert L56,1
  The Memoirs of a femme de chambre L55,290
  The Repealers L52,339
Gardiner, Samuel R. IU
Garland, Mrs.Col.
  see Pisani, Marianna
Garmeson, J.
  see Lippincott, J.B. & Co.
Garner, Mrs.Col.
  see Pisani, Marianna
Garner, Rev.T.P. L84,157
Garnett, J. IU
Garnett, Richard IU
Garnier L90,259 284
Garrett, Edward
  see Mayo, I.F.
Garsia, M.F. IU
Garsia, Dr.W.Marston IU; UC(Bentley-
  end of B)
Garside, F. L5,110; IU
Garstin, Norman L5,307
Garvey, Michael A. L82,280-1; L93,199-200;
  L117B,13
Gaskell, Miss Annie L5,253; IU; UC
Gaskell, E.C. IU
Gaskell, [S.] IU
Gasparin, Valerie de
  The Poor ye have always with ye L36,45
Gaspey, Thomas L90,139; L91,82
  The Self-condemned L53,146; L117A,8

Gasthaus & Bären L63,142
Gattie L117A,17
Gatty, Horatia IU
Gaye, Miss Selina L5,177; L94,254 257
Geater, Mrs. L85,371-2
Geisel, Mrs.A. IU
Gellie & Barrie L84,257
General Post Office L86,138; L89,114
The Gentleman's Magazine IU; UC(Bentley-
  end of B)
Geoghegan, Miss Mary L5,238
Geographical Society of Fena UC(Kunze)
George V (King of Great Britain) IU
George, Anita
  Memoirs of the Queens of Spain L36,158-9
George, Henry IU
Gerard, Emily IU
Gerard, Miss Frances A. L5,57; L22,359
Gerard, J.F. L90,91; L117A,17
Gerard, John L67,254 260; L88,337
Germains, Victor Wallace UC
Gerrare, Wirt L5,22
Gersdorff IU
Gerson, Edmund IU
Gerstean, Lewis L5,66
Gianotti, Maria UC
Gibbon, Charles L3,75; L84,294; L85,48
  126; L94,117 126; IU
  In honour bound L38,321; L39,402 451; L40,
  435; L41,514; L42,486; L59,327; L101,71
  190
  In love and war L39,269; L60,60; IU Richard
  Bentley II,3
  What will the world say? L38,338; L39,441
Gibbs, Mrs. L87,143
Gibbs, William H. L61,326; L85,379; L86,
  203; IU
Gibney, Robert D. L1,175; L26,7 16; IU
  My escape from the mutinies L36,63 209;
  L58,185
Gibson, J. IU
Gibson, James
  see Murray, T. & Son
Gibson, Miss Lizzie (L.Galbraith) L5,294
Gidley, Selina M. L5,176; L61,136-7; L85,
  297; IU
Gifford, Rev.H.G. L5,204
Gifford, Lady Helen S. IU(Dufferin & Cladeboye)
Gilbert, H.M. L86,302
Gilbert, James L81,153 158 160 165 179 182
Gilbert, Thomas L77,21-2
Gilbert, William L2,80; L5,34; L84,154; IU
  The Landlord of the 'Sun' L37,181; L38,172;
  L39,398; L40,439; L100,62
Gilbert & Field L85,18; L86,87 417 428; L88,
  198 277; IU
Gilbey, W. & A. IU
Gilby UC
Gilby, E.M. IU
Gilchrist, R.Murray L5,250
Giles, Herbert L5,89
Giles, Miss K. L5,129
Giles, Mina (Mrs.Herbert Giles) L5,255; IU

Gilks, Thomas & Edward IU
Gill, Charles F. L87,228(c)
Gill, J. L5,285
Gill, M.H. & Son IU
Gillard, Hardy L5,67
Gillert, W.F. L84,90
Gilliat, Algernon IU
Gilliat, Howard IU
Gillies, Eliza M.T. L95,118
Gillies, Robert P. L6,168; L82,114; L93,77;
  L117B,3; IU
  Memoirs of a literary veteran L7,171; L8,150;
  L36,159; L56,233
Gillings, W. IU
Gillmor, L. IU
Gillmore, Parker IU
Gilmer, J.W. L88,226
Gilsa, Baroness von L5,40
Gilson L83,184
Gindely, Anton
  History of the Thirty Years War L40,257;
  L41,236; L42,212
Giraud L84,74
Girdlestone, Rev.C. IU(Astone)
Girity, Elizabeth L74,86-103
Gisby, Miss IU
Gissing, George R. L3,159; L5,178; L85,
  425; L86,301 411; L87,52 60; IU
  The Emancipated L41,444; L64,178; L65,
  277
  Mrs.Grundy's enemies (orig.Now or never)
  L40,381; L41,520; L61,275
Giveen, Henry M.
  see Norton, Mrs.
Gladstone, Miss A.M. L5,237
Gladstone, Emily IU
Gladstone, Rt.Hon.William E. L2,51; IU
  Dean Hook L39,320; L40,426; L41,502;
  L42,505; L123,189-90 192-3
  Inaugural address L36,158; L37,134; L38,
  147; L39,432; L40,432; L41,511
Glaisher, James L2,82; L3,33; L4,81; IU
  Travels in the air L2,77; L37,137; L38,146;
  L39,145-6; L40,450; L59,234
Glaisher, William L86,45; L89,92
Glascock, Anne IU
Glascock, Henry L. IU
Glascock, William N. L91,278; L117B,17
  Tales of a tar L52,104; L68,51
Glasgow, Mrs. L5,171
Glasgow, Mrs.G.R.
  see Butt, G.R.
Glasgow Daily Mail L87,166(c) 166
Gleig, Rev.George R. L1,17; L52,139 209;
  L56,11; L71,91; L80,5; L81,28-9 46 52;
  L91,58-9; L117A,11; IU
  Allan Breck L52,331; L53,32
  Chelsea Hospital and its traditions L36,161;
  L53,250
  The Chronicles of Waltham L53,164
  The Life of Sir Thomas Munro L52,195; L68,
  86
  Memoirs of the life of Warren Hastings L53,

162; L54,312 327
  The Veterans of Chelsea Hospital L7,142;
  L54,177
Glengall, Earl of
  see Butler, Richard
Glengall, Lady IU(Glengale)
The Globe L85,195-6; L86,175; IU
Globe Parcel Express L89,105 109
Gloucester, Mary, Duchess of IU
Glover, J.H. IU
Glover, Rev.R. L5,208
Glover, R.G. IU
Glover, [S.R.] IU
Glover, W.J.S. L84,321
Gluck, Dr. L82,165
Glyde, John L89,97
Glyphographic Office IU
Godfrey, Mrs.Mary R. L3,123; L5,98 112 128
  146; L85,371; IU
  My queen L39,414; L40,174; L41,153; L42,
  157; L60,175; L123,196-7
  Unspotted from the world L39,381; L40,365
  460; L41,539; L42,497; [L60,312-14]; L61,
  8; L62,192
Godfrey, Solita IU(Godfrey,L.)
Godwin, Henry L1,106; L117A,3
  Stonehenge L55,105
Godwin, William L1,20; L117A,5
  Caleb Williams L52,151 158; L68,67 70
  Cloudesley L52,7; L68,16 18
  Deloraine L52,218; L68,94
  Saint Leon L52,158
Goff, Gerald L.J. L3,72; L4,80; L86,
  401-2(c) 404 413-14 416 429; UC
  Historical records of the 91st Argyllshire
  Highlanders L41,359; L42,225
Goldsmid, Sir Francis H. L1,43
Goldson, William IU
Good Words L63,149; IU
Goodchild, Frederick IU
Goode, F.W. IU
Goodhart, H.C. L86,171
Goodman, E.J. L3,65; L86,177 209 442; IU
  Paid in his own coin L41,467; L63,335
  Too curious L41,467 481 496; L42,473 496;
  L63,239 308
Goodman, Godfrey
  The Court of King James the First L36,159;
  L53,349
Goodman, Walter L3,113; L88,92 124-5; IU
  The Keeleys L42,363; L66,312
Goodrich, A.M.
  Leonore and the little countess L36,80; L58,
  220
Goodrich, Arthur L55,204; L117B,21; IU
Goodrich, Miss Maud L5,178
Goodrich, S.G.
  The United States of America (prop.) L52,299
  300; L81,98
Goodwyn, A.G. L94,286
[Gordon] IU
Gordon, Mrs. L85,205
Gordon, Adam L. L5,77; UC(Thurston-end of T);

UC Manuscripts, 34

Gordon, Sir Alexander Duff   L2,73; L92,187;
L117B,39; IU(Duff-Gordon)

Gordon, Brampton   L88,294

Gordon, Donald   IU

Gordon, Edward   IU

Gordon, George J.J.H.(5th Earl of Aberdeen)
L6,168; L117B,3; IU(Aberdeen)

Gordon, Gerald P.   L5,286

Gordon, Miss Harriette M.(Mrs.H.M.Smythies)
L1,181; L83,137 196; L117B,25; IU(Smythies)
The Jilt   L55,227
The Marrying man   L54,314 331

Gordon, Sir Henry W.   IU; IU George Bentley,
203+1

Gordon, Mrs.May Evans   L3,138; L4,85; L5,
90; IU

Gordon, P. & Son   L88,272

Gordon, Pryse L.   L1,40; L81,34
Personal memoirs   L52,25; L68,25-6

Gore, Mrs.Catherine G.F.   L1,19; L6,122;
L52,90 187; L55,63-7 190 215; L68,61; L81,
31 46-7 50-1 183 186 190-1 197 199 229 234;
L82,274 357 359; L83,58-60 106-7; L90,212
225 229 260-2 303; L91,21 60 123 162 171-2
190 236; L92,8; L93,215; L117A,4; IU
Abednego the money lender (prop.)   L55,124;
L69,94
The Ambassador's wife   L55,7 69
The Cabinet minister   L54,77
Castles in the air   L55,305
Cecil   L7,146; L55,69; L122,74 121
Dacre of the south   L7,146; L36,141; L54,
329
The Debutante   L55,305
The Dowager   L54,189
The Fair of Mayfair   L52,248
The Lover and the husband (ed.)   L55,11
Mothers and daughters (orig.The Season)
L122,57 121
The Opera   L52,226 228
Pin money   L52,186; L68,73
The Popular member   L7,156; L55,213
The Sketch-book of fashion   L52,249
Sketches of English character   [L7,160]

Gore, Leslie
see Mayne, Miss

Gorle, J.   IU

Gorton, C.V.   L5,205

Gorton, N.L.   IU

Gorway, Walter   IU

[Goschen]   IU(Gordon)

Gosling & Girdlestone   L83,213

Gosse, Sir Edmund W.   L3,87; L5,91; IU; UC

Gosse, Mrs.Ellen   L5,294; IU

Gosselin, Charles   L53,158 160; L81,132-4
137 161 166 168; L117B,14

Goulburn, E.M.   IU

Gould, Katherine   L3,75; L65,146; IU

Gould, Robert H.   L1,138; L58,53; L83,104

Gould, Rev.S.Baring   L2,64 71; L3,67; L5,23
53; L86,158; L94,259; IU
Arminell (pub.Methuen)   L63,302

Red spider (pub.Chatto & Windus)   L63,91-3
Through flood and flame   L37,128; L38,242;
L99,99

Goupie & Co.   L85,471

Gouverie, R.Pleydells   IU(Gouvine)

[Gouvine, R.Pleydells]   IU

Governesses' Benevolent Institution   IU

Govion Broglio Solari, Catherine de   IU

Gowans & Gray   L88,353; L89,49

Gower, George G.L.(Duke of Sutherland)
IU(Sutherland)

Gower, Lord Ronald   L85,41

Gowing, Mrs.Aylmer   IU

Gowing, Richard   IU

Gowland, Thomas A.   L86,178-9

Grädener & Richter   L60,283-5; L85,92 257
260 272; IU

Graf, J.   IU

Grafton, Duke of
see Fitzroy, H.

Grafton Examiner   L86,55

Graham, Mrs.   IU

Graham, C.   L93,119

Graham, James J.
Elementary history of the art of war   L1,168;
L36,219 222; L37,133; L38,140; L39,208;
L58,167

Graham, John   L82,69 129

Graham, R.C.   L5,96; IU(Naham)

Graham, Thomas   L1,107; L6,121; L58,268;
L82,48; L117A,20
Barba Tassi   L7,170; L8,119; L36,149;
L56,220

Grand, James   IU

Grand, Sarah
see McFall, F.E.

Grand Junction Water Works Co.   L85,222 451;
L86,440

Grange, Amy M.   L3,106; L87,194; L88,110
170; IU
Victims of fashion   L42,438; L66,114

Grant, Mr.   L84,132

Grant, Arthur   L5,205; IU

Grant, C.L.   IU

Grant, Charles   L5,189

Grant, Helen Fox   IU

Grant, Mrs.J.Colquhoun   IU

Grant, James   L95,100
The Cameronians   L3,140; L39,369; L40,
424; L60,305-6

Grant, Sir Ludovic   L5,232

Grant, Miss Maria M.   L3,90; L84,331 334
336; L85,45; IU; UC(Oliphant)
My heart's in the Highlands   L39,279; L60,
72-4
The Sun-maid   L38,144; L39,454

Grant & Griffith   L55,251; L82,355

Granville, Lord
see Leveson-Gower

Granville, Mrs.   L85,280

Granville, Alexander
With the Cape Mounted Rifles   L39,375; L40,
338; L42,403; L61,7; L85,266 268 280

Granville, Augustus B. IU
  Saint Petersburg L123,236
Granville, Rev.Augustus K.B. L5,189; IU
Granville, Catharine N. IU
Granville, Mary (Mrs.M.Delany)
  The Autobiography and correspondence L1,
  184; L2,48; L36,258 276; L37,96; L38,122;
  L39,435; L58,225-9; L94,1-23 26-52 203
Granville, Paulina B. IU
Grapel, W. L81,52 93 148 178 206 240
The Graphic, Chicago L87,154
The Graphic, London L64,247; L87,263; IU
Grattan L81,163
Grattan, E. L53,263-6
Grattan, Thomas C. L1,33; L81,61; L82,187;
  IU
  Agnes de Mansfelt L36,105
  Jacqueline of Holland L68,91; L122,73 123
  Legends of the Rhine L68,92; L122,81 123
Graves, Alfred Perceval L3,127; L5,91; L60,
  228-9; L67,148-9; L85,148; IU
Graves, Charles L. L5,218
Gray, Edward D.M. L3,112; L5,193; L86,465
  467
  The Stepsisters L41,410; L42,476; L65,189
Gray, Mrs.H.E. L5,307
Gray, Mrs.Hamilton L6,7; L117A,7
Gray, James
  see Cormack, S.G.
Gray, John A. L3,148; L88,70; IU
  At the court of the Amir L42,358; L66,314
Gray, Russell
  see Le Fanu, E.F.
Gray, S. L94,223
Gray, Thomas UC Manuscripts,39
  Correspondence of Thomas Gray and William
  Mason L36,201; L56,226; L57,15
Gray & Co. L87,101
[Grayson, Amelia] IU(Dragson)
Great Britain: H.M.Customs
  see Custom
Great Britain: H.M.Treasury L87,287
Great Britain: Lord Chancellor's Dept. L122,1
  6 138; IU
Great Britain: Paymaster General IU
Great Britain: Post Office L84,127
Great Britain: Postmaster General L86,138
Great Britain: Secretary of State for the Home
  Dept. L85,451
Great Thoughts L86,479; L87,198-9; L88,332
Great Western Railway IU
Greatbatch, William L54,204; L81,107; IU;
  [IU Unidentified, (B)]
Greatorex, R.C. L83,187-8
Greedy, J. IU
Greely, Adolphus W.
  Three years of arctic service L40,211; L41,
  306; L42,325; UC
Green, A.L. IU
Green, Miss E.M. L22,364
Green, Mrs.Eliza
  see Crawford, E.F.
Green, Miss Evelyn E.

Torwood's trust (orig.Mine own familiar
  friend) L3,182; L40,393; L41,534; L85,431
Green, Mrs.M.A.Everett (M.A.E.Wood) L1,
  148; L58,3; L62,162; L82,325 327-8; L83,
  41 232; IU; IU(Green,E.)
Green, Mrs.Montague IU
Green, Sarah E. L94,179 203 231
Green & Williams L86,199 213; UC
Greene, Mrs. L82,302 351 355 362-3; L93,201
Greenhow, Henry M. L4,78; L88,203
  The Tower of Ghilzan L42,418; L67,154
Greenhow, Rose
  My imprisonment L36,216; L37,134; L58,
  334; IU
Greenwell, W.J. L5,40
Greenwood, F. IU
Greenwood, George L5,195; L22,349
Greenwood, Grace
  see Clarke, S.J.
Greenwood, James L95,110
Greenwood, Joseph Gouge IU
Greg, Percy L85,466-7; IU; IU George
  Bentley,186+3
Greg, Thomas T. L5,154
Gregg, T.D. IU
Gregory, Geo. L88,111
Gregory, John S. L55,32 42 116; L80,13;
  L81,162; L90,87 278; L91,195; L122,15
  25-52; IU
Gregory, Son & Tozer L87,191
Greig, Mrs. L5,19
Grenfell, Dr.Wilfred L89,86
Grenville, William W.(Lord Grenville) IU
Greswell, Rev.William L5,283; L88,262
Gretton, Rev.Frederic E.
  Memory's harkback L3,175; L41,342; L42,
  514; L64,106
Grevel, Henri L3,160
Greville, Lady B.Violet L3,141; L85,267; IU;
  IU Unidentified, (A)
  Keith's wife (orig.The Squire of blackness)
  L40,371; L61,265-7; L62,318
  Zoe; a girl of genius L39,374; L40,464; L61,
  75-8; L62,318
Greville, Charles L54,59 61; L82,274-5; IU;
  UC
Greville, Sophia IU
Grey, Hon.Mrs.
  A Man without a name L7,173; L8,174; L36,
  194; L82,245 265-6 277; L117B,9
Grey, Lady Barbarina C. IU
Grey, Hon.Mrs.Caroline E. IU
Grey, Charles IU
Grey, Hon.Charles
  Some account of the life of Earl Grey L2,46;
  L36,260; L37,135; L58,258; L102,1
Grey, Mrs.Elizabeth C. L82,349 354 360 370;
  L91,146; L117B,9
  The Duke L6,168; L54,185
  The Young prima donna L6,168; L54,272
Grey, Rt.Hon.Sir George L82,164
Grey, Henry G.(3rd Earl Grey) L1,168; L82,
  272; [L94,139] ; L117A,2: IU; UC

The Colonial policy L36,160
Parliamentary government L36,37 41; L37,
132
Grey, Heraclitus
see Marshall, Charles
Grey, John L54,185 272
Grey, Rev.John Hamilton L90,177
Gribble, Mrs.Norah L5,277; IU
Grice, Miss L.
see Hutchinson, L.
Grierson, George A. L88,66 83; IU(Asiatic
society of Bengal)
Griffin, Gerald IU
The Duke of Monmouth L117B,13
Griffin, John & Co. L82,40 107 113 198 201
208-9; L83,123; L117B,12
Griffin, William IU
Griffith, Richard C.F. IU
Griffith & Co. L86,378-9
Griffiths, H. IU
Griffiths, Louise IU
Grimaldi, Joseph
Memoirs L6,156; L54,26
Grimble, Augustus L86,391 426-7
Grimshaw, Beatrice Ethel UC
Grimwood, Mrs.Ethel S.(Mrs.Andrew Miller)
L3,125; L4,77; L86,417; IU; UC
My three years in Manipur L41,367 392; L42,
284-5; L65,151; L119,116; IU Richard
Bentley II,475; UC Manuscripts,12
Griswold, Rufus W.
The Prose writers of America L36,160;
L117B,35
Grohman, W.Baillie L85,123-4; IU(Baillie)
Groom, James F. L57,108
Grosvenor, Chater & Co. L85,329-30 333
359-60 370 377; L86,175 254; L88,329-30; IU
Grosvenor Gallery Library IU
Grote, G. IU
Grove, Archibald IU
Grove, George L85,311
Grove, Captain Ross L5,111
Grund, Francis J.
Aristocracy in America L7,140; L117A,20
Grüneisen, Miss IU
Grüneisen, C. L5,103
Grüneisen, Charles L. IU
[Guarraim] L87,120(c)
Gubbins, Charles L82,165
Gubbins, Martin R. L1,155; L2,28; L83,164
An account of the mutinies in Oudh L36,57 132
244; L37,133; L38,140; L58,178
Letter to Lord Stanley L36,236
Guiccioli, Teresa
My recollections of Lord Byron L2,63; L37,
51-2; L38,137-8; L59,167
Guillemin, Amédée V. IU
The Heavens L2,63 80; L22,336; L36,308;
L37,112 135-6 144 161; L38,138-9 346; L39,
146-7; L40,256-7; L41,237; L42,226 230;
L59,47 117-18; L85,55; L102,43; L119,107;
L123,164
La Lune (prop.) L37,137

The Sun L2,77; L37,132 261; L38,139; L39,
112-13; L40,212
Guinnard, A.
Three years slavery L2,81; L37,134; L38,
240; L39,428
Guinness, Rev.Robert L87,209
Guizot, François P.G. L1,129; L2,45; L83,
159 202 239; L93,228; L117B,43; IU; UC
Address delivered in 1857 L1,143
The Christian church and society L2,46; L36,
278-9; L58,271
Corneille and his times L6,142; L36,161;
L57,84
An Embassy to the Court of St.James L2,46;
L36,89 93 119 127; L37,131; L38,141
France under Louis-Philippe L2,46; L36,215;
L37,130; L38,141
History of Charles the First L36,162
History of Oliver Cromwell L6,172; L36,163
166; L37,131 134 307; L38,142 349; L39,
113-14; L40,207-8; L41,173; L42,256-7;
L57,160
History of Richard Cromwell L1,139; L36,
209; L58,1 25
The Last days of Louis Philippe L2,46 55;
L37,137; L38,141; L39,435
Memoirs of a Minister of State L2,46; L36,
152; L37,130
Memoirs of George Monk L54,69
Memoirs of Sir Robert Peel L1,139; L36,
278; L58,63
Memoirs to illustrate the history of my time
L1,134; L2,46; L36,226 233 267-8; L37,129;
L38,141; L39,428; L57,84; L58,135 237
Shakespeare and his times L36,162; L57,84
Gulston, Alan Stepney IU
Gunton, R.T. IU
Gurney, Archer T. IU
Gurney, Edmund L89,96
Gutch, Jane L91,245
Guthrie, T.Anstey L5,102; IU; UC
Guyot, Arnold H.
The Earth and man L36,31 121; L40,429
Gwilt, Joseph IU
Gwynne, Mrs. IU
Gyles, Miss Lena L5,268

H., E. IU Unidentified
H., S.H. IU Unidentified
Hk., N. IU Unidentified
Hachette & Co. L58,93-6; L59,47 141 227-8
234 315(c); L61,133; L65,71; L66,185; L83,
113-14 124 250; L84,51 147-8 220 223 258(c);
L85,57(c) 303; L86,164; IU; UC;
UC Manuscripts,10
Hacklaender, Friedrich W.
Clara L1,136; L36,90; L58,97-103
Katherine L1,136; L36,38
The Old monastery L1,136; L36,86; L58,98
Hadden, John L85,117
Hadder, George IU

Haeston, S. L82,81
Hagan, James L84,65
Hagenbach
  Christliche Kirche (prop.) L57,225
Haggard, Frederick IU; UC
Haggard, Sir Henry Rider
  Alan's wife (pub.Spencer Blackett; A.P.Watt)
  L64,237-40
Haggard, Hale & Pixley IU
Hahn, Margareta L66,176
Hahn-Hahn, Ida M.
  Dorothy Waldegrave L3,46; L38,348; L39,
  440; L40,434
Haig, Major H. de H. L5,302
Haines L81,101
Haines, C.R. L5,110
Haines, Mrs.M.A.E. L5,302
Haines, S.C. L5,179
Hake, Rev.P. L2,58
Hake, Dr.T.Gordon L3,134; L4,79; IU; UC
  Memoirs of eighty years L41,381; L42,278;
  L65,230-1
Hakeston, R. UC Miscellaneous
Halcombe, Charles H. L88,71; UC
Haldane, Vere
  see Downes, Louisa J.C.
Haldenby, Charles F.
  see Neale, J.E.
Hale, Captain L2,61
Halford, Gerald L5,281
Haliburton, A. IU
Haliburton, Robert G. L3,77; L5,48; L84,
  319 322 331; IU
  Still life in the New World (prop.) L38,332;
  L39,209; L59,337
Haliburton, S.H. IU
Haliburton, Thomas C. L1,187; L80,26; L81,
  184 191; L82,137 233; L83,126 210; L117B,
  26; IU; IU Richard Bentley I,27;
  IU Unidentified, (A)
  The Attaché L7,157; L36,102
  The Clockmaker L7,145; L54,120; L75,108
  The Season ticket L36,81 215; L37,55
Hall, A.M. L2,69; IU(Hall,C.M.)
Hall, Anna M.(Mrs.S.Carter Hall) L117A,3;
  IU
  The Buccaneer L122,70 123
  The Outlaw L122,78 111
Hall, Augusta (Lady Llanover) L1,184; L2,48;
  L58,225-9; L83,213-15 217-28 230-1 233-4
  237; L84,76 79 149; L94,1-23 26-52; L95,
  120; IU Richard Bentley I,45; IU(Llanover)
  Good cookery illustrated L37,179; L38,180
Hall, Mrs.Charlotte L2,52; L9,81 149; IU
  Memoirs of Marshall Hall L36,269; L37,145;
  L102,16
Hall, Edward Pickard IU
Hall, Mrs.F. IU
Hall, Harold F.P.(H.Fielding pseud.) L22,355
  The Soul of a people L42,391; L67,282-5
Hall, Henry L62,81-91; L85,441
Hall, Hubert IU
Hall, J.M. L94,299

Hall, John IU
Hall, Mrs.Milly L5,133
Hall, Samuel C. L1,61; L85,392; L122,70 78
  111; IU
  Retrospect of a long life L40,373; L61,176
Haller, B.F. IU
Hallett, Charles L89,42
[Hallett, Cyril] IU
Hallett, James IU
Halliwell, J.O. IU
Halls, John J. L52,133; L68,62; L117A,22;
  IU
  The life of Henry Salt L53,53;
  UC Manuscripts,35
Hamel, Joseph von
  England and Russia L36,169; L57,302
Hamer, J. L5,87; IU
Hamerton, Isabella F.
  see Romer, I.F.
Hamerton, Robert J. IU
Hames, Ernest IU
Hamill, Mrs. L22,358
Hamilton, A.H.A. IU
Hamilton, Andrew
  Sixteen months in the Danish Isles L7,172;
  L8,174; L57,103
Hamilton, C. IU
Hamilton, Mrs.Catherine J. L5,135; L96,49;
  IU
Hamilton, Florence IU
Hamilton, Lady George
  see Hamilton, M.C.
Hamilton, Lord George F. IU
Hamilton, J.A. L5,200
Hamilton, James
  Sinai, the Hedjaz, and Soudan L1,159; L36,
  54; L58,137
Hamilton, James IU
Hamilton, Miss Lucilla L5,282
Hamilton, Lady Maud C. L5,89; IU
Hamilton, Nicholas E.S.
  An Inquiry L1,187; L36,158; L58,223; IU
Hamilton, William L52,188; L80,8
  The History of medicine L52,73; L68,72 82
Hamilton & Co. L82,129; L83,70; L85,411
  441-2; L88,271 348
Hamley, Col.E.B. IU
Hammond, Mary Anne L. IU
Hammond, William A.
  Doctor Grattan L40,408; L41,494; L42,481;
  L63,1
Hampton, 1st Baron
  see Pakington, J.S.
Hancock & Co. L83,243 252
Hancorn, Dr. L84,104
Handcock, Rev.George L5,62
Handley, A.H. IU
Hannay, David L5,109
Hannay, James L2,72; L5,15 264; L84,103
  110; IU
Hannay, R. IU
Hansard L53,343-7
Hansard, Laura C.P. IU

Hanson, Philip L5,108
Hanson, W. L60,298
Harchant & Co. L84,103
Harcourt, Alfred F.P. L4,77; L5,281; IU
    On the knees of the gods L42,412; [L67,217]
Harcourt, Rev.L.Vernon L1,176; L58,197
Harcourt, Sir William L86,369; IU
Hardie, Richard L92,188
Harding, C.T. IU
Harding, Claud IU
Harding, G.P. IU
Harding, John IU
[Hardinge, Charles] IU(Hardinge,H.)
Hardinge, Edmund S. IU
Hardinge, Edward Heathcote IU
Hardinge, George IU
[Hardinge, Henry H.] IU
Hardinge, William M. L3,53; L5,151; L86,
    106 135(c) 180; L87,196; IU
    Out of the fog L41,475; L42,471; L63,285
    The Willow Garth L40,458; L41,538; L42,
    498; L63,113
Hardman, Frederick L92,64
Hardy, Barbara N. IU
Hardy, Miss Elizabeth L6,120-31 passim;
    L82,88 90; L117A,14
    Owen Glendower L56,176-8
Hardy, Iza IU(Hard)
Hardy, Lady Mary D. IU
Hardy, Robert Burns L90,313
Hardy, Robert W.H. L1,38
Hardy, Thomas L88,173; IU
Hardy, Sir Thomas D. IU; [UC Manuscripts,
    28]
    Memoirs of Lord Langdale L7,172; L8,174;
    L36,164; L57,101; L83,82; L117A,29
Hardyman, Charles T. IU
Hare, Augustus J.C. IU
Hargrave, Miss M. L5,114
Harison, Robert IU
Harness, Col. L5,108; IU
Harness, William IU
Harper Brothers L56,240; L81,129; L84,135;
    L85,263 405 408; L86,94 121(c) 122 172-4 199
    365 367 370; IU(Harper,F.P.)
Harper's Bazaar L85,447
Harper's Magazine L61,321
Harraden, Miss Beatrice L5,246; L87,93 96
Harris, Miss L92,24
Harris, A.L. L5,286
Harris, Charles L87,192
Harris, J. IU
Harris, James (1st Earl of Malmesbury)
    Diaries and correspondence L7,155-7; L36,
    196; L55,229
    A Series of letters L2,79; L37,197; L59,219
Harris, James E.H.(5th Earl of Malmesbury)
    IU(Malmesbury)
Harris, James H.(3rd Earl of Malmesbury) L2,
    79; L55,229; L59,219; L82,342; L83,28 210;
    L84,145 158; L92,54; L117B,7; [IU George
    Bentley,85+1] ; IU(Malmesbury);
    UC(Malmesbury)

Harris, Miss Mary D. L22,355
Harris, Stanley L3,158; IU
    The Coaching age L40,220; L41,207; L42,
    178; L62,237
    Old coaching days L40,363; L61,157
Harris, Rev.Thomas IU
Harris, Captain W. L5,20
Harris, W.R. IU
Harrison, Mr. UC(Bentley-end of B)
Harrison, Mr.(Leeds) L84,321
Harrison, Mr.(Portsmouth) L81,88
Harrison, Basil L5,199
Harrison, Clifford L3,119; L86,417 440; L87,
    52; IU
    Stray records L41,372; L42,341 343 345;
    L65,123
Harrison, Mrs.E.B. L88,47(c)
Harrison, Mrs.E.H. L5,111; IU
Harrison, Elizabeth H. UC
Harrison, F. L87,174-5(c)
Harrison, Miss Fanny B. L5,175
Harrison, Frederic IU
Harrison, G.B.(Mrs.Frederic Harrison) L5,
    285; IU
Harrison, Mrs.Harold L5,273
Harrison, Harold B. IU
Harrison, Henry L82,306
Harrison, Louise IU
Harrison, Miss Lucy L62,6; L85,376
Harrison, Matilda L2,71
Harrison, Richard B. IU
Harrison, Robert IU
Harrison, Mrs.S.Frances L5,234
Harrison, W.(Leeds) L85,254
Harrison, W.(Nairn) L86,442 446; L88,209
Harrison, W.H. IU
Harrison & Sons L83,241
Harrod's Stores L88,284
Harrowby, 2nd Earl of
    see Ryder, D.
Harston, E.F.Buttermere IU
Hart, A. L82,64 66 68 81 83 87 98 114 124 132
    142 146; L117B,22
Hart, Mrs.Elizabeth A. L3,111; L85,363 367
    405; IU
    Freda L39,286; L60,98
    Wilfred's widow L40,374; L61,300
Hart, John L87,235; L88,140
Hart, Miss Mabel L5,128
Hart, Rev.R.E.S. L5,304
Hart & Co. L86,78
Harte, Francis Bret
    see Leland, C.G.
Harter, Ethel M. L3,101; L65,121; L86,426
    494
Harting, Hugh L5,300
Hartleben, A. IU
Hartlett, E. IU
Hartley, Mrs.May
    see Laffan, May
Harvey, Mrs.Anna L5,226; IU
Harvey, William L90,117
Harwood, John B. L2,56; L3,73; L5,73;

L82,106 119 121 252; L83,275; L84,42 89;
L93,178; L117A,21; IU
The Bridal and the bridle L36,113; L56,288
Helena, Lady Harrogate L39,288; L40,433;
L60,109
Lady Flavia L36,208 324; L37,56 170; L59,
73
Lady Livingston's legacy L38,314; L39,441;
L59,314; L101,125
Lord Lynn's wife L36,182 242; L37,54 174;
L59,31; L98,74
Lord Ulswater L37,182; L38,176; L59,150
Major Peter L36,314; L37,185
Miss Jane L37,198
Odd neighbours L36,187; L37,211; L38,205
Paul Knox, pitman L39,273; L60,66
Plain John Orpington L36,323; L37,220;
L38,211; L59,105
Sir Peregrine's heir L38,324; L39,446
Stamboul L7,173; L8,175; L57,162
Harwood, Philip IU
Harwood, Thomas IU
Haskell, Mrs. L84,48
Hastings, James L83,180
Hatch, Edwin IU
Hatchards & Co. L86,85
Hatter, E. L81,179
Hatton, Dr. L2,66
Hatton, John Liptrot IU
Hatton, Joseph L95,171; IU
Hatton, Robert L95,5-7
Hatton & Son L86,144
Hauptmann, Moritz
The Letters of a Leipzig cantor L41,369;
L42,275; L65,142
Haussez, C.L. d'
see Lemercher de Longpre, C.
Havard, Henry IU(Harvard)
The Dead cities of the Zuyder Zee L3,73;
L38,353 370; L39,109-10; L40,196 203; L41,
177
The Heart of Holland L3,52; L39,327; L40,
258; L41,238; L42,226
Picturesque Holland L3,73; L38,44; L39,
219; L40,315; L41,301; L42,300
Havers, Dorothy H.(Mrs.Boulger) L3,83; L5,
92; IU; IU(Boulger)
Pretty Miss Bellow L38,357; L39,443
Haw, J.Panton IU(Hour)
Haweis, Mrs.H.R. L5,130
Haweis, Rev.H.R. L5,186; IU
Hawes, Benjamin L82,272; IU
Hawker, Miss M.E. L5,226
Hawker, Pauline A. IU
Hawkes & Phelps L85,414; L87,135
Hawkins, Rev.Charles E. L2,64; L3,30; L4,
81; L57,293; L66,302-5; L88,65 68 71 76(c)
76; IU
Hawkins, Frank IU
Hawthorne, Julian L3,92 101; L85,146 267; IU
Archibald Malmaison L39,415; L40,176; L41,
150; L42,158; L123,197-8
Garth L26,2; L38,359; L39,261; L60,24

Sebastian Strome L39,321; L60,177; L123,
202-3
Hawtrey, Dr.E.C. IU(Hawtrey,R.C.)
Hawtrey, Edith IU
Hawtrey, Edward L5,94; IU
Hay, J.N. IU
Hay, Mary Cecil IU
Hay, William D. L3,156; L85,315 328; L86,
231
Brighter Britain L40,360; L41,505; L42,
502; L61,169-71
Hayden, W.H. & Co. L86,473 489-91; IU
Haydon L83,127
Haydon, Benjamin R. IU
Haydon, Rev.G.P. L85,406
Hayes, Mrs.C.C. IU
Hayes, Isaac I.
An Arctic boat journey L1,180; L36,159 162;
L37,143; L38,153
Hayes, J.Hurst L22,356
Hayhurst, H.F. IU
Hayles, B. L81,171
Hayman, Dr.Westby H.P. L5,96 207;
IU(Hayman,H.)
Haynes L84,176
Hayter, Edward IU(Haytes)
Hayter, Flora D. IU
Hayter, Laure IU
Hayward, A. L81,222; IU
Hayward, M.W. IU
Hazell, W. L88,252 263 265 269
Hazell, Watson & Viney L86,213
Hazlitt, William L1,57; L52,102; L68,51
Conversations of James Northcote L3,87;
L42,342
Hazlitt, William Carew L2,18; L84,80; L88,
57; IU
Memoirs of William Hazlitt L37,150; L59,125
Head, Sir Francis L82,97 150; IU
Head, Mrs.Julia L5,224
Head, Walter T. IU
Heal, Sir Ambrose UC
Healey, William L122,15
Healy, Miss M.
see Bigot, M.
Heare, Joseph W. L92,97
Heath, H. L81,97; IU
Heath, [J.] B. L84,86
Heath, Sir Leopold G. L4,77; L88,301 350;
IU; IU(Hurth); UC
Letters from the Black Sea L42,386
Heath, Thomas Eden IU
Heathcote, A.M. L5,190
Heathcote, Sidney J. L86,418
Heatherington, A. L94,281
Heaton, Miss Mary M. L5,101; IU
Heckethorn, Charles W. IU
The Secret societies L38,345; L39,222;
L101,57
Hector, Mrs.Annie F.(Mrs.French;
Mrs.Alexander pseud.) L2,58; L3,21 128
187; L5,39 49 57; L84,78 334; L85,150 152
209 457; L86,44 117 239; L87,93; L88,61

270; IU; IU George Bentley,183+1 403; UC
The Admiral's ward L3,160; L40,33 372; L41,29;
L42,2; L61,233-5; L119,52
The Executor L40,34 377; L41,30; L42,2;
L61,114-15; L65,67; L119,51
The Freres L39,286; L40,31 431; L41,28;
L42,2; L60,192 283-5; L119,50
Her dearest foe L38,35 363; L39,26-7 30 435;
L40,25-6; L41,24; L42,3-5; L59,334; L119,
48
The Heritage of Langdale L38,363; L39,263-5
449; L40,25; L60,14
A Life interest L41,474; L63,164-8
Look before you leap L36,190; L37,175;
L39,380; L40,27; L41,25; L42,4; L59,45;
L61,116; L65,235; L119,45
Ralph Wilton's weird L38,312; L39,408 418
446; L40,164 452; L41,154 157 159; L42,156
160; L119,49
A Second life L40,402; L41,532; L62,243-51;
L63,129; L66,289-91
Which shall it be? L37,68 277 279; L38,47
251 342; L39,29-30; L40,30; L41,27; L42,
5-6; L119,46
The Wooing o't L38,73 281; L39,28 30; L40,
28-9; L41,26; L42,6-7; L59,267; L100,189;
L119,47
Hector, Miss Ida L5,177
Hedge, Col. L81,100
Hedges & Co. L84,62
Hedley, Oswald D. L83,175
Heinemann, William L66,111-13; L87,84 180-2
186 191; IU; IU George Bentley,421; IU
Richard Bentley II,659; UC
Heldmann, Bernard IU
Helmore, Miss M.C. L5,41
Helms, Prof.A. L86,135 144 147 154; IU
Helps, Sir Arthur IU; UC
Hemans, C.J. IU George Bentley,175
Hemphill, Barbara L117A,38; IU
Hemyng, General L22,364
Henderson, E.B. IU
Henderson, E.P. IU
Henderson, H.P. IU
Henderson, W.J. L5,194
Hendriks, Herman L86,220
Hendy, Frederick J.R. L63,137
Hengelmüller, de L85,393 395 403-4 414
Henham, Ernest G. L5,305
Henley, W.E. IU(Hinley)
Hennessy, Prof. L87,53
Hennessy, Bryan IU
Hennessy, Henry IU
Henniker, Hon.Mrs.Florence L3,73; L5,240;
IU
Bid me goodbye (orig.That parting was well
made) L41,414; L42,474 480; L65,136
Sir George L41,404 429; L42,461-2; L65,
36-7
Henniker, John
Chronological peerage L36,153; L37,146
Henrietta Maria (Queen)
Letters of Queen Henrietta Maria L1,135 148;

L58,3
Henry Eugene P.L.(Duke d'Aumale)
History of the Princes de Condé L3,34; L37,
101; L38,78; L39,397; L40,421; L41,516;
L42,520; L84,133
Henry, John R. L22,364
Henry, Lucian E. L3,147; L85,364; L123,201;
IU
Henry, R. L5,17; IU
Hepworth, W. L5,175
Her Majesty's Theatre IU
Heraud, J.A.
Lives of eminent prose authors (prop.) L52,
209; L68,90
Herbert, Miss IU
Herbert, E. IU
Herbert, Edward J.(Earl of Powis) IU(Powis)
Herbert, Frances G.
A Legend of Pembroke Castle L36,165; L57,
173
Herbert, George
see Barraud, H.
Herbert, George R.C.(Earl of Pembroke) L3,
39; L4,78 88; L5,41; L26,7; IU(Pembroke)
House of Lords, 1878 L39,285
Letter to Mr.W.H.Mallock L39,285
The Political letters and speeches L42,372;
L88,120
Roots L38,280; L39,118; L40,163; L41,333
498; L42,307-8
South Sea bubbles L37,305; L38,223 271-2;
L39,119-20 430; L40,321 456; L41,304; L42,
249
Herbert, Henry J.G.(Lord Porchester)
The Last days of the Portugese constitution
L1,66; L6,173; L52,88; L68,46
Herbert, Henry W. L82,29 36 38; L117A,25
Field sports in the United States L36,154;
L56,111
Frank Forester and his friends L56,150
Frank Forester's fish and fishing L6,180;
L36,154
Herbert, Maria J.
A Legend of Pembroke Castle
see Herbert, F.G.
Herbert, Lady Mary E. L2,40; L3,46; L5,21;
L84,79 182-3; L85,477; IU; UC
Cradle lands L37,151 213; L38,151; L39,210
Edith L39,376; L40,263; L61,87
Geronimo L38,278; L39,208 235; L40,259
Impressions of Spain L37,149
Love or self-sacrifice L37,139; L38,150;
L39,210 214; L40,259; L41,269; L42,269
The Mission of St.Francis of Sales L37,139;
L38,151; L39,211; L40,261; L41,270; L42,
520
The Mother of Saint Augustine (orig.St.Monica)
L37,138; L38,152 337; L39,212 237; L40,260
A Search after sunshine L38,269; L39,211;
L40,261; L41,270; L42,520
Three phases of Christian love L37,149 167;
L38,150 368 244; L40,262; L41,271
Wives, mothers and sisters L38,368; L39,

212 238; L40,260; L41,269-70; L42,330 332; L62,295

Herbert, May (Mrs.Simpson) L3,32; L64, 282-8; L86,341

Herford, Ivan S.A. IU
Stirring times under canvas L36,298; L37, 143; L83,242; L102,55

Hering, Henry A. L5,290; L88,354

Hérisson, Comte d' IU Unidentified, (A)

Hernaman, Mrs.Claudia F. L5,259

Herouand, E. IU

Herries & Co. L85,255

Herschel, Miss IU

Herschel, A.S. IU

Hertz, Henrik
King Réné's daughter L56,86

Hervey, Charles L5, 92 106 114 150; L91,177; IU

Hervey, George W.
The Rhetoric of conversation L1,182; L36, 204

Hervieu, Auguste L53,252 255 280 282; IU

Hesford, Harry L5,126

Hetherington, Helen F. IU

Hewett, Mrs. IU

Hewitt, Miss Ethel M. L3,142; L87,193; L88, 70
In a Cinque Port L42,438; L66,118

Hewitt, W.Grailey L5,254

Hewlett, Henry G. L84,332; L86,401; IU; UC

Hewlett, Joseph T.J. IU

Hewlett, Maurice L5,251

Hextall, Frederick L75,1-105; L76,248-353

Heyward, Miss Emma J.
The Court and the desert (trans.) L36,133; L56,337

Heywood, John L85,319 330; L87,63 172; L88,48 125 222-3 276 341; L89,72

Hichens, R.S. L5,285

Hickman, Walter IU

Hicks, Charles C. IU

Hickson, A. L85,262

Hickson, Mary Agnes IU

Higbed, Robert UC

Higgins, L. IU

Higgins, Robert R. L92,90-1

Highley, Samuel IU

Hildebrand, William L94,212

Hilditch, Miss UC(Bentley-end of B)

Hill, Mrs.(edited Whately,R.) L2,50; L83, 74-6 80 137

Hill, Alexander L81,90

Hill, B. L117A,17

Hill, Benson E. L90,78 84 86 135 280 283; L91,285; L117A,23; UC
Recollections of an artillery officer L53,267

Hill, Dr.Birkbeck L87,245

Hill, Constance IU

Hill, Ellen G. IU

Hill, Frederic
Frederic Hill L3,23; L42,341; L66,66; IU

Hill, G.Birkbeck IU

Hill, Miss Georgiana L3,138; L86,495; L89,

69: IU
A History of English dress L41,382; L42,225 227; L66,5-8; L87,141 145
Women in English life L42,368; L67,52

Hill, Mrs.Georgiana L2,49
The Breakfast book L36,239; L37,29
Everybody's pudding book L36,91 135 150; L37,107 111; L38,212 334; L39,139; L40, 108; L41,215; L42,506
Foreign desserts L36,55 75 80; L37,177; L38,123; L39,204

Hill, Isaac IU

Hill, Isabel L90,89 135; L117A,19

Hill, John Spencer UC

Hill, Miss Mary C. L3,23; L66,66; L88,126 298; L89,110

Hill, Rowland IU

Hill, Thomas IU; UC

Hilliard & Co. L83,251; IU

Hillier, Arthur C. L5,58

Hillier, Charles L117B,38
A Narrative of the attempted escapes of Charles the First L1,86; L36,165; L8,174; L57,134
The Sieges of Arundel Castle L36,165; L37, 145

Hillier, George
see Hillier, Charles

Hills, Miss K.F. L5,88

Hills, M.W. L90,231

Hills, William Henry IU

Hills-Johnes, B.
see Johnes, B.

Hills-Johnes, Sir James IU; UC(Hills-Jones)

Hind, J. L5,183

Hind, James D.
see Hird, Dennis

Hind, R.W.Archer L89,116

Hindell, Francis B.S. L74,221-62

Hinkson, Mrs. L5,48

Hinshelwood, Mrs.A.Ernest L88,340

Hinshelwood, Ernest L5,298

Hinton, Frederick
Recollections of a ramble L1,145; L7,171; L8,150; L56,317

Hiorns, Mr. L89,49

Hippisley, A.J. L92,7

Hipsley, Mr. L117B,16

Hird, Rev.Dennis L67,188; L87,254 290 297; L88,236 334 355; IU
Toddle Island L42,356 362; L66,179-81; L67,106-8; L87,207

Hirst, J.Crowther
Hiram Greg L3,135; L39,355; L40,433; L60,250-1; IU

Hirt & Son L60,264 268; L85,299 431-2; IU; IU George Bentley,232+1

Hirzel, S. L64,72-3

Hissey, James J. L3,177 179 183; L4,46; IU; UC
Across England in a dog cart L41,366; L42, 168
A Drive through England L40,215; L41,212; L42,505

A Holiday on the road   L41,317 345; L42,228
231
An Old-fashioned journey L40,289; L41,391
525 531; L42,293 297; L62,220
On southern English roads L42,369
On the box seat L40,172; L41,391 525 540;
L42,293 297
Over fen and wold (pub.McM.) L42,304
Through ten English counties L42,349 362
A Tour in a phaeton L41,338
Hitchman, Francis L3,185; L5,112 141; L86,
99(c) 99 152 207; IU
Hjerleid, Mrs. L5,72
Hoare, Mrs. L83,135
Hobbes, L92,126
Hodder, George L92,248 264-5
Hodge L84,42
Hodge, Rev.Robert V. L85,361
Hodges, Mr. L89,101
Hodges, C. L93,245-6
Hodges, Rev.G. L5,59
Hodges, Sydney L3,84; L5,89; L84,298; IU
  A New Godiva L38,348; L39,437
Hodges & Co. L82,164 167; L83,97; L85,139
Hodgkin, Miss M.E. L86,227(c) 227
Hodgson, Christopher P. L2,50
  A Residence at Nagasaki L36,166 275; L58,
262
Hodgson, Edmund L83,74 93 101-2; IU
Hodgson, F.C. L5,27; L22,364
Hodgson, H.H. & Co. L86,157 327; L88,284
286; IU
Hodgson, Thomas
  see Hodgson, Edmund
Hoey, E.Maxwell IU
Hoey, Mrs.F.Cashel L2,70 81; L3,52; L5,
46 71; L85,241 250 255; L100,148; IU
Hoffman, Agnes L88,164(c); IU
Hoffman, Charles F. L1,107; L90,104;
L117A,21
  Wild scenes L54,87
  A Winter in the far west L36,170; L74,125
166
Hofland, Mrs.Barbara (B.Hoole) IU
  The Captives in India L117A,23
  Daniel Dennison L55,257
Hofland, Thomas R. L55,257; L92,58 74;
L117A,13; IU
Hogarth, George L54,101; L90,214-16; L91,
64; L117A,39; IU
  Criminal trials (prop.) L54,99
  Memoirs of the musical drama L6,180; L7,
170; L8,120; L36,166; L54,18
Hogg, George L83,234 236
Hogg, James L3,41; L59,155; L62,56-63;
L63,5; L64,20-32; L71,95; L85,446 455
L86,123 345; L87,89; IU; UC Manuscripts,14
  see London Society
Hogg, John L3,41; L60,133; L61,138 173;
L85,96 119; IU
Hogge, George IU
Holcroft, William F. IU
Holden, W.J. L96,61

Holdsworth, Miss A.E. L87,43
[Hole, B.] IU
Holl, H. L92,179
Holland, 3rd Baron
  see Fox, H.R.
Holland, Mr. L86,319
Holland, Hon.Mrs. L5,173
Holland, Charlotte IU
Holland, Francis J. IU
Holland, J.D. L90,307 311
Holland, Lawrence L5,97
Holland, Spencer L. L5,177
Hollins, Carrie L. IU(Hollius)
Hollis, Margery
  see Elliot, E.
Hollis, William L93,144
Holman, James IU
Holme, Florrie UC
Holme, Mrs.Margaret L91,54 139
Holmes, Charles John UC
Holmes, Charles R. IU
Holmes, Richard R. IU
Holmes, W. & R. L87,50; L89,108
Holmes, William R.
  Sketches of the shores of the Caspian L7,159;
  L36,166; L55,264
Holroyd, G.B. IU(Holnyd)
Holt, Henry & Co. L62,304; L67,5; L84,336;
  L85,26 92(c) 93 219 232 302 305 318 333 371
  380 394 410 431 469 480; L86,48 55 161 246
  258 329 332 442 453 471; L88,133 138 181 192
  201; IU; UC
Holt, Joseph L94,246 252 255
Holt, W. L85,182
Holte, F.T. L88,273
Holthouse L84,175 [207] 208
Holyoake, Maltus Questell L5,265; IU(Holysake)
Hombre, d' L117B,46
Hombres, d' L91,73
Home Words IU
Honan, M.B. L91,4
Honderey IU
Honourable Artillery Company L88,292
Hood, Helena IU
Hood, Henry J. IU
Hood, Jane IU
Hood, Maxwell IU
Hood, Thomas IU(Shaw,L.)
  Tylney Hall L117B,9; L122,71 123
Hood, Tom L5,35; L95,105; IU
Hook, Anne D. IU
Hook, C. L117B,6
Hook, Cecil IU
Hook, D.L. IU
Hook, Theodore E. L1,29; L53,134 347; L54,
9 30 331; L68,45; L81,236; L117A,6; L117B,
18; IU; IU Henry Colburn,1+2; UC;
UC(Bentley-end of B)
  All in the wrong (orig.Births, deaths and
  marriages) L122,88-9 118 121
  Jack Brag L6,26; L122,65 103 121
  Gilbert Gurney L122,72 109 121
  Life of Mr.Huskisson (prop.) L52,189; L68,

The Life of Sir David Baird   L52,140 191;
L68,64 84

The Parson's daughter   L53,5; L122,58 98

The Ramsbottom letters   L38,268

The Surgeon (prop.)   L122,57 97 121

The Widow and the marquess (orig.Love and
pride)   L122,72 109 121; IU Unidentified, (B)

Hook, Walter   IU

Hook, Dr.Walter F.(Dean of Chichester)   L1,
189; L2,29; L3,42; L83,198 216 225 273;
L84,68-9 112 299; IU; IU(Oxen); IU(Raper);
IU(Rapst)

The Church and its ordinances   L38,371; L39,
277 304; L40,267; L41,239; L42,178

Hear the Church   L39,386; L40,368; L41,
245; L42,227

Lives of the Archbishops of Canterbury   L1,
180 183 185; L2,50 58; L3,89; L36,154 261
277 283; L37,140 147 151 163-4 167-8 176 318;
L38,153-6 300 335; L39,148-53; L40,89-90
268-71; L41,240-3; L42,257-9 362; L58,215;
L59,8; L60,22-3; L119,88-97; L123,199-200

Parish sermons   L39,307; L40,266; L41,
238; L42,300; L123,186-7

Hooker, Worthington
Physician and patient   L36,110

Hookham, [I.]   IU

Hookham, Thomas   IU

Hoole, B.
see Hofland, B.

Hooper, J.   L5,290

Hooper, Jane Margaret (Mrs.George Hooper)
IU(Hooper,G.); UC

Hooper, Rev.Richard   L5,84; IU

Hooton, Charles   L91,34 104 119 124; L117B,
9; IU
The Adventures of Bilberry Thurland   L53,
255 277

Colin Clink   L7,146; L54,302-6; L123,147

Hooton, Mrs.Charles   L91,28

Hope, Mrs.   L5,104 208

Hope, Miss Evelyn   L5,156; L22,363

Hope, George W.   L83,105

Hope, Thomas
Anastasius   L53,174 176; L122,58; IU

Hopkins, Tighe   L5,298; L88,234-5

Hopkins, W.Watts   IU

Hopkinson   IU

Hopkinson, Arabella M.   IU

Hopley, Catherine C.   L95,23

Hoppus, John D.
Poems   L42,357

Hoppus, Mary A.M.(Mrs.Alfred Marks)   L3,
95; L5,300; L86,285 426; L88,292; IU(Marks)
Dr.Willoughby Smith   L41,418; L42,474 484;
L65,116-18

The Locket   L41,446; L42,489; L64,159

Masters of the world   L41,457; L42,491;
L64,78

Thorough   L42,439; L66,98

Horatius Flaccus, Quintus
The Odes   L3,121; L39,328; L60,143; L123,

Horbury, H.   L5,66

Horder, Percy R.M.   UC

[Hore]
Irish celebrities   L36,292

Hores & Pattison   L88,191; IU(Hires...);
IU(Hore,F.)

Horley, Mary   IU

Hormack, John   L81,67

Hornby, Edward   L1,148; L83,126

Hornby, Lady Emilia B.   L2,44; IU
Constantinople   L36,138; L37,144
In and around Stamboul   L1,148; L36,222

Horne, Richard H.   L5,86 96; L70,13; L85,1
288; L90,306; IU

Horne, Thomas Hartwell   IU

Horner, Mrs.   L5,168

Hornibrook, J.L.   L5,288

Hornung, E.W.   L5,222

Horschelt, Mrs.Mary   L59,232

Hoskins, Dr.Samuel E.   L1,89; L83,78; L93,
195; L117B,23
Charles the Second in the Channel Islands   L36,
169; L37,146; L38,149; L57,242

Hoste, Lady Harriet   L52,307 309; L117A,2

Hoste, Miss M.R.   L5,127

Hoste, Sir William
Memoirs and letters   L52,307 309

Hotten, J.Camden   IU

Hotton, Joshua (Guy Roslyn pseud.)   L5,89;
L96,47; IU; IU(Roslyn)

Houghton, Mifflin & Co.   L87,246

[Hour] , J.Panton   IU

Houssaye, Arsène
Men and women of France   L1,177; L82,179
206

Houston, Mrs.   L91,97

Houston, Harriette J.Brooke   IU

Howard, Miss   L117B,34

Howard, Mr.   UC

Howard, Anne   IU

Howard, Edward   L90,112 143 187 222; L117A,
29; IU
Memoirs of Admiral Sir Sydney Smith   L54,105
The Old commodore   L53,284
Rattlin, the reefer   L53,255 277; L122,63 99
122

Howard, George   IU

Howden, Mrs.F.A.   L5,276

Howell, Edward   L1,108; L83,55; L117B,39

Howell, Richard   L91,259; L93,79

Howey, Charles   IU(Howen)

Howison, John
European colonies   L53,113
Tales of the colonies   L52,13; L68,19

Howitt, Mary   L55,274; L56,21 54; L92,101
181; L117B,8; L122,80; IU
The Seven temptations   L53,68

Howitt, William   L1,144; L81,147 208; L82,
157 178; L83,99-100; L92,117; L117B,8; IU
The Book of the seasons   L1,18; L7,144;
L36,167; L52,135; L68,62
Homes and haunts of the most eminent British

poets L36,168; L55,272; L57,87
Howson, John S. IU
Hoyer, Miss Maria A. L5,27
Hoyle, G.H. L87,187
Hubbard, Hon.Evelyn L5,254
[Hubner, Baron] L84,241
Huddart, Miss Elinor L3,165; L4,85; L85, 355
  My heart and I (orig.Motec) L40,373; L61, 261
Huddes, James L59,319(c)
Huddleston, Lady Diana IU
Huddleston, Sir John Walter IU
Hudson, C. IU
Hudson, Frederic IU
Hudson, William Henry UC
Hudson & Kearns L88,354
Hügel, Baroness von IU
Hugessen, E.H.Knatchbull (Lord Brabourne) L3,14; L22,354; L62,177; IU(Brabourne)
  Bernerstone (prop.) L62,258
Hughes, Miss L81,195
Hughes, Miss Clive IU
Hughes, E. L5,56
Hughes, Edward IU
Hughes, H.Spencer IU
Hughes, Hugh & Sons IU
Hughes, J. IU
Hughes, James P. L3,48; L4,86; L63,104-7; L86,103; IU
Hughes, M.E.Hughes UC
Hughes, Richard L54,26; L117B,4
Hughes, Richard D. IU
Hughes, Thomas John IU
Hughes, Rev.Thomas S.
  Travels in Greece and Albania L1,59; L52, 27; L68,27
Hughes, W. L90,289
Hughes, Walter O.Hughes L3,126; IU
  The Register of Tonbridge School L41,384; L42,311
Hughes-Hughes
  see Hughes
Hugo, F.Victor IU
Hulburd, Percy L3,139; L87,159 277; L88, 124 138; IU
  Lord Hever L42,424; L67,69
  The Romance of Shere Mote L42,443; L66, 83
Hull, Edward
  Memoir on the geology and geography of Arabia L40,468; L41,298
  Mount Seir L40,219; L41,298; L62,260
Hull Booksellers' Committee L87,251
Hullah L90,172
Hullah, Mary E. L3,64; L86,200 231
  In hot haste L41,469; L42,486; L63,309
Hullmandel, Charles IU
Humbert, Aimé
  Japan and the Japanese L3,52 64; L38,299; L39,138 166; L40,285-6; L41,265; L42,509
Humboldt, C.H. IU
Hume, Andrew H. L2,21 61; L84,52 54

The Life of E.J.Eyre L37,150; L38,128; L39,402 431; L40,429; L41,519; L42,510; L59,135
Hume, Bessie IU
Hume, Eliza A. IU
Hume, James L90,267
Hume, T. L87,115
Hume, Thomas IU
Humphreys, Jennett IU
Humphreys, John Doddridge L81,66
Humphreys, W.C.C.
  The Prince of Orange L55,259; L117B,6
Hungerford, M.
  see Argles, M.
Hunolstein, Baroness L5,29
Hunt, Mr. L85,474
Hunt, Mrs. IU
Hunt, E. L86,318-19 231-2
Hunt, James H.L. L90,302; L117A,2
  Sir Ralph Esher L56,209; L122,84 125
Hunt, Mrs.Margaret L5,223
Hunt, Stephen IU
[Hunt], Thomas IU
Hunt, Thornton L84,181-2; IU
Hunt, W.Leigh IU
Hunt & Tanner L83,248; IU
Hunter, Joseph IU
Huntington, Rev.George L5,198 217; IU; UC Manuscripts,3
Huntley, Sir Henry V. L1,108; L93,10; L117B,13
  Peregrine Scramble L56,109
Hurry, W.B. L5,131
Hurst, Charles L86,350
Hurst, D. L92,44
Hurst, Thomas L81,92 148 163
Hurst & Blackett L59,161; L84,116; L85,460; L86,88
Hurton, William L1,192; L2,30; L3,24; L83, 227; IU
  Hearts of oak L36,70 125; L37,144; L58,281
  Vonved the Dane L36,264 292; L37,299; L58,260; L97,32
  A Voyage from Leith to Lapland L56,321
Huson, Thomas IU
Huston, David IU
Hutcheson, John C. L3,61; L84,224 245; IU
  She and I L38,291; L39,433; L59,294
Hutchinson, Rev.Clement UC
Hutchinson, J. IU
Hutchinson, Mrs.Louisa (Miss L.Grice) L3, 131; L5,46; IU
  In tents in the Transvaal L39,315; L40,468; L60,159; L123,195-6
Hutchinson, Peter O.
  Chronicles of Gretna Green L7,153; L91,260
Hutchinson & Co. L86,377-8 381-2 385 393; L87,181
Hutchison, W.M. L85,456 459 463
Hutter, Walter & Co. L85,476
Hutton, C. L92,75
Hutton, Catherine IU
Hutton, James L2,66

Hutton, John   IU
Hutton, John Henry   UC
Hutton, Richard H.   IU
Huxham, J.B.   L85,74(c) 75-6
Huxley, L.   L5,178
Huyghue, S.Douglass   L93,26 72; L117B,9
  The Nomades of the West   L56,199
Hygiastic Grates   IU
Hyne, C.J.Cutcliffe   L5,287

Ignatius, Father
  see Lyne, J.L.
Ihlee & Sankey   UC
Ilkley Library Co.   L85,339-40
Illustrated Bits   L86,363-7
Illustrated London News   L66,110
Illustration Company   IU
Imperial & Asiatic Quarterly Review   IU
Impey, Walton & Co.   L86,214(c) 215
Imprints   L123,228-32
Ince, Mrs.   L88,56
Ince, W.H.   IU
Inchbald, Elizabeth   IU Unidentified, (A)
  Memoirs   L52,260-263a 302
The Indian Engineer   L66,155-7
Ingham, Miss   L95,28
Inglis, Mrs.   L89,115
Inglis, H.D.   IU
Inglis, M.K.   IU
Inglis, Sir Robert H.   IU
Inglis & Leslie   L83,30
Ingram, John H.   L5,80; L85,405-6(c) 406;   IU
Inman, George Ellis   L91,100; UC
Inman, [J.] E.   IU
Innes, A.D. & Co.   L67,95-8
Innes, Miss Anne   L1,54; L90,19-20 27-8 34-5
  80; L117A,17
Innes, Mrs.Emily A.   L3,35; L63,5; L86,79
  The Chersonese with the gilding off   L40,216;
  L41,207; L63,3; L86,65
Innes, James   L86,146
Innes, R.T.A.   IU
Institute of Historical Research   UC(Spiller)
International Literary Association   IU
International News Company   L63,317; L87,
  79(c) 190
International Newspaper Agency   L61,278
Interstate Press Association   IU
Inverurie, Lady Sydney C.   IU
Inwards, Richard   UC
Ireland, Mrs.   L86,396
Ireland, Alexander   IU
Irish Education Office   L88,358
Irish Figaro   L89,106-7
Irish Weekly Independent   L87,144 146 148
Irvin, A.Jerdan   IU
Irvine, Julian   L86,236-8(c) 237-9 241 248(c);
  IU
Irving, John T.
  The Hunters of the prairie   L54,28
Irving, Pierre   L2,52; L83,254

Irving, Washington   L1,33; L6,134; L81,173;
  L82,140 184; L90,159-65; L117B,15; L123,
  152; IU
  Adventures of Captain Bonneville   L54,14;
  L57,1 62
  The Alhambra   L52,272; L57,1 62
  Astoria   L53,301; L57,1 62
  The Life and letters   L2,52-53; L36,101-2
  104; L37,156 302; L38,165; L39,454 456;
  L40,435
Irwin, Sidney T.   L5,128
Irwin, Thomas   L84,38 40
Isaacs, Nathaniel
  Narrative of travels and adventures in Eastern
  Africa (prop.)   L53,58
Isbister & Co.   L85,472

[J., W.]   IU Unidentified
Jabet, George   L1,193; L2,31; L3,49; L4,86;
  L83,207 264;   IU
  Nasology   L36,26 104 107 213; L37,204-5;
  L38,202; L39,217; L40,447; L41,384; L42,
  290; L56,95
Jabet, N.   IU
Jaccottet   L82,237
Jackson, A.W.   IU
Jackson, Lady Catherine H.C.   L2,85; L3,37
  179; L5,87 97 114-19; L17,102; L63,274;
  L64,214-16; L86,176; L102,91-170;   IU
  The Court of France in the sixteenth century
  L40,252; L41,272 352; L42,179; L62,145;
  L63,63; L86,69; L119,131
  The Court of the Tuileries (orig.The Court of
  the Restoration)   L40,347; L61,178; L119,
  130
  Fair Lusitania   L38,307; L39,217 260; L40,
  430
  The First of the Bourbons   L41,326; L42,197;
  L63,272; L119,133
  The French court and society   L39,348; L40,
  253; L60,238; L61,84; L119,129
  The Last of the Valois   L40,175; L41,271;
  L42,269; L119,132
  Old Paris; its courts and literary salons   L39,
  234; L40,448; L60,57; L119,134
  The Old regime   L39,313; L40,448; L41,272;
  L42,294; L60,152; L119,135
Jackson, Charlotte
  see Jackson, Lady C.H.C.
Jackson, G.   L88,344
Jackson, Sir George
  The Bath archives. A further selection from
  the diaries and letters   L38,283; L39,197;
  L40,422; L41,273; L42,171
  The Diaries and letters   L2,85; L3,37; L37,
  315; L38,260; L39,213; L40,436; L41,273;
  L42,185; L59,248-50
Jackson, Rev.John (Bishop of Lincoln)   L82,222;
  IU; IU(Lincoln)
Jackson, Miss Mary C.   L1,147; L2,32;   IU
  The Story of my wardship   L36,93; L58,84;

L68,101
Word-sketches in the sweet south L38,298;
L39,226; L40,463; L41,538; L42,524; L101,
95
Jackson, Richard L85,196
Jacobsen L88,299
Jacoby, Henry IU
Jacox, Rev.Francis L5,28
Recreations of a recluse L37,226; L38,213
Jakeman & Carver L86,396
James, C. L85,354
James, Charles T.C. L3,147; L88,168
The Yoke of freedom L42,422; L67,104
James, E.A. IU
James, Mrs.Edwin L94,289-90; L98,248
James, Edwin J. L5,42; IU
The Political institutions of America and
England L38,267; L40,421; L41,503
James, Mrs.Eliza A.(Mrs.William James) L1,
109; L53,206 208; L83,216; L90,93; L91,277;
L93,157 231 253 265; L117A,30
James, Florence A.
see Price, F.A.
James, George P.R. L1,26; L2,43; L6,139
144; L59,10; L77,24-82; L80,7 9 [12] 20;
L81,35 42 44 50 52 65 67 74 92 155 180 184-9
196 200 204 210 221 226-8; L90,234-5;
L117A,34; IU; IU Richard Bentley I,50; UC
Agincourt L7,156; L55,93
Arabella Stuart L7,153; L55,93
Bernard Marsh L36,141; L37,158; L38,97
Charles Tyrrell L7,139; L57,112
Darnley L52,9; L68,17
De L'Orme L52,74; L68,41
The False heir L7,151; L55,93
The History of chivalry L52,180; L68,80
The Life and time of Louis XIV L36,171;
L53,289; L76,1-23
The Man at arms (orig.Henri de Cerons) L7,
143
Memoirs of great commanders L52,210; L68,
88; L81,49
Philip Augusuts L52,160; L68,70
Rose d'Albret L7,155; L55,93
The String of pearls L7,166; L8,94; L68,74
James, Henry L5,257; IU
James, Henry IU
James, J.Barnard L5,299
James, Sir John Kingston L5,106; IU
James, M.E. IU
James, P. IU
James, William L5,63 295
James, William
The Naval history L1,109 134; L6,95; L8,34
150; L36,24 256 258; L37,157 214; L38,166-7;
L39,165 185; L40,284-5; L41,288-9; L42,
287-8; L53,206-10 263-6 269; L71,195;
see James, Mrs.Eliza A.
Jameson, Anna B. L117B,16; IU
Memoirs and essays L36,146 172; L37,158;
L55,306
Jamieson, Frances IU
Jamieson, John L95,159

Jansen, Dr.F.Gustav L3,56
Jansen, F.H. L83,69 82
Japp, Dr.Alexander Hay L5,134; UC
Jarrold & Sons L65,188a; L67,208 239; L86,
463; L88,209 281 306 313
Jarvis, Anna IU
Jay, Miss Edith K.S. L3,163; L5,306; L88,82
The Apotheosis of Mr.Tyrawley L42,426;
L67,12
Jay, G.H. L83,234
Jay, Miss Harriett L3,80; L5,102; IU
Dark Colleen (orig.Morna Dunoon) L38,58
372; L39,449; L60,36
Madge Dunraven (orig.The Lovers of Armstead)
L39,290; L60,103-4; L123,201-2; IU George
Bentley,177
The Queen of Connaught L38,341; L39,439;
L59,341-3
Jeaffreson, J.Cordy L5,97; IU
Jebb, H.G. IU
Jebb, Rev.J. L82,155 309
Jebb, Richard L84,189-90 204; IU
Jeens, Charles H. IU
Jefferies, Jessie IU
Jefferies, Richard L3,180 188; L85,448; IU
The Dewy morn L40,397; L41,89 508 541;
L42,85; L62,216
Jefferson, E. L87,279
Jefferson, Thomas
Memoirs L1,37 59
Jeir-Carleton, H. UC
Jenings, Elizabeth J.(Wickliffe Lane pseud.)
L2,30; L3,25
My good for nothing brother L36,117 177;
L38,143
Jenkins, Rev.C. L2,53
Jenkins, Mrs.Cecilia G. L91,118 137; L117B,
4
Miss Aylmer L7,143; L54,222; L81,234
Wedlock L7,146; L55,28
Jenkins, J.Edward L4,73
Pantalas L42,413; L67,224
Jenkins, Louisa Hadow (J.C.Chillington pseud)
L3,80; L87,85; IU
Dual lives L41,403; L42,457
Jenkins, Mary Bradley IU
Jenkins, Robert C.
The Last crusader: Cardinal Julian L36,255;
L102,14
Jenkins, William R. L87,162
Jenner, Mrs.Katharine L. L3,150; L5,163;
L85,420 422; L86,275; IU
In London town (orig.David Everest) L40,391;
L62,137
In the Alsatian mountains L40,386; L41,500
514; L42,509; L62,52
Katharine Blythe (orig.In quietness and
confidence) L40,417; L41,515; L63,80
Love or money L41,429; L42,490; L65,
15-17 145
A Western wildflower L40,345; L61,159
Jenner, Stephen L2,70
Jenner, Rev.Stephen L1,182

Jennings, Alfred L94,308
Jennings, Cecil F. UC
Jennings, George H. IU
Jennings, J.Frances IU
Jennings, J.W. L85,204
Jennings, S.J. IU
Jephson, Esq. L2,71
Jephson, Richard M. L3,66; L5,48; L85,160
184 262 370 374 379; L95,251; L101,141; IU
The Girl he left behind him L38,357-8; L39,
433 456; L40,432; L41,512; L42,484
He would be a soldier L38,358; L39,242;
L40,264; L41,489 495; L42,466 472; L60,
195
A Pink wedding L39,331
The Red rag L39,351 353 371; L40,318-19
Tom Bullekeley L38,294; L100,277
Jerdan, William L1,31; L6,78; L52,137;
L68,63; L81,193; L82,167 356 358 361; L90,
69; L92,143; L117A,2; L117B,29; IU; UC
Jerdein, Mrs. L2,74; L5,16
Jerningham, Hon.Frances
The Jerningham letters L4,33; L42,366-7;
L66,240-4
Jerningham, Sir Hubert E.H. L2,63; L5,20;
L59,167; L84,118-19; IU
Jerome, J.T. IU
Jerrold, Blanchard UC
Jerrold, Douglas L53,314-16; L81,199; UC
Jerrold, Evelyn D. L5,47 92 145; IU;
IU(Fenold); UC
Jerrold, Sidney UC
Jerrold, Walter IU
Jervis, J.Chester IU; IU(Kavanagh)
Jesse, Clifford Heneage L84,276
Jesse, Edward L1,109; L93,2; L117B,27; IU
Anecdotes of dogs L36,175; L55,188
Jesse, J.Heneage L2,46; L56,70 201; L83,
143 267; L84,39 201; L117B,21; IU; UC
George Selwyn L7,151; L36,175; L39,400;
L55,158-62
Literary and historical memorials of London
L7,163; L8,34; L36,174; L37,159; L38,167;
L39,431; L56,27
London and its celebrities L7,170; L8,120;
L36,174 243; L37,159
Memoirs of celebrated Etonians L3,80; L38,
353; L39,214; L40,436; L41,210; L42,503;
L59,328
Memoirs of King Richard the Third L36,206
243 272; L37,157; L58,263
Memoirs of the Court of England during the
reign of the Stuarts L6,165; L7,141 143 148;
L36,25 172; L54,201
Memoirs of the Court of England from the
Revolution in 1688 L55,48
Memoirs of the life and reign of King George III
(? pub.) L36,243; L56,232
Memoirs of the Pretenders L7,158; L36,173;
L55,261
Jesse, William L83,182-3; L92,81
Jessop, Miss Esther L58,303; L83,246
Jessop, William H.B.

Flindersland and Sturtland L36,300; L58,303
Jeune, F.H. IU
Jewell, Robert IU
Jewry, Laura
Kirkholme Priory L55,347; L117B,8
Jewsbury, Geraldine E. L1,181; L2,54; L3,
111; L5,86; L83,228; L94,1-58 67-9 71
74-6 79 82-99 103-4 123 150 203 207 214;
L95,17-19 45 49-50 57 75-6 79-90 96 123
181-4 190 200 221 250 279 286; L96,18-21
24-8 33 44 50 58-9 63-8 283-4; L97-L101;
IU; IU(Clark,E.)
Jewsbury, Maria Jane IU; IU Unidentified,(A)
Jex-Blake, S.
see Blake, S.
Jobbins, J.R. IU
John, Eugenie (E.Marlitt pseud.) L39,322;
L70,196
In the councillor's house L3,73; L38,361;
L39,427
The Second wife L3,73; L38,336; L39,448
Johnes, B. IU(Hills-Johnes)
Johnes, Elizabeth H. L3,148; L60,214; L61,
224; L85,250 276 303 334
Johnes, Sir J.H.
see Hills-Johnes, J.
Johns, Catharine IU
Johns, Louisa IU
Johns, Richard L90,181; L91,83 87; L92,139;
L117A,38; IU
Legend and romance L54,122; L81,216
The Schoolfellows L7,145; L54,282
Johnson, Lady (Dowager) IU
Johnson, Rev. L82,250
Johnson, C. IU
Johnson, Prof.Charles F. L5,200-1 248;
[L63,96]
Johnson, Charles H. L86,405 432-3 441
Johnson, Cuthbert W. IU
Johnson, George W. L56,66 92; L70,283;
L117B,33
Johnson, Henry C.R. L2,76; IU
A Long vacation in the Argentine Alps L37,
160; L38,168
Walter Raleigh Sinjohn L37,284; L38,245
Johnson, I.Hernaman IU
Johnson, R.B. IU
Johnson, R.W.M. L3,62; IU
Johnson, Samuel IU
Johnson, Rev.W. L5,72
Johnson, W.S. L85,140(c) 140 274
Johnston, Dr.
The Conspiracy L52,246
Johnston, Miss L57,190
Johnston, Rev.B.W. L57,190; L117A,34
Johnston, Frederick IU
Johnston, Grace L.K. L3,152; L4,47; L5,23;
L86,370; L87,157; L88,254; IU
Alasnam's lady L40,349; L61,185
The Halletts (orig.Senior and junior) L41,430;
L42,486; L65,5
A Hurricane in petticoats (orig.Great
Grandmama Severn) L41,448; L42,485; L64,

151

In spite of herself L41,411; L65,224-7
The Indian uncle L42,429; L66,298
The Mischief-maker L42,413; L67,219-23
A Rash verdict L42,416; L67,195
A Troublesome pair (orig.P's and Q's) L42,
442; L66,73
Venetia's lovers L40,401; L41,537; L42,
497; L62,261
Johnston, R.W. L87,173
Johnston, Ran
see De la Condamine & Johnston
[Johnston], Robert W. IU
Johnston, William L1,151; L83,133 155; L100,
121
Nightshade L36,45 53; L58,123
Johnstone, Miss Elizabeth M. L5,258
Jolly, Emily L2,61; L84,53; IU
The Cypresses L36,180; L37,82; L59,88;
L98,146
Jonas, Sophie IU
Jones, Mr. UC Manuscripts,29
Jones, Mrs. L85,422
Jones, Ann IU
Jones, Arthur Bassett IU
Jones, C.A.
see Selous, Miss
Jones, C.W.F. L88,309
Jones, D. L84,188
Jones, Miss Dora M. L5,297
Jones, Rev.E.A. L85,198
Jones, Edward IU; UC
Jones, Ernest C. IU
Jones, H.E. L5,261
Jones, Rev.Harry L5,263
Jones, Rev.Henry B. L1,73; L82,338; L83,
48; L117B,19
Adventures in Australia L36,177
Jones, Henry R.Bence IU
Jones, J.H.H. UC
Jones, J.M. IU
Jones, James Athearn L1,16
Lights and shadows of American life (orig.
Tales of the western hemisphere) L1,51;
L52,114 116; L68,55-6
Stories of American life L1,51; L52,114 116;
L68,55-6
Traditions of the North American Indians (orig.
Tales of an Indian camp) L52,46; L68,34
Jones, John T. L52,98; L68,49
Jones, Lydia IU
Jones, Richard Llewellyn IU(Llewellyn)
Jones, T.H. IU
Jones, T.Mason L2,19
Old Trinity L37,212; L38,205; L59,127
Jones, Miss W. IU
Jones, William L82,89; L91,297 299; L92,1
40-1; L93,56 59-62 73-5 93-4 102 106-8; IU
Jones, William IU
History and mystery of precious stones L39,
331; L40,199; L42,116; L123,212-13
Jones, William A.
see Jones, James A.

Jones, William Cairns L5,293
Jones & Ward L81,108
Jordan, Donald IU
Jordan, Ellinor L. IU
Jordan, F.W. IU
Jordan, Frederick W. L3,162; L5,186
The Spanish verbs L42,322a
Jordan, W.E. L5,39
Joubert, F. IU
Journal de Genève L87,41 43
[Jouveaux, A.] IU
Jouvet & Co. L85,407 445; L86,159 295 352
436-7; IU(Furne); UC
Jowett, B. IU
Joy, Dr. L93,84-5
Joyce, Charles IU
Joyce, Felix L90,23 25
Joyce, Herbert L3,90; L4,86; L87,104-5 108;
IU
The History of the Post Office L42,336; L66,
18
Joyce, John L82,276; L93,166-70
Joyer, Arthur J. L83,58
Joynes, J.L. L5,134
Julian, John L84,244
Junot, Laura (Duchesse d'Abrantes)
Memoires L39,395; L40,361 444; L42,339
343; L61,226; L119,162; UC Miscellaneous
Jupp, Richard F. L5,294
Justi, Carl
Life of Winckelmann L3,106; L39,370; L40,
337
Juta, J.C. & Co. L85,290 306; L86,312; L87,
271-2(c) 273 298(c) 299; UC

Kand, McNally & Co. L87,65
Kantzow
see De Kantzow
Karani & Co. L86,499
Katscher, Leopold IU
Kaudacheff, Princess Mary L63,129
Kaufmann, J.B. IU
Kavanagh, Miss Julia L2,72; L3,107; L5,25;
L60,71; L83,36; L117A,28; IU Richard
Bentley I,23-4 26; IU; UC; UC Manuscripts,
47
Daisy Burns L6,151; L36,178; L57,7
Forget-me-nots L39,278; L40,431; L41,510;
L42,483
Madeleine L36,177 179; L37,165; L56,102
Kaye, Sir John W. L1,87-8; L56,295; L82,
168 173 202-3 213-14 305; L83,41 66; L117B,
37; UC
Administration of the East India Company
L36,179; L57,118
History of the war in Afghanistan L36,178-9;
L37,166; L38,171; L56,297; L57,116
Life and correspondence of Charles, Lord
Metcalfe L36,179; L57,258-66
Life and correspondence of Henry Tucker L36,
56 64; L37,165; L38,170

Passages in the life of Gilbert Arnold L38,
129 210

Kean, Ellen IU

Kearney, Mrs.G.M.V. L87,149-500(c) 167 201

Keate, Edward L5,169

Keatinge, Dr.J.V.R. L84,131-2; IU

Kebbel, T.E. L5,40

Keddie, Henrietta L3,99; L4,48; L5,259;
L87,118; L88,152; IU
Honor Ormthwaite L42,423; L67,81
Lady Jean's vagaries L42,440; L66,32

Kedson, Miss M. L86,311

Keeley, Mr. IU

Keeling, Miss E.D.Esterre L5,204

Keene, A.G. L5,202

Keene, Edwin L1,157; L83,111 146; L93,300
Sydney Fielding (orig.Saverne) L58,81

Keene, H.G. L22,359

Keese, Oliné
see Leakey, C.W.

Keeton, Miss A.G. L5,18

Kegan Paul & Co. L61,104-5; L65,192-5; L86,
326 429 469; L88,257 324; IU(Paul)

Keil, Ernst L60,236-7; L85,131; IU

Keily & Endean L86,54

Keith, H.C.A.(Philip Kent pseud.) L5,194 270;
L28,192; L88,248; IU; IU(Kent,P.)

Kellner, Leon L88,254

Kelly, F.M. IU

Kelly & Co. L3,20; L62,56-63; L63,21 179;
L64,23; L84,41 126 130 292 332(c); L85,435;
L86,87 130 174; L87,128; IU

Keltie, John S. IU(Nature)

Kelty, Mary A. L117B,38
A Devotional diary L36,142
Life by the fireside L7,174; L8,200; L36,
185; L57,228; L82,295
The Real and the beau-ideal L36,109

Kemble, Miss A.F. IU

Kemble, Mrs.Frances A. L3,109; L5,183
249; L85,58 68 86 164 248 300-1 316 412;
L86,91 228; IU; IU(Remble); UC
The Adventures of Mr.John Timothy Homespun
L41,461; L42,478
Far away and long ago L41,456
Further records L41,352; L42,198; L64,
221-3; L119,112
Notes upon some of Shakespeare's plays L39,
390; L40,353; L41,289; L42,289; L61,147-8;
L119,113
Poems L27,70; L40,286; L41,501 516; L42,
248; L62,126-8
Record of a girlhood L39,284 295; L42,519;
L60,94 136-7; L119,110; L123,186-7
Records of later life L39,387; L40,352 445;
L41,530; L42,519; L61,149-52; L119,111

Kemble, John Mitchell IU

Kemp, E.E. IU(Kemp,G.)

Kemp, Miss Emily G. L5,307

Kempe, J.A. L85,375

Kempe, John A. L88,90 169

Kempt, Robert A. L2,15; L5,91

Kemsley & Elkington L85,271; UC

Kenealy, Dr.Arabella L3,92; L87,137(c) 137
139-40 146(c) 147 150; IU
Molly and her man of war L42,442 447; L66,
68-9

Kenealy, Edward L91,212 251; L92,208; IU;
UC

[Kenimer], Henry IU(Keiman)

Kennard, Mrs.Esther (Mrs.R.P.Kennard) L62,
92-6; L85,447 470

Kennard, Mrs.Nina H. L3,162; L5,90 144; IU
Hélène (orig.Swift as a shadow) L40,383;
L62,50

Kennard, Richard P.A. L85,401 423 426-7(c)
429-30; IU
A Life of Lord Westbury (prop.) L3,170; L40,
338; L41,320; L42,511; L62,69-100

Kennedy, Rev.Dr. L84,33

Kennedy, Agnes G.C. IU

Kennedy, Benjamin H. IU
Ely lectures L39,382; L40,246; L41,509 514
519; L42,506; L61,85

Kennedy, Charles L92,169 236-7

Kennedy, H.Arthur L5,220

Kennedy, John P. L81,115
Rob of the bowl L54,164

Kennedy, Patrick L94,288

Kennedy, Rev.R. IU

Kennedy, Dr.R.Hartley L1,74; L117B,33
Narrative of the campaign in Sind and Kaubool
L7,144; L54,300

Kennedy, Theo. L2,68

Kennedy, Thomas L84,44

Kennedy, W.P. L82,294 306-7

Kennett, Richard J. L1,35; L52,15; L68,21;
L74,125-79

Kenney, Charles L. L3,96; L92,92; IU

Kenney, Rosa L. IU

Kent, Charles L85,222; IU

Kent, Philip
see Keith, H.C.A.

Kent, S.Harriet
Within the Arctic circle L38,360; L39,227;
L40,462; L60,26; IU

Kent, W. L86,380

Kent, W. IU

Kent, W.Ridley IU

Kent & Co. L83,79

Kenyon, Arthur R.
Letters from Spain L36,180; L57,269

Kenyon, John IU

Keon, Anne D.(Mrs.Miles G.Keon) L3,117;
IU; UC

Keon, Miles G. L2,42; L83,82; L84,147
Dion and the Sibyls L36,318; L37,89; L38,
124; L39,429; L40,427; L59,86; L98,
129-37 171 182
Harding the money-spinner L39,308; L60,
127; L85,140; L123,185-6

Keppel, George T.(6th Earl of Albemarle) L82,
161; L117A,29; IU(Albemarle)
Memoirs of the Marquis of Rockingham L7,
172; L8,165 174; L36,104; L57,52
Narrative of a journey L52,182; L68,81

Keppel, Hon.Sir Henry   L82,224 231 234 266-7
276; L117A,38; IU
The Autobiography L3,114; L4,40; L42,359;
L67,28-33
A Visit to the Indian Archipelago [orig.Voyage
of the Meander] L36,181; [L57,140 169]
Keppel, Lady Louisa L100,22
Keppel, William C.(Viscount Bury; 7th Earl of
Albemarle) L2,60; L84,45; IU(Albemarle);
UC(Albemarle)
Exodus of the Western Nations L36,184; L37,
30; L59,12
Kerkadec, Solange de IU
Kerr, Mrs. L88,206
Kerr, Mrs.J.H. L5,106 175; IU
'Kerr, Reid'
see Bell, F.
Kerr, Robert L3,125; L85,147; IU
His Excellency the Ambassador Extraordinary
L39,317; L60,182-4; L123,196-7
Kettle, Miss Mary R.S. L2,87; L3,56; IU
Kettle, Rupert L92,88
Key & Co. L81,35
Keys, Rev.J.L. L87,192
Kidd, Robert B. L1,158
A Delineation L36,108; L58,44
Kidson, Eastwood L5,134
Kiegan, John IU
Kilvert, Francis
Memoirs of the life of Richard Hurd L36,76
Kimball, Richard B. L1,110; L2,78; L3,32;
L82, 52 65 68 70 81 84 124 240; L83,147 241-2;
L117B,4; IU; UC
Virginia Randall L37,262; L38,243; L39,433
Kimbley, J. L86,46(c)
Kinder, Miss L. L1,54
Kindon, J. UC(Windon)
King, Miss A.Fielder L5,141
King, B.B. L91,204
King, Elizabeth A.(Mrs.Moss King) L5,129;
L85,448; L86,109 285; L88,165; IU
The Diary of a civilian's wife L40,221; L41,
212; L62,218
Italian highways L42,370; L67,102
King, Mrs.Harriet B. L3,86; L92,12 48 104;
IU
Letters from Muskoka L38,372; L39,282;
L40,438; L41,519; L42,512
King, Henry S. IU
King, Henry S. & Co. IU
King, John IU
King, Madge L3,112; L86,477
Cousin Cinderella L41,412; L65,207
King, Mrs.Moss
see King, E.A.
King, Paul H. IU
King Richard
Narrative of a journey L53,257
King, Richard Ashe L3,19; L85,465 473
A Coquette's conquest (orig.A Goodly outside)
L40,406; L41,506; L62,283
Kinglake, Alexander W. IU
Kinglake, J.A. L83,57

Kinglake, [Robert] Arthur IU
King's College Hospital IU
King's College School L123,148-50
Kingsbury & Co. L85,435
Kingsford, Mrs.Nina L5,94; IU
Kingsley, Charles L5,88; IU
Kingsley, Frances E. IU
Kingsley, Dr.George H. L3,39; L4,86; IU;
UC
South Sea bubbles
see Herbert, G.R.C.
Kingsley, Henry L3,65; L5,42; L84,181;
L100,135; IU; UC Manuscript,36
Reginald Hetherege L38,310; L39,445; L59,
312
Kingsley, Mary IU
Kingsley, Mary Henrietta IU
Kingsley, Maurice L5,178
Kingsley, Sarah M.K. IU
Kingston, Frances S. IU
Kingston, William H.G. L92,59 121; L117B,14;
IU
The Circassian chief L55,175; L82,307 323
The Prime minister L55,177
Kinlock, Arthur L95,13-14
Kippis, Andrew
The Life of Shaftesbury L1,58; L52,154;
L53,196-200; L68,68
Kirkland, Mrs.C.M. L93,100 111
Kirkland, Walter L22,356
Kirkpatrick, Rev.Alexander F. L85,223-4
Kirkwood, James
see Clark, R. & R.
Kitchin, Clifford L5,112
Kitchin, F.Harcourt L22,360
Kitto, Dr.John IU
Kitton, Frederick G. L5,207; L88,355 358;
IU; UC
Kleinau, Henriette IU
Kleinau, J. L84,153
Klingender, Dickson & Kiddle L67,122; L88,
181-3
Knesebeck IU
Knight, Charles L122,60; IU
Knight, George L94,305
Knight, Hubert B.Finlay L3,114; L86,477 480;
L87,177 213; L88,117
The Courage of Sylvia Fulgent L42,448; L66,
50
A Girl with a temper L41,410; L65,211
Knight, J.Hamilton L86,223
Knight, J.Harcourt L89,64
Knight, Maria D. IU
Knight, William H. L2,54
Diary of a pedestrian in Cashmere L36,130
132; L37,164; L58,313
Knighton, Lady Dorothea L6,25; L90,191;
L117A,35
Memoirs of Sir William Knighton L36,181;
L37,166; L54,16; IU
Knipe, Miss M. L22,355
Knollys, Francis IU
Knollys, William W. L2,71; IU

Knott, Alfred IU
Knowles, [James] Sheridan L93,96; IU
Knowles, Sir James Thomas IU
Knowles, John L1,49
  Life and writings of Henry Fuseli L52,94;
  L68,47
Knowling, George F.S. IU
Knox, G. L92,70
Knox, Miss Theodoria L2,70; L5,16; IU
Kobell, Luise von
  Conversations of Dr.Dollinger L3,75; L41,
  370; L42,181; L65,146; L119,100
Köhler, A.C. IU
Koniglich Sachs Kreishauptmannschaft L60,309
Kopta, F.P. IU(Kapta)
Kortright, Miss L83,150
Kortright, Mrs.Fanny A. L1,152; L83,135;
  IU
  Anne Sherwood L36,247; L58,130
Kotzebue, Otto von
  A New voyage round the world L1,62; L52,
  162; L68,71
Kreyser, Henry L90,252 277
Kuhe, Ernest IU
Kuhe, Wilhelm L3,169; L4,49; L88,148 157
  159; IU
  My musical recollections L42,371; L67,85;
  UC Manuscripts,37
Kunze, George F. UC

L., C. IU Unidentified
L., W.R. IU Unidentified
Lablache, Miss Fanny R.L. L5,100; IU
La Bonninière de Beaumont, G.A. de
  Ireland L54,211
Lace, Miss UC
Lacroix & Co. L2,56; L59,14-19; L83,251
  275
Lacy, Walter IU
Ladvocat, Mr. L81,142
The Lady L86,52
Laffan, May (Mrs.Noel Hartley) L3,103; L5,
  97; L60,199; L85,28 286 400; IU(Fraser,J.);
  IU(Hartley); UC(Hartley)
  Christy Carew L39,327
  Flitters, tatters and the counsellor L39,328;
  L40,246; L60,158; L123,191-2 203-4
  The Hon.Miss Ferrard L39,236; L60,55
Lahee, J. & Co. IU
Laidlaw, F.Allan IU
Laird L86,118; IU
Laird, Macgregor
  Narrative of an expedition into the interior of
  Africa L38,178; L42,405; L53,309 311;
  L117A,40
Lake, Miss Barbara L5,102; IU
Lake, Sir Henry A. L1,145; L83,116 121-2
  126 138 236; L93,272
  Kars and our captivity L1,135; L36,50; L58,
  65
  Narrative of the defence of Kars L36,51;

L37,178; L39,398; L58,114
Lake, Miss Nesta L5,161
La March L93,184
Lamartine, Alphonse de
  see Lamartine de Prat, M.L.A. de
Lamartine de Prat, Marie L.A. de L1,111;
  L2,33; L3,20; L117B,10; IU
  Memoirs of celebtrated characters L1,134;
  L36,39-40 172-3; L37,146 176; L38,179; L41,
  521; L42,406; L57,120-6
  A Pilgrimage to the Holy Land L53,158 160;
  L90,64 67-8
  Twenty-five years of my life L2,40; L37,102;
  L38,175; L59,227-8
Lamb, Lady C. L90,120
Lamb, Charles UC Manuscripts,39
Lamb, Henry & Co. IU
Lambert's Monthly L86,370-1
Lamington, 1st Baron
  see Cochrane, B.
Lamson, J.W.
  Rook's Dene L38,360; L39,443-5
Lamson, W.O. IU
Lancaster L5,70
Lancelot du Lake (pseud.) IU
Land & Water L64,51-2 57-9; L86,261
Landells, Ebenezer IU
Lander, Richard
  Records of Captain Clapperton's last expedition
  L1,36; L52,40; L68,32
Landers, J. L5,107; IU
Landner, William IU
Landon, Miss Letitia E.(Mrs.Maclean) L1,49;
  L53,64; L80,17 28; L90,46; L117A,2; IU;
  UC(end of L)
  Francesca Carrara L52,268
  Romance and reality [L68,48 49] ; L122,80
  124
Landon, Rev.Whittington H.
  Lives of the Greek classicists (prop.) L52,
  176; L68,80
Landor, Edward W. L1,110; L6,106; L117A,
  20
  The Bushman L56,52
Landor, Walter S.
  Andrea of Hungary L36,101; L83,77
  Letters and other unpublished writings L42,
  384; L67,236 306-8
Landseer, Thomas IU
Lane, Murray IU
Lane, Richard James IU
Lane, Wickliffe
  see Jenings, E.J.
Lane-Fox, Florence UC
Lang, Emma IU
Lang, Mrs.Louisa L5,304
Langbridge, Rev.Frederick L86,201; IU
Langdale, Lady L83,83
Langdale, Hon.Charles L1,131; L2,34; L3,26;
  L83,95-6 101
  Memoirs of Mrs.Fitzherbert L36,49; L58,46
Langdon, Rev.Charles L83,63
Langham, Ada L5,202

Langhorne, C.H.   L92,56 67
Langhorne, W.H.   IU
Langston, Rev.Charles J.   L5,174
Langton, Robert   IU
Lankester, Phebe   IU
Lanman, Charles   L82,86 90 219
  Adventures of an angler in Canada   L36,183
Lansdowne, Henry P.(Lord Shelburne)   IU
Lanyon, Florence L.   IU
Larking, Col.   L5,225
Larpent, Francis S.
  The private journal   L36,183; L57,177
Larpent, Frederic de H.   IU
Larpent, Sir George G.   L57,177-9; L82,269
  316 319; L117A,37
Lascelles, M.A.   IU
Lascelles, Rowley   IU
Lasteyrie du Saillant, C.P. de
  The History of auricular confession   L1,139
Latham, Dr.Robert G.
  Norway and the Norwegians   L6,134; L54,165;
  L117B,15
Lathrop, Lorin A.   L5,264
Latimer, Mrs.E.
  see Wormeley, E.
La Touche, Mrs.Maria
  The Clintons   L57,212; L117A,27
Laube, Florence   IU
Laughton, Sir John Knox   IU
Lauriat, C.E.   L88,89
Lavers, William   L95,206 210 215 245 259 265;
  IU
Lavisse, Ernest
  The Youth of Frederick the Great   L3,81;
  L41,365; L42,335; L65,71
Law, Mrs.   L5,25
Law, Miss Alice   L5,280; L22,368; IU(Hall,H.)
Law, Edward (1st Earl of Ellenborough)
  History of the Indian administration   L3,66;
  L38,298; L39,206; L40,245; L41,513; L42,
  508; L59,299
  A Political diary   L39,357; L40,245; L41,
  292; L42,517; L60,196
Law, Georgiana C.E.   IU
Law, James P.   L75,159-98
Law, Margaret   IU
Law, Richard   L88,234(c) 235
[Lawden], Augusta   IU(Lowden)
Lawless, Hon.Emily   L5,179; IU
Lawrence   L88,208
Lawrence Brothers   L88,253 269
Lawrence & Bullen   L87,65 67
Laws, Edward   L5,227; IU
Lawson, Canon   L5,204
Lawson, J.   L1,74; L5,246; L88,228; L117B,
  19; IU
Lawson, J.A.   IU
Lawson, Miss Roberta   L86,487
Lawson, William J.
  The History of banking   L36,184; L56,228;
  L83,77
Lay, John   L90,301
Layard, Miss Amy   L5,198

Layard, Florence L.   L64,209-10; IU
Layard, George Somes   L5,221; L88,116; IU
Layman, Thomas   IU
Layton, Charles   L83,40 65 81 133 186; L85,
  390; L86,59 97 99(c) 99; IU(Hagton)
Lea, Miss Elizabeth
  Provincial neighbourhoods (prop.)   L52,298;
  L81,97 102
Lea, Henry   L83,191
Lea & Blanchard   L82,77 84 197 211; L117A,4
[Leach], N.   IU
The Leader   IU
Leakey, Caroline W.(Oliné Keese pseud.)   IU
  The Broad arrow   L3,45; L36,68; L40,107;
  L41,186-7; L42,456; L58,195; L63,201; L86,
  134 331
Leakey, Miss Emily   L3,45; L63,201
Lean, Florence
  see Marryat, Florence
Lear, Edward   L1,89; L57,5; L82,193 307;
  L83,72 146; L117B,40
  Journals in Southern Calabria   L57,147
Leary, Thomas H.L.   IU
Leatherdale, G.F.   L5,272; IU
Leathley, Miss Emma   L3,175; L4,87; IU
Leathwick, W.G.
  see Starbuck, W.G.
Leavitt, George A. & Co.   IU
Le Breton, John   L5,35
Le Buée, William   IU
Lechmere, Lady   L5,219
Lecky, Elizabeth   IU
Lecky, W.   L5,93; IU
Ledger, Rev.   L85,310
Ledhuy   L117A,19
Ledos de Beaufort
  see Beaufort
Ledru, Charles
  Modern causes célèbres (prop.)   L56,63
Lee, Frederick G.   IU
Lee, H.Austin   L84,329
Lee, H.B.   IU
Lee, Mrs.Harriet   L81,69; IU
Lee, James   IU
Lee, M.S.   IU
Lee, Richard   IU
Lee, Robert
  Last days of Alexander   L36,189; L37,178;
  L38,179; L39,434
  History of the discoveries of the circulation of
  the blood   L36,192; L37,174
Lee, Robert J.
  An Explanation of the movements of the iris
  L37,181; L38,177; L39,426
Lee, Mrs.Sarah
  [Stories of strange lands (pub.Moxon)]   L1,61;
  L52,164; L68,72; L73A,193
Lee, Mrs.Susan R.(Curtis Yorke pseud.)   L3,74;
  L5,205; L86,207 209 359 457
  Hush (orig.Idols)   L41,468; L42,514; L63,
  331; L65,188a; L67,239
Leece & Co.   L84,119
Leech, Ann (Mrs.John Leech)   IU

Leech, Miss C.E. L3,78; L4,87; L85,474;
IU; UC
Leech, John L54,148; L55,52 138; L83,255;
L86,412; IU
One hundred and seventy designs and etchings
L36,241; L37,170; L38,177
Portraits of children of the mobility L3,78;
L7,146; L38,177-8; L39,166 238; L40,425;
L41,208; L42,502
Leeds Saturday Journal L86,252
Leemann, E.A. IU
Leeper, Miss Jane L5,302; IU
Lees, Captain L83,158
Lees, Elliot L5,269; IU
Leete, Jessie L5,194
Le Fanu, Miss Eleanor F.(Russell Gray pseud.)
L2,74; L84,130; IU(Gray)
Never for ever L37,206; L38,201; L59,138
Le Fanu, George Brinsley IU
Le Fanu, Joseph S. L2,43; L3,36; L5,17;
L59,138; L83,251-2 264 273; L84,39-40 57
66 154; L95,166-8; IU; IU George Bentley,
57+1
All in the dark L37,20; L59,106
Chronicles of Golden Friars L37,83; L38,
119; L59,229
Guy Deverell L36,198; L37,65-6 171; L38,
44; L39,419; L40,69; L41,67; L42,85; L59,
29 50
The House by the churchyard L36,174; L37,
66; L38,76; L39,419; L40,70; L41,68-9;
L42,86; L62,272-4; L119,39
In a glass darkly L38,259; L40,69-70; L41,
69-70; L42,87; L59,266; L119,40
A Lost name L37,183; L38,178
The Purcell papers (orig.Irish stories) L3,
127; L39,337; L60,228-9; L67,147-9
Uncle Silas L36,140 199; L37,64 67 294;
L38,46; L39,419; L40,69; L41,67-8; L42,
88-9; L58,317; L62,272-4; L119,38
Wylder's hand L36,140 246; L37,66 269;
L38,253; L39,420; L98,15
Le Fanu, [Thomas] Philip S. IU
Le Fanu, W.R. L85,303; L87,289
Lefevre, Charles S.(1st Viscount Eversley)
IU(Eversley)
Lefroy, Miss F.C. L5,107
Lefroy, Mrs.Isabella L3,102
A Scots thistle L41,417; L42,475; L65,138
Le Gallienne, Richard IU
Legge, Lady Anne IU
Legge, William (4th Earl of Dartmouth)
IU(Dartmouth)
Legge, William Walter (5th Earl of Dartmouth)
IU(Dartmouth)
Le Gros, W.B. L90,258; L91,22
Fables and tales of Pompeii L36,182
Leigh, Mrs. IU
Leigh, C.A. L5,67
Leigh, Chandos L81,91; IU
Leigh, Cholmondeley A. L3,118; L84,163;
IU(Austen-Leigh)
Leigh, Elizabeth M.

Medora Leigh L2,76; L37,197; L38,189;
L39,425; L40,443; L41,522; L42,490; L59,
217
Leigh, Felix IU
Leigh, Hon.Mrs.Frances B. L3,164; L4,87;
IU
Ten years on a Georgia plantation L40,375;
L41,500 536; L42,517 522; L62,8-14
Leigh, H.S. L2,15
Leigh, James E.A. L2,22; IU(Austen-Leigh)
Lady Susan L3,118; L37,170; L38,32; L39,
16-17; L40,17-18; L41,19 31; L42,9-10;
L61,244-6; L119,25
A Memoir of Jane Austen L37,25; L38,83;
L39,434; L40,17; L41,19 31; L42,9; L59
206; L61,244-6; L67,1 133
The Watsons L39,16-17; L40,17-18;
L41,19 31; L42,9-10; L61,244-6; L119,
25
Leigh, James Wentworth IU
Leigh, John S. L57,302; L117A,20
Leigh, Miss M.Austen L67,1; IU(Austen-Leigh)
Leigh, Percival L93,197-8; L117B,19
The Comic English grammar L7,145; L36,
129
Portraits of children of the mobility
see Leech, J.
Leigh, S. L94,131
Leighton, Mrs. L5,156
Leighton, Sir Baldwyn L2,87; L3,50; L5,49;
IU
Agricultural labour L38,267; L39,208; L40,
421; L41,512
Depauperisation L38,351; L39,207; L40,427;
L41,508
The Farm labourer L38,267; L39,207; L40,
430; L41,512
The Late Thomas W.Robertson L38,346
The Lull before Dorking L37,259; L38,173;
L39,426; L40,442; L41,512
Leighton, John IU
Leighton, Mrs.Mary L3,155; L64,64; L86,217
Leighton & Co. L84,53; L88,271
Leinbach, Louie IU
Leir-Carleton, H. IU
The Leisure Hour IU(Macauley)
Leitch, James L94,111 127
Leitner, Dr.G.W. L88,173
Leland, Charles G.(Francis Bret Harte pseud.)
L5,84 95 114; L60,130; IU
Le Marchant, Sir Denis IU
Memoir of third Earl of Spencer L3,93; L38,
364; L39,223; L40,325; L41,521-2; L42,513
Le Marchant, Sir Henry D. L2,34; L3,93;
L84,317 326 329(c); IU
Breakers ahead L36,156
Trades unions L37,252; L38,200; L39,425
Le Marchant, Sarah E. IU
Lemercher de Longpré, Charles (Baron
d'Haussez)
Great Britain in 1833 L53,9; L117A,14
Le Messurier, Augustus L3,94; L4,88; L86,
256-7(c) 285-8(c) 320 343; L87,144 211; IU

From London to Bokhara L41,343; L42,197
Le Mesurier, Miss L5,305; L88,299
Lemon, Mark L90,209-10 246 256; L92,276;
  L93,291; IU
Lennard, H.B.
  see Lennard, Thomas B.
Lennard, Thomas B. L3,175
Lennox, Lord William P. L91,20 171; L117B,
  10; IU
  Compton Audley L7,146; L55,1-6
Leon, E. de L5,81
Leonard, R.Maynard L87,72
Leonards, Lord H. IU
The Leopold Institute IU
Lepsius, Carl R.
  Discoveries in Egypt L36,184; L82,241
Lernard, John P. IU
Leroy, Miss Amélie C. L3,84; L5,158; L86,
  179; L87,145 152 154 168
  Joan Vellacot (orig.A Man's mistake) L41,
  473; L63,287
  The Power of the past (orig.We that are strong)
  L42,444; L66,71
Leslie L93,292
Leslie, C.R. IU
Leslie, Robert C. L5,293
Leslie, Mrs.Thomas IU
Le Soudier, H. UC
Le Sporto Illustrato L88,276
Lester, Charles E.
  The Glory and the shame of England L55,61;
  L117B,15
Lester, Henry J.
  Struggles in falling L36,68 81; L58,177
Lester, Horace F. L3,146; L86,211; IU
  Hartas Maturin L41,466; L42,485; L64,33
L'Estrange, A.G. L2,79; L84,156 163 177-8;
  L95,51-5 59; IU
L'Estrange, Guy L3,28; L5,62; L22,345;
  L64,95 291-3; L86,119 346; IU
L'Estrange, Col.W.P. L3,41; L4,87; L87,222
Levack, Miss (Reay Mackay pseud.) L5,130
Lever, Charles J. L81,242; IU; UC
Leveson-Gower, Granville George (Earl
  Granville) IU(Granville)
Levieu, Edward L83,170
Levy, Miss Amy L5,110 153-4
Levy, Arthur
  The Private life of Napoleon L41,386; L42,
  291
Lévy, Michel Frères L1,154; L60,21; L62,
  276; L63,231-3; L83,121 159 161 180 182;
  L84,146 180; L85,147; L86,149 155 158; IU
Levy & Müller IU
Lewes, George H. IU
Lewin, Ross
  The Life of a solider L53,36; L117A,3
Lewin, Walter L5,249
Lewis L86,445(c)
Lewis, Mr. L85,198 204
Lewis, Angelo E. L5,184
Lewis, Edward L2,22; L59,134; IU
Lewis, G.C. IU

Lewis, G.H. L92,233
Lewis, G.M.
  Tour of Italy (prop.) L54,59
Lewis, Rev.Gerrard L5,173 195-7
Lewis, J.W. L82,286 303
Lewis, James (Charles Masson pseud.) L92,
  87; L117B,19; IU(Masson)
  Narrative of various journeys L55,118
Lewis, Mrs.Janet L85,48
Lewis, Kate Terry IU
Lewis, Lady Maria T.(Lady M.T.Lister) L1,
  178; L58,196; L83,187; IU
Lewis, Miss Mary A.
  Two pretty girls L3,137; L39,364; L40,459;
  L60,302-3; IU
Lewis, Matthew Gregory UC Manuscripts,39
Lewis, Rev.S.L. L5,137
Lewis, T.Hanson L5,99; IU
Lewis, Sir Thomas Frankland IU
Lewis, Rev.W.G. L1,174; L2,53; L3,29;
  L58,203
Lewis, W.Knapton L5,206
Lewis, Wilmarth Sheldon UC
Lewis & Lewis L85,94; IU
Leys, John K. L4,75; L5,185; L88,229 288
  Under a mask L42,414; L67,209-12
Lias, J.J. IU
Library Bureau Ltd. L88,335-6 338
The Library Company L83,253; L84,64 124;
  IU
The Library Table IU; IU(Literary Table)
Libri, E. IU
Libri, Guglielmo L57,84 160; L58,1 63 135
  237; L82,242; L83,173 201 203-4 206-8;
  L117A,35; IU; IU Unidentified,(A)
Lichtenberger, F. IU
Liddell, Mrs.Christina C.F.(C.C.F.Tytler)
  L3,97; UC
  Jonathan L38,364; L39,279; L60,4 6
Liddell, Henry IU
Liddon, Henry Parry IU
Lieber, Franz L81,135
  On Civil liberty L36,185; L57,253-8
  Reminiscences of an intercourse with Niebuhr
  L53,172
Lietch, Alice L94,102
Lieven, Dorotheya K.(Princess)
  Correspondence L3,28; L41,346 352 356;
  L42,504; L64,95 291-3
Life IU
Ligacs, N.M. L84,149
Limond, Margaret S. IU
Lincoln, Bishop of
  see Jackson, J.
Lindall, Edwin L84,179
Lindesay-Bethune, Sir John Trotter IU(Lindsay)
Lindsay, Lady C.Blanche E. L3,97; L5,132
  172; L86,198 378 386; IU
  Bertha's earl L41,430; L42,480; L65,27
  Caroline L41,463
Lindsay, Lady Charlotte IU
Lindsay, J.T.
  see Lindesay-Bethune

Lindsay, Lady Sarah E.   L3,164; L4,87; L85,
394
A Few choice recipes L40,379
Linklater, J. & A. L82,210; L84,60
Linskill, Mary (Stephen Yorke pseud.)   L3,180;
L85,466; L86,54 57; IU; IU(Smurthwaite)
Between the heather and the Northern sea
L40,222; L41,434 505; L42,90; L62,235;
L65,73; L119,41
Cleveden L41,98; L42,91; L65,191-5; L119,
44
The Haven under the hill L40,444; L41,91 513;
L42,92 95 485; L62,320; L65,73; L119,42
In exchange for a soul L41,77; L42,93; L65,
115; L119,43 82
Tales of the North Riding L41,496; L42,94;
L65,268 328-34
Linton, E.L.
see Lynn, E.
Lippincott, J.B. & Co. L2,86; L60,157; L65,
158 205; L66,141-7 151-4; L82,200; L84,
112-13 127 155 225; L85,245 265 277 432 455
474; L86,74 88 97 107 109 143 183 218 339 413
463 475 494; L87,41 210 214-16 216(c) 217 259;
L88,222; IU; IU(Garmeson)
Lister, Miss Edith L5,237
Lister, Lady Maria T.
see Lewis, Lady M.T.
Lister, Thomas H. L1,41; IU
Arlington L52,264
Epicharis L6,173
Liston, Charles L3,176; L62,202-9; L85,451
463; IU
Litchfield, J.P. L90,276
The Literary Gazette L80,4 7
Literary & Scientific Institution, Slough IU
Literary Union Club IU
The Literary World L82,60; L88,85;
IU George Bentley,174
Little, A.Clarke IU
Little, Mrs.Alicia
see Bewicke, A.
Little, Brown & Co. L66,307; L82,120 133
141 156 160; L84,127 168; L85,87 91 191 263
415
Little Folks IU
Litton, Rev.Edward A.
A History of the Church of England (prop.)
L36,241; L82,300; L83,89
The Living Age UC
Llanover, Lady
see Hall, Augusta
Llewellyn, R.L.J.
see Jones, R.L.
Lloyd, C.D.Clifford IU
Lloyd, E.C.A. IU
Lloyd, Eleanor
Valeria L39,318; L60,160-1; L123,193 195;
IU
Lloyd, Francis L1,111; L91,221; L92,215;
L117B,20; IU
Hampton Court L7,157; L55,241
Lloyd, J.B. L117A,18

Lloyd, Llewellyn L1,47 142; L82,319-20 325;
L93,225
Field sports of the north of Europe L1,54;
L52,23 193; L68,24 86
Lloyd, Richard IU
Lloyd & Co. L86,421
Lluellyn, Lady IU
Loader, William L82,15-17 290 292-3 305;
L83,98 191-2 256
Lobb, Harry IU
[Lock], John Griffith IU(Loch)
Lock, S.R. IU
Locke, Ada Blanche IU
Locker, Mr. IU
Locker, Arthur L26,43; L86,196;
IU(The Graphic)
Locker, Frederick L5,87; IU
Lockhart, John Gibson L81,98; L82,242 245
249 254 258; IU
Lockwood L5,73
Lockwood, Mr. L85,25
Lockwood, Mrs. L85,27 29-30
Lockwood, Henry IU
Lockwood, M. L82,25 80 127 139 149 214; L83,
38 93 98 108
Lockyer, Sir Joseph N. L2,63; L59,117-18;
L84,46 50 53-4 76 95 163; L102,43; IU
Lockyer, Mrs.Winifred L2,79; L84,142; IU
Locock, Miss Frances L2,81; IU
Biographical guide to the Divina Commedia
L37,305; L38,174; L39,400 426; L40,441;
L41,505
Loewe, Rev.Dr.Louis L86,74 85-6 179 184;
IU; IU George Bentley,203+2
Loftie, Rev.William John IU; UC
Loftus, Thomas IU
Logie, Cosmo IU
Lohmeyer, John H. L55,324; L92,280-1
Lomax, J.Acton L5,159
[Lomme, G.Laurence] IU
London Booksellers' Society L87,229; IU
The London Journal IU
London Library IU(Harrison, R.);
UC Manuscripts,20
London Stationers' Company IU
London & North-West Railway L86,375
Londonderry, 3rd Marquis of
see Stewart, C.W.
[Lonergon], E.Argent IU
Longfellow, Henry W. L91,179-80 232; L117A,
28; UC
Outre-mer L74,125 175
Longfellow, Mountfort L81,143
Longman & Co. L66,125 231-4; L67,122; L81,
230 345; L82,169; L83,85-6 88 99 105; L87,
47-9 51(c) 52 69 71 79 127 235 285; L88,59
86(c) 87 125 250 260; L89,78 96; L90,5 40 69;
L117A,24; IU; IU Richard Bentley II,657+1;
UC; UC Manuscripts,11
Longworth, Maria T.(Lady Avonmore; Hon.Mrs.
Yelverton) L2,43; L3,62; L5,44; L83,227;
L84,240-4; IU
Martyrs to circumstance L36,266-7; L37,

287; L58,261
Teresina in America L38,329; L39,225;
L40,457; L41,535; L42,521; L101,203
Teresina Peregrina L38,307; L39,225; L40,
457; [L59,311]
Lonsdale, Earl of
see Lowther, William
Lonsdale, James J. L3,121; L60,143; L123,
191; IU
Lord, Mrs.Catherine L5,107; IU
Lord, Grace IU
Lord, John K. L2,60; L84,51 78
The Naturalist in Vancouver Island L36,207;
L37,179; L39,455; L59,84
Lord, Walter F. L4,72; L5,228 290; L22,
359; L88,113 184 291(c); IU(Lord,F.)
The Lost empires L42,385; L67,232
The Lost possessions of England L42,361 368;
L67,60
Lothian, Lady C.H.M. L88,120; IU;
IU(Lathian)
Lott, Emmeline L2,60; L84,54 56 66 104;
L98,173
English governess in Egypt L36,152; L37,
173 181; L38,179; L59,80
Loudon, Mrs.Jane (Miss Webb) L1,64
Loudon, Mrs.Margracia
Fortune-hunting L52,276
Loughran, J. L89,102
Louis, Alfred H. L1,192; L2,52; L83,224;
L85,432
The Conference and the crisis L38,118; L39,
453
England and Europe L36,81; L58,253
Louis, Philippe I IU Unidentified,(A)
Loumyer, Henry L85,204; IU
Lovell, John W. L64,266; L86,323 330 332
335 352 354-5 377 381 384 421 423 456;
IU George Bentley,259
Lover, Henry W. L5,134; IU; UC
Lover, Samuel L54,12 161; L81,231 235; L91,
8 36-9; L117A,28; IU; UC
Rory O'More L122,67 105 122
Lovett, Amelia IU
Low, Charles Rathbone L3,117; L4,87; L5,
105; L85,352 403; IU
History of the Indian Navy L39,284; L40,435
457; L41,245; L62,115; L67,75
A Memoir of Sir Garnet J.Wolseley L39,289;
L40,339 343; L41,162 223; L42,260 510; L60,
99; UC
Low, Miss Frances H. L86,79
Low, Sir Hugh
Sarawak L36,187; L56,64; L117B,34
Low, William Henry IU
Low, Sampson & Co. L64,26; L82,92 101 105
208 239 281 283; L83,35 152-3 205 210 218 239
241; L84,134 167-8 170 [171] 206 249-50 302
307(c) 309-10 313-15(c); L85,218 409; L86,81
280 288; L87,238 239(c) 240; IU(Sampson)
[Lowden], Augusta IU
Lowe, William L56,118; L92,140 155
Lowell, J.Russell L85,214; [IU(Sackville)]

Lowenstam, Leopold IU
Lowes, Russell IU Unidentified,(C)
Lowndes, George R. L3,101
Camping sketches L41,372; L42,180; L65,
171
Lowry, H.D. L5,43
Lowth, G.T. L5,76
Lowther, William (2nd Earl of Lonsdale)
IU(Lonsdale)
Lucas, David IU
Lucas, John IU
Lucy, Sir Henry W. L3,177; L5,180; IU;
UC(end of L)
East by west L40,293; L41,216; L42,188;
L62,227
Luffmann, F.C.B. L5,289
Lumley, Benjamin L2,15; L83,217 219; IU
Sirenia L36,99 120; L37,233; L38,220
Lumley & Co. L84,179
Lunn, J. L92,68; IU
Lupton, J. & A. L85,405
Lupton, Miss Margaret (Mrs.Stennett)
Maud L36,198; L57,226; L117B,36
Lyady, Thomas L90,188
Lyall, Sir Alfred C. L88,264; IU
Lyddy L92,207
Lyell, Charles IU
Lynch, Miss L5,82
Lynch, Mrs.E.M. L5,259
Lynch, William IU
Lynch, William F.
Narrative of the United States expedition L36,
187
Lynd, William UC
Lyndhurst, Lady Georgiana IU
Lyndhurst, Rt.Hon.Lord John L83,201; IU
Lyndon, Mrs. L85,317
Lyne, Francis L84,194-6 225-6
Lyne, Rev.Joseph L.(Father Ignatius pseud.)
L2,84; L85,407; IU; UC
Leonard Morris L37,294; L38,173; L39,215;
L40,287; L41,519; L42,488; L59,252; L84,
175
Lyne, Louisa G. IU
Lynedoch, Lord Thomas IU
Lynn, Miss L82,96
Lynn, Elizabeth (Mrs.E.L.Linton) L2,64; L3,
161; L5,123 148 158; L61,260; L84,31 247;
L86,74 139; L95,178; L98,110; L117B,19;
IU(Linton); UC Manuscripts,47
Amymone L56,88
The Autobiography of Christopher Kirkland
L40,407; L41,503 513; L42,477; L62,310
The Girl of the period (orig.Saturday mornings)
L40,326; L41,512; L42,508; L62,30
Paston Carew L40,158; L41,527; L63,
123-6 270
The Rebel of the family (pub.Chatto & Windus)
L5,45 55; L60,180-1
Patricia Kemball (pub.Chatto & Windus) L5,
45
Lyon, Chaloner L5,58
Lysaght, Mrs.Elizabeth J. L3,38; L86,77

299; IU
  Sealed orders L40,416; L41,532; L63,47
Lysons, Rev.S. L82,95
Lyte, Cecil Maxwell L5,100
Lyttleton, Lord George W. IU
Lytton, Lady Betty L5,184
Lytton, Bulwer
  see Bulwer
Lytton, Lady Constance G. IU
Lytton, Cuthbert IU
Lytton, Edward R. L63,35; L86,69

M., Captain L94,294 298
M., A. IU Unidentified
M., D.L. IU Unidentified
Maberley, Mrs.Col. L83,29
Maberly, W. L84,48
Macarthur, Son & Beckford L60,78-93
Maccall, William IU
McCallum, Mary IU
McCape, Alexander L91,167-70
MacCarthy, Daniel
  The Free lance L7,156
MacCarthy, Justin L3,76
  The Ladies' gallery
  The Rebel rose
  see Praed, R.C.M.
Macartney, Major L22,356
MacCausland, Dr.Dominick L1,151; L2,35;
  L3,26; L61,274; L94,142; IU
  Adam and the Adamite L36,134; L37,187 204;
  L38,184 345; L39,114-5; L40,192-3; L41,
  315 394; L42,161
  The Builders of Babel L37,178; L38,184 351;
  L39,115-6; L40,193-4; L41,315
  The Latter days L36,72 74; L37,187; L38,
  185
  Sermons in stones L36,82 133 141 220 306;
  L37,185 203; L38,186 292; L39,116-7 454;
  L40,211; L41,315; L58,36
  Shinar L37,200; L38,185
MacCausland, Emily S. L61,274
MacCausland, Ernest J. IU
MacCausland, M.F.H. IU
McClintock, Letitia IU
McClise, Daniel IU(MacLise)
M'Clure, Sir John David UC
McClymont, W. L5,285
MacColl, Norman IU; UC
McCrea, Miss L82,182
McCrie, George L5,277
McCullagh, W.T.
  see Torrens, W.T.M.
Macdonagh, Michael L5,300; L22,355 363;
  L88,237
Macdonald, A.H.Moreton
  see Moreton, A.H.M.
Macdonald, Etienne J.
  Recollections of Marshal Macdonald L41,368
  380; L42,310 313; L65,127-30 154; L119,87
MacDonald, George IU

Macdonald, Mosse L5,110
Macdonell, John L5,298; IU
Macdowall, M.W. IU
McDowell & Co. L87,153
Maceroni, F. IU
McEvoy, Bernard IU
MacEwen, Alexander L3,130; L61,109
  The Need for protection L39,334; L40,312;
  L41,530
  Reasonable protection L39,394; L40,312;
  L41,530; L61,126
McFall, Mrs.Frances E.(Sarah Grand pseud.)
  L3,29; L5,155; L66,111-13; L87,122-4;
  IU(Grand); UC(Grand)
  Ideala L41,460 541; L42,487; L64,90-1;
  L119,119
Macfarlane, Miss L5,69
Macfarlane, Charles L53,228; L80,2; L117A,
  17
Macfarlane, Harold L5,62
Macfarren L5,68
Macfarren, Lady C.Natalia L102,175
McGee, William H. L87,144; UC
MacGhee, Rev.R.J.Leslie L2,45
  How we got to Pekin L36,294; L58,289
McGlashan, James & Gill L82,368; L83,97
  252; L84,39 48-9 63; [L85,189]
McGouran, James
  The Will L55,339
McGowan, James
  see McGouran, J.
Macgregor, Mrs. L88,240
McGrigors Bank L89,113
McIan, Ronald R. IU
MacIntosh, Maria J.
  Alice Montrose L36,192; L57,198
McIntyre, James L93,11
MacIvor, A. L5,288
Mackarness, Mrs.M.A.
  see Planché, M.A.
Mackay, Alexander
  The Western world L36,190; L56,137; L82,
  99; L117B,12
Mackay, Dr.Charles L1,75; L2,76; L5,150;
  L6,130; L59,217; L82,126; L83,69; L86,
  107(c); L91,70; L117A,36; IU
  The Hope of the world L7,143; L36,191
  Memoirs of extraordinary popular delusions
  L7,141; L36,190; L54,83
  The Thames and its tributaries L7,144; L53,
  13
Mackay, Eric L87,124 127; IU
Mackay, Mrs.J.Hayward L88,132
Mackay, Kenneth
  The Yellow wave L4,68; L42,431; L66,
  227-9
Mackay, Mary (Marie Corelli pseud.) L3,15-16
  18-19 142 149; L4,37; L5,185; L86,282 324-5
  385 391 395 407 423 451 453 456 481 491(c) 492;
  L87,62 65-6 76 84 123 131 135 159(c) 215 221
  225 225(c) 226 236 238-9 299 300-1 302-3(c);
  L88,68 78 79-80(c) 80 84 88 155-6 203;
  IU Richard Bentley II,474: IU(Corelli);

UC(Corelli)
Ardath L41,108-9 452; L42,56; L64,136
224-31; L119,143
The Hired baby L41,422; L42,467; L65,98
Romance of two worlds (orig.Lifted up) L40,
415; L41,56 110 529; L42,57-8; L63,39-43
245; L119,140
The Soul of Lilith (orig.A Strange experiment)
L41,74 416; L42,59 475; L65,149 309; L119,
145
Thelma L41,57 67 484; L42,60-1; L63,
222-9; L64,17-18; L119,142
Vendetta L40,53 160; L41,55 74 537; L42,
62; L63,121 211; L119,141
Wormwood L41,109 139 436; L42,63-4 498;
L64,327-32; L65,43; L119,144
Mackay, Reay
see Levack, Miss
Mackay, William
The Popular idol L3,87; L38,352; L39,436;
L62,105; IU
MacKellar, P. IU
MacKenna, Stephen L95,172-3
Mackenzie, C.F. L83,127
Mackenzie, Charles
Notes on Haiti L1,66; L52,100; L68,50
Mackenzie, Charles Finch L92,164
Mackenzie, Colin
The Crisis in India L36,55
Mackenzie, Miss Gertrude P. L5,306
Mackenzie, Helen (Mrs.Colin Mackenzie) L1,
112; L58,140; L82,326 332 335; L117A,32
Life in the mission L36,34 191; L38,122;
L57,236 245-6
Mackenzie, Miss Jessie L5,287
Mackenzie, Kenneth R.H. L57,225; L82,304
315; L117A,8
Mackenzie, Keith S.
Narrative of the second campaign L1,76;
L55,111; L117B,31
MacKenzie, Mary J.
Lectures on miracles L38,200
Lectures on parables L38,200
Private life L38,200
MacKenzie, Morell IU
McKern, G. & Sons L87,190 199(c) 201
Mackeson, R. L2,61
MacKillop, Henry F.
Reminiscences of service in New Zealand
L36,192; L82,96
Mackinnon, Daniel
The Origin and services of the Coldstream
Guards L52,290
Mackinnon, Hamilton L63,77; L85,315 389;
L86,50 80 96 373; L87,110; L88,102(c) 102
106 259; IU; UC
Mackinnon & Co. L61,97-101; L63,79; L85,452
Mackintosh, A.E. L5,251
Macklin, W. L82,127
Macknight, Florence IU
Macknight, Thomas L83,49; L117B,3
The Rt.Hon.Benjamin Disraeli,M.P. L36,
143; L57,282

Mackulin, Mrs.Nellie L5,165
MacLaughlin, Louisa E.
Our adventures during the war
see Pearson, E.M.
McLean,·Donald L83,56
Maclean, John
Notes of service in Hudson's Bay L6,180
Maclean, Mrs.Letitia E.
see Landon, Miss L.E.
Macleay, O.S. L5,99
MacLeod, Alfred IU
McLeod, Miss Camilla L5,91; IU
McLuhae, Mrs. L92,199
Maclure & Co. IU
MacMicking, Robert
Recollections of Manilla L1,68-70; L36,193
MacMicking, Thomas L83,70; L117A,14
Macmillan, Maurice IU
Macmillan & Co. L59,117-18; L66,200 244-7;
L85,218 444; L86,119; L87,220 220(c) 221 292
299; L88,353; L89,43 72 124 126 130 134
135-6(c); L96,227 247; L115,247-9 257-65
287-305; IU; UC; UC(Foster)
Macnamara, F.Nugent IU
Macnaughton, Sarah IU
Selah Harrison L42,408; L67,276; L89,49
McNeile, Hugh UC
Macniven & Cameron UC
Macniven & Wallace L88,301 308 310
Macpherson, William IU
McQueen, Georgiana IU
McQueen, W.M. IU
Macquoid, Gilbert S. L5,186
Macquoid, Mrs.Katherine S. L2,84; L3,44;
L5,23 43 50; L84,139 143 228; L85,464; IU
Louisa (orig.Among the olives) L40,401; L41,
519; L62,265
Pictures across the Channel L38,271; L39,
433
Rookstone L37,256; L38,215; L39,439; L59,
242; L100,84
Too soon L38,293; L39,438; L59,301
Macquoid, Thomas R. IU
McReynolds, George W. L53,276; L81,170
Macrone, John L53,341-5; L117A,29
Macrorie, W.K. IU(Macione)
[Mactin, John] IU
Madden, Dr. L83,41
Madden, John L88,208; IU
Madden, Richard R. L1,56; UC
The Mussulman L52,118; L68,57
Maddock, Miss E.M. L5,284
Madeley, G.E. IU
Madox, John
Excursions in the Holy Land L52,333; L90,
45 47 56; L117A,24
Madox, M. IU
Maessenhausen, von L85,365
Magee, James L. L94,125 128 134
Magennis, Peter IU
Maginn, Charles A. IU
Maginn, D.W. L81,59
Maginn, Dr.William L90,195; L91,11 14 33

102 140 178; IU; UC

Shakespeare papers   L36,210 214; L37,195; L38,200

Magnusson, Eirikur   L83,278; L84,29 47 145; IU

Maguchelli, Mrs.   L85,249

Mahon, Lord
see Stanhope, Philip H.

Mahony, Rev.Francis S.   L90,119 200-1; L91, 76-8 196 210; L92,182; L117B,33; IU

Facts and figures from Italy   L36,150; L56, 35-8

Mahony, Martin F.
Checkmate [orig.Deguseau]   L36,65; L58, 176; L83,163

The Mail, London   IU(Garnett,J.)

Maillard, Annette M.
The Compulsory marriage   L6,150; L57,13; L117A,22

Main, Robert   L2,61

Maitland, A.   IU

Maitland, Mrs.E.Fuller   L5,199

Maitland, Edward   L3,55; L84,234; L95,251; IU

By and by   L38,282 286; L39,450; L59,296; L100,155; L101,2 4

Maitland, James A.   L2,68; L5,16

Maitland, Miss Margaret Mary   L5,202

Majendie, Lady Margaret E.   L3,131; L4,88; L5,103 140; L85,447; L86,66 157 258; IU; UC(end of M)

Fascination   L39,345; L60,225

Once more   L40,382; L42,523; [L61,304]

Out of their element (orig.Transplantation) L40,397; L41,526; L62,200

Past forgiveness (orig.Etienne's revenge)   L41, 453; L42,493; L64,120

Precautions   L41,480; L63,241

Sisters-in-law   L40,410; L41,533; L42,495; L63,27

The Turn of the tide   L39,372; L40,459; L61, 79-81

Major, Albany F.   IU

Major, Michel   IU

Makinson, Joseph   UC

Malan, Rev.A.H.   L5,252; IU

Malcolm, Col.   L83,157 166

Malcolm, E.H.   L93,130

Malcolm, Mrs.Georgiana   L1,164; L58,125

Malet, William W.
An Errand to the South   L36,134; L37,193

Malheiro, Manuel   L85,28 31-2

Malins, Sir Richard   IU

Mallan & Ripsher, Mesdames   L86,159 391; L87,58 133; IU

[Mallanti, J.]   IU

Malleson, F.A.   IU

Mallet, J.L.   L82,196

Mallet-Dupan, Jacques F.
Memoirs and correspondence   L36,195; L57, 76-8

Mallett, Cyril   L5,34 90

Mallett, J.Reddie M.   L3,136; L4,88; L5,276

285; L87,285; L88,68 91; IU
A Life's history   L42,367; L67,184

Mallett, Mrs.S.G.   IU

Mallett's Printing Office   IU

Mallock, Cecil   IU

Mallock, Mary M.
A Younger son's cookery book   L4,67; L42, 370 388; L67,73; IU

Mallock, William H.   L3,151; L62,187; L63, 238; L65,232-3; L85,331; L86,258(c) 471(c); L88,135 141 312 343; IU

Atheism and the value of life   L40,244; L41, 533 539; L42,161-2; L119,121

In an enchanted island   L41,343; L42,243 245; L65,196-200

The Old order changes   L40,467; L41,479 497; L42,470 489; L63,152

Social equality   L40,348 423; L41,164-5; L42, 316; L61,219-22; L119,120

Mallock, Mrs.William H.   L85,434

Malmesbury, Earl of
see Harris, James

Maloch, Miss   L92,182

Malone, R.Edmond
Three years' cruise   L36,208; L57,308; IU

Malortie, Baron Carl von   L3,113; L5,102; L85,94-5; IU; IU George Bentley,180+; UC

Diplomatic sketches   L39,296; L40,427

Mr.Gladstone and the Greek question (Dip. sketch III)   L39,317; L123,198-9

Malot, Hector
Conscience   L3,23 125; L41,422; L42,481; L65,84-9

No relations   L3,103 125; L39,329 361; L40, 82 346 446; L41,79; L42,104 409; L60,187-9; L61,161

Malse, Edith   IU

Manchester Examiner & Times   IU

The Manchester Guardian   L87,142 152 183; IU

Mancur, J.H.   L92,84

Maning, Frederick E.
Old New Zealand   L38,356; L39,218 241; L40, 309-10; L41,185 293 311; L42,294 298 337 344; L84,316; IU

Mank, William   IU

Mann, Alice   IU

Mann, Mrs.Mary E.(Mrs.Fairman Mann)   L3, 88; L5,284; L86,223-4 301 364 394 397; L87, 63 189; IU

A Lost estate   L41,460; L42,489; L64,76

One another's burdens   L41,443; L42,492; L64,180

Perdita   L41,407; L42,461; L65,272

A Winter's tale   L41,431; L42,498; L65, 59-61

Manners, Mrs.Catherine (Lady Stepney)   L117A, 23; IU(Stepney)

The Heir presumptive   L53,56 64

The New road to ruin (orig.Lorevaine)   L52, 124; L68,59

The Three peers   L7,143; L54,274-6

Manners, James J.R.(Duke of Rutland)
IU(Rutland)

Manners, Walter E.   IU
  Marquis of Granby (pub.McM.)   L42,261; L67,
  312-15; L88,175
Manners-Sutton, Mrs.   IU
Manning, Miss Anne   L1,170; L2,55; L3,57;
  L83,161-5 167 189 191 194 231 241 259; L84,
  72 121 128; L97,149; L98,141; L99,31 140;
  IU
  Belforest   L36,181; L37,34; L38,95; L59,
  37
  Diana's crescent   L37,99; L38,123; L59,172
  The Ladies of Bever Hollow   L36,231 237-8;
  L58,173
  Lady of limited income   L37,303; L38,174
  The Lincolnshire tragedy. Passages in the
  life of the faire gospeller Mistress Anne
  Askewe   L37,124; L59,113
  Lord Harry Bellair   L38,290; L39,446; L59,
  307
  Meadowleigh   L36,148; L37,193; L39,454;
  L58,331
  Monks Norton   L38,318; L39,426
  Story of Italy   L36,75 80; L37,237
  Town and forest   L36,210; L37,245; L38,240
  Valentine Duval   L36,212; L37,299
  Village belles   L36,62 81
Manning, Miss G.E.   L86,340
Manning, Henry E.   IU
  Modern society   L37,194; L38,182; L39,400
  425; L40,445; L41,500 522; L42,513
Manning, James A.   L93,3-5; IU
Manning & Co.   L81,171
Mansfield, R.B.   L87,222; IU
Mansfield, Richard   IU Unidentified, (A)
Manson, Edward   L5,298; IU
Manston, Rev.Augustus   L5,292; IU
Maquay, W.   L81,92
Mar, Earl of
  see Erskine, J.F.
March   L91,134 138
March, Leopold G.F.   L1,76; L82,256; L93,
  112; L117B,21
  A Walk across the French frontier   L7,173;
  L8,174 200; L36,196; L57,130
Margoliouth, Rev.Moses   L82,71 73 76 103
  125-6; L117B,22
  History of the Jews   L8,150; L36,198; L56,
  272
  A Pilgrimage to the land of my fathers   L36,
  197; L56,244
Margollé, E.
  Volcanoes and earthquakes
  see Zurcher, F.
Marillien, M.   IU
Maringer, Peter
  A Victim of the Falk laws   L3,119; L39,416;
  L40,171; L41,151; L42,159; L123,191-2
Mario, Jessie W.   L84,102 117
Mariotti, Mme.Eva   L5,32
Marjoribanks, E.   L53,30
Mark, W.   L86,457
Markham, Dr.   L58,137
Markham, Frederick   L1,112; L2,40; L6,166;

L82,236 348; L117B,35
  Shooting in the Himalayas   L36,56 69; L57,
  275
Marks, Mrs.   L87,263
Marks, Mrs.Mary A.M.
  see Hoppus, M.A.M.
Markwick, Edward   L5,197
Marlborough, Duke of
  see Churchill
Marlborough, E. & Co.   L88,170
Marlborough, F.   IU
Marlitt, E.
  see John, Eugenie
Marne & Son   L85,190
Marryat, Augusta   IU
Marryat, Emilia
  see Norris, E.
Marryat, Florence (Mrs.Ross Church; Mrs.Lean)
  L2,40 78; L3,36; L5,20; L84,52 78 98 116
  138-9; IU(London Society);
  UC(Desart-end of D); UC(Lean)
  The Confessions of Gerald Estcourt   L37,88;
  L38,144; L59,144
  For ever and ever   L37,126; L38,128
  The Girls of Feversham   L37,169; L38,143;
  L59,184
  Gup   L37,138
  Her Lord and master   L37,108
  Life and letters of Captain Marryat   L37,315;
  L38,263; L59,265
  Love's conflict   L36,191; L37,175
  Mad Dumaresq   L38,295; L39,450; L59,309
  Nelly Brooke   L37,207; L38,201; L39,442;
  L59,160; L99,92
  No intentions   L38,310; L39,403 424; L40,
  447; L41,523; L42,492
  Petronel   L37,220; L38,207; L59,224
  The Prey of the gods   L37,213; L38,210; L39,
  442
  Too good for him   L36,202; L37,88
  Veronique   L37,264; L59,204
  Woman against woman   L36,314; L37,267
Marryat, Frank   L82,43
Marryat, Frederick   L1,67; L6,133; L53,222
  224; L81,39 130; L90,18; L117A,31; L122,
  62 77 96 110 124 126; IU; UC
  The Dog fiend   L53,222 224; L56,10
  Jacob Faithful   L54,124
  Japhet in search of a father   L54,124
  The King's own   L54,124; L68,40
  Life of Lord Napier (prop.)   L53,220 259-62
  Mr.Midshipman Easy   L54,124
  Newton Forster   L54,124
  The Pacha of many tales   L54,124
  Percival Keene   L55,315 322-3
  Peter Simple   L54,124
  The Phantom ship   L56,10
  Valerie (pub.Colburn)   L55,341
Marsden, A.P.   L88,191
Marsden, Rev.John B.   L1,133; L82,347; L93,
  237 241-6 249 255-6 264 283; L117A,32
  History of Christian churches and sects   L36,
  28 82 92-3; L37,191 193; L38,198; L57,284-6

Marsh, Anne L82,40 50-1 55 57 59; L93;29; L117A,39; IU(Marsh-Caldwell); UC
Norman's bridge L36,213; L55,326; L56, 216
The Protestant reformation in France L7, 163; L8,34 111; L55,326; L56,216
The Triumphs of time L7,155; L55,221
Two old men's tales L122,92
Marsh, J.T. L84,56
Marsh, John B. IU
Marsh, John T. L1,135
Marsh-Caldwell
see Marsh
Marshall, Mrs. IU
Marshall, A.H. IU
Marshall, Arthur L95,285
Marshall, Charles (Heraclitus Grey pseud.)
Armstrong Magney L37,23; L59,130
Glum-glum L2,18; L37,136; L38,142
Marshall, Miss Christabel L5,297
Marshall, David IU
Marshall, Miss E.M. L85,146
Marshall, Mrs.Florence A. L3,52; L64,70; L86,333 390 465; IU
Marshall, H.F.C. IU
Marshall, James C. IU
Marshall, Rev.John L93,210
Marshall, Mrs.Ord L5,237
Marshall, Thomas IU
Marshall & Son L82,125 218; L89,104
Marsland, George
A Basket of fragments L36,139; L37,42; L38,98; L94,151-2; IU
Marston, Edward L83,55; L86,359a 360(c); IU
see Low, S. & Co.
Marston, Miss Lina L5,285
Martelli, Charles
The Naval officer's guide L1,112; L36,57 69; L53,99
Martelli, Mrs.Charles L1,112; L117A,40
Martin, Mr. L93,13
Martin, A.P. L88,255(c)
Martin, A.Patchett L5,179; IU
Martin, Mrs.A.Patchett L5,237
Martin, Albinus L5,70; L84,157; IU
Martin, Benjamin E.
In the footprints of Charles Lamb L41,359; L42,244
Martin, C.E.M. IU
Martin, E. le Breton IU
Martin, Mrs.Frederick E.M. L3,27; L22,347; L86,315 323 383 399 402 431 443 443-5(c) 449; L87,43 233 236(c)
An Australian girl L41,425 441; L42,463; L64,204-8; L66,170; UC Manuscripts,12
The Silent sea L41,415; L42,475; L65,162-8
Martin, John L53,216; L117A,6; [IU(Mactin)]
Martin, Mrs.Mary Bell
Julia Howard L56,250; L117B,7
Martin, Mrs.Mary E.(Mrs.Herbert Martin) L3,131; L5,265; L87,207 274; L88,182 292

339; IU; UC
Britomart L42,450; L66,30; L67,208
Out of the workhouse L42,420; L67,127
Martin, R. IU
Martin, Theodore L90,319
Martin, Miss Violet F. L3,30; UC
An Irish cousin
see Somerville, E.A.
Martin, William L91,283; L117B,28
Martineau, Harriet IU; [IU(Martinson)]
Martyn, Benjamin
The Life of Shaftesbury
see Kippis, A.
Marvin, Charles IU
Marzials, Theo. L5,107
Mason, A.E.W. L5,245
Mason, A.J. IU
Mason, C.W. L5,274
Mason, Charles S. IU
Mason, Finch L5,162; L67,322-4; L86,302 455; L87,44; IU(March)
Mason, Henry Watts L2,33; L59,195-6
Mason, Maria IU
Mason, R.L. L2,66
Mason, Thomas M.
Life of Dean Swift (prop.) L60,190; L123,215
Massalska, Hélène
Memoirs of the Princesse de Ligne L3,63; L41,318; L63,231-3 243-5
Massey, William L1,22; L52,106; L90,92; L117A,31
Alice Paulet L52,96; L68,47 52
Fitzwiggins L7,141; L54,199
Lionel Wakefield L53,97
Sydenham L52,36; L68,31
Massie, John L5,58
Massie, William
see Massey, William
Massina, A.H. & Co. L86,58
Masson, Charles
see Lewis, James
Masson, David IU
Masson, G.
A French reader
see Brette, P.H.E.
Master, Mrs.Ethel A.
see De Fonblanque, Ethel
Masterman, Miss
Antony L57,64; L117B,6
Masterman, Austin L91,79
Masterman, J.
see Baker, Victoria
Masterman, Rev.Thomas L57,64
Masterton, R.K. L5,294
Mathers, Helen B.(Mrs.H.A.Reeves) L3,82 91 172; L5,85 113; L84,333-4; L85,8 97 147 153 155 177 177-9(c) 312 334 415-19 433 438 471-4; L86,58 185 316 349 352 377; L87,255; L88,63 85(c) 85 155 164 164(c); IU George Bentley, 175+1; IU(Reeves); UC(Reeves-end of R)
As he comes up the stair L38,339; L39,231 410; L40,167; L41,151 157; L42,155; L60, 29

Cherry ripe   L38,119; L39,262 287; L40,79;
L60,16 31 65; L62,173
Comin' thro the rye   L38,339 354; L39,53;
L40,80-1; L41,80 125; L42,105-6; L119,36
Eyre's acquittal   L40,395; L41,509; L62,167
Land o' the leal   L39,406; L40,161; L41,152;
L60,112-14 126
My Lady Greensleeves (pub.Low, S. & Co.)
L39,303; L85,98 167
Sam's sweetheart   L40,79-80; L41,81; L42,
107; L62,164-5; L64,301
The Token of the silver lily   L39,239; L40,
332; L41,306
Mathew, L.   IU
Mathews, Mrs.Anne   L92,100 130; L93,52;
L117A,38; IU; UC(Bentley-end of B)
Memoirs of Charles Mathews   L7,140; L53,
347; L54,9 163; L81,239
Mathews, Charles (jnr.)   L6,43; L54,9
Mathews, Charles (snr.)   IU
Mathews, Elkin   IU
Mathews, H.B.
see Mathers, H.B.
Mathews, Mrs.I.Wallas Penfold   IU; UC
Mathews, John J.   L94,144
Mathias, Fanny (Mrs.G.H.D.Mathias)   L3,54;
IU
Mathias, Rev.G.H.Duncan   L2,75; L59,146;
L81,91; IU(Mathias,D.)
English B.A.'s and Prussian freshmen   L37,
201; L38,191; L39,425
Matthews, H.W.   L22,353
Matthews, Miss Helen B.
see Mathers, H.B.
Matthews, W.G.M.   IU
Matthey, A.   IU(Gatty,H.K.F.); IU(Motthey);
UC
Maturin, Mrs.   L81,71
Maturin, Charles R.
Melmoth the wanderer   L41,418; L42,460
Maud, C.G.   IU
Maud, Miss Constance   L5,110; L22,349
Maud, J.W.   UC
Maude, Richard W.   IU
Maule, W.   IU
Maule, Rt.Hon.Sir William H.
Memoir of the early life   L3,175; L38,261;
L39,402 425; L40,443; L41,509; L42,506
Maull & Fox   L66,201
Maurenbrecher, Miss   IU
Maurice, John F.D.   UC
Eustace Conway   L52,214; L68,93
Maury, Richard L.   IU
Mawer, Mrs.   L85,361 363; L86,232
Maximilian (Emperor of Mexico)
On the wing   L37,186; L38,204
Recollections of my life   L2,32; L37,199;
L38,199; L39,430
Maxwell, Cecil   IU
Maxwell, J. & R.   L59,148; L63,118; L83,
244-5 247; L84,65; L85,84 270 272 278
279(c); L86,64 65 107-8; IU
Maxwell, Lucy   IU

Maxwell, Mrs.Mary E.(M.E.Braddon)   IU
Maxwell, W.B.   L5,133
Maxwell, Mrs.W.H.   L83,91
Maxwell, Rev.William H.   L1,62; L54,145-7
197; L55,85 107-10 113-16; L56,179-83; L81,
27 38 54 79 118 138 160 172 208 213 222; L90,
186; L91,9; L92,165-8 170-1 173 210 241
244-7 260 282 287 293; L93,22-3 28 40; L117A,
7; IU; IU Richard Bentley I,11+1 11+2 20+1;
IU(Santir)
The Adventures of Captain Blake (orig.My life)
L122,88 100 122
The Bivouac   L122,65 101-2 122
Brian O'Linn   L54,12 150; L55,285
Erin-Go-Bragh   L36,78; L37,194
The Fortune of Hector O'Halloran   L55,107;
L122,84 114 122
Stories of Waterloo   L52,80; L68,20 41
The Victories of the British armies   L7,141;
L54,85 97 156
Wild sports of the north (prop.)   L55,285;
UC Manuscripts,10
Wild sports of the West   L52,78 [341]; L68,
42
May, Ada   L94,113; L98,10
May, Miss Bessie (Mrs.Radford)   L5,270
May, Mrs.Georgiana M.
see Craik, G.M.
Mayer, Brantz   L57,313-16
Mayer, Mrs.Gertrude Townshend   L3,88; L5,
122 264; L22,361; IU; UC(Beard)
Sir Hubert's marriage   L38,370; L39,445
Women of letters   L42,342
Mayer, Joseph   L84,324; IU
A Trio of worthies: early exhibitions of art in
Liverpool
see Boyle, Frederick
Mayer, S.R.Townshend   L3,99; L5,87 105;
L60,8 222
Mayers, F.H.Madan   L5,129 195-7
Mayhew, Athol   L86,197; IU
Mayhew, E.   L90,291
Mayhew, Henry   L91,92
Mayhew, Horace   L92,264; L93,70; UC
Mayne, Miss (Leslie Gore pseud.)
Annie Jennings   L2,79; L37,26; L38,77
Mayo, Mrs.Isabella F.(I.Fyvie; E.Garrett
pseud.)   L3,155; L71,72; L85,326(c) 327
Mrs.Raven's temptation   L40,361; L61,199
The Mystery of Allan Grale   L3,122; L40,411;
L41,522; L63,19
Mayo, Miss Katharine   L5,56
Mayo, William S.   L82,85
Mazucelli, Mrs.Nina E.   L5,110; IU
Mead, George B.   IU
Meadows, Drinkwater   L82,324; L91,229-31;
L97,21; IU
Meason, George   IU
Meason, M.Laing   L5,99; IU
Medina Pomar, Duke de   IU
Medwin, Captain   L91,195
Medwin, T.   IU
Medwin, Thomas   L54,20; L81,118; L90,175;

L117A,20

The Angler in Wales   L36,209; L53,76; L83, 182

Meer, Eugène van der   IU

Meetkerke, Mrs.   L5,84 131; IU

Meikleham, Robert S.   L1,127; L83,66 93-4 97 100; IU
The Origin and progress of the steam engine   L36,239; L37,238

Melbourne, Lord William L.   IU

Melbourne Age & Leader   L62,40

Meldon, G.W.   L86,495

Melfort, Count Edouard   L1,113; L81,150; L117A,30

Melhuish, Emily M.   IU

Meller, W.   L91,101

Mellor, Henry J.   L53,154

Melville, G.Whyte   IU; IU(Whyte-Melville)

Melville, Herman   L57,43; L82,30 147 166 212 219; L117A,3; IU
Mardi   L56,148
White jacket   L56,205

Melville, Whyte   L5,44 89

Melville & Co.   L87,121

Mengens, R.   IU

Menkes, Sigmund   L5,85

Menzies, G.K.   L5,283

Menzies, J. & Co.   L85,273; L86,90 188; L87,293; L88,232 352; IU

Meredith, Mrs.   L22,356

Meredith, John B.   L81,53 100

Merewither, Francis L.S.   L90,288 293

Mérimée, Prosper   L6,149; IU
Demetrius the imposter   L36,208
The History of Peter the Cruel   L36,200; L56,166

Merivale, Herman C.   L5,75 147; IU

Merivale, W.   IU

Merle, Mr.   L93,19

Merle, William H.   L117B,4

Merrick, L.
see Miller, L.

Merridew, H.M.   IU

Merrifield, Charles W.   L57,123; L83,42; L117B,18

Merrill, Selah
East of the Jordan   L39,374; L40,242; L41, 216; L42,506; L61,92-4

Merriman, Henry S.
see Scott, H.S.

Merriman, Dr.Samuel   IU

Merritt, Anna Lea   IU

Méry, Mme. de   L93,63

Metcalf, Lady   IU

Metcalfe, Dr.R.Ives   IU

Meteyard, Eliza   IU

Methodist Book & Publishing House, Toronto   L87,230(c) 266

Methuen, Rev.Henry H.   L1,90; L2,37; L88, 308; L117B,13
Life in the wilderness   L7,161 166; L8,52 94; L36,209 212

Methuen & Co.   L86,430; L88,163 176 193: IU

The Metropolitan, New York   IU

Metternich-Winneburg, Clemens von
Memoirs   L3,122 124 129 144; L39,301 346; L40,292-3; L41,278 500; L42,277; L60,144 165-70 204-9 279; L123,213-15; IU;
UC Manuscripts,15

Metternich-Winneburg, Richard von   L3,129; L60,144 165 204-6; L85,50 159 165 168-70 229 232 249 366;
see Montgelas, Count

Metze, Mrs.   L91,5-7

Meves, Augustus
The Dauphin-Louis XVII   L3,112; L38,124; L39,453 455; IU

Meves, William   IU

Mew, Miss Charlotte M.   L22,349

Mew, Egan   L5,231; L88,298

Mew, James   L3,81; IU

Mexborough, Earl of
see Savile, J.H.

Michie, Archibald   L90,232-3

Michon, Jean H.
Narrative of a religious journey in the East   L36,200; L57,244
The Nun   L2,55-6; L36,214; L37,205; L59, 14-19

Middlemass, Jean   IU

Middleton, Charles   L93,122

Middleton, Charles I.   IU

Middleton, Hastings Burton   UC

Middleton, Miss J.A.   L5,169

Midgley, F.   L87,100

Midland Educational Company   L88,303

Mignan, Robert   L1,65; L54,91

Mignaty, Mme.Marguerite A.   IU
Sketches of the historical past of Italy   L38, 371; L39,218; L40,295; L41,499 513; L42, 508; L85,16

Mignet, Francois A.M.
The History of Mary, Queen of Scots   L36, 208-9; L37,192-3; L38,140 198; L39,117-18; L40,208-9; L41,174; L42,222; L56,307

Milbank, Lady   L86,434-5

Miles   L88,112

Miles, George Edward   UC

Miles, Laurence   IU

Miles, T.   L81,90

Mill, Jane   IU

Mill, John Stuart   IU

Miller, Mr.   L81,128

Miller, Mrs.Ann   L81,58

Miller, Cincinnatus H.(Joaquin Miller)   L3,58; L5,96; L84,242; IU(Miller,J.)
Life among the Modocs   L38,293; L39,400 430; L40,467

Miller, Florence Fenwick   IU

Miller, Mrs.[Hugh]   L83,157

Miller, J.M.   L87,277

Miller, Joaquin
see Miller, C.H.

Miller, John   L53,5 32; L54,34 93 162-4 191; L81,193; L82,22-3 138; L117A,36

Miller, Leonard (Leonard Merrick pseud.)   L3,

126; L88,270
  Violet Moses L41,424; L42,497; L65,79;
  L67,199-202
Miller, Lydia F.
  Passages in the life of an English heiress
  L6,106; L117B,31
Miller, T.M. L89,78
Miller, Thomas L81,58
Miller, W.C. L5,175; UC(Garcia-end of G)
Millingen, Dr.John G. L81,36; L92,29;
  L117A,33
  The History of duelling L7,143; L54,[189]
  195-7
  Jack Hornet [L55,245]
  Stories of Torres Vedras L54,32
Millington, Powell
  see Synge, M.
Millington, Rev.T. L5,75
Mills, Francis IU
Mills, John L91,131
Milman, Miss Constance L5,241; IU
Milne, Mrs. IU
Milne, Sir Alexander L85,14
Milner & Co. L86,486 497
Minchin, Harry C. L5,262
The Minster IU
Mitchell, Donald G. L92,255-7 261
Mitchell, Edmund L5,135
Mitchell, Edward C. L5,278; UC
Mitchell, Miss Julia L5,157
Mitchell, T. L81,118 163; IU
Mitchell, W.Foster IU
Mitchell, Walter IU
Mitchell & Hughes UC
Mitchell's Royal Library IU
Mitchison, Mrs. L5,178
Mitford, Dr.G. L52,116; L53,72-4; L68,56;
  L81,164-5
Mitford, Rev.John L56,226-7; L57,15; L82,
  148; L93,104; L117B,26; IU
Mitford, Miss Mary R. L1,51; L52,116; L68,
  56; L81,125; L92,62; L117A,25; L123,1-12
  215; IU; UC(Prouting)
  Belford Regis [L53,72-6]
  Letters of Mary R.Mitford L2,88; L37,183;
  L38,183; L40,444; L59,243; L84,157
  The Life of Mary R.Mitford L2,79; L37,184;
  L38,182; L39,172; L40,444
  Recollections of a literary life L36,67 201;
  L37,192; L40,295; L41,161-161a; L42,305-6;
  L57,44-9
Mitlingen, Dr. L91,75
Moberley, Alfred L5,56
  Lady Valeria L3,122; L40,433; L41,520;
  L63,176
Moberly, Miss L.G. L22,354 363
Moeller, Mme. de
  Gertrude L52,63; L68,37
Molesworth, Sir William IU
Molliva, Charles W. L93,87
Molloy, Fitzgerald L5,218; L86,348;
  IU Unidentified, (A)
Molloy, James Lynam L5,206; IU;

UC Manuscripts,40
Molyneux, E. IU
Molyneux, Georgina
  The Curé d'Ars L37,73; L38,114; L59,189
Mommsen, Dr.Theodor L2,32; L3,25-6; L4,
  50; L42,343; IU
  History of the Roman republic L3,44; L4,31;
  L40,300; L41,329; L42,218; L63,137-40;
  L66,100-7
  History of Rome L2,32 83; L3,34 120-1 124
  140 180; L4,41; L22,336; L36,195 266 279-80
  313; L37,188-91 195 200-1 308; L38,192-8;
  L39,167-71; L40,243 296-300; L41,246-51;
  L42,212-17 376-7; L58,265-6; L62,306-9;
  L63,76 98; L119,83-5
Monck, Hon.Frances E.O.
  My Canadian leaves L41,368; L42,515
Moncrieff, Miss IU
Moncrieff, A.R.Hope L95,222
Moncrieff, William A. L67,167-9; L86,113
  178 326 377 384 455; L88,91 112 142 185 204
  213 282 304 325 329 331 359; L89,47 51 69 78;
  IU; UC
Money, Alonzo
  Sévastopol, our tent in the Crimea L1,130 135;
  L58,48; L83,92 106 108-9; L93,266 268 274-5
Money, George H.
  Sévastopol
  see Money, A.
Money, Harriott E.E. L3,60; L86,169-70;
  IU; UC
  A Little Dutch maiden (orig.Jack: a South
  African sketch) L40,105; L41,465 484; L42,
  468 488; L63,192
Monk, Charles J.
  The Golden Horn L36,202; L56,274
Monkhouse, Cosmo W. L5,109
Monkland, Mrs.Anne C. L91,125; L117A,37
  The Nabob's wife L53,303
  Village reminiscences L53,1
Monkswell, Lady Isabella L63,82-4; L86,93;
  IU
Monro, Rev.Vere
  A Summer ramble in Syria L53,152; L117B,
  19
Montagu, Anne P.D.(Marquise de)
  Memoirs L2,20; L37,202; L38,181; L39,
  216; L40,445
Montagu, Basil IU; UC
Montagu, Elizabeth IU
Montagu, Lady Mary Wortley
  Letters and works L6,16; L53,216
Montagu, Lord Robert IU
Montaignac, Baroness de L2,20; L84,128 137
  149 156; IU
Montalembert, Charles F.R. de
  The Insurrection of Poland L2,46; L36,123
  Memoir of the Abbé la Cordaire L36,126;
  L37,196
Montalembert, Countess Eliza R. de L53,81-5;
  L81,156-7; L117A,22; IU
Montalk, Mme. de L92,262
Montamerli, Countess IU(Commission Italienne)

Montbard, G. IU

Montbrisson, Count L82,190

Montefiore, Arthur
see Brice, A.M.

Montefiore, Sir Francis L4,72; L88,228
The Princess de Lamballe L42,378; L67,
64-5

Montefiore, John (John Norman pseud.) L5,
90-91; IU

Monteiro, Mrs. L85,314

Montgelas, Count L60,165; L85,44 46-7 106
110-11 119-23 130 132 140; IU; IU George
Bentley,180+1 180+6

Montgomery, Alexander IU

Montgomery, Carmichael L5,40 289; L22,354

Montgomery, Miss E. L5,68

Montgomery, Emily L5,21

Montgomery, Hon.Mrs.Fanny C.
see Wyndham, Hon.F.C.

Montgomery, Miss Florence S. L2,78; L3,40
109 140 159-60 165; L4,51; L66,27; L82,230;
L85,193 269 412; L86,47; L88,92 108; L89,
53; IU
The Blue veil L40,307; L41,280-1 284; L42,
453 455
Colonel Norton L42,433; L66,231-5; L119,
155
Herbert Manners L39,354; L40,180; L41,
157 285
Misunderstood L37,207 300; L38,188-9 303;
L39,173-4; L40,301-2; L41,279-80 285; L42,
100-1 469; L119,151; UC Manuscripts,41
Moral tales for children L40,163; L41,280-1
Seaforth L39,283 314; L40,306; L41,282-3
286; L42,101-2 104; L119,152; L123,207-8
Thrown together L38,56-7 262; L39,175;
L40,303; L41,281-2 284; L42,102-3; L119,
153
Thwarted L38,304; L39,176; L40,304; L42,
496
Tony L42,409
The Town-crier L38,328; L39,177; L40,180
305; L41,157 285
Transformed L40,163; L41,283-4; L42,472;
L119,154
A Very simple story L37,263; L39,407; L40,
162; L41,156
Wild Mike and his victim L38,326; L39,178;
L40,162 301; L41,156 286; L42,498

Montgomery, Jessie Douglas L5,183 300; IU

Montgomery, Miss K.L. L5,306; L22,367

Montgomery, Mabel IU

Montgomery, Robert IU; UC Manuscripts,16

Moodie, John W.D.
Ten years in South Africa L42,405; L53,120;
L81,135; L117B,11

Moodie, Mrs.Susanna (S.Strickland) L1,114;
L2,38; L82,222 228 237 284 301 328 343 352
371; L83,61 113; L94,260; L95,8 15; L98,
205; L117B,11; IU; UC Manuscripts,42
Flora Lindsay L36,203; L57,299
Life in the clearings L57,237; L84,116
Mark Hurdlestone L36,203; L57,154

The Monctons L36,204
Roughing it in the bush L36,94 202; L57,81-3
World before them L37,380; L38,252

Moody, Mrs. L83,261

Moody, Sophy
What is your name? L36,99; L37,194; L58,
333; L97,266; IU

Moody & Andreae L86,333 344

Mookerjee, C.P. UC

Moon, Bessy IU

Moon, G.Washington IU

Moore L81,163

Moore (Poco Mas pseud.)
Scenes and adventures in Spain L55,251

Moore, Mrs.Alicia L1,91; L82,349-51; L83,
158; L117A,28
Rosalind and Felicia (orig.The Sisters) L82,
351

Moore, Arthur L22,368

Moore, Beatrice IU

Moore, Mrs.Bessie IU

Moore, C.W. IU

Moore, George L5,182

Moore, J.J. & Co. L85,350-1; L86,225 338;
L88,100 153 226; IU

Moore, John L81,63; L93,53

Moore, Mary
Autumn manoeuvres L3,42; L40,412; L41,
503; L63,44-6

Moore, Thomas L80,16; L91,13; IU; UC

Moore & Hayward L81,192

Moorhouse, Miss E.Hallam L22,356

Moorsom, Mrs.Florence IU

Moorsom, William S. L1,190; L2,36; L83,
188 238
Historical record of the Fifty-Second Regiment
L36,278; L37,195; L38,199; L39,424; L58,
199; L85,127
Letters from Nova Scotia L52,54; L68,36

Moran, Edward R. L117A,40; L122,65;
IU(The Globe)

More, Rev.C.A. IU

More, Robert L91,182 198

Morell, J.R. L93,151; IU

Moreton, Hon.Augustus H.M. L91,240; L92,
33 95 185-6 253; L93,51 152-3

Morford, Henry L94,317

Morgan L80,21

Morgan, Augusta IU

Morgan, Sir Charles L53,118

Morgan, E.S. L82,267; L122,25-30

Morgan, Letitia IU

Morgan, Mary IU

Morgan, Richard W. L1,75; L117B,11
The Fortunes of Roger de Flor L6,88; L117A,
21; IU(Johnson,C.)
Raymond de Monthault L57,180

Morgan, Lady Sydney (Sydney Owenson) L1,171;
L83,58 139; L117A,25; IU; UC
Passages from my life L1,134; L36,58; L58,
190
The Princess L53,118; L74,37 181

Morgan, William IU

Moriarty, G.P. L5,223
Morice, Thomas R. IU
Morier, James J. L90,132 230; L91,142;
L117A,8; IU
  Abel Allnutt L6,45; L53,312
  The Adventures of Hajji Baba L53,175; L122,
  58 121
  Ayesha L74,1 37 86 181; L122,75 122
  The Man of honour, and The Reclaimed L53,
  62
  Martin Toutrond L7,166; L8,76 94; L36,204
  The Mirza L54,324-6
  St. Roche L7,165; L8,35; L56,29
  Zohrab the hostage L122,61 122
The Morning Advertiser L82,162
The Morning Chronicle L82,366 369
The Morning Herald L82,366 369
The Morning Post L84,259
Morpeth, Viscount IU
Morran L83,270
Morris, Arthur L54,169; L82,304
Morris, Charles
  Lyra Urbanica L6,22 165; L7,140; L36,205;
  L54,169
Morris, Georgiana K. IU
Morris, Herbert L83,245-6
Morris, Kate IU
Morris, Lily O'Conner IU
Morris, Miss Maria O'C L83,73
Morris, Mowbray W. L5,77-8 99 135; IU
Morris, William O'Connor L2,84; L5,73 77
  123-24 143; L84,183; L87,223; IU
  The Campaign of 1870-1 L37,258; L38,105
  L39,201 233; L40,426
Morrison, Geo.H. L5,161
Morrison, Walter IU
  see Palestine Exploration Fund
Morton, Charles H. IU
Morton, John G. IU
Moscheles, Charlotte IU
Moss, H.W. IU
Mostyn, Sydney
  see Russell, W.C.
Motley IU
Mott, Mrs. L89,74
Mouhot, Marie IU
Moulton, Louise Chandler IU
Mowbray, William T. IU
Moxton, William L91,284
Mozley, Edith IU
Mozley, James Bowling IU
Mozley, John R. L5,217; L22,339; L89,40;
  IU
  A Vision of England L42,332; L67,271
Mudford, William L91,233-5 242; L117B,11
  Stephen Dugard L7,143; L54,271
Mudie, Charles E. L82,82 93 174 329 333 338
  342; L83,100 137 151 165 176 182 205 215 236
  240 245 253 269 271; L84,52 81 106 127; L85,
  4 99 150 231 251-2 311-13 324 416 472; L86,
  102-3; L87,75 194 204 237 255; L88,101 277;
  IU Richard Bentley I,33 46-7; UC
Mudie, Christabel IU

Mudie, Miss Christina L5,109
Mudie, Mary IU
Mudie's Select Library IU;
  see Mudie, C.E.
Mueffling, F.C.F. von
  Passages from my life L57,136
Muegge, Theodor
  Switzerland in 1847 L36,205
Muhammad Ibn'abd Allah
  Solwan L36,98
Muir, W.J.Cockburn
  Pagan or Christian? L36,65; L58,221
Mulford, Prentice L5,81; IU
Mulgrave, Lord
  see Phipps, C.H.
Mulholland, Rosa (Lady Gilbert) L5,41; UC
Mullan L82,74 145; L83,51 84
Mullen, Samuel L85,15 41 192 271 324 419;
  L86,62
Müller, F.Max L83,228; L84,324; IU
Müller, Mathilde IU
Mulley, Miss Jane L5,180; IU
Mulock, Miss (Mrs.Craik)
  Cleomenes L82,302
Mulock, Thomas IU
Munby, Arthur J. L5,245; IU
Munden, T.S.
  Memoirs of Joseph S.Munden L7,153; L91,
  250
Mundt, Clara
  Frederick the Great L36,69
Mundy, Godfrey C. L82,198 255 263; L83,49
  96; L93,150; L117A,7
  Our antipodes L36,36 206; L57,95-7
Mundy, Howard L. L88,187-8(c)
Munnings, Andrew IU
Munnings, James L2,70; L5,21; L102,83-5
Munnings, John IU
Munnings, S. IU
Munro, Edith IU
Munro, Georgina C. L117B,30; IU
  Charles Harcourt L7,150; L55,98
  The Voyage of life L7,155; L55,197
[Munsion & Bordeaux] IU
Munster, Earl of
  see Fitzclarence, G.
Munton & Morris L86,485
Muntz, A.Irving L5,247
Murphy, Sir James Joseph UC
Murray, Dr. IU
Murray, Mrs. L84,86
Murray, Mrs. IU
Murray, A.G. IU
Murray, A.H.Hallam IU
Murray, Alexander L1,115; L117B,23
  Doings in China L55,145
Murray, C.Grenville L5,174
Murray, Mrs.C.L. IU
Murray, Rt.Hon.Sir Charles A. L82,292-3;
  L117B,26; L122,93; IU
  The Great cardinal (prop.) L55,233
  The Prairie-bird L7,153; L55,13 15; L83,
  114; L122,93

Titus Tipcock (prop.) L55,249
Travels in North America L7,140; L36,207; L54,175
Murray, Mrs.Clara G. L57,192
Murray, Mrs.E. L83,250
Murray, Elizabeth A. IU
Murray, Hon.Erskine L83,128
Murray, Eustace C.G.
  Droits et devoirs L36,207; L57,192; L117A, 19
  From Mayfair to Marathon L36,199
  Walter Evelyn L57,192
Murray, Frank L88,227 241 281 283
Murray, Hon.Mrs.Grenville L93,145-6; L117A,37
Murray, Hon.Henry L83,114
Murray, John L53,174 176; L82,48 321; L86, 80 369; L87,78 227(c) 228; L89,122 122(c); L122,58; IU; UC
Murray, John Fisher L91,149 207 298; L92, 11 42-3; L117B,8; IU
  The World of London L55,248
Murray, Hon.Robert D. L1,90; L82,49-50 205; L83,43; L117A,22
  The Cities of Andalucia L7,174; L8,200; L36,206
Murray, T.Douglas IU
Murray, Thomas & Son L61,9; L86,243; IU
Murray, V.M. IU
Murray & Wilson IU
Murray's Magazine IU
Murrell, Captain H. IU
Murthwaite, S.S. IU(Smurthwaite)
Musgrave, George M.
  The Parson, pen, and pencil L7,165; L8,52 95; L56,59; L117A,33
  Reminiscences of Paris [L8,95]
Musgrave, H.
  see Beadon, H.
Musset, Louis C.A. de
  The Poet and the muse L39,362; L40,316; L41,527
Musters, L.C. IU
Myers, Ernest J. L3,48; IU; UC(Bentley-end of B)
  Lord Althorp L41,350 387; L42,274; L64, 277-9
Mylius, Karl M. IU
Myres, M. IU

N., H. L91,148; [IU Unidentified]
Nadal, E.S. IU
Nants, William IU
Napier, Mrs. L5,202
Napier, Alexander IU
Napier, Sir Charles L1,169; L82,123 177 276; L83,147; IU
  The History of the Baltic campaign L1,135 150; L36,51; L58,110
Napier, Sir Charles James· IU
Napier, E. L93,121 131-3; IU

Napier, Mrs.Robina L3,124; L5,127; L85,143 149 181 195 197 233 240 256 374-5; L123,215; IU; IU(Bunser); UC
Napier, Sir William F.P. L90,275; IU
Nares, Edward
  Memoirs of William Cecil L123,236
Nash, Mrs. UC Miscellaneous
Nash, Mrs.Albert IU
Nash, Hon.Mrs.Arthur L5,258
Nash, Augusta IU
Nash, E.Rowland IU
Nash, Edward Henry IU
Nash, Rev.H.H.Ashley L89,79
Nash, J.Hartopp IU
Nash, M.Fleetwood IU
Nash, R. IU
Nash, T.A. L5,145
Nash, Thomas A. IU; UC(Bentley-end of B); UC
  The Life of Richard, Lord Westbury L3,97; L41,320; L42,511; L63,100
Nasir al Din (Shah of Persia)
  A Diary L39,324; L40,462 465; L41,508; L42,506; L123,211-12
Nassau Steam Press L85,274-6(c)
Nast, C.L.R. IU
Natali, Dr.Vincenzo L84,47
Nathusius, Marie L102,18
  Step by step L1,156; L36,80; L38,228
National Bank of Scotland L86,471 472-4(c)
National Review L85,373
National Telephone Company L61,243 279-83; L86,268 339 374 440; L87,278-9; L88,96 110 114 337; L89,116
Nature IU
The Nautical Magazine L88,197 224
Naylor, Mrs. L86,145
Naylor, Elizabeth IU
Neale, Rev.James E.(Haldenby,C.F.pseud) L56,22-6; L82,13 27 37 56 292; L117A,10; IU; IU(Waldenby)
  Experiences of a gaol chaplain L122,90 125
  The Life of Edward, Duke of Kent L6,180; L36,210; L56,194
  The Life-book of a labourer L7,169; L8,119; L36,210; L56,194
Neale, Susanna L94,162 233
Neale, W.J.Nelson IU
Neale, William Johnson IU
  Cavendish L52,238 242 245 279; L69,26; L73A,111
Neave, Sir Digby
  Four days in Connemara L1,131; L7,173; L8,175; L36,211; L57,175; L117B,20
Nebel, Charlotte E.
  The Great day of atonement L36,40-1; L58, 140; L83,136
Needham, J. L81,169
Neill, Miss J.W. IU
Neill, John M.B.
  Recollections of four years service in the East with H.M.Fortieth Regiment L7,159; L55, 270; L117B,19

Nelson, Charles IU
Nelson, Miss F. IU
Nelson, G.F. L87,45-6 61
Nelson, W.F. L5,200 231
Nesbit, E.
 see Bland, Mrs.
Nesbitt, J.J. IU
Nesfield, Henry W. L3,134; IU
 A Chequered career L39,359; L40,466; L41,
 189; L42,182; L60,278
Nesfield, William Eden UC
Ness, Mrs.Bertha L85,131; IU
Netley L86,173(c)
Neumann, Mrs. IU
Neveu, Gabrielle L94,149
Neville, Thomas H.G. L3,114; L4,88;
 IU(Olympic Theatre)
 The Stage L38,355; L39,217 222; L40,308;
 L41,533 542; L42,520
Nevills, Ralph L5,309; IU
New, Francis C.
 The Visiting justices L37,35; L38,243
New South Wales Bookstall Company L86,
 477(c); L88,177 183
New Telephone Co.Ltd. L64,132
New York Commissioners of Fisheries IU
New York Eclectic Library IU
New York Herald L83,60; IU
Newark, Major L5,267
Newby, Mr. L92,220
Newby, Mrs.Emma L1,162; L83,147
 Margaret Hamilton L36,228 231; L58,150
Newcastle Courant L85,86
Newcombe, G.Hubi L5,220
Newcome, W.M. IU
Newcomen, Mr. IU
Newdigate, Mrs.Edward L95,195
Newman, E. IU
Newman, Miss Hilda L5,261
Newman, John IU
Newman, John Henry UC Manuscripts,4
[Newton]
 Levant (prop.) L36,279
Newton, Miss IU
Newton, Mr. IU
Newton, A. & Co. L81,234
Newton, A.L. L54,145-7
Newton, Miss Ada L5,160
Newton, Mrs.Lucy Hay L5,254; L86,497;
 IU(Hayhewton)
Newton, S. L81,209 229
Newton, T.C. L83,205
Newton & Eskell L86,203
Nicholay, Rev. L117A,14
Nicholl, Mrs. L5,227
Nicholl, David L94,198
Nicholl, Edith M. IU
 Observations of a ranch woman (pub.McM.)
 L42,250; L67,304; L89,56
Nicholls, Archibald J. L88,168
Nicholls, J.B. IU
Nicholls & Leatherdale IU
Nicholls, White & Co. L86,334 403; L88,87 246

Nichols UC Manuscripts,26
Nichols, F.M. IU
Nichols, J. IU
Nichols, J.B. UC(Bentley-end of B)
Nichols, John Gough IU
Nichols, T.L. IU
Nichols, W.W. L87,218
Nicholson, Arthur E. IU
Nicholson & Son L83,165
Nicholson, W. & Sons L86,105(c) 105-6; L87,
 247-8(c) 248
Nicolas, Lady L82,301
Nicolas, Sir Nicholas H. L1,24; L7,161; L55,
 343; L117B,32; IU
 A History of the Royal Navy L7,162; L8,
 34-5; L36,212
 Memoirs of Sir Christopher Hatton L7,162;
 L36,212; L55,330
 Memoirs of Sir Sydney Smith (prop.) L55,317
 343
 see Barrow, John
Nicolas, Mrs.Sarah UC
Nicoll, Henry G. IU
Nicoll, W.Robertson IU
Nicolls, Edith IU
Nicols, Arthur L3,56 139; L86,242 296 336
 338 403
 Wild life and adventure L40,98 156; L41,
 184-5 309; L42,330 524; L63,183-4
Niemann, August
 Ephraim L3,92 160; L40,368; IU
Nimmo, J.C. & Bain IU
Nisbet & Co. L67,320; L82,355
Nix, Miss Mary C. L88,153-4
Nixon, J.St.Arnaud L5,209; L86,160
 A Chronicle of two months L41,449; L42,464
Noble, James Ashcroft L5,57
Noel, Major L84,141
Nohl, Dr.Karl F.L. L3,94; L85,2 58; IU
 An Unrequited love (orig.An Episode in the life
 of Beethoven) L3,73; L36,323; L37,205;
 L38,233; L39,199; L59,90-91a
[Nollit, A.] IU(Rollit)
The Nonconformist IU
Nops Electrotype Agency L86,319
Nordan, Max IU
Norgate, G.L. L5,170; L22,355 359; IU
Norman, Charles B.
 The Corsairs of France L63,190
Norman, John
 see Montefiore, J.
Normanby, Marquis of
 see Phipps, C.H.
Norris, Emilia (E.Marryat) UC
Norris, William E. L3,171; L5,147 163; L22,
 353; L31,ii; L67,255-8 320; L85,405 465;
 L86,115 118 188; IU
 A Bachelor's blunder (orig.A Romance of
 English life) L40,78 413; L41,83 125; L42,
 107-8; L62,267-8; L119,54
 Major and minor L41,85 480; L42,108-9
 490; L63,146-9; L119,55
 Miss Shafto L41,82 144 450; L42,109-10;

L63,296-7; L119,57
Mr.Chain's sons (orig.The three brothers)
L41,428; L42,491; L64,174; L119,58
The Rogue L41,82 94 471; L42,111; L63,
143-5; L119,56
Thirlby Hall L40,78 389; L41,84 535; L42,
112 496; L62,112-14; L119,53
Norrish, George R. IU
North, Captain L5,183
North, Christopher
see Wilson, John
North British Colour Works IU
The North Star, Darlington IU
North Western Educational Company L86,307
Northcote, J.Spencer IU
Northcote, James
Life of Titian L1,57; L52,102; L68,51
Memoirs (prop.) L54,22
Northcote, John L85,217
Northern Assurance Company L87,244-5; L88,
300 307 321; L89,47 123
Norton, Mrs.(Henry M.Giveen pseud.) L22,367
Norton, Mrs.Caroline E.S. L1,39; L82,120-3;
IU; IU Henry Colburn,1+3
The Undying one L68,48
Norton, G.C. IU
Norton, Theodore IU
Norway, Arthur H. IU
The Government official
see Riddell, C.E.L.
Norwich, Bishop of
see Pelham, J.T.
Norwich Union Insurance Company
IU Richard Bentley II,7-8
Nostitz, Mathilde P.
Travels of Doctor and Madame Helfer L3,110;
L39,282; L40,434; L60,67-8
Notes & Queries IU
Notley, Mrs. L2,71
Notley, Mrs.Frances E.M. L3,113 116 118;
L4,52; L85,86 104; L100,67; IU
Cordelia L39,291; L60,134; L123,182-3
Love's crosses L39,290; L60,100-1; L61,
102
Olive Varcoe L39,319; L40,83-4; L41,86;
L42,113; L60,149; L123,197-8
Red Riding Hood (pub.Hurst & Blackett) L40,
453
Nott, Miss L87,129
Nottage, Hawkes IU
Notter & Clarke L87,144
Novello, Ewer & Co. L65,142 174-6; L86,435
486 488; IU
Nowlan, Frank IU
Noyes, Snow & Co. IU
Nugent, Edmund C.
Anderleigh Hall L36,323; L37,21; L38,80;
L39,448
Nugent, G. IU
Nunns, Miss Theodora L5,308

Oades, Mrs. L84,90
O'Brien, Miss Alice L5,279; L88,182
Anthony Blake's experiment L4,79; L42,419;
L67,139-41
O'Brien, Augustin P. IU
Petersburg and Warsaw L36,133; L37,210;
L38,205
O'Brien, Sir George L4,79; L88,185
O'Brien, J.T.M. IU
O'Brien, John IU
O'Brien, Sir Patrick L57,310
Journal of a residence in the Danubian
principalities L36,216; L57,291
The Observer, London IU
O'Byrne, Mr. IU
O'Callaghan, Desmond L5,269
O'Connell, Mrs. L5,168
O'Connell, Catherine M.
Excursions in Ireland L7,173; L8,174; L36,
215; [L57,126]; L82,145
O'Connell, John
Recollections and experiences L6,180; L36,
214; L56,135; L117A,32
O'Connell, P.G. L5,263
O'Connell, T.F. & Son L67,27; L89,64
[O'Connor, C.P.] IU
Odgers, Miss L5,173
O'Donel, Charles L82,303
O'Donnell, B.L. IU(Donnell)
O'Donoghue, D.J. IU(O'Douglas)
[O'Driscoll, W.J.] IU
Ogden, J. & Co. L60,104; L85,61; L86,120
158; IU
Ogilvie, Sir Andrew M.J. UC
Ogilvie, G.Stuart L85,142
Ogle, Elizabeth IU
Ogle, John W. IU
Ogle, Wilfrid IU
O'Halloran, G.B. L5,260; IU
Old Calabar
see Vismes, Prince de
Oldershaw, Rosa J. IU
Oldfield, F.H. IU
Oldfield, R.A.K.
Narrative of an expedition
see Laird, M.
Oldham, Miss A. L5,222
Oliphant, [Charles] W. IU
Oliphant, F.R. IU
Oliphant, H.Ellen IU
Oliphant, Mrs.M.
see Wilson, M.O.
Oliver, Captain IU Richard Bentley II,539
Oliver, J.B. L5,173; IU
Oliver, Samuel P. IU; UC
Oliver & Boyd L57,68; L82,180; L83,240;
L85,64 67 76; L87,210; L88,232 284; L89,
46 123
Olley, Charles W. L86,302; L87,109
Ollier, Charles L5,205; L6,102 143; L117B,7;
IU
Ollier, Edmund L5,108; IU; UC
Ollier, Emily IU

Ollier, James   L90,67 292; L117A,16
Ollivant, Charles   L86,145
Olmsted   L83,117
Oltan, G.R.   L83,266
Olwen, Prof.   L83,224
O'Mahony, John   L87,148
O'Meara, Barry E.
Napoleon at St.Helena   L41,320 344 358; L42,
290 292; L119,161; IU
O'Meara, J.B.   L90,136; L91,243-4 263-4
O'Meara, J.M.   IU
O'Meara, Miss Kathleen (Grace Ramsay pseud.)
L3,63; L86,167 169; L101,160; IU
Madame Mohl   L40,184
Narka   L41,471; L63,263
The Old house in Picardy   L40,457; L41,486;
L63,109
A Salon in the last days of the Empire   L38,
297; L39,221; L40,454; L101,60
O'Neil, John   L5,225
O'Neil, Maurice   L5,285
[Onsley, G.]   IU
Onslow, C.J.   IU
Opie, A.   IU
Oppenheim, E.Phillips   L3,14; L88,86 151 334
The Mystery of Mr.Bernard Brown   L42,426;
L67,14-16
Oppert, E.   L87,112(c)
Ordish, T.Fairman   L86,345; L87,155
O'Reilly, Andrew
Reminiscences of an emigrant Milesian   L36,
215; L117A,37
O'Reilly, Arthur   L82,195 197 232
O'Reilly, Charles W.   L1,77; L56,146
Oriental Translation Fund   L6,25 67; L80,9;
L81,111 113 131; L90,43 54 71 76 270; L117B,
45
Orlebar, Frederica S.
The Adventures of the moon-faced princess
L41,464; L42,477 488; L63,325
Ormathwaite, Lord
see Walsh, J.B.
Ormerod, Eleanor A.   IU
Orr, Mrs.   L5,76
Orr, A.   IU
Orr, John   UC
Orr, Margaret   IU
Orr & Co.   L117B,12
Orsay, Alfred G. d'   L82,136; IU
Orsay, Harriet F. d'   IU
Ortmann, Emmy   UC
Osborn, D.H.   IU
Osborn, Laughton   L83,44
Osborn, Montagu   IU
Osborne, Catherine J.   IU
Osborne, N.   IU
Osborne, Lord Sidney G.   L26,55; IU
Osborne, Lord William G.   IU
Osbourne, Charles   L2,71
Oscar II (King of Sweden and Norway)
Charles XII   L38,354; L39,214 311; L40,231;
L41,507-8; L42,502; L123,195-6
Osgood & Co.   L87,153 155 268; L88,174; IU

O'Shaughessy, Major   L93,142
Osman, W.   L92,13
Ossington, Viscountess   IU
Ossoli, Sarah M.(Marchioness)
see Fuller, S.M.
O'Sullivan, John L.
Union, disunion and reunion   L2,48; L36,162;
L37,242; L38,231
Otten, T.A.   L84,158 168
Ottley, Edward B.   IU
Otway, Rt.Hon.Sir Arthur   L87,153
Ouida
see Ramé, de la
Our Continent Publishing Company   L61,216
[Ouseley, G.]   IU(Onsley)
Ouseley, Sir William   L1,52; L52,4 29 31;
L68,14 28-9
Outram, Leonard   UC
Ouvry, Peter T.   IU
The Overland Mail   UC
Overton, E.
see Edersheim, E.
Owen, East   L5,300
Owen, Ellen M.   IU
Owen, Mrs.J.A.   L87,261
Owen, William F.
Narrative of voyages   L52,329
Owenson, Miss Sydney
see Morgan, Lady S.
Owgan, Dr.   L2,52
Oxenden, Miss Maud   L5,35
Oxenford, John   L5,45; L92,4-5; IU
Oxford, Bishop of
see Wilberforce, S.
Oxford & Cambridge Review   IU
Oxford University Press   IU
Ozanne, Mrs.   IU
Ozanne, James W.   L5,83; IU

P., W.   IU Unidentified(X.,A.M.)
[Packham, John]   IU
Paetel   L86,143-4; IU(Deutsche Rundschall)
Page, Mrs.   L95,124
Page, Mary Alice   IU
Page, William   IU
Paget, John C.   L5,270; L117B,3; IU
Paget, Miss M.Maud   L5,295
Paget, Mary M.   IU
Pain, Albert E.   L5,287
Pakington, John S.(1st Baron Hampton)
IU(Hampton)
Palestine Exploration Fund   L2,80; L3,33; L59,
225; L61,131-2; L85,40; L123,216-17; IU
see Besant, W.; P.E.F.Quarterly Statement
Palfrey, Dr.   L83,174
Pall Mall Gazette   L86,94 389; IU; IU George
Bentley,188; IU(Morley)
Pallen, Dr.Montrose A.   L86,175
Palliser, Fanny   L95,194; IU
Palmé   L85,66
[Palme, A.H.]   IU

Palmer L84,169
Palmer, C. IU
Palmer, E.H. L5,173; IU
Jerusalem
see Besant, W.
Palmer, Francis L83,226
Palmer, Francis Paul L92,120
Palmer, H.P. L5,299
Palmer, H.Vaughan IU
Palmer, J. L94,121 163 168 178 301 303
Palmer, John McAuley UC
Palmer, M.A. IU
Palmerston, Henry J.
see Temple, H.J.
[Panizzi, A.] IU
Papendiek, Charlotte L.H.
Court and private life in the time of Queen
Charlotte L40,93; L41,200; L63,194; L86,
105
Papillon, C.G. IU
Papin, M. L66,309; IU
Pardoe, Miss Julia S.H. L83,91; L117B,33;
IU
The Court and reign of Francis the First L36,
217; L40,90; L41,273 285; L42,180 183;
L56,172; L63,170-1
The Life of Marie de Medicis L41,356; L42,
266; L64,314
Louis the Fourteenth L36,217; L40,115; L41,
274 374; L42,270-1; L55,308
The Rival beauties L55,308
Pardon, Charles F. L86,54
Paris, Dr.John A. L90,6-7 11 32
Life of Sir Humphry Davy L53,242-4; L68,66;
L77,1-20; L80,4
Philosophy in sport L52,166; L68,74
Parker, Hon.Augusta
see Bethell, A.
Parker, E.H. L5,247
Parker, Eric L5,286
Parker, F.Hardyman L5,181
Parker, George IU
Parker, J.W. & Son IU
Parker, Joseph IU
Parker, Kenyon C.S. L85,430
Parker, Louis N. IU
Parkins & Gotte L86,431
Parkinson, C. L22,354
Parkinson, J.C. L2,63; L63,181; L86,124
363; IU; UC Manuscripts,10
Parkman, Francis
History of the conspiracy of Pontiac L36,218;
L57,19; L82,143 152 154
Parnell, Rev.Frank L85,41
Parnell, Reginald L5,59
Parr, George L60,154 223 310; IU
Parr, Harriet IU
Parr, Mrs.Louisa L3,120; L5,121 135-6;
L40,158; L85,260; L86,80 151 161; L87,206;
IU; UC
Adam and Eve L39,313 364; L40,86-7 420;
L41,87; L42,114; L60,154-7 285
Dorothy Fox L39,341 418; L40,88; L41,88;

L42,115; L60,223
Loyalty George L41,474; L42,489; L63,
247-9
Robin L39,389; L40,353; L60,310
The Squire (pub.Cassell) L41,472
Parry, Griffett IU
Parry, T. L82,49
Parry, W. L64,289-90
Parry & Co. L82,128 238
Parsons, Florence Mary W. L5,292; IU
Partoris, F. IU
Partridge, Mrs. L123,1-12
Partridge, S.W. L91,185
Partridge & Co. L83,98; IU
Pascoe, Charles E. L85,257; L94,141; IU
Pascoe, James
The Brigantine L36,106; L37,39; L58,305
Passow, Athenaea L85,29; L86,141; IU
Paston, George
see Symonds, E.M.
Patent Lever Watch Manufactory L92,298
Paterson, Arthur H. L3,115; L5,246; L87,154
The Daughter of the Nez Perces L42,441;
L66,77-82
Paterson, Augusta IU
Paterson, William IU
Patmore, Georgiana IU; UC
Patmore, K.A. L5,305
Patmore, P.G. L93,14; IU
Paton, Andrew A. L82,112; L117A,12
The Goth and the Hun L36,218; L56,329
The Mamelukes L7,171; L8,150; L56,323
Paton, F.Noel L5,56
Paton, Walter B. L5,197
Patterson, Miss L5,76
Pattinson, H.S. L5,217
Pattisson, Mrs.Pierre L5,295
Paul, Benjamin H. L57,76; L117B,36
Paul, Sir John IU
Pauli, George R.
The Life of King Alfred L7,172; L8,174; L57,
93
Paulin L82,93 154 157 189 194 207; L117A,2
Pawsey & Hayes L87,199
Payn, James L2,1; L3,45; L5,81; L71,273;
L85,43; L95,99; L100,249; IU
At her mercy L38,309; L39,437
The Best of husbands L38,323; L39,399 432;
L40,467; L41,505
A Woman's vengeance L38,266; L39,437;
L59,268; L100,138 140
Payne, Geo.P. L90,312; L91,17 65 113-15
Payne, John L2,72; L5,19
Payton, Charles A. L95,205 230
Peach, Robert E.M. L36,273; L37,197; IU;
UC
Peachey, Miss C. L92,214 227-8; L117A,38
Peachey, James P. L56,166; L83,95
Peacock, Bligh UC
Peacock, Eleanor IU
Peacock, F.M. IU(Peacock,E.)
Peacock, Florence L5,211
Peacock, Thomas L. L117A,30; L122,60;

L123,215 222-3; IU
The Works of Thomas L.Peacock L38,316;
L39,184-5; L40,314 450; L41,301 374; L42,
301; L60,162; L84,286
Peacock, W.E. IU
Peacock & Goddard L61,22-75 passim; L85,
439-40 449 451-2 464
Peacocke, Gerald L. L5,88; IU
Peake, Charles
The Saucy Jack and The Indiaman L53,337;
L117B,10
Peake, Richard B. L81,240; L91,106 110
126-7 129; L92,78; L117B,29; IU
Peara, Henry IU
Pearce, James L5,111
Pearce, Nathaniel
Life and adventures L52,133; L68,62
Pearce, Robert R. L92,79-80; L117B,15; IU
A History of the Inns of Court L7,165; L8,
35; L36,217; L56,6
Memoirs of Wellesley L6,165; L7,160; L36,
84; L55,301; L82,323
Peard, Frances M. L3,161; L4,70 140 153;
L85,368 392 471; L86,80 252 416 423; L87,
190 193; L88,229 231 244 267 354; L89,58 64;
IU; UC
Alicia Tennant L40,417; L41,503; L63,55
The Baroness L41,419; L65,100
The Career of Claudia L42,418; L67,179-83
Contradictions L40,380; L61,308-12
The Country cousin L41,456; L42,480
His cousin Betty L41,475; L42,485; L63,267
An Interloper (orig.A French story) L42,439
444; L66,52
Near neighbours (orig.The Town councillor's
family) L40,98 404; L41,90 524; L42,115-16;
L62,279; L63,25
Paul's sister L41,458; L63,333
The Swing of the pendulum L42,445; L66,54
Peard, George S. L1,140; L83,71
Narrative of a campaign in the Crimea L36,
49
Pears, E. L5,24
Pears, H.V. IU
Pearse, Hugh Wodehouse L88,212; IU; UC
Pearson, Miss L5,37
Pearson, Cyril Arthur L65,201-3; L86,469
478 487; IU(Pearson's Weekly)
Pearson, Emma M. L2,87; L3,35; L84,210-14
216 224 226-7 293; IU; IU(MacLaughlin)
Our adventures during the war L37,258; L38,
83; L39,403 453; L40,420
Pearson, George L85,278 401; L86,133(c) 170
316 469; IU
Pearson, Hugh IU
Pease, Joseph Whitwell UC
Peat, John IU
Pebody, Charles L5,81; IU
Peebles & Son L85,204 304
Peel, Jonathan
The Peels L39,249; L85,30; IU
Pégot Ogier, Eugène L2,89; L3,52; L84,147;
IU

The Fortunate Isles L2,77 81; L37,113;
L38,131; L39,428; L40,431; L59,213
Pelham, Cressett Thursby IU
Pelham, John T.(Bishop of Norwich)
UC(Norwich)
Pellew, E.F. L5,212
Pellico, Silvio
Life of the Marchesa Giulia Falletti Di Barolo
L37,125
Pelly, Sir John H. L55,177 179
Pemberton, Mrs. L83,274
Pemberton, Harriet Childe L5,126; IU(Childe)
Pemberton, Helen L94,158
Pemberton, Thomas E. L3,155; L4,79; L86,
261 314 390 442; IU
The Life of T.W.Robertson L41,375; L42,
267; L65,238-42 301-2
A Memoir of Edward A.Sothern L41,342 353;
L42,278 281; L64,134
Pembroke, Earl of
see Herbert, G.R.C.
Pembroke, Lady G.F. L4,78; L88,207 211
226; IU
Penn, Mary E.Stanley L5,98; IU
Pennefather, F.W. IU
Pennell, Henry C. L5,71 180; IU
Pennington, Canon IU
Penny, Richard L5,288; IU
Penrose, Mrs.H.H. L5,263
Penrose, M. IU
Pentland, Joring J. L89,107 111 115
Pepe, Guglielmo
Memoirs L55,337; IU
Pepper, Prof. L88,87(c)
Pepys, Lady Charlotte M.
Lady Avice L36,182; L56,335; L82,150
Pepys, Maria IU
Pepys, Philip H. L1,92; L93,162; L117A,26
Constance Tyrrell L57,145
Pepys, Samuel
The Life, journals and correspondence L6,173;
L53,274 307
Memoirs L7,142
Pepys, Walter L5,215
Perceval, Beatrice IU
Perceval, Cecil H. IU
Perceval, E.A. IU
Perceval, Emma C. IU
Perceval, Spencer George IU
Percy, Miss A.B.Isabel L1,91; L57,165; L82,
113 116 230 247 250; L93,127 161; L117B,41
Percy, Algernon Heber L88,181; IU
Percy, Hon.Charles B. L56,29 246; L82,71;
L117B,41
Pereira, Mme.Louise L5,131; L88,238
Perkins, A. IU
Perks, Mrs.Hartley L5,52
Perks, Lily IU
Gift and weirds L42,424; L67,56-8; L88,107
Perowne, Connop F.S. L5,43
Perowne, Rev.John J.S.(Dean of Peterborough)
L3,148; L60,216-18; L85,166 208 280 287
290-2; IU

Perrin & Co. L66,34-7; L87,112 114 122 206;
L88,278 283 285
Perrotin L82,361
Perry, James H. L85,128; IU
Magneopathy L36,212; L38,212
Peterborough, Dean of
see Perowne, J.J.S.
Peters, F.H. L86,115 146; IU
Petherick, Edward A. L71,213; L85,115 200
203 220 258 260 475; L86,122 281 338 409 412
454-5; L87,48 81-2 84 89 115 203 225 233-4
238 241 268 280; UC; UC Manuscripts,11
Petit du Noyer, Anne M.
The Correspondence L41,349; L42,505; L64,
209-10
Pettigrew, Thomas J.
Life of Lord Nelson L40,309
Peyronnet, Viscountess F. de IU(De Peyronnet)
Pfitzer, Wilhelm UC
Phelps, Miss Emma Maude L5,203
Phelps, Sidgwick & Biddle IU
Philip & Andrew L83,247
Philip, Son & Nephew L86,188 190
Philips, Francis C. IU
Phillimore, Mrs. L22,359
Phillimore, Miss C.B. IU
Phillimore, Miss Elinor L5,238; L87,173
Phillimore, Rt.Hon.Sir Robert J. L1,133;
L56,248; L117A,2; IU
Phillipps, Sir Thomas IU; UC Manuscripts,29
Phillipps Wolley
see Wolley
Phillips, Mrs.Augustus L94,238 242 249
Phillips, Charles
Napoleon the Third L36,224-5; L37,219
Phillips, Emma Watts L5,216
Phillips, Miss F. L88,295
Phillips, Mrs.Frances L52,260 263a
Phillips, Georgiana L94,182
Phillips, H. IU
Phillips, Janet IU
Phillips, John South L5,204
Phillips, Montagu L.
Worlds beyond the earth L1,93; L58,22;
L117B,27
Phillips, S. L5,45
Phillips, Samuel IU
Phillips, T. IU
Phillips, Sampson & Co. L1;115; L82,179-80
198 300; L117B,32
Philpott, C. IU
Phipps, Beatrice H. IU
Phipps, Constantine H.(Lord Mulgrave)
The Contrast L52,266; IU(Normanby)
Phipps, Constantine O. IU
Phipps, Hon.Edmund L56,86; L82,31
Phipps, G.D. IU
Phipps, Pownoll R. IU
Phipps, Rev.Pownoll William L3,147; L5,210;
L85,10; L87,202 240; L88,193; IU
Chalfont St.Giles L42,372; L67,110
The Life of Colonel Pownoll Phipps L42,345
Phipps, Ramsay W. L5,206 304; L86,282 392;

L88,333; L117B,36; IU; IU George Bentley,
180+7 181+1 181+2
The Lives of the marshals of the First
Napoleon (pub.McM.) L42,361; L65,39
Phipps, Richard UC
Phipson, Dr.Thomas L. L2,77; L3,86; L84,
169-70; IU
Biographical sketches L38,136; L39,254;
L40,195-6; L41,177; L42,401; L60,10
The Storm and its portents L39,292; L60,107
Pichot, Joseph J.M.C.A.
The Life and labours of Sir Charles Bell L1,
134; L36,67 132
Pick-me-up L86,374
Picken, Andrew
The Black Watch L53,41 43
Picken, John C. L53,41 43; L117A,20
Pickering, Miss Ellen L81,197 201 213; L90,
44 97 178; L91,18; L117A,23; IU
Agnes Serle L53,101
The Heiress L52,304
The Merchant's daughter L53,235
The Prince and the pedlar L54,98
The Squire L54,24
Pickering, Sidney L5,231
Pickering, T. IU
Pickersgill, John IU
Pickersgill, R. IU
Pickford, John IU; UC
Pickthall, M.W. L5,63
The Pictorial World IU
The Picture Magazine IU
Piddington, Miss Rose M. L1,185; L2,50;
L86,193(c) 194 195(c) 195; IU
The Last of the Cavaliers L36,71 119 129;
L37,61 67 112; L38,45; L39,25; L40,54;
L41,107-8; L42,8; L58,191; L119,78
Piesse & Son L86,405-6; L88,177; IU
Piggot, John IU
Pigon, Francis IU
Pigot, E.E. L94,185
Pigott, Harriett
The Private correspondence of a woman of
fashion L52,288; L53,109
Pigott, Mary IU
Pigott-Carleton, Mrs.Henrietta (Lady
Dorchester) L5,175; IU; UC
Pile, William L88,270
Pilkington, H. L81,57
Pillersdorff, Franz X. von
Austria in 1848 and 1849 L6,180; L7,170
Pim, Bedford T. IU
Pinhorn, C.A. IU
Pinker, James B. IU
Pinkerton, John
Literary correspondence L1,64; L52,21;
L68,23
Pinkerton, Thomas A. L3,121; L85,123; IU
Crossford L39,310; L60,138; L123,190-1
Pinkney, Francis L53,38; L117A,5
Pinto, Leite & Co. L85,40
Piper, Count IU
Piper, F.H.C. IU

Piper, William L77,21-2
Piper & Co. L82,341; L83,54 99
Pisani, Countess Marianna (Mrs.Col.Garner)
L1,116; L69,154; L81,133 143 150 201-2;
L83,35 124; L90,65-6; L117A,28; IU
The Convent and the harem L7,172; L8,150;
[L57,50]
Vandeleur L53,277; L81,143 150 201
Pitchford, Rev.W.M.Watkins L5,269
Pitman, Coulson B. L5,203; L63,212-14;
L86,167 191-2 208; IU
Planche, J.K. L84,177
Planché, James R. IU
Planché, Matilda A.(Mrs.Mackarness) L2,81;
L3,38; L84,195 228; [L99,238];
IU(Mackarness)
A Mingled yarn L38,266; L39,443
A Peerless wife L37,222; L38,209; L39,
443; L59,241
Plarr, Victor L5,224
Platnauer L86,84
Plato
Selections L36,290 294; L37,79; L38,112;
L58,279
Platt, William L83,122
Plautus, Titus M.
The Captives L3,173; L39,201 208; L40,
230; L41,209
The Haunted house L37,211; L38,148; L39,
210 213; L40,258; L41,253; L42,227
Plenge, Rev.Johan L5,34; L100,118; IU
Plesner L5,70
Plesner, Augusta L2,74; L84,164; IU
Plomer, Mrs. L1,116
Plomer, Mrs.Anne H.
Kate Devereux L56,301; L117B,16
Plon, E. & Co. L60,279-81; L63,59 202 327;
L64,307; L65,127; L84,225; L85,78 107 118
128-9 132-6 148 164 206 231 237 239 241 249
253(c) 253 255; L87,61 89; IU; IU George
Bentley,180+4; UC
Plon, Eugène
Thorvaldsen L3,52; L38,286; L39,226; L40,
457; L41,388 520; L42,261
Plumley, Miss L2,82
Plumley, Miss L5,40
Plumley, Miss M.F.A. L2,87; L3,48; L84,
214; IU
Plumptre, Mr. L81,164
Plumptre, C.C.M. L22,364
Plunkett, Arthur H. L54,213-21; L91,61
Plunkett, Oliver L2,63
Poco Mas
see Moore
Polack, Joel S.
New Zealand L6,44; L54,89; L117B,4
Polehampton, Rev.Arthur L2,39; L3,90; L94,
79
Kangaroo Land L36,100-1; L37,218; L38,
211; L58,285
Polehampton, Rev.Edward L1,165; L58,188;
L83,187
Polehampton, Rev.Henry S.

Memoir, letters and diary L1,165; L36,61-2;
L37,218; L38,211; L58,188
Polehampton, Rev.Thomas S. L1,165; L2,39
Poles, Stefan L5,77; IU
Police Superintendent L89,100
[Pollak, Robert] IU
Pollard, Mrs.A.D.(John Pomeroy pseud) L2,48;
L83,261; L94,218 227; L97,107 135 176; L98,
59
Opposite neighbours L36,252; L37,211; L97,
234 238
Raising the veil L36,219; L37,226; L38,216;
L58,292
Pollard, A.O. IU
Pollard & Co. L85,148
Pollock, Emma Jane IU; UC(end of P)
Pollock, Guy C. IU
Pollock, Hugh IU
Pollock, Lady Juliet L5,82 113 131; L85,20
27; IU; UC(end of P)
The Story of Marie Dumont L40,351; L61,
154 191
Pollock, Walter H. L3,81; L4,53; L5,47 113
122; L62,36; L86,162; IU; UC(end of P)
A New book of sports (ed.; orig.The Games of
the world) L40,244; L41,290; L42,289; L62,
290-1
Polwarth, Lady Harriet IU
Pomar, Duke de
see Medina
Pomeroy, John
see Pollard, A.D.
Ponsonby, Rt.Hon.Sir Henry L86,423 424(c)
Pontifex, Hewitt & Pitt L86,394
Poole, John L53,127; L54,322; L81,116;
L117B,45; IU
Oddities of London life L54,67 73
Poole, Stanley L. L5,58; IU
Poole, Rev.Thomas E.
Life in Sierra Leone and the Gambia L1,117;
L7,170; L8,120; L117B,26
Poole, W.T. IU
Poorten-Schwartz, A. van der IU(Schwartz)
Poorten-Schwartz, Ada van der IU(Ada);
IU(Schwartz)
Poorten-Schwartz, J.M.W. van der L3,60 98;
L4,53a; L5,236 275; L22,353; L65,91; L86,
368 410 412 447 450; L87,91 94 170-1 174(c)
174; L88,62 63-4(c); L89,56; IU George
Bentley,250-86 passim 300+1 356+1 391+ 416+1;
IU(Schwartz); UC(Schwartz)
God's fool L41,144 421; L42,96 112 475;
L65,90; L119,60; UC Manuscripts,12
The Greater glory L41,405; L42,97 459;
L65,220-3 315-19; L119,159
Her memory (pub.McM.) L67,278
My lady nobody L42,95; L66,294; L119,146
An old maid's love L41,78 433; L42,98 493;
L65,3; L119,59
The Sin of Joost Avelingh L41,89 424; L42,
99 496; L65,160; L119,61
Pope, Henry E. L1,183
The Corsair and his conqueror L36,67

Popham, C.V. IU
Popham, H. IU
Popham, Radford & Co. L88,188
Porchester, Lord
 see Herbert, H.J.G.
Porsell, Frederick Y. IU
Portens & Co. L87,105
Porter, Miss E.J. L85,317 337
Porter, Mrs.Gerald L5,152
Porter, Jane L52,256; L68,91; L81,49 60;
 IU; UC Manuscripts,17
 The Scottish chiefs L91,144
Porter, John A. L5,253
Porter & Coates IU
Portman, Miss S.Blanche L5,72; IU
Post Office
 see Great Britain
Postans, Mrs. IU
Postans, M.
 see Young, Marianne
Postans, Mrs.P. L81,235
Postans, Robert R. L92,118; L93,148 171;
 L117A,19; IU; UC
Pott, James L85,324
Potter, Sandford & Kilvington L86,362; IU
Potters, J. IU
Poulet, Malassis & Co. L83,191 193
Pound, W. L84,58
Powell IU
Powell, George E.J. L2,27; L3,23; L84,
 94-7
Powell, George H. L5,162; L87,241(c) 241
 243(c) 243; L88,332; IU
Powell, H.Y. L85,54; IU; UC
Powell, Mrs.Myddleton L94,122 133
Powell, S.W. L5,302
Powell, Thomas (George Clark pseud.)
 Florentine tales L6,103; L117A,25
 Tales from Boccaccio L1,99; L6,97; L69,
 114
Powell, W. IU
Power, Ellen IU
Power, Frederick L57,210
Power, Harriet L94,209
Power, Miss Marguerite A. L82,53
Power, Victor O'Donovan UC
Power, William G.T. UC
 Impressions of America L53,178; L117B,12
Power, Sir William J.T. L1,77; L82,293;
 L117B,4
 Recollections of a three years residence in
 China L57,210
Powis, Earl of
 see Herbert, E.J.
Powles, J.Fleetwood IU
Pownall, Miss D.Beaty L5,263
Powys, Miss Norah L5,53; L88,250 315(c);
 IU
 In a country town L42,417; [L67,193]
Poynter, Miss E.Frances L3,50; L5,125;
 L86,282 289 331
 The Failure of Elizabeth L41,443; L64,
 169-71

Poynter, Miss H.M. L5,45
Poyntz, Albany
 A World of wonders L55,190
Poyntz, Isabella H.(Lady Cork) IU(Cork)
Poz (pseud.) IU
Praed, Campbell L85,234; IU
Praed, Mrs.Rosa C.M. L3,136; L5,138; L85,
 412 414; L86,45 196; IU; UC
 Affinities L40,405; L41,504; L62,292-3 325
 The Ladies' gallery (orig.Binbian Jo) L41,
 463; L63,304
 Miss Jacobsen's chance L40,467; L41,489;
 L63,115
 Policy and passion (orig.Longleat of Kooralbyn)
 L39,360 377; L40,97 450; L41,91 188-9; L42,
 468; L60,286
 The Rebel Rose L41,469; L42,494; L63,306
Praet, Jules van
 Essays on the political history L2,73; L37,
 222 264; L38,244; IU(Van Traetz)
Prager, Mme. L86,128
Pratt, E.J. L86,308
Pratt, Henry IU
Pray, Isaac C. L91,282; L117B,9
Prélat, T. IU
Prendergast, Dr. L5,56
Prendergast, Francis L60,190; L123,215; IU
Prendergast, Thomas
 The Mastery of language L2,33; L36,167;
 L37,217; L38,211
Prescott, William H. L1,118; L36,46 89; L82,
 18 69 124 134 144 166 191 210 244 297 308;
 L83,38 47 50-3 55 61 64 74 79 85 114-15 118
 120 125 171; L91,56; L93,257; L117B,28; IU
 Biographical and critical miscellanies L7,159;
 L36,18 23; L37,220; L55,254
 History of the conquest of Mexico L7,152 156;
 L8,35; L36,15 17 20; L55,186; L56,235 240
 History of the conquest of Peru L7,163; L8,
 34-5; L36,16 18 20; L56,14-16
 History of the reign of Ferdinand and Isabella
 L7,148 160 170; L8,120; L36,15 17 19; L54,
 7; L55,46; L56,235-8
 History of the reign of Philip the Second L36,
 16 19 21 47; L57,320-7; L58,26-7 37-8; L68,
 98
Press Cutting Agency L86,313-14
Preston, T.R.
 Three years in Canada L54,278; L117B,5
Pretyman, I. IU
Prevost, Miss C.M. L5,207
Prevost, F.
 see Battersby, W.H.
Price, Miss Ada M. L5,284
Price, Miss Eleanor C. L3,47; L5,238; L86,
 116 229 359 368; L87,57; L89,90; IU
 Alexia L40,441; L41,496; L42,477; L63,156
 The Little one L41,434; L42,490; L64,341-6
 Miss Latimer of Bryans L41,408; L42,460;
 L65,249
 Off the highroad (pub.McM.) L42,504; L67,
 300
 Red Towers L41,461; L42,494; L64,88

Price, Florence A.(Mrs.F.A.James; Florence
  Warden pseud.) L3,186; L5,234; L63,186;
  L85,475; L86,338 390 400-1 428; L89,103(c);
  IU(James,F.); IU(Warden)
  A Dog with a bad name (orig.The Iron hand)
  L40,405; L62,287-8
  Ralph Ryder of Brent L41,417; L42,475;
  L65,125
  Those Westerton girls L14,300; L41,426;
  L42,473; L65,24-6 65
  The White witch L3,122; L40,399; L41,539
  A Witch of the hills L41,462; L64,62
Price, J. L90,315
Price, S.Lowell IU
Price Bros. & Co. L86,198 253
Prichard, Iltudus T. L2,57
  How to manage it L36,184; L37,141; L38,
  148; L59,32; L98,79
Prideaux, Miss S.T. L5,190
Prideaux, William Francis IU; UC
Prideaux, X. IU
Priestley, R.M. L85,144 308; L86,340 347
Primrose, Archibald P.(Earl of Rosebery)
  IU(Rosebery)
Pringle, Mrs. L5,97; IU
Pringle, Rev.A.D. IU
Printers' Pension Corporation IU; UC(Miller)
Printing & Allied Trades' Association IU
Prior, James
  Life of Goldsmith (prop.) L53,122; L122,58;
  [IU Unidentified,(A)] ; UC
Prior, Katharine F. L55,27
Pritchard, Henry Baden IU
Pritchard, Rev.R. L83,36
The Prize-Winner L85,403
Probyn, Ericson L5,253
Probyn, J.W. IU(Prabyn)
Procter, Mrs.A.
  see Wood, Annie
Procter, Bryan W. IU
Procter, Richard A.(Barry Cornwall pseud.)
  L5,26; IU
Procter, Miss Zoe L5,309
Proctor, Mrs.A.B. L5,185
Proctor, Fred. UC
Proctor, Richard A. L2,72 80
Proctor, Samuel L122,11
Professional & Mercantile Institute IU
Prothero, Rowland E. IU(Ernle)
Protheroe L81,185
Prouting, Frederick J. UC
Provincial Welsh Insurance Company L83,233
Pryce, Miss Daisy Hugh L5,147; L88,168; IU
  Goddesses three L42,421; L67,112
Pryce, Miss Margaret F. L5,150
Pryce, Richard L5,223
Public Opinion L85,87; L86,89; L89,96
The Publishers' Association L67,291-3; L89,
  122; L123,116; UC(Poulton); UC Manuscripts,
  11
Publishers' Circular IU
Publishing & Printing Stock Company, Hamburg
  (formerly J.F.Richter) L64,309

Puddicombe, Edward L96,13-16
Puddicombe, Miss Julia L84,192; L95,127 133
  208 224 226 233 243 246
Puliga, Comtesse de L5,289
Pulitzer, Albert IU
Purcell, Edmund S. IU
Purchas, John IU
Purchas, Major R.E. L5,169
Purkess & Co. L86,112
Purkis, E.L. L5,108
Puseley, D. IU
[Puthingham & Co.] L81,208
Putnam, G.P. & Sons L62,187 229-30; L66,
  319-22; L82,63 68 77 86 90 99; L83,240; L84,
  165; L85,12 322 331 469 471-3 475; L86,55 69
  259 259(c); L87,62 87 114 119(c) 161 165 185
  191 212-13; L88,72 176; L117A,5; IU
Putnam, Gertrude A. IU
Pycroft, James
  Oxford memories L3,20; L40,178; L41,294;
  L42,517; L63,21-4
Pyke, Rivington
  see Ainscough, James
Pyne L117B,20

Quaritch, Bernard L86,462; IU
Quarry, Miss Alice L5,151
The Queen L88,314
Queensbury, Marquis of
  see Douglas, J.S.
Quekett, Mrs.Marion L5,304
Quentin, Charles
  see Quin, C.
Quiller-Couch, Miss Mabel L5,305
Quilter, Welton & Co. L86,483
Quin, Miss Clara (Charles Quentin pseud.) L3,
  153; L85,327 330
  A Fearless life (orig.Wrought out) L40,360;
  L61,201
Quin, Michael J.
  A Steam voyage L53,166 168; L117A,28
Quittery, Harry IU
Quivogne de Montifaud, Marie A. IU

R., A.B. IU Unidentified
R., P. IU Unidentified (R.,C.)
Rachel, Madame IU
Rackstraw, Miss IU
Radclyffe, Edward IU
Radford, Mrs.
  see May, Bessie
Radhalai, Mrs. L86,324
Rae, John L5,176
Rae, Julia E.S. L3,23; L65,84-9; L86,406
Rae, W.Fraser L3,57; L4,55; L5,193 229;
  L22,349 358; L86,134 275 278; L89,49; IU;
  UC(Rivington)
  An American duchess L41,432; L42,478;
  L65,77

Egypt today L41,377; L42,188; L65,245
Maygrove L41,446; L64,196-9
Miss Bayle's romance L40,95; L41,488;
L63,195
A Modern brigand L41,470; L63,337-40
Sheridan L42,358 387; L67,3-5 99
Rahn, Norman L85,198
Raikes L81,195
Raikes, George A. L3,174; L63,174; L85,
162; L87,210(c); IU
The Ancient vellum book L41,360; L42,167;
L65,34-5
Historical records of the First Regiment of
Militia L38,219; L39,423; L40,452; L41,
252; L42,224
The History of the Honourable Artillery
Company L39,311 335; L40,223; L41,251-2;
L42,219-20; L123,212-13
Roll of the officers L40,218; L41,252; L42,
312
The Royal Charter of Incorporation L42,313
The Strength of the British army L37,20;
L38,232; L39,422; L40,455; L41,534; L42,
521
Raikes, Harriet L1,184; L2,47; L58,252;
L82,91 298; L83,35 216; IU
The Marriage contract L56,189
Raikes, Rt.Hon.Henry Cecil
A Selection from the poems L3,124; L42,
357; L66,237
Raikes, Henry St.John L3,124; L22,342; L66,
237; L87,290; L88,54; IU
The Life of Henry C.Raikes (pub.McM.) L42,
251; L67,298
Raikes, Thomas
Private correspondence with the Duke of
Wellington L1,184; L36,262; L58,252; L97,
10
A Visit to St.Petersburg L54,61; L117B,5;
IU
The Railway & General Automatic Library Ltd.
L65,199-200; L86,476
Railway Guide & General Printing Works UC
Raine, G. L87,219
Raine, Miss Jane L22,353
A Royal smile L42,415; L67,228
Ralph, John
The Lives of the Poets-Laureate
see Austin, W.S.
Ralston, William R.S. L5,27; IU
Ram, R.A. IU
Ram, Stephen L5,75
Rambaut, Miss Beatrice L5,32; L22,354
Ramé, Louise de la (Ouida pseud.) L2,20; L25,
90; L84,75; L98,175; IU(De la Ramée)
Ramsay, Miss Catherine M. L4,78; L5,308;
L22,353
Miss Drummond's dilemma (orig.The Paying
guest) L42,425; L67,40
Ramsay, Dorothea IU
Ramsay, Grace
see O'Meara, K.
Ramsay, Rina IU

Ramsay, Robert W. L5,164
Ramsay, Thomas IU
Ramsden, Lady Helen G. L3,106; IU
Speedwell L42,443; L66,75
Ramsey, Mrs. L22,355
Ramsey, Miss Alicia L5,27
Rand, McNally & Co. L87,72
Randolph, Mrs. IU
Randolph, Edmund IU
Randolph, L.W. L93,137
Randolph, Anson & Co. IU
Ranke, Leopold von IU
Civil wars and monarchy in France L57,158;
L82,238 240; L83,137; UC
Ranken, W.Bayne L5,74
Rankin, Francis H. L91,46 51; L117B,3
The White man's grave L53,205; L81,233
Ransom, Arthur L5,286; L22,353
Raper, R.G. L84,331; IU(Rapst)
Ratcliffe, Mr. L85,85
Ratcliffe, Dunbar & Co. L87,279
Rathbone, A.S. L86,284 493; L87,165 187;
L88,53
Rathbone, Benson L3,60; L59,290; L65,82;
IU
Rating Assessment Committee L84,247; L85,
194
Rauschmann L88,137
Raven, John Hardy IU
Raven, Mathilde
The Two brothers L56,248
Rawlinson, Cecil J. L88,155
Rawlinson, L.L. IU
Rawnsley, Drummond IU
Rawnsley, Rev.H.D. L85,145; IU
Raymond, George L91,199; IU
Raymond, Walter L3,111; L5,269; L86,430;
L87,119; L88,154
Taken at his word (orig.It look like truth) L41,
415; L42,497; L65,133
Reach, Angus B. L83,32; IU
Read, F.J. L88,75
Read, Hollis
The Hand of God in history L56,224
Read, William & Co. IU
Reade, Mr. L5,24
Reade, A.A. L5,174
Reade, Charles L1,92 175; L2,42; L5,141;
L9,166; L58,108; L82,341 343; L83,37 58 60
128-9 140-1 168-9 175 235; L93,230 301;
[L94,25]; L95,189; L96,17 30; L117A,35;
IU; IU Richard Bentley I,25+1: UC
Christie Johnstone L36,32 124; L37,228;
L75,336-44
The Course of true love L9,81; L36,34
It's never too late to mend L36,31 221 285-6
The King's rival L38,218; L39,399 422; L40,
452; L41,527; L42,509
Masks and faces L38,218; L39,399 422; L40,
452; L41,528 541; L42,280
Peg Woffington L36,32 124; L37,228; L38,
219; L55,294; L75,336-44
A Perilous secret L3,176; L40,106 398;

L41,92 527; L42,117; L62,202-9; L65,114
[Poverty and pride] L38,219; L39,422; L40,
453; L41,528; L42,301
Three dramas L36,45
Reade, Compton L5,90; L62,149-60; L86,51;
L88,214 216(c); IU
Reade, Emma C.(Mrs.Compton Reade) L3,72;
L39,219; L88,214; IU
Rose and rue L38,315 329; L39,439 456;
L40,453; L41,531; L42,494; L59,318; L101,
153
Reade, John Edmund
Cain the wanderer L52,149
The Revolt of the angels L52,149; L68,67
Reade, Winwood IU
Reading, Bradfield L88,245(c)
Ready, Arthur L5,218
Reay, Stephen L86,44
Redding, Cyrus IU
Redfield, J.S. L1,177; L82,206
Redfield & Panton L82,179
Redford L5,69
Redgrave, Miss L82,158
Redman, J.H. L2,71; IU
Redmond, Miss IU
Redmond, Philip L22,359
Redway, George L88,231
Redwood, B. IU
Reed, Miss L5,176
Rees, A.Willesley L5,165; IU(Reis)
Rees, George L89,45
Rees, Owen IU
Reeve IU
Reeve, Henry IU
Reeves, H.A. L60,96-7; L85,167; IU
Reeves, Mrs.H.A.
see Mathers, H.B.
Reeves, John Sims UC
[Regant], Harriette C. IU
Rehbaun, Frederick IU
Reid, Andrew UC
Reid, George William IU
Reid, M. L94,225
Reid, Mayne L1,189; L2,43 49 70; L3,31;
L84,84; IU
The Bandolero L37,47; L38,216; L59,120
The Child wife L37,73; L59,163
The Headless horseman L37,148; L38,219;
L59,121
The Wild huntress L36,262; L58,250
Reid, Mrs.Mayne L86,186 191
Reilly, Dr.Robert L5,221
Reinige, Louis UC
Relfe Brothers L88,319
Religious Tract Society L86,470
Rellstab, Heinrich F.L.
Eighteen hundred and twelve L7,168; L8,94
Remanda, S. IU
Remnant, Richard IU(Revenant)
Remnant, W. L83,135 168 190; IU(Renmant)
Remnants & Edmonds
see Edmonds & Remnants
Remy, Georges IU

Remy, Virginia Georges IU
Renan, Joseph E.
Studies in religious history L3,186; L40,220;
L41,304 307; L42,317; L62,270 276; L63,142
Rendall, Edward D. L5,169
Rendall, Godfrey L5,167
Rendall, Vernon L5,278; L87,241 242(c)
Rendle, William L5,171; IU
Renny, Mary IU
What to do with cold mutton L2,55; L3,101;
L36,216-7; L37,268 309; L38,249; L39,188;
L40,442 461; L41,312; L58,336 336a; L59,89
Repository of Arts & Co. IU
Reshir, Emir IU
Retail Newsagents' & Booksellers' Union L86,
462; UC
[Reuss, Miss] L85,105
Reuter's Telegraphic Company IU
Revail L83,271 273 275
Revans L82,194
Revue Britannique L87,64 66; IU
Reynolds, Frederick
The Dramatic tourist (prop.) L52,44; L68,33;
IU
Reynolds, Henry R. IU
Reynolds, John Hamilton L55,5-6; L90,255;
L91,164; L92,145-6; IU
Reynolds, Paul R. L66,260-2 282-3; L67,146
211; L88,90 96 111 115 118 154 157 160 192 218
282 349-51 357; L89,42 76 104
Reynolds, Thomas IU
Rhoades, Walter L22,354
Rhodes, Miss Elsie L5,296
Ribton, Mrs.T. L5,39
Ribton, William L90,245
Rice, Mia Knowles IU
Rich, O. L53,172; L55,61; L117A,27
Richards, Blanche Brinsley IU
Richards, Brinsley (jnr.) L86,479
Richards, Florence B. UC
Richards, Harriet IU
Richards, Henry Brinsley IU
Richards, James Brinsley L3,163; L5,63 155;
L71,158; L85,355 390 406; L86,66 73 224 395
474 477; IU
The Alderman's children L41,426; L42,479;
L65,119
The Duke's marriage L40,413; L41,507 510;
L42,481; L63,29-31
Prince Roderick L41,451; L64,108-9
Seven years at Eton L40,217 374; L41,319
394; L42,314; L61,263
Richards, Thomas L81,57
Richards, W.L. L87,277 278; IU
Richardson, Coke L58,177
Richardson, Mrs.Constance L1,117; L117B,4
Memoirs of Louisa, Queen of Prussia L56,42
Richardson, Henry W. IU
Richardson, James
Travels in the great desert L6,154 159; L42,
404; L56,55 170; L117B,34
Richardson, Lieut.John
Frascati's L1,38

Richardson, Sir John L90,113-15; L117A,26
Richardson, Robert L5,219
Richmond, Duke of UC
Richmond, G. IU
Richmond, George L88,59
 see Smith, Charles E.
Rickard, G.B. IU
Rickert, Miss Edith L22,355
Ricketts, E. IU
Riddell, Mrs.Charlotte E.L.(C.E.L.Cowan)
 L1,153; L2,73 90; L3,21-2; L4,56; L5,73
 144; L83,135; L84,293; L85,424 440 446;
 L86,96 167; L87,177 237(c) 238; L89,55;
 IU; UC
 Berna Boyle L40,95 395; L41,94-5 505; L42,
 118-19 479; L62,135-6 281
 A Bid for fortune (orig.Michael Gargrave's
 harvest) L42,439 500; L66,108-10; L67,280
 Daisies and buttercups L39,387; L40,359;
 L61,134 140-1
 George Geith of Fen Court L40,96; L41,95-6;
 L42,118-20; L62,272-4; L119,136
 The Government official L40,468; L41,491;
 L42,484; L63,154
 A Mad tour L41,421; L42,515; L65,106
 Mitre Court (orig.A Tale of the great city)
 L40,411; L41,522; L62,181-3
 The Mystery in Palace Gardens L39,341 366;
 L40,92-3; L41,93; L60,275-6 289-91 295
 Ruling passion L36,39; L58,134
 The Senior partner L39,365 395; L40,94 454;
 L60,288-91
 A Struggle for fame L40,377; L61,313
 Susan Drummond (orig.Three wizards and a
 witch) L3,41; L40,94 389; L41,93; L42,120;
 L62,56-63 281
Riddell, Vaisey & Co. L87,99; IU
Riddle, Rev.Joseph E.
 History of the Papacy L56,278; L57,200;
 L82,282-3; L83,45-6; L117A,37
Rideal, Charles F. UC
Ridge, William P.(Warwick Simpson pseud.)
 L3,162; L4,79; L88,61; IU
 A Clever wife (orig.A Brace of talents) L42,
 428; L66,287
Ridgway, Miss E. L3,143; L85,279
 Dorothy's troth L39,371; L40,241; L41,213;
 L61,9-11
Ridgway, James IU
Ridgway, T.G. IU
Ridley, J.W.W. IU
Rigby, F.E. IU
Rigby, Roger L91,288-9 292-3
Rigby, W.E. L86,233 351
Rimboult, J.H. IU
Rinder, S. IU
Rintoul, R.S. L53,34
Rions, M. L88,67
Ripon, Earl of
 see Robinson, F.J.
Rippingille, Edward V. L91,238-9; L92,3
 221-3; IU
Ripsher

 see Mallan
Rising, Eleanor IU
Risk, Margaret M.F. IU
Risos, Mme.A. L3,64; L4,88; L22,344; L87,
 118
Ritchie, Mrs.Anne L86,269; IU; UC
Rivenhall, Edward L84,168 184 320; L85,29
 445; L86,111 170 187 223 384; L87,45 70 111
 135 258; L88,74 105 212 257; UC
Rivington, Arthur W. IU
Rivington, Emily IU
Rivington, Margaretta IU
Rivington & Son L61,53 65; L62,183 302; L67,
 31-3; L83,90-1 268-70; L84,99 239 246; L85,
 319 320(c) 427 436 446(c) 463; L86,127(c) 192
 244 248(c) 248-9; L87,53; L89,118 127-9;
 L95,61-71; IU; IU George Bentley,414+1: UC
Robbers, J.G. L85,54 60 355 391
Roberts L83,38
Roberts, Mrs.Alexander L5,199
Roberts, C. IU
Roberts, Lord Frederick S. L3,166; L4,65;
 L22,330 336; L88,265(c); L89,74; IU;
 IU George Bentley,270 287 468; UC(end of R);
 UC Manuscripts,11 21
 Forty-one years in India L42,355 373-4
 379-83 392-4; L66,193-211; L88,269; L89,
 42 59 71; L115,222 260 291-3 300-4; L119,
 165; L123,178
Roberts, J. IU
Roberts, J.S. L5,79
Roberts, Miss Jane
 Two years at sea L53,45; L81,116-17 136
 142 168
Roberts, W. L5,296; IU
Roberts, W.A. IU
Roberts Brothers L85,53 141 141(c) 395; L86,
 93 482 497; L87,41 58; IU
Roberts & Evans L89,118
Robertson, Miss A.Fraser L5,131
Robertson, Miss Anne L94,234
Robertson, Charles M. L67,247-8
Robertson, David L83,242
Robertson, Eric L5,252; UC
Robertson, George & Co. L84,65; L85,61 115
 201-2(c); L88,252; L89,109-10; L95,248;
 IU; UC
Robertson, Herbert L86,49
Robertson, J.E. IU
Robertson, M. IU
Robertson, T.W. L65,242; IU
Robertson, Thomas C. L1,128; L82,298
Robertson, William L83,96 136 138 148 244
Robins, Arthur L2,54; L94,164
 Black Moss L36,166; L37,33; L38,94; L59,
 22-3; L98,16
Robins, Miss Gertrude M. L3,24; L86,78 167
 A False position L41,477; L63,261
 Keep my secret L40,415; L41,516; L63,53-4
Robins, Miss Mabel H. L22,363
Robinson L2,67
Robinson, Charles Clough L2,72; L5,22
Robinson, Charles Horace IU

Robinson, Miss Emma   L2,56; L83,276; L84
50; L94,189-91 229
  Christmas at Old Court   L36,164; L37,80;
  L58,338
  Dorothy Firebrace   L36,182; L37,90
Robinson, F.   L85,189
Robinson, Frederick
  Diary of the Crimean War   L36,235; L58,50;
  L83,102
Robinson, Frederick J.(Earl of Ripon)   IU(Ripon)
Robinson, G.K.   L86,337; L88,209
Robinson, Rev.Hayes   L5,92
Robinson, Heaton B.   L52,329; L90,53; L117A,
14
  Memoirs of Sir Thomas Picton   L53,138 182-4
Robinson, Mrs.Janet   L5,36
Robinson, Lionel   L86,211; IU(Johnison)
Robinson, Mary G.
  The Life of James Kelly O'Dwyer   L7,172;
  L8,174; L36,180; L57,128; L82,217
Robinson, Nellie   UC
Robinson, Nugent   L5,22; L95,157
Robinson, P.A.   L88,160(c)
Robinson, R.Hayes   IU
Robson, H.   L81,127
Robson, Miss Isabel Stuart   L5,168 237
Robson & Sons   L60,244-5 276 288-91 295; L61,
  140-1; L62,281; L85,9 238 240 307 316
  321-2(c) 322; L86,48 50; IU
Rochau, August L. von
  Wanderings through the cities of Italy   L7,174;
  L8,200
[Roche]
  London (prop.)   L36,98
Rochester, Bishop of   L88,84
Rockliff, I.Russell   IU
Rodenberg, Julius   IU(Deutsche Rundschall)
  England, literary and social   L3,81; L38,352;
  L39,220; L40,453; L41,509; L42,507
  King 'By the Grace of God'   L37,31; L38,170;
  L39,432
Rodwell, J.   L81,45
Roe, Mrs.Harcourt   L5,297
Roebuck, Henrietta   IU
Roebuck, Rt.Hon.John A.   L84,111 145; L92,
  292; IU; UC
  Lives of the Prime Ministers of England (prop.)
  L40,434; L82,194 199 204
Roffe, W.   L88,244; IU
Roffen, Randall T.   IU
Rogers, E.S.   L54,22
Rogers, James E.T.   L3,98; L4,82; L5,79
  87 104; L84,322; IU
  Epistles, satires and epigrams   L38,367;
  L39,220; L40,320; L41,217; L42,507
Rogers, Sara B.
  Life's way   L42,411; L67,234; L88,293
Rogers, W.A.   IU
Roget, John L.   L3,44; IU
Rolfe, Elizabeth R.   IU
Rolfe, P.   L84,49-50; IU; IU George Bentley,
  372 374
Rolfe, Philemon   L5,215

[Rollit, A.]   IU
Rolls, Charles   L81,81
Rolls, Henry   IU
Romer, Isabella F.   L6,57; L8,35; L82,52;
  L93,38-9; L117B,22; IU
  The Bird of passage; or Flying glimpses of many
  lands   L56,141; L84,154; L100,3
  Filia Dolorosa   L56,222; L57,70 74
  A Pilgrimage to the temples and tombs   L7,161;
  L55,319
  The Rhone   L6,173; L7,151; L55,168
  Sturmer (orig.Tales of a wanderer)   L7,147;
  L55,30
Romilly, George T.   IU
Romilly, John   IU
Romilly, Sir Samuel   IU
Rooke, Octavius   L85,21
Roope, Charles J.   L5,303; IU
Roose, Miss Pauline   L5,222 288
Roper   L82,71
Roper, Arthur A.   L5,151
Roper, R.Ormsby   L59,60-7
Roscoe, Edwards S.   L5,69; L22,365; L95,144
  179; IU
Roscoe, Mrs.H.   L5,186
Roscoe, Thomas   L1,31; IU
Roscoe, William   [IU]
  Life of Leo the Tenth   L40,188
  Lorenzo de Medici   L40,185
Rose, Agnes R.   IU
Rose, Cowper   L1,41
Rose, Edward   L5,102
Rose, George   L54,63
Rose, George   IU
Rose, Rt.Hon.George   IU
  The Diaries and correspondence   L1,134 176;
  L36,64 142; L58,197
Rose, Rev.Henry J.
  The Emigrant churchman in Canada   L1,78;
  L36,149; L82,51; L117B,41
Rose, Rev.Hugh J.   L3,102; L5,49 107; IU
  Among the Spanish people   L39,232; L40,421;
  L41,502; L42,501; L60,48-51
Rose, John C.   L5,206
Rose, William G.
  Three months leave   L54,63; L117A,38
Rosebery, Earl of
  see Primrose, A.P.
Roskell, Ogden & Co.   L81,161 176
Roslyn, Guy
  see Hotton, J.
Ross, Emma Mary   UC
Ross, J.W.   L93,113
Ross, Janet   L5,217; IU
Ross, Sir John
  Memoirs of Admiral Lord de Saumarez   L54,1;
  L81,219; L117B,8
Ross, R.B.   IU
Ross, Miss Thomasina   L1,53; L56,113-15;
  L90,12-13 36 57 79; L92,249-50; L117A,17
Rossedome, L.   UC
Rossi, Miss   L5,155
Rosslyn, Earl of   L5,62

Rothshott, Ramis IU
Roundell, Mrs.Julia A.E.   L5,250; IU
Rousseau, L.   IU
Roussell, Stuart IU
Routledge, George & Sons   L3,140; L57,1;
   L60,63 87-93 305-6; L62,173 192; L63,163;
   L64,83; L82,46-7 94 103 141 148 152-3 221;
   L83,67 74-5 80-2 85 87 92 95 108 143 172 174
   196; L84,51 58 64 123 293; L85,15 17 168 182
   256 377 436 438-9; L86,143 168 470(c) 470
   474(c) 476; L117B,35; IU
Routledge, James IU
Rowan Alexander IU
Rowbotham, John F.
   The History of music   L41,380; L42,224 227;
   L61,277; L65,286-91; L87,68; L88,59; IU
Rowe, J.R. & Sons   L86,403
Rowley, George W.   L73B,7
Royal Academy of Arts   IU
Royal Asiatic Society   IU
Royal Engineer Institute   IU
Royal Exchange Insurance   L83,242; L84,76
   175; L85,66 77 88 188 197 332 333 376 378 387
   400-2 443 462 465 473; L86,71 75 161 176 212
   284 [344] 411 488; L87,136 227 232 236; IU
Royal Literary Fund   IU
Royal Naval College   L87,187(c)
The Royal Society, Melbourne   L83,237
Royle, C.   L5,83
Rudolph, F.C.J.(Crown Prince of Austria)   L3,
   184
   Travels in the East   L3,183; L40,335; L41,
   536; L42,324; L62,64-8; L85,421;
   UC(Clowes)
Rule, Frederick   IU
Rupe, Lupton   L90,247
Ruschenberger, William S.
   Narrative of a voyage   L54,93; L117A,24
Rush, Benjamin   L59,298; IU
Rush, Richard
   A Residence at the Court of London   L7,159;
   L38,283; L39,403 423; L40,454; L41,506;
   L42,503; L53,11; L55,279; L59,298; L117A,
   13
Rushforth, George   L5,226
Russ, Miss H.M.   L5,299; L22,368
Russell, Miss   L5,48
Russell, Amy   IU
Russell, Mrs.Annie
   The Pet of the consulate   L3,142; L39,378;
   L40,449; L61,88; L85,282-3; UC(Pigott)
Russell, C.H.   L5,271; IU
Russell, George   L5,162
Russell, Howard   L83,83
Russell, J. & Sons   IU
Russell, J.H.   L86,200
Russell, John   IU
Russell, Lord John   L1,119; L2,41; L3,18;
   L60,33; L84,97; L85,11 13; L117A,40; IU;
   IU(Barber,C.M.)
   The Life and times of Charles J.Fox   L6,155;
   L36,175-6 245 250; L37,224-5; L38,217; L39,
   423; L40,451; L58,192

Foreign policy of Great Britain   L38,204
Russell, Rev.John   UC Manuscripts,45
Russell, John Howard   IU
Russell, Rachel E.(Lady Butler)
   The Prophecy   L2,44; L36,302; L37,37;
   L58,295-6
Russell, Tom   L5,279
Russell, William C.(Sydney Mostyn pseud.)
   L3,51; L5,34; L85,346 369 373 376; IU
   As innocent as a baby   L38,318; L39,437;
   L59,317
   Captain Fanny   L38,369; L39,438-9; L40,
   466; L41,506; L42,480; L60,13
   A Dark secret   L38,331; L39,438
   The Deceased wife's sister   L38,314; L39,429
   The Mystery of Ashleigh Manor   L38,289;
   L39,451; L40,446; L59,306; L101,60
   An Ocean free-lance   L39,359; L40,99 449;
   L41,97-8; L42,118; L60,271-4 309; L64,
   161-2
   Which sister?   L38,277; [L59,295]
Russell, Sir William Howard   L83,70; IU
Rutherford, John   IU
Rutherford & Son   IU
Rutland, Duke of
   see Manners, J.J.R.
Rutland, George   IU
Rutt, John T.   L1,43; L54,193 267; L117B,5
Ryan, Edward   L81,171-2 178; L90,133 211;
   L117A,19
Ryan, M.M.   L5,268; IU
Rybot, Victoria
   see Baker, Victoria
Ryde, H.T.   IU
Ryder, B.F.   IU
Ryder, Dudley (2nd Earl of Harrowby)
   IU(Harrowby)
Ryder, Edward A.   L5,95; L63,71; L71,74;
   L86,86; IU
Ryder, Mrs.Edward A.   L86,165
Rydill, L.R.   L88,172

S., Gerald H.   L93,97
S., L.J.   IU Unidentified
Sabin & Sons   L85,21 368; L88,145; IU
Sackett   L83,244
Sadleir, Michael   UC
Sadler, Joseph   L73B,7
Sadler & Jameson   L82,331
Sage, Edward   IU
[Sahumé, H.Anthony]   IU
Saint Albans
   see Beauclerk
Saint Amant, de   L84,239
St.Andrews, Bishop of   L85,398
Saint Aubyn, Rev.John H.
   The Elopement   L54,48
   Hugo the Fourth (prop.)   L52,315
Saint Clair, George
   The Buried city of Jerusalem   L40,459; L41,
   300

Saint Clair, Thomas S.
  A Residence in the West Indies and America
  L52,337; L81,174; L117A,23
Saint Elme, Ida L90,108-10; L117B,45; IU
Saint George, Mrs.Flora K.E. L5,307; L88,
  308
Saint Germans, Earl of
  see Eliot, E.G.
St.James' Gazette L62,222
St.James's Magazine IU
St.James' Society L82,224
Saint John, Bayle L92,39 53 60-1 86; L117A,
  19; IU
  The Eccentric lover L55,235
Saint John, Lady Isabella L81,105-6; L90,
  29-30; L117A,14; IU
  Mrs.Cleveland and the St.Clairs [orig.The
  Legacy] L53,37
  Wedded life in the upper ranks [L83,103]
Saint John, James A. L1,78; L81,41 209;
  L83,71; L92,196 204 301; L93,1; L117A,25;
  IU
  The History of ancient Greece L7,148; L40,
  166; L55,81; UC Manuscripts,15
  The Lives of celebrated travellers L52,203
  Sir Cosmo Digby L55,180
  Tales of the Ramad'han L53,125
Saint John, Molyneux IU
Saint John, Percy B. IU
  French Revolution L92,6; L117B,38
Saint John, Sir Spenser L86,85
[St.John-Brenon, Fannie] IU
St.John's Hospital, London IU
St.Peter's Church, Chalvey IU
St.Stephen's Review IU
Sainte Marie, le Comte de L92,122; L117B,2
Saint-Maur, Edward A.
  Letters, remains and memoirs L3,106 151;
  L41,379; L42,276; L65,232-3
Saintsbury, Mr. IU
Saitner & Sons L60,167
Sala, Bessie L87,184; IU
Sala, George A. L1,171; L2,63; L5,17; L36,
  323; L83,165 174 181; L86,113(c); L94,25;
  L97,77; IU; UC
  Autobiography (prop.) L40,157; L41,193;
  L42,163; L63,181; UC Manuscripts,10
  A Journey due north L36,59; L58,181-3
  Lily L36,242; L58,112
Sala, Henrietta C.F. IU
Sale, Mrs. L5,238
Salisbury, Lord
  see Cecil, R.A.
Salm-Salm, Agnes (Princess) IU
  Ten years of my life L3,99; L38,343; L39,
  221; L40,457; L59,324-6
Salm-Salm, Felix C.(Prince
  My diary in Mexico L37,229; L38,226
Salmon, Arthur L. L5,230; L22,354
Salmon, Edward L5,137
Salmon, Joseph L86,326
Salt, Henry S. L3,32; L5,176; L86,315; L88,
  108; IU
  The Life of Henry D.Thoreau L41,353; L42,
  264; L64,322-5; L67,54; L119,103
Salter, P.King L3,66; L86,166
  Whitepatch L41,476; L42,498; L63,259 311
Salter, Rev.W. L90,70
Salvin, F.H. L86,405(c)
Salway, C.C. L88,171
Sambonifacio, Elisa di IU
Sambrooke, Thomas G. L55,108-10
Sampson, John L87,43
Sampson, M.B. L90,254
[Samson, Joseph] L81,200
Samuda L2,21; L84,155
  Bertha Devereux L37,46; L38,92; L39,447
Samuel, Rev.J. IU
Samuel, Morris L. L92,229
Sandars, W.Collett L5,85 103; IU
Sandbach, Mrs.Margaret L1,119; L117A,11;
  IU
  Spiritual alchemy L57,66
Sandbach, Tinne & Co. IU
Sanders, H.M. L5,295; L22,349 354 357 360
  363 366 368
Sanders, Rev.J. L2,15
Sanders, W.H. IU
Sanderson, S. L85,454; IU
Sanderson, William IU
Sandford, Sir Daniel L81,37
Sandford, M.G. IU
Sandifer
  see Smith, W.H. & Son
Sands, Robert IU
Sansom L84,177
Sargent L5,69
Sargent, Herbert Howland IU; UC(end of S)
Sargent, J.Y. IU
Sartoris, Adelaide
  Past hours L3,138; L4,85; L39,355; L40,
  314
Sartoris, F.U. L5,211; IU
Sassoon, Alfred L63,17; IU
Sassoon, Mrs.L. IU
The Saturday Review L85,266; L86,215; L62,
  290-1; IU
Saunders, Francis W. IU
Saunders, Frederick L1,150; L2,44; L83,103
  106 130; L93,290
  Evenings with the sacred poets L2,16; L37,
  111; L38,221; L39,222; L59,220
  Pastime papers L40,192; L41,302; L42,517
  Salad for the social L36,52 122; L37,236;
  L58,62; L83,109
  Salad for the solitary L57,249
  Salad for the solitary and the social L40,185;
  L41,305; L42,318
Saunders, James L94,80
Saunders, John L2,77; L3,27; L84,150; L85,
  169
  Hirell L37,164; L59,194
Saunders, Trelawney
  An Introduction to the survey of Western
  Palestine L39,393; L40,466 468
Saunders, W.H.Patten L2,48; L88,297(c);

L94,221-2
  Black and gold   L36,180; L37,33; L59,33;
    L98,87
Saunders & Ottley   L54,124-44; L81,33; L90,
    128; L117A,31; L122,62
Saunders's News-Letter, Dublin   IU
Savage, M.W.   L81,33-4; L82,196 273 277
Savile, Hon.Charles S.   L92,147 151 189-91
    234 271; L94,167 170 174 208; L117B,15
  Karah Kaplan   [L7,150]; L55,57
Savile, John H.(5th Earl of Mexborough)
    IU(Mexborough)
Savile, William   IU
Savile Club   L85,323; IU(Hood,H.J.)
Savill, Frances M.   IU
Saville, Miss   L5,90
Saville, Miss S.E.   L5,129
Saville & Edwards   L83,254 258; L84,34
Savinon, W.L.   IU
Saxby, Jessie M.E.   L5,210
Saxon, A.O.   L82,146; L117A,24
Saxon & Co.   L86,393
Sayce, Rev.Archibald H.
  The Ancient Hebrew inscription   L39,357
Scadding, S.W.   L5,237
Scadding, W.   L88,199-200(c)
Scargill, William P.
  Tales of a briefless barrister   [L123,22]
Scarlett, Sir James   L90,9
Scarth, Alice M.E.   IU
Scharling, Carl Henrik   L3,88; L84,293; IU
  Nicolai's marriage   L3,83; L38,363; L39,
    446
  Noddebo Parsonage (orig.Cecilton)   L2,55;
    L37,86 206
  The Rivals   L37,223; L38,215
Schenley, E.W.H.   L68,37
Schfeldt, Fritz   IU
Schiller, Johann C.F. von
  Correspondence with Körner   L56,75
Schindler, Johanna   IU; UC
Schlagentweit   L83,231
Schleuning, A.   IU
Schlueter, Dr.Joseph   L2,58; L3,29
  A General history of music   L36,188; L37,230;
    L42,402; L59,1
Schmalz, Miss Flora   L5,63; IU
Schmalz, Rosa   IU
Schmidt, A.   IU
Schmieden, Else   L3,151; L85,412
  Self deception (prop.)   L3,166; L40,346; L61,
    163-7
Schmitz, L.   IU
Schnitzler, Johann H.
  Secret history of the Court of Russia   L8,35;
    L117B,34
Schock, Helene   L85,267
Scholastic Trading Company   L88,313
School Board for London   L86,155
Schorer, J.H.   L86,386
Schott & Co.   IU
Schoultz, Anna von   L55,231; L117B,30
Schrader   L83,184

Schreiner, Mrs.Olive   L88,283
Schultz, M.M. & Co.   L85,85
Schultz, Marie   IU
Schultz, R. & Co.   IU
Schulze, Adolphus   L62,115; L67,75; L82,108;
    IU; UC
Schulze, Bertilde   IU
Schulze, F.   IU
Schumacher, Gottlieb
  Across the Jordan   L40,181; L41,297
  The Jaulan   L41,328
  Pella   L41,328
Schumann, Robert A.
  The Life of Robert Schumann   L3,56; L41,
    357; L42,265; L64,282-8
Schwartz, Marie S.
  Elvira, Lady Casterton   L3,73; L38,320;
    L39,402 440; L40,429; L41,509; L42,482
Sclater, P.L.   L64,40
Scoble, Sir Andrew R.   L1,139; L56,307; L58,
    25; L82,226 257 309 312 314 317 347 353;
    L83,43; L93,204 216 280; L117A,26; IU
Scoble, P.L'Estrange   L94,154; IU
  Unidentified,(A)
Scoones, Rev.R.D.   L5,86 97 121
Scoones, William D.   IU
Scopes, Gowing   UC Manuscripts,11
Scott   L82,163
Scott, Lady Caroline L.   L1,144; L83,103-4
    109 112; L117A,14
  Exposition of the types and antitypes   L36,97
    111; L37,232
  The old grey church   L36,91; L58,60
  Trevelyan   L53,32; L74,37 181; L81,104;
    L122,61 123
Scott, Charles H.   L1,94; L83,63-4; L117B,7
  The Baltic   L57,318
Scott, Sir Claude E.   IU
  Adventures of the South Army   L56,257
Scott, Clement   L2,65; IU
Scott, Col.Courtenay   IU
  Invasions of India
  see Scott, Margaret
Scott, Miss Eva   L5,141; L22,365
Scott, Sir George   L81,104
Scott, Lady Harriet A.   IU
Scott, Hugh S.(H.S.Merriman pseud.)   L3,67;
    L5,286; L66,160; L67,43; L86,178 214 267
    336 359 400; L88,43; L89,57 65 65-6(c) 68;
    IU; UC(Scr...)
  The Phantom future   L41,458; L42,493; L64,
    66
  Prisoners and captives   L41,435; L42,493;
    L64,333; L65,63
  Suspense   L41,447; L64,157
  Young Mistley   L41,476; L42,105; L63,276;
    L64,176
Scott, James   L81,96 112-12 118; L90,38-9
    42; L117A,22
Scott, Mrs.[James]   L81,129
Scott, Margaret (Mrs.Courtenay Scott)   IU
  Invasions of India   L3,119; L39,306; L40,
    434; L41,515; L60,123; L123,183-4;

UC(Scr...)
Scott, Montague L83,256
Scott, P. IU
Scott, P.
  Domestic manual L1,60; L73A,193
Scott, Patrick L2,17
  Legends of a state prison L37,238; L38,231;
  L39,403 431; L40,439
Scott, Redna (pseud.) L88,69(c) 69; IU
Scott, Samuel P.
  Through Spain L40,188; L41,307; L42,516
  522
Scott, T.H. L95,95
Scott, Thomas L85,349; IU
Scott, W. L82,172
Scott, Walter Ltd. IU
Scott, Rev.William L83,167; IU
  Austria and Italy L36,68
Scott-Stevenson, Esmé IU
Scotter, Sir Charles L88,278
Scottish Club L85,415
Scribe, Augustin E. L3,42; L38,284
Scribner, Charles' Sons
  see Scribner & Welford
Scribner & Welford L60,168-70 208-9 299-300;
  L61,92-4 226; L63,98 171 199; L64,315; L65,
  154 279; L82,213 272-3; L83,176 184; L84,
  147 162 209; L85,161-2 166-7 218 229 243 249
  254 256 260 263 273 295 335 417 434-5 450; IU;
  IU(Welford); UC
  see Baker & Scribner; Bangs, L.W.
Scribner's Magazine L86,169
Sealy, Thomas H. IU
  The Porcelain tower L7,147; L36,140; L92,
  294; L117B,25
Seames, M.J. IU
Searle, Thomas L53,203
Seaton, R.C. L5,172
Seccombe, Captain T.S. L84,200; IU
Secker, Charlotte IU
Secker, E.H. UC
Sedgwick, Catharine M. L117B,18
  Clarence L1,37
Seeley, Robert B.(Edmund Clifford pseud.)
  The Greatest of all the Plantagenets L36,254;
  L37,76; L38,113; L59,235-7; L70,29 139;
  L83,211
Seguin, A. L91,48
Sehfeldt, Fritz IU
Seifferth, Charles B. UC
Sekon, G.A. IU
Selby, H.P. IU
Sellers, Miss Edith L5,262-3; IU
Selous, Miss (Mrs.C.A.Jones) L5,235
Selous, Edmund C. L86,197; IU
Selous, Frederick C. L3,146; L4,56; L22,
  336; L85,289; L86,115 155 267; L87,82 83(c)
  83 130 132(c) 132-3 138(c); L88,243; IU
  A Hunter's wanderings in Africa L39,372;
  L40,272; L41,349 393 513; L42,228-9; L61,
  82; L65,169; L119,114; IU George Bentley,
  232+1 232+2; UC
Selous, Mrs.Frederick C. L86,148 150-1

Semmes, Raphael
  My adventures afloat L37,254 310; L38,227
Senior, Mary C.M.
  see Simpson, M.C.M.
Serfaty, Solomon UC
Sergeant, E.F.Adeline L3,158; L5,222; L85,
  353; L86,77 217 245(c) 349 404; L87,57 60;
  IU
  Beyond recall (orig.Out of the land of Egypt)
  L40,372; L61,250
  Esther Denison (orig.A Woman of today) L41,
  459; L42,483; L64,68
  Name and fame L41,438; L42,492; L64,303
  No saint (orig.Paul Hernshaw) L40,416; L41,
  524; L63,51
  An Open foe (orig.The Ravenscrofts) L40,391;
  L41,526; L42,492; L62,139
  The Story of a penitent soul L41,423; L65,75
  237 251-4
Sergeant, Lewis
  Name and fame
  see Sergeant, E.F.A.
Sergel, Charles H. L87,298; L88,50
Serrell, Dr.George L5,292; L22,357 365 368
The Servants' Own Paper L87,145
Sessions, H.C. L95,242
Seton, Malcolm C. L5,42
Seton & Nicholson L83,194
Severn, Emma
  Anne Hathaway L7,158; L55,243; L117B,19;
  IU(Severne)
Severn, Joan Ruskin IU
Severne, Miss A.M. L5,105; IU; IU(Swerne)
Seward, Anna L94,296
Sewell, Miss IU
Seyboldt, Fr. L83,182
Seymour, Edward A.
  see Saint-Maur, E.A.
Seymour, Frederick IU
Seymour, G.H. IU
Seymour, J. L87,267(c)
Shadwell, Sir Charles F. IU
Shadwell, J.E.L. IU
Shadwell, L. L5,65
Shadwell, Lancelot M. IU
Shaen & Roscoe L84,137
Shaftesbury, Earl of
  see Cooper, A.A.
Shakespear, H.Hope IU
Shakespeare, William IU
  The Prince's Shakespeare L2,75; L3,54;
  L37,222; L38,190; L39,434; L59,146
Shakspeare, John
  see Oriental Translation Fund
Sharp, Miss Evelyn L5,296
Sharpe, J. L83,32
Sharpe, J.E. IU
Sharpe, Sutton L81,224; L91,147; L122,3
Sharpley, Miss C.E. L87,49
Shaw, John
  A Tramp to the diggings L57,152
[Shaw, L.] IU
Shaw, N. L82,43

Shaw, Dr.Norton L1,180
Shaw, Thomas B. L92,177
Shaw, Mrs.Walrond L5,292; L88,152
Shaw & Roscoe IU
Shee, Martin A. L2,37; L84,43; L100,136;
  IU; UC
  The Cream of a life L36,149; L37,84; L58,
  323; L97,264
Sheehan, F. IU
Sheehan, John L2,73; L5,15-16 46 53; L85,
  91 93 101; L91,294; L92,73 106 112 123;
  L95,180; L96,42; IU
Shehan L82,288
Sheil, Richard L. IU
Shelburne, Lord
  see Lansdowne, H.P.
Sheldon, G.W. IU
  see Appleton & Co.
Sheldon, Gilbert L5,58
Shelley, Lady L5,175
Shelley, Lady Jane IU
Shelley, Lady Louisa E. IU
Shelley, Mrs.Mary W. L1,46; L117A,11;
  L122,59; IU
  The Fortunes of Perkin Warbeck L52,82;
  L68,44
  The Life and letters L3,52; L41,339; L42,
  511; L64,70
  Lodore L53,7
Shenton, Henry C. IU
Shepard, E.Clarence L1,140; L6,128; L117A,
  20
  Francia L36,53; L56,299; UC Manuscripts,47
Shepheard, H. IU
Shepheard & Co. L86,451; L87,94 102
Shepherd, F.Waller L3,49; IU
  Made in heaven L38,282; L39,432; L96,33;
  L100,152
Shepherd, Sarah IU
Shepherd, William A.
  From Bombay to Bushire L36,52; L58,116
Sheppard, Dr. L5,80
Sheppard, Rev.Nathan L2,85; L5,42; L100,
  191; IU
  Shut up in Paris L37,237 293; L38,222; L95,
  83-9
Sherer, C.J. L89,86; IU
Sherer, John IU
Sheridan, Mrs.Frances
  Carwell L1,39; L52,50; L68,35
Sheridan, J. IU
Sheridan, Louisa H. IU
Sheriff, Frank F. L5,167
Sherratt & Hughes L88,232 288 291
Sherwill, Markham L90,100-1 122-3; L117A,
  18
Sherwood & Co. L81,163
Shew, Mrs.Elizabeth L. L3,35; IU
  If men were wise (orig.Wrayburn) L42,445;
  L66,58
Shield, Miss Alice L5,203
Shilleto, A.R. L5,194
Shillibeer, Miss Elizabeth M.A. L76,26-245

Shillibeer, H.W. L81,217
Shipley, Orby L83,28; IU
Shippard, Lydia A. IU
Shipton, Miss Helen L5,282
Shoberl, Frederick L1,55; L53,318; L90,31
  320 322; L117A,15
Shoberl, William L1,59; L55,63; L90,49 55
  58; L93,214 225; L117A,16
Shorrock L5,95
Short, G. L95,21 35-7
Short, John L5,67 74
Shrimpton L81,61
Shuldham, Dr.E.B. L5,68; L22,367
Shute, R. IU
Sibbald, W.A. L5,268
Sibley, Mrs. L82,159
Siborne, William
  History of the Battle of Waterloo L40,232
Siddons, J.H. L5,105; IU
Sidgwick, Mrs.Cecily L3,99; L5,293
  Mrs.Finch Brassey (orig.Whincliffe) L42,452;
  L65,311; L67,91-4
Sidney, Hon.Adelaide A.W.
  Home and its influence L7,163; L8,34
  Sadness and gladness L7,166; L8,52; L56,
  90; L117B,16
Sier, Henry N. IU
Sieveking, A.Forbes L5,146
Siewers, Carl (King of Sweden) L5,188
Sikes, F.H. L5,280
Silas, Ferdinand L83,253
Sillard, P.A. IU
Sillence, Miss L89,112
Sim, William L84,91
Sime, David IU
Simeon, Stephen L. L3,81; L65,130; L86,408
  430-1; L87,139; IU; UC(end of S)
[Simes, Adelie G.] IU
Simmonds, Peter L.
  Curiosities of food L1,173; L36,60 63; L37,
  232
Simms, G. L81,151 214
Simms & McIntyre L57,112; L82,130 180 183;
  L92,149 156 159; L93,89 91 125-6; L117B,23;
  IU
Simon, Jules F.
  Natural religion L1,133-4; L36,33 42; L37,
  236; L38,232; L58,93-6; IU
Simpkin, Marshall & Co. L81,79 84-5 102 163;
  L82,27 41; L83,98; L86,185 295 308 458;
  L87,128; L88,219 251 289 348; L89,52 104; IU
Simpson, Mrs. IU George Bentley,467
Simpson, Rev. L84,133
Simpson, Alexander L1,93; L55,179; L92,32;
  L117B,30; IU
  The Life and travels of Thomas Simpson L7,
  158; L55,266
Simpson, George & Co. L86,140 155; L87,148
  195; L88,134 137 207 275-6 280 294; IU; UC
Simpson, John P. L92,235; L93,15 41-2 122;
  L117B,34; IU; IU(Dramatic ...)
  Gisella L56,46
  Letters from the Danube L7,164; L8,34;

L56,33
The Lily of Paris L56,129
Second love L7,160; L55,313
Simpson, Leonard F. L1,79; L56,75 127;
L117B,2
Simpson, Mrs.Mary C.M.(M.C.M.Senior) L3,
138; L85,261; IU
Simpson, Mrs.May
see Herbert, May
Simpson, Pinder IU
Simpson, Thomas
Narrative of the discoveries on the north coast
of America (orig.Hudson's Bay Company
expeditions) L7,152; L55,177 179
Simpson, Warwick
see Ridge, W.P.
Simpson & Renshaw L85,248 333; L86,57; IU
Simrock, Carl J.
Faust L6,105; L36,53
Sinclair, Miss Catherine L1,121; L57,247;
L82,106 149 343; L83,26 49 52 91 111; L92,
22 37-8; L93,259; L117A,14; IU
Beatrice L36,114; L57,54-6
Common sense tracts L36,52
Cross purposes L36,52; L58,120-2
Sinclair, Donald IU
Sinclair, George A. L5,149; IU
Sinclair, Rt.Hon.Sir John
Correspondence L52,68; L68,38 88 91; L80
1; L81,40 42
Sinclair, Miss May L5,266; L87,188; L89,
52-4; IU; UC
Singer, S.W. L52,153; L68,68
Singleton, Mary M.(Lady Currie;Violet Fane
pseud.) IU(Currie)
Sinnett, Edward P. L1,62; L52,162; L54,286;
L68,71; L90,140 183 242; L117B,36
Sinnett, Mrs.Jane L82,286-7 290; L92,202 231
258-9 278-9; L93,202; L117B,37
Sinnett, Percy
see Sinnett, Edward P.
Sisley, Thomas A. L5,215
Skeat, C. L85,369
Skelton, Emma A. L95,47; IU
Skene, Miss L2,70
Skene, A.P. L3,126; L85,127; IU
Skene, Miss F.M.F. L5,65 276; IU
Skene, Felix IU
Skene, Mrs.J.H. L82,255 261 310-11
Skene, James H. L1,120; L2,72; L3,17; L4,
82; L5,128 173; L82,345 353; L83,29 72 129;
L85,433; L93,284-5; L117A,23; IU
Anadol L36,99
The Frontier lands of the Christian and the Turk
L57,171
With Lord Stratford in the Crimean War L40,
363; L41,539 541; L42,524; L62,24
Skerry, J.W. L85,160
Skinner, A.M. L90,273 285
Skinner, Mrs.Ann L53,233
Skinner, John E.H. L2,25; IU
After the storm L37,20 311; L38,228; L59,76
Roughing it in Crete L37,241; L38,233

Skinner, Thomas L117B,15
Adventures during a journey [L7,110]; L53,
233 277
Excursions in India L52,258
Skoltowe, F. L94,206 244
Skrine, Mrs.Mary L5,155; L22,365
Slack, Henry J.
The Ministry of the beautiful L7,170; L8,119;
L83,76
Slack, John L86,310-11
Slade, Mrs. L87,188
Slade, Sir A. L2,69
Slade, Mrs.Evelyn M. L66,44-8
Slade, Florence B.
see Breton, Florence B.
Sladen, Douglas B.W. L5,200; IU
Slater, Walter L5,221
Slatter L81,202
Sleath, Francis G. L86,125
Sleath, John IU
Sleeman, Lady A.J. L58,165; L83,154 158
Sleeman, H.A. L83,159
Sleeman, Henry A. L1,161
Sleeman, Sir William H.
A Journey through the Kingdom of Oude L1,134
161; L36,225; L58,165
Sleigh, Burrows W.A. L1,80; L82,346 352 354;
L83,34; L117A,35
Pine forests L57,229
Slidell, Alexander L81,127; L90,116; L117A,
27
The American in England L53,203
Spain revisited L53,218
Slough Board of Guardians L85,205
Slough & Upton Curate's Fund IU
Sly, Stephen & Wilson IU
Smales, E.C. L5,180
Smallfield, F. L5,192; IU
Smallwood, Edward L117A,22
Smart, Alice Hawley IU
Smart, H.B. L85,269
Smart, Hawley L2,77; L3,51 54; L5,26; L84,
140 150 161; L101,97; IU
Bitter is the Rind L37,45; L38,86; L100,43
Breezie Langton L37,52 58 289; L38,42 97;
L39,271-2; L40,100-1; L41,98-9 125; L42,
121; L63,317-21; L119,80
Cecile L37,297; L38,106; L39,401 432; L40,
424; L41,506; L59,253; L100,114
Race for a wife L37,236; L38,213; L99,252
Two kisses L38,332; L39,421; L59,329
Smart, R.H. L85,111 113-14(c); IU
Smart, R.L. IU
Smeaton, J. L117B,21
Smedley, Menilla Bute IU
Smelt, Captain R. L2,71
Smith, Miss L81,58
Smith, Miss (A.G.Vaughan pseud.)
The Romance of a court L2,50; L84,62; L37,
227; L38,216; L98,200
Smith, A.Bruce IU
Smith, A.J. L86,336 356
Smith, A.M. IU

[Smith, A.W.] IU

Smith, Adolphe L5,80; L101,25 38; IU

Smith, Albert R. L55,294; L82,333; L117B, 27; IU
  Adventures of Mr.Ledbury L7,153; L40,178; L41,194; L42,162-3; L122,78 112-13 123
  The Fortunes of the Scattergood family L7, 158; L122,78 112 123
  The Marchioness of Brinvilliers L40,178; L41,195; L42,469; L63,163; L122,76 110 123
  The Physiology of evening parties L55,120-3; L117B,12
  The Struggles and adventures of Christopher Tadpole L55,328
  The Wassail-bowl L7,149; L55,123 138

Smith, Miss Anne M.C. L2,54; L94,136; L101,223
  The Two Anastasias L36,168; L37,247; L38, 237; L98,65 71
  Work-a-day Briers L37,281; L38,248

Smith, Dr.Archibald
  Peru as it is L54,95; L117B,20

Smith, Arthur L83,194 197 199; IU

Smith, Augusta A.Varty L3,94; L86,407-10 412 414 416 418-19 422 425 427 437 440; L96, 203-10 203-10(c); IU; UC Manuscripts,23
  Matthew Tindale L41,420; L42,492 500; L65, 94-6 110

Smith, Beaumont L2,72

Smith, Charles E. L87,95 107 213
  see Richmond, George

Smith, Miss Constance L3,184; L4,71; L5,233; L22,356; L67,321; L86,342; L88,237-9 252; IU
  The Backslider L42,417; L67,186
  The Repentance of Paul Wentworth L41,454; L64,104
  The Riddle of Lawrence Haviland L41,439; L64,280

Smith, Miss E.M. L5,160

Smith, Miss Eleanor L3,183

Smith, Elizabeth E.(Mrs.Elton Smith) L90,48; L117A,21
  The East India sketch-book L52,286; L53,27
  The Three eras of woman's life L53,78; L81, 139

Smith, Evangeline J. UC

Smith, G. L63,86; L65,268; IU

Smith, George L5,236; L82,191-2

Smith, George & Co. IU George Bentley,356

Smith, George Barnett L5,90; IU

Smith, George M. L41,iv ix

Smith, Gerard W. L3,144; L85,258; IU

Smith, Goldwin IU

Smith, Rev.Gregory L5,299

Smith, H. L3,80

Smith, H. IU

Smith, H.Stinton IU

Smith, Harriet
  see Smith, Maria P.

Smith, Herbert Greenhough L3,75; L5,193 212-14 228; L87,269 274; L89,76; IU(Strand)
  Romance of history L41,370; L42,309

Smith, Horatio L1,32; L81,131; L117A,5; IU
  Gale Middleton L52,284; L53,32
  The Involuntary prophet L53,180

Smith, J.Caldecott IU George Bentley,265+2

Smith, J.H. IU

Smith, J.O. & Linton, W. IU

Smith, J.R. L117B,3

Smith, J.William IU

Smith, James L53,242-4; L82,285; L117A,5

Smith, Rev.John L53,274 307; L117B,16

Smith, Dr.John Gordon
  The English army at Waterloo L1,36; L52,42; L68,33

Smith, John Thomas
  A Book for a rainy day L7,159 270; L54,50
  Nollekens and his times L3,87; L42,351
  The Streets of London L1,172; L36,59 71; L37,234; L38,220; L39,421; L54,50

Smith, Mrs.John Thomas L54,50; L117A,31

Smith, Maria P.
  Castle Deloraine L6,131; L38,112; L56,331; L82,128 130-1; L117A,21

Smith, Matheson J. L94,202 216

Smith, Mrs.Matilda L3,122; IU

Smith, Montagu L91,30

Smith, O. L91,237

Smith, P.Horton IU

Smith, Percy Caldecott L86,474; L87,50; IU

Smith, Philip L94,187

Smith, Reginald Bosworth UC

Smith, Roandeu A.H.Bickford L3,68; L4,82; L22,342; L87,93 99 101(c) 107 128(c) 182; L88, 126 357; L89,51
  Cretan sketches L42,390
  Greece under King George L42,336-7

Smith, Robert Vernon L1,120; L83,118-19; L93,279; L117B,10; IU

Smith, Samuel S. IU

Smith, Seba L82,88

Smith, Rev.Sydney L67,250-65; L89,57

Smith, [T.] G. IU

Smith, Thomas L5,28

Smith, Thomas B. IU

Smith, Thomas R. IU

Smith, W.(F.C.pseud.)
  Anonymous poems L6,121; L69,143; L78,76; L117A,14

Smith, W.H. & Son L82,33 56; L83,67 212; L84,33 41 67 115-16 129 131; L85,199 266 268 443; L86,125(c) 313 326 464; L87,232; L88, 218 287; IU

Smith, W.J. L86,236 355

Smith, W.Luff IU

Smith, W.Paterson UC

Smith, W.R. IU

Smith, William UC(Bentley-end of B)

Smith, Sir William IU; UC

Smith, Sir William Sidney IU

Smith, William & G. IU

Smith, Elder & Co. L81,93; L82,295; L83, 258; L84,113; L88,46 49; IU

Smith & Seale L88,246 256 261

Smithers, Leonard L86,428

Smythe, George A.F.(7th Viscount Strangford)
L82,186; IU(Strangford)
Angela Pisani L3,19; L38,331; L39,401 430
Smythe, [Percy] IU(Strangford)
Smythe, Percy E.F.(8th Viscount Strangford)
A Selection from the writings of Viscount
Strangford L37,255; L38,224; L59,203
Smythies, H.M.G.
see Gordon, H.M.
Smythies, William Yorick L83,196; IU
Snelgrove, A.G. IU
Snell, Mme.A. L83,144
Snodgrass, John L5,107; IU
Snow, Mrs.Owen L5,294
Snow, William Parker L2,88; L87,124; IU
Soames, C. L5,66
Soane, George L92,25
Society L85,408; IU
Society for Promoting Christian Knowledge L7,
82 188-214; L8,passim
Society of Antiquaries of London IU
Society of Authors
see The Authors' Syndicate
Sodenstjerned, Mathilde von IU
Solomon, Miss B. L22,366
Solomon, Montague Granger IU
Somers, Earl of
see Cocks, J.S.
Somers, Robert L94,220
Somerscale, W.E. L81,154 156
Somerset, Aylmer IU
Somerville, Miss Edith A. L3,29; L86,235
355; L87,89 92 95 98; IU; UC
An Irish cousin (orig.An experiment) L41,452;
L64,98
Somerville, Elizabeth L94,265
Somerville, H.G. L3,153; L5,130; L85,358-9
423 430; L88,169; L89,50
Curiosities of impecuniosity L42,367; L61,
268-72; L62,252-7
Somerville, John L5,194
Sommariva, Marchesa de IU
Sophar, M.W. L86,205
Sophia, Electress of Hanover
Memoirs L3,155; L41,337; L64,64
Sotheby, Wilkinson & Hodge L82,19; L117B,
46; IU
Sotheran, H. & Co. L63,170; L82,302; L84,
125 158 208; L85,408
Soule & Bugbee L85,415
The South London Gazette IU
Southam, S.Clement IU
Southee, S. L83,163; IU(Soutbie)
Southey, [Car.] IU
Southey, Robert UC; UC Manuscripts,39
Southgate & Co. L59,43-4; L83,88 119 121
126-7 152 155
Southwell, Edmund M. IU
Southwell, T.Martin IU
Sowden, Mr. L84,38
Soyer, Alexis B. UC
Spackman, Netta UC
Spalding, Henry IU

Spalding, Thomas IU
Spalding & Hodge L83,98 100 102-3 107 259;
L84,74; L85,309 358; L86,159 218; IU
Sparrow, Arthur G. IU
Sparrow, Walter Shaw L5,308
The Spectator IU; IU(Hutton,R.H.)
Spedding, Sarah F.
Corbie's Pool L3,149; L39,392; L40,344;
L61,144-5
Speed, E.J. IU
Speedy, Mrs.Cornelia M. L3,178; L5,157;
L86,91 188
My wanderings in the Soudan L40,294; L41,
522; L62,233-4
Speight, Thomas W. L3,75; L85,206 211 254;
IU
In the dead of night L38,323; L39,451
The Mysteries of Heron Dyke L39,351; L40,
446; L41,523; L42,490; L60,248
A Secret of the sea L38,359; L39,437
Spence, Miss Catherine H. L2,54
The Author's daughter L37,23
Mr.Hogarth's will L36,218; L37,142; L59,83
Spence, James L2,44; L3,27; L83,236; L84,
299; IU
The American Union L36,280; L37,231; L58,
273; L102,26
On the recognition of the Southern Confederation
L36,164; L37,231; L38,230; L39,421
Southern independence L36,149; L37,231;
L38,230; L39,421
Spence, John L77,106-9
Spence, R.M. IU
Spencer, Lord George J. IU
Spencer, H. L84,326
Spencer, J. & T. IU
Spencer, Mary J. IU
Spencer, William Robert IU
Spender, Lily IU
Spenser, Edmund
Poems L40,384; L41,303; L42,315; L62,6
Spicer, H. & Co. L86,343
Spicer, Henry IU
Spicer, James & Sons IU
Spicer, William L5,24; IU
Spielhagen, Friedrich
The Breaking of the storm L3,98; L38,370;
L39,240
Spiller, Robert Ernest UC
Spinkan, Gustave L85,409
Spooner, Elizabeth IU
Spooner, Louisa M. L94,112 135 137
The Sporting Gazette IU
Spottiswoode & Co. L62,239; L82,102; L83,
113 238 241 265-6 276; L84,55-6 73 77; L85,
265 311 328 353-4 356 461-2 466; L86,296 342
354 356-7; L94,73; IU; IU Richard Bentley I,
29-32; UC
Sprague & Co. L86,382(c)
Sprigge, Sir Samuel Squire IU
Spriggs, J.F. L88,211
Spring, Mary IU
Springall, Stephen IU

Spurston, Heycrofts L86,353
Staal, Marguerite J. de
  Memoirs L39,252; L40,453
Stace, Mr. L81,165
Stacpoole, H. de Vere L3,148; L4,80; L5,
  257; L87,219; L88,116
  The Intended L42,435; L66,158; L67,125
Stacy, H.W. L86,218
Stallard, C. IU
Stamp, Edmund L84,128-9
The Standard, London L84,281; L86,420; IU
Standing, Percy Cross L5,302
Stanford, Mr. L86,162
Stanford, Mr.E. L86,353
Stanford, Edward IU
Stanhope, Lord Arthur P. IU
Stanhope, Gilbert L22,368
Stanhope, Lady Hester L. IU
Stanhope, Philip D.(4th Earl of Chesterfield)
  The Letters L7,157 173; L8,189 200; L36,
  194; L54,187; L55,276-7
  The Wit and wisdom L38,325; L39,101-1a;
  L40,216; L41,538; [L65,205]
Stanhope, Philip H.(Lord Mahon) L6,99; L8,
  92; L55,276; L84,247; L117A,34; IU
Stanisby, Miss UC(Bentley-end of B)
Stanley, Arthur P.(Dean of Westminster) L85,
  243 280; IU; UC(Executors)
Stanley, Edward H.(15th Earl of Derby)
  IU(Derby)
Stanley, Francis IU
  St. Petersburg to Plevna L39,281; L40,455;
  L60,77
Stannard, Arthur IU
Stannard, Mrs.Henrietta E.V.('J.S.Winter')
  L5,199
Stannton, M.A.A. IU
Starbuck, A.B. IU
Starbuck, William G. L2,38; L83,263; L94,
  119 157 161
  Latimer's luck L36,240; L37,169; L59,55;
  L98,106 124
  A Woman against the world (orig.Arcady) L36,
  157; L37,275; L38,250; L58,337; L97,272
  279 285; L98,9 66
Starker, James IU
Starting, W.F. IU
Statham, H.Heathcote L88,248; IU(The Builder)
Statham, Reginald IU
Stationers' Company IU
Staunton, T.H.
  The Family and school geography L36,263;
  L37,234; L38,232; L58,222; L83,232
Stead L86,101-2
Stead, William Thomas L88,148 281; UC
Stebbing, Miss Beatrice (Mrs.B.Batty) L1,179;
  IU(Batty); UC(Batty)
  Truth answers best L36,74; L63,237
Stebbing, Henry L94,155
  Lives of the Italian poets L36,84 122; L37,
  233; L58,210
Stedman, Algernon M.M. L63,302; L86,189
Steede, M. L5,295

Steeds, J.P. IU
Steele, Mrs. L5,19
Steele, Anna C. L2,68; IU
Steele, L.Edward L5,26
Stein, B. & Co. L86,309 336 346
Steinmetz, Andrew
  History of the Jesuits L56,73; L117B,38
  Tobacco L36,53; L58,117
Steinmetz, L. IU
Steinmetz, Mrs.M.A. IU
Stennett, Mrs.
  see Lupton, M.
Stent, Rev.P. L1,122; L117A,5
Stent, William D.
  Egypt and the Holy land L55,173; IU
Stephen, Miss IU
Stephen, Alexander C. IU
Stephen, Charlotte IU
Stephen, Leslie L85,173; IU
Stephen, Miss R. L5,33
Stephens, A.J. L82,356-7 359; IU
Stephens, Ann S.
  Fashion and famine L36,157; [L83,48]
Stephens, H.M. L5,209
Stephens, Henry P. IU
Stephens, John L. L81,205 232
Stephens, William R.W.(Dean of Winchester)
  L3,91; L4,58; L85,88; L87,50; IU
  Christianity and Islam L38,329; L39,250;
  L40,425; L41,208; L42,502-3; L60,52
  The Life of William F.Hook L38,356; L39,
  230 350; L40,204-5 265; L41,167-8 288; L42,
  262 510; L60,110 298; L119,99; L123,185-6
  188-9
  A Memoir of Baron Hatherley L40,311 350;
  L41,287; L42,514; L61,252-4
  Memorials of the South Saxon See of Chichester
  L38,355; L39,216; L40,291; L41,287; L42,
  513
Stephenson, Agnes L3,94; L60,2 40; IU
Stephenson, Emily L3,94; L60,2 40; IU
Stephenson, Robert IU
Stephenson, William IU
Stephenson-Hall, W. L81,153
Stepney, Lady Catherine
  see Manners, C.
Sterling, John L52,214; L81,49
Steuart, John A. L22,357
Stevens, Augusta de Grasse IU
Stevens, B.F. L67,117; L87,231 278; L88,73
Stevens, G.L. L5,227; IU
Stevens, Henry L83,120
Stevens, John L.
  History of Gustavus Adolphus L40,218; L41,
  253; L42,220
Stevens, N. L95,109
Stevens & Sons L85,419(c)
Stevenson, Andrew L81,220
Stevenson, D.M. L5,156
Stevenson, Joseph IU
Stevenson, M.E.
  see Carter, M.E.
Stevenson, Robert L. L5,94; IU

Stevenson, Mrs.Scott L85,221
Stewart, C.S. IU
Stewart, Caroline IU
Stewart, Charles W.(Marquis of Londonderry)
  L1,25; L81,57 197 219-20 229; L117A,39;
  IU(Londonderry)
  Narrative of the war L52,65; L68,37
  Recollections of a tour in the north of Europe
  L36,189
Stewart, W.
  Narrative of his escape from the Americans
  (prop.) L53,95
Stibbs, E.W. IU
Stickney, S.
  see Ellis, S.
Stiff, G. L6,118; L117A,39
Stifter, Adalbert
  Pictures of rural life L8,120
Stigand, Isabella S.E. IU
Stigand, William L5,24; IU
Stiles, John IU
Stirling, Rev.C. UC(Norwich)
Stirling, John L68,93
Stirling, William IU
Stisted, Miss Georgiana M. L5,235
Stock, Elliot L86,450; L87,143; IU
Stock, St.George IU
Stock, W. L87,267; L88,297
Stocker, Miss Constance H.D. L3,181; L5,
  183; L85,455
  Between the acts L40,400; L41,505; L62,
  224-6
Stocqueler, J.H. L92,16-18 110-11
Stodart, G. L63,62 94; L86,293 295 316
Stodart, Maria IU
Stokes, Rev.Louis L3,142; L5,174; L85,280;
  IU
Stone, C.J. L94,285 300 302
Stone, Elizabeth L117B,6
  Chronicles of fashion L7,158; L55,164
  Miss Pen and her niece L55,154
  William Langshawe L7,149; L55,133
Stoneham, F. & E. L86,171; L88,94 96 99(c)
  100; L89,43 49
Stoney, Rev.W. L5,266
Storkhausen, O. von IU
Story, Alfred T. L3,24; L5,254; L86,439
  458 466 469; L87,59 132 183 202(c); IU; UC
  James Holmes and John Varley L42,354;
  L66,191
  The Life of John Linnell L41,363; L42,266;
  L65,92
Stothard, Anna E.(Mrs.A.E.Bray) L82,314;
  L117B,13; IU(Bray)
  Courtenay of Walreddon L7,155; L55,211
  Henry de Pomeroy L7,148; L55,54-5
Stott, David L86,276 280 338 411 413 462
Strafford, Lord IU
Strahan, A. IU
Straker, William L92,203; L117A,36; L117B,
  35
The Strand Magazine IU
Strang, M. L92,144

Strange, E.F. L5,249
Strangford, Lady E.A.
  see Beaufort, E.A.
Strangford, Viscount
  see Smythe
Stredder, Sarah L94,291-3
Street, Alfred B. L82,65 68
  Frontenac L6,180; L36,157
Street Brothers L85,266
Street, George & Co. L61,237; L62,38-40;
  L85,32 351 358 393; L86,105; IU
Street, H. IU
Streeten, C.A. IU
Stretton, Charles L2,50; L83,247
  Memoirs of a chequered life L36,282; L37,
  235; L58,293; L102,35 40
Stretton, Edward B. IU
Stretton, Hesba L2,70; L99,155; IU
Strickland, Agnes L2,61; L57,184; L82,275
  356; L83,37 131-2; L94,283; L117B,43; IU
  How will it end? L36,242; L37,141; L59,81
Strickland, Elizabeth IU
Strickland, Jane IU
Strickland, Samuel
  Twenty-seven years in Canada West L1,87;
  L7,173; L8,200; L57,184
Strickland, Susanna
  see Moodie, Mrs.S.
Strickland, W.J. IU
Stringer & Townsend L82,36
Stringfellow, F. L86,115
Stritch, B. L92,65 286
Stronach, George IU
Strong, Herbert A. L3,173; IU
Strong & Hanbury L87,125 194 200(c) 281; L88,
  112 215
Stuart, Captain L85,269
Stuart, Alex. L5,159
Stuart, Arthur
  see Cochrane, Arthur
Stuart, Charles Pole IU
Stuart, Miss G.B. L5,199; L87,173; L88,43
  45(c) 45 53(c) 53
Stuart, Miss H. IU
Stuart, J. L5,161
Stuart, J.W. IU
Stuart, McDougall L83,230
Stuart, Robert M. IU
Stuart, Thomas P. L87,227(c)
Stuart, de Rothesay, Lady Elizabeth M. IU
Stubbs, Miss Laura UC
Stubbs, Rev.William L1,185; L2,50; L94,
  64-6; L95,1; L102,29-42 45-79 87-9 179-81;
  IU
Sturge, Mrs.Jane L3,110; L60,67-8 172; L85,
  54; IU
Sturgess, John IU
Sturgis, Howard O. L22,353
Sturgis, Russell L83,79 83 87
Styles, John
  Dictionary of churches and sects (prop.) L52,
  230
Suffield, Lord Edward H. IU

Suliga, Countess de IU
Sulivan, Robert L3,43; L4,81; IU
  The Agent of Broome Warren L37,124; L38,
  87; L59,244; L100,98
Sullivan, Mrs. IU
Sullivan, Mrs.Arabella J. L81,132; L117A,8
  Recollections of a chaperon L122,81 124
  Tales of the peerage and peasantry L122,82
  124
Sullivan, Sir Edward R. L1,177; L83,42-3 45;
  L93,236; L117A,32
  Rambles and scrambles in America L57,
  148-50
Sumner, Charles IU
Sumner, George L5,33; IU
The Sun, London L87,198; L88,225; IU
Sun Fire Insurance L65,102; L86,100 343
[Sünndrop] UC
Surr, Thomas S. L1,63
Surrage, Mr. L122,94-6
Surtees, W.E. L53,303
Sutcliffe & Birch L81,106
Sutherland, Duke of
  see Gower, G.G.L.
Sutherland, Dr.
  Autobiography of an Indian Army surgeon L1,
  160; L36,170; L57,221; L117B,29
Sutter, Miss Julie L3,174 178 180; L4,59;
  L42,365; L62,231; L64,189-92; L86,285 305;
  L88, 97 101 146 156-62 164 188-9 203 205 216-17
  316-18 321 324-5 360; L89,46 48 50; IU
  England's greatest problem (prop.; orig.Wanted,
  the upper ten) L67,48
Sutton & Co. L88,351
Swain, J. & Co. L86,171-2 176-7; IU; UC
Swaine, Mrs. L5,247
Swan, Rev.C. L81,62
Swan, Sonnenschein & Co. L86,53 475-7; IU;
  IU George Bentley,261+1
Sweetman, Miss Elinor M. L5,278
Swift, P.D. L89,73(c); UC Manuscripts,11
Swire, Mrs.Elaine A. L5,306; IU
Sylvester, James J. IU
Symes, Fraser IU
Symmons, E. & Sons L85,90 222 267 460 470;
  L86,291 375 447 461 464; L87,91 153 281;
  L88,108-9 119-22 126 135 138 141 143-4 205(c)
  249 347; L89,58 70 84-5
Symmons & Bolton L84,164; L86,386
Symon, James D. L5,24
Symonds, Miss L5,250; L22,349
Symonds, Emily M.(George Paston pseud.)
  L88,330; L89,44 52 54 125; IU
Symonds, Miss Margaret L89,69
Symonds, William S.
  Stones of the valley L36,41; L58,124
Symons, A. L5,219
Symons, George James IU; UC(end of S)
Synge, Mark (Powell Millington pseud.) L5,
  131; IU
Syrett, Miss Netta L5,299
Szemere, Bertalan
  Hungary from 1848-1860 L36,78; L82,232; IU

Tabrum, Arthur H. UC
Tagore, Devendranath IU Unidentified,(A)
Tait, Archibald C. IU
Tait, J.Selwin & Sons L66,221; L88,72 95 110
Talbot, F. L5,64
Talfourd, T.N. IU
Talleyrand-Périgord, C.M. de L80,27
  The correspondence of Prince Talleyrand L3,
  52 138; L39,363; L40,326; L41,209; L42,
  503; L60,281 299-300
Taplin, S.A. IU
Tapparelli D'Azeglio, Massimo
  The Maid of Florence (orig.Nicolo de Lapi)
  L36,195; L57,167
Taranaki News IU(Brown,C.)
Taraporevala, D.B. & Co. L88,176; L89,93
Tarpey, Mrs.J.T.Kingsley L5,291
Tarpey, W.Kingsley L5,270; L88,279; L89,
  79; IU
Tarr, William H. L86,79
Tarry, Captain G.C. L5,292
Tarver, H. IU
Tarver, Helen A. IU
Tasburgh, Mr. L81,141
Tasma
  see Couvreur, J.C.
Tauchnitz, Bernhard von (Baron) L59,208-10
  270 310; L60,30 64-5 126 136-7 243; L61,
  180-3; L62,325; L63,169 265 308; L64,142
  176 316; L65,1 38 59 63 151 237 247; L66,85
  133-5; L67,22 50-1 246; L84,50 82 188 229;
  L85,167; L86,394; L87,263; IU; IU(Uhlmann);
  UC
Tautphoeus, Jemima von (Baroness) L1,157;
  L2,28; L5,20; L66,27; L82,138 148 332;
  L83,109-10 141-4 146 150 160 162 164 177 193
  199 253; L117A,27; IU
  At odds L36,289; L37,67; L38,61; L39,54;
  L40,106; L42,160; L58,217
  Cyrilla L6,155 173; L36,138; L38,48-9;
  L39,56; L40,105; L57,155
  The Initials L7,169; L8,119; L36,144 147
  171 221; L37,46 61 71; L38,36; L39,57-8;
  L40,102-3; L41,99-100; L42,122; L56,201;
  L58,219; L119,137
  Quits L36,88 213; L37,62 66 73; L38,37;
  L39,59; L40,104; L41,100-1; L42,123; L58,
  141-2 219; L119,138
Tayler, Charles B. IU
  Not of the world L36,211; L37,245; L38,240
Tayler, J.W. L94,169 177
Taylor, Miss IU Unidentified,(A)
Taylor, Miss Alice L5,267; L22,366; L87,
  159; IU
Taylor, Francis L94,171-3
Taylor, Frederick Winslow UC
Taylor, Helen B.
  Soups, savouries, sweets L41,340 498; L42,
  320; L64,92-4; L86,232 343 456 478; L87,216
Taylor, Henry R. L84,326
Taylor, Miss Ida A. L3,43; L5,272 303; IU
  Allegiance L40,455; L41,504; L63,111
Taylor, J. IU

Taylor, James L81,198 202
Taylor, John IU
Taylor, John E. L1,154; L82,70 74 260; L83,
68 117 125 193; L93,82-4 208-9; L117A,29
Taylor, John G.
The United States and Cuba L7,171; L8,150
Taylor, Marianne Cooke IU
Taylor, Meadows L83,236; L91,143; L92,115;
L117B,9; IU
Confessions of a thug L36,40; L54,103
Tippoo Sultaun L54,263-5
Taylor, Philip Meadows L91,213-15; IU
Taylor, R. L85,381
Taylor, Richard S. L61,14-75 passim; L86,
379 382
Taylor, Richard W.C.
Introduction to a history of the factory system
L3,71; L4,82; L41,265; L42,241-2; L63,102
Taylor, T. & Sons L81,204
Taylor, T.C. IU
Taylor, Tom L92,34-6; IU
The King's rival
Masks and faces
Three dramas
see Reade, C.
Taylor, Miss Una A. L5,61
Taylor, W.G. L83,183
Taylor, Whately C. L5,186; L54,211; L91,
254 262 267; L92,200-1 217; IU;
[IU(Coquilla)]
Taylor, William Cooke L117B,7; IU;
[IU(Coquilla)]
Memoirs of the House of Orleans L7,167;
L8,95; L56,162
The Revolutions of Europe L7,151; L55,166
Romantic biography L7,148
Taylor, Hoare & Box L86,496; L87,50
Taylour, Virginia L3,63; L64,295-9; L86,348
Teague, Rev.J.Jessop L5,212; IU
Tebbitt, Stanton IU
Teeling, Mrs.T.L.L. L5,110; IU
Tegg, Thomas L52,220 254 256 277; L68,96;
L73A,35; L123,137
Telephone Company L85,363
Tempest, Lord Ernest Vane IU
Temple, Sir Edmond
Travels in Peru L1,47; L52,32 34; L68,30;
IU
Temple, F. IU
Temple, Sir Grenville IU
Temple, Henry J.(3rd Viscount Palmerston)
IU(Palmerston)
Selections from private journals L37,219;
L38,208; L39,184
Temple, N. IU
Temple, Hon.W.Cooper L84,252; IU
Templer, John C. L57,289; L82,330-1 360;
L117A,37
Tenison L83,78
Tenison, Lady Louisa M.A. L82,286
Tennant, George L84,55
Tennant, Gertrude IU
Tennent, Sir James E.

see Emerson, J.E.
Tenniel, Sir John L83,154 176 180 243; IU
Tennyson, Miss Mary H.
see Folkard, M.H.T.
Terry, Daniel IU
Testard, Henri IU
Thacker & Co. L82,334; L83,257; L88,231(c)
290; L89,80 108
Thackeray, Rev.F.St.John L5,260
Thackeray, J.D. IU
Thackeray, W.M. L82,345; L83,170; L90,197
204; UC
Thackwell, Edward J. L1,122; L83,82; L93,
303; L117B,11
Narrative of the Second Sikh War L56,280
Theobald, Sir Henry Studdy IU
Thienemann, K. IU
Thiers, Louis A. IU
History of the French Revolution L36,24 286
288; L37,244; L38,241; L39,187 362; L40,
199 328; L41,254; L42,221 348-9 351; L53,
318; L66,151-4 178; L92,44; L117B,17;
L123,146
Thing, Harriet B. IU
Thios, W.A. IU
Thirlwall, Connop (Bishop of St.David's) L40,
463
Essays, speeches and sermons L39,336; L40,
330; L41,308; L42,522
Letters of Connop Thirlwall L3,142 148; L39,
367; L40,331 468; L41,163-4; L42,270; L60,
210-18; L61,224; L119,102
Thirlwall, John L60,210; IU
Thirlwall, Thomas J. IU
Thiselton, Mrs.Elizabeth L9,135; L58,245
Thisted, V.A.
Letters from Hell L2,24; L3,60 174 178 180;
L4,59; L37,180; L38,177; L40,291 354; L41,
274-5 345 392; L42,454-5; L59,126; L62,231;
L64,189-92 289-90
Thistlethwayle, James Seymour IU; UC
Thistlethwayte, Mrs.Tryphena F. L1,123;
L117A,34
Memoirs and correspondence of Dr.Henry
Bathurst L1,87; L36,21; L57,223
Thomas, Bertha L3,146; IU
Elizabeth's fortune L3,20; L40,109; L41,
493; L63,179
In a cathedral city L39,393; L40,351; L61,
152
The Violin-player L39,343; L60,244-5
Thomas, C.G. L88,255
Thomas, J.L. IU
Thomasson, John P. IU
[Thomes, A.] IU
Thompson, A.Hamilton L5,303
Thompson, A.T. IU
Thompson, Alfred IU
Thompson, C.Leonard IU
Thompson, G. L83,27
Thompson, Rev.Henry L5,95; IU; UC
Thompson, John IU
Thompson, Margaret W. IU

Thompson, Reginald IU
Thompson, Springale IU
Thompson, W. IU(Thomson)
Thoms, Peter P. L75,108-58; L77,83-105
Thoms, William J. L6,128; L82,46-7; L90,
 257 314 316; L92,137; L117A,35; IU; UC
 Extraordinary characters (prop.) L6,128;
 L55,268
Thomson, Dr.Anthony T. L55,296; L92,103;
 L117A,35
Thomson, D.Spencer
 The Heiress of Somerton L1,123; L36,89;
 L57,204; L82,288; L117B,10
Thomson, Miss Henrietta L2,26; L84,89 96;
 IU(Alexander,H.)
Thomson, J.G. L84,174
Thomson, James
 see Thomson, Richard
Thomson, K. IU
Thomson, Mrs.Katharine L82,211 212 273 285
 324; L83,61 135; L92,103 124-5; L117A,15
 The Chevalier L7,156; L55,223
 Constance L53,40
 The Heir of Sherborne L36,164
 The Lady of Milan L7,159
 Memoirs of the Jacobites L7,159-60; L55,238
 Ragland Castle L7,151; L55,146
 Tracey L55,332
 The White mask L7,153; L55,170
 Widows and widowers L7,149; L55,91
Thomson, Mowbray
 The Story of Cawnpore L1,174; L2,53; L36,
 62 73 118; L37,246; L38,238; L58,203
Thomson, Richard L90,148 166-8 263
Thomson, T.R.H.
 A narrative of the expedition to the River Niger
 see Allen, William
Thoré, Theophile L56,127
Thornbury, W. L95,78
Thornley, Jer. IU
Thornton L38,239
Thornton, Conway L5,231
Thorold, Richard
 see Astley, Sir John
Thorpe, William G. L3,137; L4,78; L86,438
 480; L89,126; IU
 The Still life of the Middle Temple L41,375;
 L42,321; L65,152; L66,23
Thredder, J. L83,29
Thring, G.Herbert
 see The Authors' Syndicate
[Thuig] , Herrick B. UC
Thurston, B.W. IU; UC(end of T);
 UC Manuscripts,34 44
Thurston, William L5,181; IU
Thwaite, W.H. L91,95-6
Thynne, Lord Charles L2,68
Thynne, F.J. IU
Thynne, John Alexander (4th Marquis of Bath)
 IU(Bath)
Thynne, R. L88,217
Ticknor, Reid & Fields L82,68 79 322
Tiddeman, L.E. L5,288; L88,340

Tieck, Sophie
 The Peasant and his landlord L56,21 54
Tillotson & Son L85,463; L86,245(c); IU
Tilly, Harry L83,158
Tilt, Julia
 The Old palace L1,161; L36,194 224; L58,
 169
Timbs, John L1,188; L2,48; L3,38; L82,221;
 L83,195 211; IU
 Anecdote biography L36,264 282-3 292; L37,
 249; L38,236-7 242 342; L39,121-3; L40,
 209-10 213-15; L41,179-80; L42,163-5; L58,
 211; UC Manuscripts,43
 Anecdote lives of the later wits and humourists
 L38,306; L39,124-5
 A Century of anecdote L36,290; L37,248;
 L58,332
 Club life of London L36,300; L37,248; L59,
 48
 Doctors and patients L38,273 361; L39,120-1
 434; L40,197; L41,182; L42,185
 English eccentrics L37,250; L59,101
 Lives of wits and humourists L36,282; L39,
 123-4; L41,181; L42,165-6
 London and Westminster L37,251; L38,236;
 L39,421; L40,441
 Romance of London L36,196; L37,247; L59,
 48
The Times, London L66,255; L67,221-3; L82,
 58 75; L83,164; L84,225; L85,407; L88,210
 274; IU; UC(Bentley-end of B); UC(Delane)
The Times of India L88,239
Timins, D.T. L5,44
Tindal, Acton IU
Tindal, Charles H. IU; UC
Tindal, Mrs.Henrietta E.(Mrs.Acton Tindal)
 L4,77; L5,70; L84,335; IU
 Rhymes and legends L39,332; L40,319; L41,
 530; L42,519; L123,209-10
Tinling, Rev.J.F.B. L88,315
Tinniswood, Mrs. L86,281
Tinsley, Mrs.Annie
 see Turner, A.
Tinsley, Charles L83,185
Tinsley Brothers L83,239 247 265 270; L84,
 291
Tinsleys Magazine L59,340(c); IU
Tisdall, Charles E. IU
Tissot, Victor
 Unknown Hungary L3,132; L39,349; L40,
 334; L60,230-5
Tit Bits L86,234(c) 234-6 241(c) 241 244(c)
 368 368(c) 369; IU
Tocklington, Miss IU
Tod, H.M. L89,103(c); UC(Chaplin)
Todd, Mrs. L86,123 131 132
Todhunter, John L22,361
Toker, Mrs. L83,92 94
Tolfrey, Frederick L91,25-7; IU
Tollemache L87,220
Tollemache, Mrs. IU
Tollemache, Beatrix L. IU
Tollemache, Hon.Mrs.Lionel L5,287

Tomalin, James B. L91,31
Tomasson, Miss Beatrice L62,1-4; L85,380
Tomkins, Thomas UC Manuscripts,46
Tomlins, Thomas E. L81,70
Tomlinson, Rev.C.W. L5,106
Tomlinson, William R. IU
Tondini, Caesarius IU
Toogood, Frederick L84,268
Toogood, Harriet L2,30; L3,24; L84,279;
  L94,241; IU
  The Treasury of French cookery L37,251;
  L38,238-9; L39,226; L84,129
Toogood, William IU
Tooke, Arthur William L91,91; L117B,5
Tooke, N.P. IU
Toole, J.L. L85,277
Tooley, Sarah A. IU
Topham, C. IU
Topping, Charles
  see Wrigley & Co.
Torquay Directory L84,217
Torrens, W.T.McCullagh L3,119; L87,213;
  IU
  Twenty years in Parliament L41,38; L42,327;
  L65,243
Tortell, W.J. L83,44 46
Tottenham, Miss Blanche M.L. L3,128
  Who wins-loses
  see Young, A.S.C.
Toulmin, Camilla L91,62 69; IU(Tonkmin)
Tournaillon, E.H. IU
Tourt, T. L86,269 294 396
Tower Furnishing Finance Company L86,131
Towley, George Makepeace IU
Towne, Lieut. L53,28 103; L117A,13
Townsend, Mrs. IU
Townshend, C.Hare IU
Townshend, Mrs.Chambery L5,271
Townshend, Rev.Tyler L5,27
Toynbee, Mrs.Helen L5,303; IU
Toynbee, Paget UC
Toynbee, William L5,255; L88,299 324(c); IU
Traherne, Harriet M.A. IU
Travers, Eaton A. L86,431(c)
Travers, F.
  see Ellicott, F.
Treadway, G. L88,199-200(c)
Tregaskis, James UC
Tregellas, Mrs. L88,52
Trelawny, Edward J.
  Adventures of a younger son L1,20; L81,146;
  L117A,8; L122,59-60
Tremlett, Rev.Francis W. L3,137; L5,65;
  L37,252; L85,418; L86,240; IU
  God's way of answering prayer L39,396 452;
  L40,458; L41,255
  Hymns and anthems for churches L37,263;
  L38,234; L39,186 204; L40,333; L41,255
  The Sword and its retributions L38,234; L39,
  396 452; L40,458; L41,255
  Vivisection L38,233; L39,396 452; L40,458;
  L41,255
Trench, Rev.H.Francis

L1,94; L5,68; L82,61 63; L92,93 113; L117A,
  32; IU(French); IU(Trenet)
  Diary of travels in France and Spain L55,256
  Memoir of her late Majesty (prop.) L56,214
  Scotland, its faith and its features L55,300
  A Walk round Mont Blanc L56,57
Trench, Maria M.F.
  Journal abroad L37,254; L38,235; L39,399
  449; L40,459; L41,515; L42,509
Treuttel & Wintz L81,36
Trevelyan, Sir Charles L83,111
Trevor, Rev.James L83,252 260; L84,28-9
Trevor, Mrs.Philip L5,152
Trikes & Caftahl L63,229
Tristram, W.Outram IU
Trollope, Mrs. L5,37
Trollope, Anthony L1,162; L5,51; L83,156-7;
  L122,109; IU; UC
  The American senator (pub.Chatto & Windus)
  L59,330
  The Three clerks L36,69 170 227; L37,55 63
  67; L38,41; L39,60-60a; L40,108-9; L41,
  101-2; L42,124; L58,152-4; L119,37
Trollope, Miss C.A. L5,308; L22,359
Trollope, Frances L90,141-2 189 287; L91,71;
  L117A,26; L122,69 107; IU
  The Life of Jonathan Jefferson Whitlaw L53,
  201 240 256
  One fault L7,142
  Paris and the Parisians L53,156; L80,16
  A Romance of Vienna L53,240 280; L54,46;
  L81,200
  The Temporal history of the Pope (prop.) L53,
  237
  Tremordyn Cliff L53,150
  The Vicar of Wrexhill L53,240 252 256; L122,
  123
  A Visit to Italy L7,149; L53,240 281
  The Ward L7,146; L54,309
  The Widow Barnaby L122,71 108 123
Trollope, Frances Eleanor (Mrs.T.Adolphus
  Trollope) L3,98; L65,274; L86,224; L87,
  64; IU
  Black spirits and white L38,370; L39,271;
  L60,19; L67,118-20
  Frances Trollope L42,364; L66,292; L67,36
  Madame Leroux L41,440; L42,491; L64,
  245-7
  That unfortunate marriage L41,462; L64,80
  That wild wheel L41,414; L42,476; L65,140
Trollope, Henry M. L86,52
Trollope, Thomas A. L2,85; L3,40; L5,26
  152; L64,80; L65,274; L85,1 11 94; L86,
  126(c) 128 134 138 266 334 433; IU
  Durnton Abbey L37,257; L38,120; L39,438;
  L100,46
  The Stilwinches of Combe Mavis L38,265;
  L39,438; L40,455; L100,159
  The Story of the life of Pius the Ninth L39,
  248; L40,449; L60,27-8
  What I remember (orig.My autobiography)
  L41,318 344 534; L42,518; L63,204; L64,
  184-5

Trotter, Coutts IU
Trübner & Co. L1,124; L57,253; L82,310 335
  337 369-70; L84,164 285 289 332(c) 333; L85,
  148; L117A,40; IU
  see Kegan Paul & Co.
Trueba y Cosio, J.T. L1,63; L117A,3; IU
  Paris and London (orig.Satanic records) L52,
  174; L68,78
  Salvador, the guerilla L52,292
Truslove & Hanson L88,334
Tschopp, Teresa L89,95(c)
Tua, Major Giacinto L67,170; L88,171
Tubbs, Mrs.F.Cecilia L59,1; L83,266
Tucker, Admiral IU
Tucker, C.N. L94,256
Tucker, Henry S.
  Memorials of Indian government L36,240
Tucker, Jedediah S. L1,95; L117B,31
  Memoirs of the Earl of St.Vincent L7,151;
  L55,156
  Naval financial reform L7,168; L8,94; L38,
  242
Tucker, Marwood L3,63; L96,41; IU
  Michael Tresidder L37,321; L38,260; L84,
  188; L100,92
Tuckerman, Charles K. L3,131; L4,80; L67,
  115 143-5; L88,44(c); IU
  Personal recollections L42,360; L66,316 323
Tuckerman, Henry T. L83,130; L93,226;
  L117A,3; IU
Tuckey, Miss Janet L5,83; IU
Tudball, Charles D. IU
Tudor, Elizabeth E. IU
Tugwell, George
  On the mountain L36,297; L37,246; L58,290;
  L102,37
Tupling, John IU
Tupper, Martin F. L91,268; L92,26 30;
  L117B,31; IU; UC
  An Author's mind L7,147; L55,36
  The Crock of gold L7,153; L55,209
  Heart L7,153
  The Twins L7,153
Turco, E. L86,148
Turgenev, Ivan S.
  Smoke L2,78; L3,70; L37,253; L38,226;
  L39,274; L59,175; L70,123; L99,167
Turnbull, David L81,32 62
Turner, Alfred L58,27
Turner, Alfred T. L5,144; L22,365
Turner, Annie (Mrs.A.Tinsley) L82,349; L83,
  185; L117A,38
  Margaret L36,197; L57,214 280; L82,298
  Women as they are L57,280
Turner, Charles J.Ribton UC(Ribton)
Turner, Dawson L1,64; L52,21; L68,23
Turner, E. IU
Turner, Edgar L5,250
Turner, Henry L5,74
Turner, J.Hudson L90,244; L91,173
Turner, Mathew J. L53,276 278
Turner, R. L87,166
Turnerelli, Edward T.

Russia on the borders of Asia L57,272; L117B,
  25
Twain, Mark
  see Clemens, S.L.
Tweeddale, Captain
  The Griffin's aide-de-camp L6,70; L7,150;
  L117B,42
Tweedie, Mrs.Ethel B. L5,256; L88,285; IU
Twemlow, Miss Fanny L63,57; L86,78 81
  82-4(c) 205
Tweney & Co. L86,402
Twisden L1,52
Twiss, Horace IU
  Events and characters in the reigns of George I
  and George II (prop.) L56,160; L82,20-2
  Life of Lord Eldon (pub.J.Murray) L54,71
Twiss, Sir Travers L5,171; IU; UC
Tylee, Edward Sydney L5,201
Tyler L87,76(c)
Tyler, H.W. IU
Tyler, Sir Henry L85,175
Tyler, Rev.James E. L1,124; L117B,2; IU
  Henry of Monmouth L54,75
  The Worship of the Blessed Virgin Mary L7,
  155; L55,219
Tyler, John L85,94
Tyndale, John W.W. L1,95; L6,124; L83,77;
  L117A,20
  The Burger and Brighton Leonora L7,167;
  L8,95
  The Island of Sardinia L7,166; L8,76 94;
  L56,107
Typographic Etching Company L85,379
Tyrrell, Mrs.Christina L3,92; L60,242; L85,
  264 364; IU
Tyson, Miss L5,232
Tytler, Christina C.F.
  see Liddell, C.C.F.
Tytler, Miss M.E.Fraser L3,170; L4,82; IU
  Transplanted L40,381; L61,306; L62,38-40
Tytler, Patrick F. IU
  England under Edward VI and Mary L7,139;
  L54,181-3; L81,55; L117B,7

U.S.A.: Vice Consul General L85,251
Uhlmann & Co. IU
Underdown, Miss E. L22,353 364
United Service Company L84,59 61
United Service Gazette IU
United Service Magazine, Philadelphia L87,150
United State Geological & Geographical Survey
  L85,170
United Telephone Company
  see National Telephone Company
Unwin, Jane C. IU
Unwin, Thomas Fisher L86,281; L88,296; IU;
  UC
Upcott, William L117A,18; IU
Upton, Miss Alice L89,95
Upton Old Church, Slough L84,191
Upton-cum-Chalvey Charities IU
Urlin, R.Denny IU

Urmston, H.B. IU
Urquhart, David
  The Pillars of Hercules L7,169; L8,111;
  L56,125
Uttley, Thomas F. L86,487 489

Vachell, Horace A. L3,154; L4,74; L87,265;
  L88,171 182 186; L89,76 93(c); IU
  A Drama in sunshine (pub.McM.) L42,500;
  L67,273-5; L88,356
  The Model of Christian Gay L42,432; L66,
  217-19
  The Quicksands of Pactolus L42,420; L67,
  156-7
  The Romance of Judge Ketchum L42,425;
  L66,221
Vacher, Eliza IU
Vaillant, V.J. L5,78 88
Valentine, Mrs.L. L87,191
Valles, Baron de los
  see Auguet de Saint-Sylvain, L.X.
Vallings, E.Harold L3,97; L87,113 257; L88,
  68; IU
  A Month of madness L42,428; L66,300;
  IU Richard Bentley & Son (Manuscript Dept.)
  A Parson at bay L42,434; L66,189
  The Transgression of Terence Clancy L42,
  450; L66,25
Valmer, George IU
Valpy, Abraham J. L52,56 60 62; L81,39-40
Valpy, Leonard Rowe L85,131; IU
Valpy, R. L52,56 60 62
Vandam, Albert D. L3,100; L5,244; IU
Vanherman, E. IU
Van Homrigh, A.H. IU(Scientific Press)
Van Homrigh, S.R. IU
Vanity Fair IU; UC
Vardy, A.R. IU
Varley, Isabella (Mrs.G.Linnaeus Banks) L2,
  60; L5,24; L84,67; L98,230; IU(Banks)
  God's providence house L36,297; L37,31;
  L38,144; L59,75
Varnals, P. L86,73
Vase, Gillan IU
Vaslyn L90,298-300
Vaughan, Miss L85,110
Vaughan, A.G.
  see Smith, Miss
Vaughan, C. L5,73
Vaughan, Cleveland IU
Vaughan, Rev.John L5,239; L88,280; IU
Vaughan, Herbert M. L5,304
Vaughan, Virginia IU
Vaughan, W.F. IU
Veitch, John Leith L3,139; L85,264 343 354;
  IU; UC
  A Daughter of the Pyramids (orig.Kem) L41,
  437; L42,482; L64,269
  King Lazarus L39,368; L40,437; L61,1
Veitch, Miss Sophie F.F. L2,57; L5,35; L99,
  273; L100,15; L101,134; IU

Wife or slave (orig.Juggernauth) L37,314;
  L38,246; L40,461; L59,257; L100,88 149
Wise as a serpent L37,282; L38,247; L59,
  202
Velhagen & Klasing L85,476
Vellner, Leon IU Unidentified,(A)
Venables, Gilbert IU
Venables, H. IU
Venis, J. L88,60
Venn, Susanna C. L3,169; L85,417; L87,198;
  L88,50; IU
  The Dailys of Sodden Fen (orig.Eight hundred
  acres) L40,390; L62,132-4
  Some married fellows L41,406; L42,462;
  L65,270
Venning, Rose L5,207
Vereker, Col. L85,301 302(c) 302
Vereshchagin, Vasily V.
  Vassili Verestchagin (orig.Sketches of an
  adventurous life) L41,319 322; L63,214; L86,
  100; IU
Verrier L65,235
Vertannes, Z. UC
Vervoitte, Anna IU
Vibart, Col. L87,141
Vicars, Rayleigh L87,85(c) 85
Vicary, John Fulford IU
Vicary, M.
  Notes of a residence at Rome L7,164 [168];
  L8,52 95; L56,43-4; L117A,34
Vickers, Henry L85,144 185 185-7(c) 187 223
  298
Vickers, J.W. & Co. L84,260
Vickery, T. L80,13
Vickriss, Frances
  The Priest miracles of Rome L56,333
Vigée le Brun, Marie L.
  Souvenirs L3,114; L39,294; L123,184-5
Vignolles, Rev.J.O. L5,234
Villari, Linda IU
Villemain, Abel F.
  Life of Gregory the Seventh L3,48; L38,287;
  L39,209
Villiers, Charles Pelham IU
Villiers, H.Montagu IU
Vincent, Col.H.A. L5,301
Vines, Mrs. IU
Viney, Edmund
  see Christian, E.V.B.
Virgil
  Bucolics, Georgics and Aeneid L2,51 58-9;
  L3,53 135-6; L36,131 281; L37,286 288; L38,
  257-8; L39,192; L40,342-3; L41,314; L42,
  335; L58,283; L59,112
Virtue, G. L91,144
Virtue & Co. L85,265 291 295 349 382 384 387
  402
Vismes, Prince de (Old Calabar pseud.) L3,58;
  L5,77; L84,239 249; IU
  Over turf and stubble L38,279; L39,433;
  L100,[255] 270
  Won in a canter L38,306; L101,91
Vizetelly, Edward H. L5,241; IU

Vizetelly, Henry L82,248-50; L95,92; IU
Vogel, B.G. L52,151; L68,67
Vokins, William IU
Voss, Sophie W.C.M. von
  Sixty-nine years at the Court of Prussia L3,
  94; L38,362; L39,223; L40,325; L41,535;
  L42,521; L60,2
Voysey, Rev.Charles IU
Vrangel, Baron Ferdinand von
  Narrative of an expedition (pub.Harper & Bros.)
  L54,280
Vyse, Griffin W. L85,194 196; IU; UC

[W.H.O.] UC Manuscripts,44
W., P.T. L5,82
W., W.H.C. L92,134
Waddington, Horace L2,69
Waddington, Miss Julia R.
  Newstoke Priors L55,71; L91,270-1;
  L117B,3
Waddington, Richard L6,154; L56,319; L82,
  169 287 311 315 317; L117A,21
Waddington, S. L5,100; IU
Wade, A.G. IU
Wade, J.Augustine L90,124 146-7 152 154-5
  158 170 182 194 213; L91,90; L117B,46; IU
Wageman, Thomas IU
Wahlmuth, Eugenie IU
Wain, W.J.Carruthers L85,282-3 308; L86,
  110-11 113
Waite, Samuel L84,257
Wakefield, Edward G.
  England and America L53,34; L117A,25
Walch & Sons L89,99
Walcott, Rev.Mackenzie L83,235; IU
Waldegrave, Countess of IU Richard Bentley I,
  35
Waldegrave, George E.(7th Earl) L55,150-4;
  L90,26; L117A,12; IU
Waldegrave-Leslie, Howard George UC
Waldie, John UC
Walford, E. IU(Gentleman's Magazine)
Walford, R.S. IU
Walford, Thomas L83,121
Walker, Mrs. L85,53
Walker, Bettina L3,25; L86,337 376; IU
  My musical experiences L41,354 371; L42,
  283-4 515; L64,271; L65,174-6; L119,105
  Songs and sonnets L3,64; L4,88; L22,344;
  L42,340
Walker, Charles R. L3,93; L4,82; L64,
  217-18; L86,266
Walker, Miss Ellen
  The Confessor L56,282-4; L117B,37
Walker, J. & C. IU
Walker, James L94,210
Walker, James & Co. L81,40-1 80
Walker, Miss L.A. L5,203
Walker, Mrs.Mary A. L4,77; L5,93; L22,
  339; IU
  Old tracks and new landmarks L42,389;

L67,240-3
Walker, N.Bailey IU
Walker, Robert L74,105-20
Walker, Thomas A. L3,93; L86,153
  The Severn tunnel L3,93; L41,326 354; L42,
  319; L64,218; L66,155-7
Walker, William L81,49; L88,208
Walker & Boutall L88,147; UC
Walker & Laycock L86,172 174
Walkes, W.R. L5,166
Walkey, Harriet UC
Walkley, A.B. L5,180
Wall, Mary IU
Wallace, Miss Ellen L82,182 184; L117B,35;
  IU; UC Manuscripts,47
  The Clandestine marriage L7,144
  King's cope L7,169; L8,111; L56,196
  Margaret Capel L55,288
  Mr.Warrenne L56,45
Wallace, Lady Grace L1,136; L58,98-103;
  L83,90 117 194; L93,297
Wallace, Percy R. L5,280; UC
Wallace, William IU(The Glasgow Herald)
Waller, Bryan Charles L5,157; IU
Waller, James L83,156
Waller, John Frances L5,84; IU
[Wallford] IU
Wallick, Dr. L82,38 40
Wallington, Nehemiah
  Historical notices L37,283; L38,248; L59,
  197
Wallis, J.F. L93,31-2 35
Wallop, B. L93,80
Wallop, Lady Camilla (Miss C.Fellowes) L5,
  40 130
Walmsley, Hugh M. L2,83; L3,54; L4,81; IU
  Branksome Dene L37,312; L38,96; L39,435;
  L100,167
  The Life guardsman (orig.The Lost Prince)
  L37,166 171; L38,171; L39,435; L59,233
Walond, R.F. L1,125; L92,206 274-5; L93,
  99; L117B,38
  Memoirs of Dr.Blenkinsop L57,163
Walpole, Hon.Frederick L2,45; L82,153 188
  302 344; L83,39-40 250; L84,73 207; L93,69
  123; L97,182; L117A,28; IU
  The Ansayrii, and the Assassins L56,218;
  L57,58
  Four years in the Pacific L7,167; L8,95 111;
  L56,133
  May and September L37,198; L38,190; L59,
  133
Walpole, Horace L1,146; L55,150-4; IU
  Journals L1,132; L36,38
  Letters L1,149; L6,180; L7,152; L8,49;
  L36,226 233; L37,278; L40,190; L41,275-6
  365; L42,271-2; L53,226; L54,187; L55,194;
  L56,227; L58,68-80 239; L62,322-4; L66,42;
  L91,91; L117A,12; L117B,5 25; IU George
  Bentley,176
  Letters addressed to the Countess of Ossory
  L1,120; L7,165; L8,52 76 94; L80,21
  Memoirs of the reign of King George the Third

L7,155 158
[Walpole, I.] IU
Walpole, Spencer H. L52,307 309; L81,115
Walsh, John B.(1st Baron Ormathwaite)
  Lessons of the French Revolution L38,280;
  L39,217; L40,438; L41,520; L42,512;
  IU(Ormathwaite)
Walsh, Robert L81,209
Walsh, William S. L5,222
Walter, James L83,136
Walters, Dr.Alan L3,144; L5,240; L22,364;
  L87,43; IU; UC
  A Lotos eater in Capri L41,382; L42,275
  277; L65,255
  Palms and pearls L41,369; L42,302; L65,
  112; UC Manuscripts,12
Walters, F.G. L5,308
Waltes, J. IU
Walton L5,67
Walton, William
  The Revolutions of Spain L6,53; L53,286 288
Warburton, Bartholomew E.G. L82,14 48 54
  62 67 91 133; L88,151(c); L92,285 288; IU
  Evenings at sea
  see Warburton, G.D.
  Memoirs of Prince Rupert L7,167; L8,81 95;
  L56,49 70; L117B,30 36
Warburton, George D. L1,158; L82,60 75;
  L83,31 147; L92 225 289; L93,49; L117B,36;
  IU
  The Conquest of Canada L36,35 130; L56,
  168; L58,146
  Evenings at sea L7,169; L8,119; L56,207;
  L69,234
Warburton, Thomas Acton L6,112 117; L82,26;
  L92,183; L117B,36
  Rollo and his race (orig.The Footsteps of the
  Normans) L7,165; L8,52-3; L56,68
Ward, A. UC
Ward, Sir Adolphus W. L3,78-9; L59,39;
  L86,318 322; L95,12; IU; UC
Ward, B.W. L88,96(c); L89,93; UC
Ward, Charles A. L5,185; IU
  Literary London L40,168
Ward, H.E. L5,174
Ward, Harriet L82,45-6 185; L93,12 116-18
  212; L117B,14
  Helen Charteris L7,166; L8,53; L56,100
  Recollections of an old soldier (orig.Col.Tidy's
  memoirs) L7,168; L8,94
Ward, Henry L87,244
Ward, Henry Baynes IU
Ward, James L92,251-2; L117A,6
  A Voice from the Danube L56,210
Ward, Rev.N.J. L5,157
[Ward, R.G.] IU(Ward,R.P.)
Ward, Rawdon UC
Ward, Rowland L85,388-9
Ward & Downey L86,156
Ward, Lock & Co. L67,253; L83,87 89 92 139
  277; L84,122 278 278(c) 292(c) 302; L88,335;
  IU
Ward, Mills & Co. L85,318;

UC(Garcia-end of G)
Warden, Florence
  see Price, F.A.
Wardleworth, Mr.W. L85,17 361 458; L86,
  69-70(c) 70 72 236 343 349 432; L88,333;
  IU(Wasdleworth)
Waring, Laura Scott L94,267-75
Warlow, Rev.G. L5,75
Warne, Frederick & Co. L64,85; L82,141-2
  L84,47 49 81 160 184; L85,96; L86,227; IU
Warner, Anna B.
  Say and seal
  see Warner, S.B.
Warner, Miss Susan B. L1,186; L58,235;
  L83,130 138 147 195 199-201 203; IU; UC
  Say and seal L36,83 98 108; L58,235
Warner, W.Harding IU
Warren, Sir Charles L3,105; IU
  The Temple or the tomb L39,365; L40,328;
  L41,300; L42,522
  Underground Jerusalem L3,52; L38,165;
  L39,227 234; L40,334; L85,3
Warren, Cusack IU
Warren, Count Edward de L1,96; L57,156-7
  244; L82,260; L83,27 31 107 110; L93,288-9;
  L117A,14
Warren, F.R. IU
Warren, Fanny IU
Warren, George F.L. (2nd Baron de Tabley)
  IU(De Tabley)
Warren, John B.L.(3rd Baron de Tabley) L2,
  73; L3,31; L4,84; L85,125; IU(De Tabley)
  Hence these tears L37,311; L38,259; L39,
  438
  Ropes of sand L37,225; L38,215; L59,198;
  L99,221
  Salvia Richmond L39,288; L40,454
  A Screw loose L37,229; L38,220; L59,168
Warren, John Esaias L92,300; IU; IU Richard
  Bentley I,21
Warren, Samuel IU
Washbourne, Robert L88,248
Washington, George IU
Wass, Charles IU
Wassermann, Mrs.Lillias L3,139; L85,264
  A Man of the day L39,368; L40,443; L61,3
Waterfield, William L5,185 210; IU
Waterford, Marchioness of IU
Waterlow & Sons IU
Waters, Cyril A. L5,193
Waters, Mark L85,433
Watkins, George IU
Watkins, Lizzie IU
Watkins, Miss Lydia M. L3,114; IU
Watkins, Rev.U.G.F. L5,28
Watson L86,104
Watson, Alfred E.T. L3,168; L5,40; L85,388;
  IU
  Racecourse and covert side L40,317; L41,498
  531; L42,306; L62,32-4
Watson, E.H.Lacon L5,247 257
Watson, Mrs.Elizabeth S.(E.S.Fletcher) L3,
  110; L4,71; L86,456; IU; UC

A High little world L41,413; L65,185
His fault or hers L42,412; L67,204
Watson, Frank L5,160
Watson, Henry L81,238
Watson, James IU
Watson, Mrs.Lily L3,84; L88,73 175 272; IU
  The Vicar of Langthwaite (orig.The Professor's
  daughter) L42,449; L66,19; L67,206
Watson, Miss Mary L5,39
Watson, R.Llandaff IU
Watson, W.J. IU
Watson, William & Co. IU
Watson Sons & Co. L86,372
Watt, Alexander P. L5,241-3; L63,91-3 126
  267; L64,151 200 237-40 248-65; L65,311;
  L66,160 188 224-6 253; L67,8-9 12 43 91-4
  150-3 268 275 312 317; L86,96-7 116 129-30(c)
  172 186 264 267 304-5 310 329-30 332 334 425
  451 466 489; L87,176 180 189-90 204 209-10
  215 218 233 260 263 266 267(c) 268; L88,43
  48-9(c) 77 95 150-1 153 157 163 202 230-1
  233(c) 233 236 252 255 264 270 280 287 313 320
  326-8 343 349 355-6 358; L89,44 67 69 75 84
  87-8 92 94 102 104 108 111; IU;
  IU(Blackett & Watt)
Watt, John UC
Watters, Augustus L5,279
Watts, Alaric Alexander L1,18; L52,13 135;
  L53,68; L68,19 62; L81,47; IU
  Scenes of life L52,17
Watts, Alaric Alfred L3,50; L4,80; L85,410;
  IU
  Alaric Watts L40,222; L41,194; L42,501;
  L62,130
Watts, Henry L. L92,108
Watts, William H. L54,67; L117A,29
Waugh, Alexander IU
Waugh, Mrs.Ellen L3,166; L61,163-7; L85,
  365 380 411 413; IU
Waugh, John IU
Waugh & Cox L83,30
Weatherhead, D.Hume
  Madagascar, past and present L36,193; L42,
  402; L56,8
Weatherly, Frederic E. L5,iv 74 88 125 133-4;
  L86,426; L95,239; L96,32 40; IU
Webb, Mrs.Annie L1,97; L2,62; L82,58;
  L83,38 123-4 143 145 189-90; L84,55; L93,
  25; L117A,8
  Idaline L36,44 49; L37,274; L57,312
  Marco Griffi L36,79; L37,274; L58,204
  The Martyrs of Carthage L36,33 105-6; L37,
  273; L38,249 334; L39,215; L56,203
Webb, Egerton L90,218 238
Webb, Miss J.
  see Loudon, Mrs.J.
Webb, Rev.L.B. L83,190
Webb, Miss Rosamond A. L59,197; IU
Webb, Mrs.Wilfred L5,256
Webbe, Cornelius L90,282; IU
Webber, H.F.Incledon IU
Weber, A. L89,109
Weber, J.J. IU

Webster, B.O. IU
Webster, Benjamin N. IU
Webster, Geo. L90,226
Webster, Miss Grace L1,125; L117B,11; IU
  Raymond Revilloyd L36,93
Webster, James
  Travels through the Crimea L1,56; L52,11;
  L68,18
Webster, Richard IU
Webster, William H.B.
  Narrative of a voyage (orig.Chanticleer's
  voyage) L53,93; L90,95 98; L117A,29
Weddle, Miss Isabella L3,139
  A Man of the day
  see Wassermann, L.
Wedmore, Cecil L3,168; L85,399
Wedmore, Sir Frederick L3,104 168; L5,82
  98 125; L22,342; L87,191;
  IU(Burlington Fine Arts Club)
  Pastorals of France L39,277; L40,313; L61,
  107
  The Pictures of the seasons L40,382; L41,
  528; L42,518
  Studies in English art L38,343 351; L39,229
  352; L40,323-4; L41,305; L42,318; L60,18
  277; L101,184
Wedmore, Miss Millicent L5,130
The Weekly Dispatch L80,17
Weekly Echo L85,477 478(c)
The Weekly Sun L87,157
Weidmann L3,180; L62,306-9
Weigall, Mrs.C.E. L5,160; L22,365; UC
Weise, Arthur J.
  The Discoveries of America L40,190; L41,
  213; L42,186; L62,229-30
Weiss, Dr.Alvys L89,107
Weld, Charles R. L91,105
  The Search for Sir John Franklin L56,325;
  L83,69
Weldon, C.E. IU
Welford, Charles
  see Scribner & Welford
[Welldon, G.] IU
Welldon, Rev.J.E. L84,122
Wells, Julia IU
Wells, Nathaniel A. L92,107
  The Picturesque antiquities of Spain L7,160;
  L55,283
Wells, Sir Thomas Spencer IU
Welton, Jones & Co. L88,88 216 336; IU
Wemyss, Mrs.Erskine L5,207; L87,65
Wendon, E.I. IU
Went, G.M. L5,140
Were, R.E. IU
Werne, Ferdinand
  Expedition to the White Nile L7,169; L8,95;
  L56,146
Werner, A. L5,205
Werner, E.
  see Buerstenbinder, E.
Werry, Eliza F. IU
The Wesleyan Times UC(Forster-end of F)
West L92,119

West, Miss Eva   UC
West, Mrs.F.   L83,192
West, H.   IU
West, Maria J.   IU
West, Theresa C.J.
  A Summer visit to Ireland   [L1,96] ; L56,20;
  L117B,23
Westall, W.   IU
Western Daily Mercury, Plymouth   IU
Western Union Telegraph Company   L86,390
Westley, F.   L90,223 227
Westley, J.J.   L82,95
Westminster, Marchioness of   IU
Westminster, Lord Robert G.   IU
Westminster Conservative Association   IU
Westneath, Lady Emily A.   IU
Weston, F.M.   UC
The Weston Mercury   L86,147 151; IU(Western)
Wetherell, N.   IU
Wetmore, F.R. & Co.   L85,19
Weuve, Cécile   IU
Weyman, Stanley J.   L5,220; L67,150-3
Weymouth, J.W.   L83,149
Whalley, B.   L93,105
Whalley, P.C.   L5,239
Whalley, Thomas S.
  Journals and correspondence   L36,48 54; L37,
  271; L58,278
Wharncliffe, Lord
  see Wortley, J.A.S.
Whately, Richard (Archbishop of Dublin)   L1,
  191; L82,82; IU; IU(Dublin)
  Mental culture   L36,53
  Selections   L2,50; L36,50 120 128; L37,268;
  L38,253; L39,420; L40,461; L41,532; L42,
  520
Whatman, C.   IU Unidentified,(A)
Whatman, C.E.   IU
Whealler, Anson   IU; UC
Wheatley, Henry B.   L5,74 76; IU
Wheeler, [A.] H.   IU
Wheeler, George H.   L5,212
Wheeler, Stephen   L67,236 306-8; L89,91 94
  97-8 100-1; IU
Wheelwright, Edith G.   L3,150; L4,79; L88,
  55 311 333; L89,90; IU
  Anthony Graeme   L42,430; L66,285
Whetham, John W.B.
  Western wanderings   L38,322; L39,431 434;
  L40,461; L41,538; L42,524
Whetham, Maria A.B.   IU(Boddam)
Whewell, Rev.William   L83,225; IU
Whichcote, Lady Isabella E.   L2,78; L5,21; IU
Whishaw, Frederick   L5,252
Whitaker, Harold   L5,274
Whitaker, J. & Son   L85,191; L87,297;
  IU(Whitaker's Almanack)
Whitbread, Gordon   IU
Whitbread, J.   IU
Whitcombe, Mrs.   L5,78
Whitcombe, Mary E.   IU(Whitcombe,H.P.)
  Bygone days in Devonshire (orig.Legends of
  English counties)   L38,297; L39,100; L40,

424; L41,506; L42,502; L59,173-4; [L99,
  167] ; IU(Church,F.); IU(Hughes,R.D.)
Whitcombe & Tombs   L85,424
White, Mrs.   L5,244
White, Miss A.K.M.   L5,273; IU
White, Miss Annie   L5,296; L22,358
White, Charles   IU
White, F.V. & Co.   L64,27; L84,244; L85,
  286; L88,140-1
White, Col.H.   IU
White, James   L91,208-9 274; L93,138-40;
  L117A,36; IU
  English country life   L55,135-6
White, Percy   L5,189
White, W.A.   IU
White & Allen   IU
White, Allison & King   L88,243
White, Druce & Brown   L89,119
Whitehall Rooms   L89,49
Whitehead, Alfred   L53,51
Whitehead, Charles   L1,135; L55,73-81; L90,
  126 156 202 317; L91,109 154 184 205-6 249
  253 261 265 269 272-3; L92,114 176; L93,71
  252; L117A,40; L117B,27; IU
  The Earl of Essex   L54,332
  Richard Savage   L42,423; L122,74 123;
  UC Manuscripts,18
Whitehead, Miss Emma   IU
  Pierce Falcon, the outcast   L53,51; L117A,31
Whitehead, Mrs.Sarah R.   L82,279 340; L117B,
  5
  Nelly Armstrong   L36,211; L57,188
Whitehouse, Felix M.   L95,107 155
Whiteing, Richard   IU
Whitelocke, R.H.   IU
Whiteside, J.W.   IU
Whiteside, Rt.Hon.James   L1,79; L82,24 35
  45 97-8 247 258 290 295 305; L93,263; L117B,
  39; IU
  A Guide to the antiquities of Rome   L36,236
  Italy in the nineteenth century   L7,168; L8,
  52 76
  The Vicissitudes of the Eternal City   L8,95
Whitford, C.E.S.   L5,113
Whiting, Miss Mary Bradford   L3,107; L5,274;
  L86,421
  Denis O'Neil   L41,419; L42,474; L65,108
Whitling, Henry J.   L93,54-5
  Pictures of Nuremberg   L56,116-24
Whitman, James   IU
Whitney, Mrs.Charles A.   L89,44
Whittaker, I.   L63,96
Whittaker, Rev.John W.   L1,65
Whittaker & Co.   L81,105 153 163; L82,41;
  L83,94-5 97; L84,43; L117B,18;
  IU(Whitaker)
Whitting, H.J.   L92,155
Whittingham & Wilkins   L84,298; L85,324-6;
  IU(Chiswick Press)
Whittle, James   L93,82-3
Whymper, Charles   L64,39
Whymper, J.W. & Co.   L84,46; IU
Whymper, Sir William   L92,193-5

Wickham, Rev.Hill D.   L58,278; IU
Wickham, William   IU
Wickham, Rt.Hon.William
  The Correspondence   L37,282; L38,245; L39,
  452; L40,462; L41,507; L42,503
Wiedmann   L86,120 120(c) 121
Wieler, Miss   L3,59
Wiffin, King & Co.   L83,67
Wigan, James   L83,89; L117A,19
Wigg, E.S. & Son   L86,316
Wiggins, John
  The Monster misery of Ireland   L55,206;
  L117B,18
Wight, Orlando W.
  Quinland   L58,139; L83,132-4
Wightwick, George   L83,135
Wigram, W.Knox   L2,73; L3,67; L4,81; L5,
  18; L93,18 78
  Five hundred pounds reward   L37,127; L38,
  134; L39,439; L59,140; L99,21
  Twelve wonderful tales   L3,44; L37,283; L38,
  247; L39,453 455; L40,337 467; L41,308;
  L42,523; L62,15-20
Wigston, W.F.   L5,179
Wilberforce, Edward   L2,67; L5,66; L93,188;
  IU; UC
Wilberforce, Samuel (Bishop of Oxford)   L82,
  54 200 205 208; IU; IU(Oxen); UC
  National life   L36,26; L58,106
Wilcox, A.M.   L5,104; IU
Wilcretz, Count Henry   IU
Wild, Elizabeth E.   IU
Wild, John James   IU
Wilde, Lady Jane F.   L3,174; L85,442
  Driftwood from Scandinavia   L40,241; L41,
  214; L62,188-90
Wildes, George & Co.   L53,218; L81,130
Wildey, Dr.   L5,218
Wilding, E.   IU
Wilkes, J.   IU
Wilkins, Miss   L82,324
Wilkins, William Noy
  Art impression of Dresden   L36,238; L37,271;
  L38,250; L39,226; L94,175
Wilkins, William Walker   IU
Wilkinson, Mrs.C.A.M.   L93,43-6
Wilkinson, Emily L.   IU
Wilkinson, J.S.   IU
Wilkinson, John   IU
Wilkinson, Thomas E.   IU
Wilkinson, W.H.   L5,233; L86,385
Wilkinson, William Irving   IU
Wilks, John   L91,220 226-8; L117B,14
  The Tory baronet   L7,147; [L55,40]
Willard, Mrs.Florence J.   L3,45; L86,117;
  L88,227; IU
  Pictures from Paris   L2,81; L37,54; L38,
  209; L39,424
Willdey, C.J.   IU
[Willert, J.]   IU
Willes, J.   L5,233
Willes, J.S.   L58,38
Williams, Mrs.   L83,264

Williams, A.   IU
Williams, A.M.   L5,260
Williams, Mrs.A.S.   UC
Williams, A.W.   L86,229-30(c)
Williams, C.Woolmer
  Incidents in the history of the Honourable
  Artillery Company   L3,89; L41,327; L63,329
Williams, Charles H.   L64,4-13
Williams, Charles R.   L3,177; L4,80
  Some professional recollections   L40,329;
  L41,501 535; L42,521; L62,46; IU
Williams, Charles W.   L92,213 226
Williams, D.E.   L1,50; L91,130
  Life of Sir Thomas Lawrence   L52,66 169 216;
  L68,77 94 95
Williams, E.   L82,35
Williams, Mrs.E.   UC
Williams, Miss E.Abdy   L5,181
Williams, E.P.   L82,41
Williams, Rev.Edward A.   L1,178; L2,49; L3,
  28
  The Cruise of the Pearl   L36,328; L58,205
Williams, Eliza   L74,37-84
Williams, Folkstone   L90,151
Williams, Francis Edgar   IU; UC(end of W);
  UC Manuscripts,15
Williams, Frederick S.   L3,87; L86,199 230
  The Midland Railway   L41,iii 331 393; L42,
  282; L64,4-13
  Our iron roads   L41,iii 331 390 393; L42,295
  297; L64,4-13
Williams, H.L.   L5,226
Williams, Howard   L5,18; L86,71
Williams, J.   L5,205
Williams, General James   L2,49; [L83,263];
  L84,44; IU
  The Rise and fall of the model republic   L36,
  105; L37,272; L38,252; L39,420; L40,462
  The South vindicated (pub.Longmans)   L37,273;
  L38,253; L39,420; L40,462
Williams, James   L3,127; L4,77; L86,381
  382(c) 412; IU
  Sketches of village buildings   L41,361; L42,
  321; L65,29-30
Williams, M.Paolo   L39,443
Williams, Mrs.M.T.   L86,198
Williams, Rev.Morris P.   L5,282
Williams, R.H.Oakley   L22,361
Williams, Sydney   L84,107 186 193
Williams, W.H.   L5,55
Williams, W.W.   IU
Williams, Watkin Wynn   UC
Williams & Norgate   IU
Williamson, J.R.   L5,250
Williamson, John   L75,108-58
Williamson, W.   IU
Williamston, Fred.   IU
Willing, Mr.   L84,124
Willis, Auguste Maria   IU
Willis, E.C.   L25,222
Willmets, Clara L.   IU
Willoughby & Co.   L84,90
Wills, Rt.Hon.Sir Alfred   L1,152; L83,145

Wanderings among the High Alps L36,223;
L58,56
Wills, G. & Co. L85,476
Wills, Harry L85,118
Wills, W.G. IU
Wills, W.H. L83,269; L84,67; L90,184-5 294
Wills, Dr.William L2,20; L3,79; L58,301
Wills, William John
  A Successful exploration L2,20 46; L3,79;
  L36,196 305; L37,270; L38,333-4; L58,301
Willy, E.C. L26,7
Wilmere, Mrs. L82,327
Wilmot, Mrs.Barbarina (Baroness Dacre) L81,
  65; IU(Dacre)
Wilmshurst, T.B. IU
Wilson L82,32
Wilson, A. IU
Wilson, Alfred W. L89,112
Wilson, Mrs.Annie L5,278
Wilson, Mrs.C.B. L90,228 240 296-7
Wilson, C.J. L90,105 153 217 265 305 308;
  L91,23 84 145 165 193 257; L92,23; L117B,24
Wilson, C.W. L83,256-7
Wilson, Sir Charles W.
  The Recovery of Jerusalem L2,80; L3,33;
  L37,236; L38,214; L39,186 236; L40,317
  325; L41,295 499; L42,307; L59,225
Wilson, Crawford L117B,6
Wilson, E. L81,92
Wilson, Mrs.Elizabeth L52,276
Wilson, F.Collins L5,44
Wilson, Miss F.Mary L5,247
Wilson, Flora M.E. IU
Wilson, Dr.George L83,63; IU
Wilson, H.Schütz L5,70; IU(Wilson,F.S.)
Wilson, Helen K. IU
Wilson, J. IU
Wilson, J.I.
  see Wilson, C.J.
Wilson, Miss J.M. L86,417
Wilson, John (Christopher North pseud.)
  UC Manuscripts,39
Wilson, John Crawford L1,126; L57,294-7;
  L82,370; L83,78 80; L93,286
  Jonathan Oldaker L36,90
Wilson, Margaret O.(Mrs.M.Oliphant) L82,131
  137 145 171 174 176-7 215 217 318 323 336;
  L84,150; L87,242(c) 242; L117A,30;
  IU(Oliphant)
  John Drayton L36,176; L57,24-40
  The Melvilles L36,199; L57,28-40 114
Wilson, Melvill L82,176 186-7
Wilson, R. L85,2
Wilson, S. L87,268
Wilson, S.R. L87,274
Wilson, Samuel L92,152-3
Wilson, Thomas Cornelius L54,73; IU
Wilson & Mackinnon L85,459 465-6; L86,496
Wilton, Miss L5,23
Wimphen, Rachel IU; UC
Winchilsea, Earl of
  see Finch-Hatton, G.J.
Winckworth, H.R. IU

Windham, Captain L88,200 210 212 258 262 266
Windham, General Sir Charles
  Crimean Diary (pub.Kegan Paul) L42,374
Windham, W.A. IU
Windrop, S. L87,285(c)
Windsor, Dean of L86,347
Windsor Rose & Horticultural Society IU(Rose)
Windsor & Eton Express IU Richard Bentley II,
  674
Wingate, F.R. IU
Wingate, R.E. L86,367
Wingfield, Hon.Lewis S. L3,107; L85,410;
  L86,211 224 233 358; L87,112; IU
  Abigel Rowe L40,388; L62,122
  Barbara Philpot L40,414; L41,505; L42,479;
  L63,37
  In Her Majesty's keeping (orig.The House of
  bondage) L39,342; L60,221
  Lady Grizel L39,274; L40,159 438; L41,
  106-7 520; L42,129-30 488; L60,59
  The Maid of Honour (orig.Lorge) L41,436;
  L42,491; L64,335
  My Lords of Strogue L39,318; L123,198-9
  Wanderings of a globe-trotter L41,339; L64,
  86
Wingfield, William F.
  A Tour in Dalmatia L36,71
Winkfield, Miss L5,93
Winkworth, H.R. L84,249
Winkworth, Susanna IU
Winn, Dr. L5,64
Winsley, Francis L56,209
Winslow, Forbes B. IU
Winslow, Lyttelton S.F. IU
Winson & Newton L59,2
Winston, J. IU
Winter, C.Gordon IU
Winter, Christopher T.
  Six months in British Burmah L36,66; L58,
  180
Winter, J.S.
  see Stannard, H.E.V.
Winterburn, G. & Co. L87,90
Winthrop, Florence E. IU
Wirgmann, Colonel L5,98
Wise, Henry A. L117A,7
Wister, Mrs.S.B. L5,290
Witham, William IU
Withy, Thomas IU
Witt, John G. L4,74; L22,345; L88,285 290(c);
  IU
  Then and now L42,386; L67,213-15
Wives & Daughters L86,375
Wohl, Miss Yanka L88,136
Wohlauer, F. L3,98; IU
Wolferstan, Esther Kate
  Philip Leigh L3,59; L5,80; L38,302; L39,
  450; L101,83; IU
Wolff, H.W. UC
Wolff, Miss Helen L3,33; L87,78; IU
Wolff, Rt.Hon.Sir Henry D. L82,218; L93,66
  88 135; L117B,29; IU
  Blondelle L36,111; L57,132

Madrilenia L57,9

Wolff, Joseph IU

Wolffsohn, Mme.Lily L3,106; L5,109; L85, 12 123 335; IU; UC

Wollaston, J.T.Burton IU

Wolley, Sir Clive Phillipps L3,154; L5,60-61; IU(Phillipps-Wolley)

Savage Svanetia (orig.The Land of Schamyl) L40,376; L41,499 534; L42,316; L61,209-13

Sport in the Crimea L39,375; L40,323; L41, 534 540; L42,317; L61,83

A Sportsman's Eden L41,332; L42,319-20

The Trottings of a tenderfoot L40,367; L41, 533-4; L42,518 522; [L62,179]

Wolseley, Garnet J.(Viscount) L3,130; L4,62; L61,248; L86,299-301(c); L87,54-5(c) 59 74-5 77 86 88 91(c) 155(c) 162-4(c) 269; L88, 142 268; IU

The Life of John, Duke of Marlborough L40, 169; L41,325; L42,263 353-4 388; L62,48; L65,264; [L66,125]; L71,194; L87,220; L119,157; UC Manuscripts,11

Wolseley, Sir George L5,100

Woltmann, Alfred F.G.A. IU

Holbein and his time L2,68 81 88; L37,161; L38,152; L39,402 427; L40,434

Woltmann, E. IU

Wood, Miss A. L5,48

Wood, Miss Anna Cogswell L3,111; L86,451 454; L87,59 159

Westover's ward L41,413; L42,476 481; L65,182-4

Wood, Miss Annie (Mrs.Procter) L3,73; L85, 131; IU; UC

Love or pride L38,299; L39,447

Wood, Charles W. L2,67; L3,122; L4,63; L60,141; L84,236 240 251 321; L85,2 125 146 427; L86,164 191 328 338 415; L87,45 87 260 284 288(c) 288-9 292 293(c) 293-4 296; L88,51 54 56 118 152 158 178 200 201(c) 295 298 310 349; L89,49 100 131 135-6(c); L115,243; IU; IU George Bentley,317; IU Richard Bentley II, 604+1; UC Manuscripts,24

The Cruise of the Reserve Squadron L40,230; L41,309; L42,179; L62,117-20

In the Black Forest L40,365 441; L41,310-11; L42,242; L61,235

Letters from Majorca L41,333 390; L42, 272-3

Memorials of Mrs.Henry Wood L42,350 366 378

A Month at Gastein L38,294; L39,418 449; L40,445

Round about Norway L39,354; L40,320

Through Holland L39,269 275; L40,330 337; L41,310 390; L42,326

Under Northern skies L40,107; L41,311; L42,329

Wood, Edward J. L2,31

Curiosities of clocks and watches L37,277; L59,116

Giants and dwarfs L37,380; L59,147

Wedding day L3,74; L37,300; L38,246

Wood, Elizabeth L94,79

Wood, Ellen (Mrs.Henry Wood) L2,47 65 69 89; L3,14; L14,201 345-8 352 354 386; L15, 67-68a; L22,363; L41,110-12 145-9 395-402; L42,128 130-55; L46-L51; L83,245 258-9; L84,64 160-1 [173] 193 236 283; L87,293-4; L115,214-21 245 250-6 286 294; IU; UC

Adam Grainger L38,366; L39,97; L40,420

Anne Hereford L38,71-2; L39,61-2; L40, 116; L41,113

Bessy Rane L37,49 307; L38,22-3 85; L39, 63-4; L40,117-18; L41,114; L59,230

The Channings L36,293-4 303; L37,54 60 70 266; L38,17-18; L39,64-5; L40,119-20; L41, 115; L58,286-7; L60,141

Court Netherleigh L39,379 394; L40,156-7 426; L41,116-17 507; L42,480; L61,90

Dene Hollow L37,298; L38,55 120; L39,66-7; L40,120-1; L41,117-18

East Lynne L36,271-2 274-5 316; L37,57 59; L38,15-16; L39,67-8; L40,122-3; L41,118-19; L58,267; L97,56; L123,261

Edina L38,82; L39,255-6 429; L40,123-4 428; L41,120

Elster's folly L38,64; L39,69; L40,125; L41,121

Featherston's story L41,451; L42,483

George Canterbury's will L38,67; L39,70-1; L40,126-7; L41,122

The House of Halliwell L41,437; L42,486-7

Johnny Ludlow L38,311 317 330; L39,24-5 350 366 427; L40,128-30 158 404 437; L41, 123-4 514-15; L42,487

Lady Adelaide's oath L37,57 68 180 320; L38, 21; L39,72-3; L40,131; L41,126; L59,129

Lady Grace L41,479; L42,489

A Life's secret L38,70-1; L39,73-4; L40, 132-3; L41,127

Lord Oakburn's daughters L38,47-8; L39, 75-6; L40,134; L41,128

The Master of Greylands L38,75 295; L39, 76-7 425; L40,135-6 443; L41,129-30 523; L42,490

Mildred Arkell L38,63; L39,78; L40,137; L41,130-1

Mrs.Halliburton's troubles L36,143 299; L37, 48 60 70 266 319; L38,19-20; L39,79-80; L40, 138-9; L41,131-2; L58,297

Orville College L38,362; L39,81; L40,140; L41,133

Oswald Cray L38,54; L39,82-3; L40,141-2; L41,134

Parkwater (orig.Told in the twilight) L38,350 369; L39,84; L40,143; L41,135

Pomeroy Abbey L39,293 315-16; L40,144-5 450; L41,136 528; L42,493; L123,188-9

The Red Court Farm L38,68; L39,85-6; L40, 146; L41,137

Roland Yorke L37,227 260; L38,25-6 220; L39,87; L40,147-8; L41,138

St. Martin's Eve L38,65; L39,90; L40,150-1; L41,140-1

The Shadow of Ashlydyat L36,244 271; L37,

63 72-3 267; L38,52-3; L39,88-9; L40,149;
L41,139-40; L58,328; L59,38; L97,87
The Story of Charles Strange L41,466; L42,
495
Trevlyn Hold L38,66; L39,91-2; L40,152;
L41,141-2
Verner's pride L37,308; L38,24; L39,93-4;
L40,153-4; L41,142-3
Within the maze L38,69 270; L39,94-5; L40,
155; L41,143-4
Wood, Ellen N. IU
Wood, H.F. L5,186
Wood, Mrs.Henry
see Wood, Ellen
Wood, Mrs.John G. L89,40
Wood, Rev.John G. L3,77; L5,221; L86,185;
IU
The Dominion of man L41,330 394; L42,186;
L63,299-300; IU Richard Bentley II,343
Wood, M.J. IU
Wood, Mary A.E.
see Green, M.A.E.
Wood, R.M. IU
Wood, Roland A.
see Wood-Seys, R.A.
Wood, Rev.William L5,307
Wood, William H. UC
Wood & Sharwood L117A,11
Wood-Seys, Mrs.L.H. IU
Wood-Seys, Roland A.(Paul Cushing pseud.)
L3,36; L86,67
A Woman with a secret (orig.Arrows and traps)
L40,412; L41,539; L63,33
Woodburne, G.Lancaster L85,283
Woodbury Permanent Photographic Printing
Company L85,115 124 170; IU; IU(Fry,J.W.)
Woodd, Basil & Sons IU(Wood,B.)
Woodd, Charles H.L. IU
Woodfall, Thomas L92,131
Woodfall & Kinder L83,167
Woodrow, C.A. IU
Woods, Mrs. L5,28
Woods, Mrs.Margaret L. L3,55; L5,206;
L87,277; IU
Lyrics and ballads L41,340; L42,273 275;
L64,115-19
A Village tragedy L40,87; L41,482 490; L42,
474 499; L63,205; L64,142; L119,122
Woods, N.A. L83,84
Woods, Thomas L91,252
Woods, Dr.Thomas
The existence of the deity L36,236; L37,272;
L83,203-5
Woodthorpe, Col.R.B. IU
Woodward, Captain L82,253
Woodward, Miss
The Renaissance (prop.trans.) L3,47; L38,
285
Woodward, B.B. IU
Woodward, Bettina E. IU
Woodward, Francis
Masterpieces of Sir Robert Strange L38,308;
L39,422; L40,456; L41,523; L42,514

Woodward, [W.] N. IU
Woodward, Dr.William L5,273
Woolcott, John S. L61,96; L85,296
Woollam, Wilfred L5,216; L89,119
Woollcombe & Jago L81,50-1
Woollright, Henry H. L3,118; L4,64; L86,
498; L87,41; L88,171
History of the Fifty-seventh Regiment L41,
376; L42,223
Woon, F.Dillon L5,298
Wordsworth, Charles IU
Wordsworth, Fanny G. IU
Wordsworth, Gordon IU
Wordsworth, R. IU(Wordsworth,A.)
Workmen's Hall & Institute, Blaengarw UC
Wormeley, Elizabeth (Mrs.E.Latimer) L92,
219; L117B,26; IU(Latimer)
Worsfold, William B. L3,123; L4,65; L87,44;
L89,101; IU
The Valley of light (pub.McM.; orig.The Vaudois
country) L42,3 250; L67,302
A Visit to Java L41,376; L42,328-9; L65,257
Wortley, Lady Emmeline C.
Travels in the United States L7,171; L8,150;
L36,90; L37,312; L38,251; L39,419; L40,
463; L56,309-14
Wortley, James A.S.(1st Baron Wharncliffe)
L53,216; L81,172; L117A,10; IU
Wortley, John S.(2nd Baron Wharncliffe) L54,
69
Wotton, Miss Mabel E. L5,184 248; IU
Word portraits of famous writers L41,323;
L42,521
Wrangel, Ferdinand von
see Vrangel, F. von
Wraxall, Charles Edward IU
Wraxall, Sir F.C.Lascelles L2,53; L83,260-1;
L93,95 114-15 172; L94,104; L98,7; L100,77;
IU
Remarkable adventurers L36,113; L37,275;
L58,306; L97,196
Wraxall, Lady Jane L53,185-93; L81,159 166
169; L117B,13; IU
Wraxall, Sir Nathaniel W.
Memoirs L1,132; L36,243; L37,276; L53,
185-93
Wrench, Rev.Dr. L55,264
Wright L83,120
Wright, Edward UC
Wright, Rev.H.V. IU
Wright, Ichabod C. L82,189; IU
Wright, J.M. IU
Wright, Rev.J.P. L5,168
Wright, J.W. L83,153-4
Wright, John L54,187; L55,194; L81,228;
L91,136; L117B,5
Wright, Margaret B. L5,291; L22,356
Wright, Robert L2,61
Wright, Thomas L82,66; L117B,38; IU
England under the House of Hanover L7,163;
L8,52; L37,279; L56,77
Narratives of sorcery and magic L56,230
Wright, Thomas L5,183 IU

Wright, W. L83,110 129
Wright, William A. L67,18; L87,184 186; IU
Wrightson, Richard H. L1,191; L83,108
  A History of modern Italy L58,23
Wrigley, James & Son L59,102 148; L64,28;
  L84,72-4 80 159; L85,25 47 347; IU; UC
Wrottesley, Hon.George L1,126; L58,201; IU
  Life and correspondence of Sir John Burgoyne
  L38,270; L39,200; L42,406; L59,258-9;
  [L84,198]
Wrottesley, Mrs.George L1,126; L117B,46
Wrottesley, Margaret A. IU
Wyke, C.Lennon L92,49; IU
Wykes Bros. & Mantle IU
Wyld, James IU
Wyndham, Hon.Fanny C.(Hon.Mrs.Montgomery)
  The Bucklyn Shaig L2,56; L36,200; L37,28;
  L59,77-8; IU(Montgomery,F.)
Wynn, Emily W. IU
Wynne, Miss L5,179
Wynne, Mrs.Catherine A.S. L2,61; L3,68;
  L84,164 174; L94,264 306; IU
  A Horrid girl L38,46; L39,442
  A Life in a love L36,175; L37,173; L38,180;
  L59,56
  Margaret's engagement L37,186
  My insect queen L37,203; L38,165
  Sister May L37,262; L38,221; L39,446;
  L59,251
  The Story of a kiss L41,481; L63,252
Wyse, Miss L5,220; L86,250

Yates L81,122
Yates, Edmund H. L2,62; L3,181; L5,i; L41,
  496; L42,499; L84,58-9 62 102; L85,467 479;
  L86,44; IU; UC
  Broken to harness L37,69 320; L59,42-4
  Edmund Yates L40,186 253 466; L41,218;
  L42,507; L61,256
  Our pleasant vices (prop.) L62,297
Yates, Dr.Holt
  Wanderings in Palestine (prop.) L53,70; L81,
  136
Yates, William UC
Yelverton, Hon.Mrs.M.T.
  see Longworth, M.T.
Yonge, A. L82,354
Yonge, Miss C.M. IU
Yonge, Charles D. L1,137; L2,51 58-9; L3,
  53 135-6; L58,86-9 283; L60,129 151; L83,
  73 95 105 111-12 118 181 262 266; L84,61 81
  92-5 97 99 [159]; L85,409; L86,264; L93,
  278; IU
  Dictionary L36,29 47 112 123 151; L37,286-9;
  L38,255-7; L39,189-91; L40,340-2; L41,
  313-14; L42,333-4; L58,30 58 214 304; L59,
  112; L68,97
  The History of the British Navy L36,95; L37,
  285; L38,254-5; L58,319-21; L59,112; L94,
  109; L123,157-9
Yonge, Miss Fortescue L5,89

Yonge, J.B. IU
Yonge, Rev.John E. L59,111-12; L60,129
Yorke, Curtis
  see Lee, S.R.
Yorke, Philip J. L57,136
Yorke, Stephen
  see Linskill, M.
Young, Miss L117B,31
Young, Miss Amelia S.C.(Miss Minnie Young;
  Pamela Sneyd pseud.) L3,133 145; L87,99;
  IU(Young,Minnie)
  Jack Urquhart's daughter (orig.Shadows) L39,
  388; L40,354; L41,515; L61,123-5; L63,278
  Point-blank L40,394; L41,528; L62,175
  Who wins-loses (orig.No appeal) L41,403;
  L42,463; L65,324
Young, Charles George IU; UC Manuscripts,28
Young, Sir Charles L. L95,177; IU
Young, E. & J.B. & Co. IU
Young, G. L81,149 179-84
Young, Miss G.Julian L5,231
Young, Gerald IU
Young, H.Savill IU
Young, Henry IU; IU(Young,H.)
Young, Henry & Sons L86,310 330; L87,280
Young, Henry Schultess L59,260-4; L84,193
  210 215-23 227-32; L95,102 116 121 125-41
  146-50 154 162 192 196-8 202-17 224-9 231-7
  240 243-6 254-78 281-3; L96,1-10 13-16 61;
  L123,264-7; IU; IU George Bentley,169+2
Young, Rev.James L84,229; L95,271 281-2;
  L96,6 10 14-15
Young, Jane H. IU
Young, Julian C. IU
Young, Lambton IU
Young, Mrs.Marianne (M.Postans)
  Our camp in Turkey L58,5-7; L117B,25
Young, Miss Minnie
  see Young, A.S.C.
Young, Murdo L82,130; L117B,31
Young, Selina Elizabeth C. IU
Young, W.Siddons IU
Young & Vallings L81,48
Younge, W. IU
Your Wellwisher (pseud.) IU
Yule, H. IU

Zimmern, Miss Alice L5,281
Zimmern, Miss Helen L5,60; IU
Zoological Society of London L86,285(c)
Züngling, Paul IU(Jungling)
Zurcher, Frédéric
  Volcanoes and earthquakes L37,263; L38,244;
  L39,401; L59,141; L61,133

BENTLEY PERIODICALS

The Argosy Magazine L10,29; L11,27-8 153-4
  172-85 190-190a; L12,206-3ͻ 240-1; L13,

194-225; L14,160-1 168-9 172 302-89 passim;
L15,64-5 132-42; L37,284; L38,374; L39,458;
L40,486; L41,546 563; L42,540; L123,217-18
Bentley's Miscellany L6 passim; L8,30-1 73-4
88-9 113 118-19 147 151 170-1 189 200; L9,
140; L10,145; L36,109 232; L37,48; L53,
292-301 328-33; L58,9; L59,94 157 166; L76,
26; L90 passim; L91 passim; L115,87-8;
L116 passim; UC Manuscripts,47
Bentley's Quarterly Review L1,190; L36,70
186 229; L37,44; L58,186; L83,166
The British Army & Navy Review L2,21 61;
L10,177-8; L36,307; L37,19; L115,117
Colburn's New Monthly Magazine L10,218;
L59,166; L73B,1
Colburn's United Service Journal L73B,1; IU
The Literary Gazette L115,1-12
London Society L9,189; L10,33 74-6; L11,
147 187-8; L37,180 324; L38,390; L59,155;
L64,20-32; L84,171-2 215; L103; L105;
L107; L115,118-208; L123,124; IU
Men and Women of the Day L14,221-4 335;
L63,282; L64,211; L86,281
see Barraud, H.
Palestine Exploration Fund Quarterly Statement
L2,80; L3,33; L38,206; L39,180; L40,311;
L41,294
The Picture Gallery L36,86; L37,219; L38,
211; L39,424
St.Stephen's Chronicle L2,22; L37,240; L38,
229; L59,134
The Temple Bar Magazine L2,62 68; L5; L10,
162-74 191-200 215-21 231 233-233a; L11,
36-42 81-101; L12,23-30 46-52 181-205; L13,
23-31 45-50 174-91; L14,30-46 67-77 153-7
167 272-301 373-5 388-90; L15,18-23 29-33
108-21; L22,349-68; L25,89-228 passim;
L26,passim; L27,119-43; L28,173-204; L36,
319-22; L37,325-45; L38,375-88; L39,
459-73; L40,471-85; L41,547-62; L42,
526-539a; L45; L59,102 148; L75,355; L84,
125 176; L86,110 125; L115,266-7 296-9;
L123,218-22; UC Manuscripts,47
Young England L6,88-93

BENTLEY PUBLISHER'S SERIES

Bentley's Burlington Library L38,388; L39,
455; L123,224-5
Bentley's Cabinet Library UC Manuscripts,9
Bentley's Empire Library L39,405-18
Bentley's Favourite Novels L123,168
Bentley's Greek & Latin Classics (prop.) L58,
86-9
Bentley's Popular New Series of Two Shilling
Volumes L36,158
Bentley's Railway Library L36,27
Bentley's Standard Novels L1,21; L36,22 40
48 248-9 295-6 309-12; L37,27; L52,126 128;
L68,71 76-7; L80,12; L83,68; L115,91-101
Family Classical Library L52,56 60 62 277;

L123,137
The Juvenile Library L1,31; L52,137 178 277;
L68,63; L123,136-7
The National Library L1,18; L52,277 281;
L123,136-7
The Parlour Bookcase L36,26

TITLES BY ANONYMOUS OR UNIDENTIFIED
AUTHORS

Les Anglais et L'Inde L38,178
Contrition and constancy L55,204; L69,104;
L117B,21
The Court and the desert
see Heyward, E.J.
Crimean diary IU Unidentified, (B)
The Duke of Cousin L7,140
English satirists (prop.) L36,77
Flotsam and jetsam IU Unidentified, (B)
The Foreign exclusives in London
see Campbell, C.S.M.
Hennebon L117A,3
Hermit IU Unidentified, (B)
Historical sketches IU Unidentified, (B)
A History of English literature L36,77
Hungary & Transylvania L7,141
Juggernauth
see Veitch, S.F.F.
A Little anecdote in rhyme IU(Little)
The London apprentice (prop.) IU Unidentified,
(B)
Ministerial recollections (prop.) IU
Unidentified, (B)
Miscellaneous legends (prop.) L36,185; L37,
196
The Paying guest IU Unidentified, (B)
La Plainte de Thérouanne IU Unidentified, (B)
A Popular history of architecture (prop.) IU
Unidentified, (B)
Practical economy
see Scott, P.
Princess of the theatre (prop.) L36,179
Service afloat L53,16-22
The Unhappy one L37,17
Was he successful L36,17